Winter's Dreams

Winter's Dreams

Glen Cook

SUBTERRANEAN PRESS 2012

Winter's Dreams Copyright © 2012 by Glen Cook.
All rights reserved.

Dust jacket illustration Copyright © 2012 by Raymond Swanland.
All rights reserved.

Interior design Copyright © 2012 by Desert Isle Design, LLC.
All rights reserved.

First Edition

ISBN
978-1-59606-360-0

Subterranean Press
PO Box 190106
Burton, MI 48519

www.subterraneanpress.com

Table of Contents

Song from a Forgotten Hill ... *9*

And Dragons in the Sky ... *19*

Appointment in Samarkand ... *51*

Sunrise ... *53*

The Devil's Tooth ... *75*

In the Wind ... *111*

The Recruiter ... *151*

The Seventh Fool ... *159*

Ponce ... *165*

Quiet Sea ... *179*

Darkwar ... *209*

Enemy Territory ... *237*

The Waiting Sea ... *257*

Winter's Dreams ... *269*

Song from a Forgotten Hill

We were trapped in a world where tomorrow was yesterday. The fire had come three times and gone, and now we were back where our fathers had been a hundred years ago. There were some—"Toms," I've heard them called—who went into slavery as if it were their birthright, but there were also those who fought and died rather than hoe in some redneck's field. Most of those who fought did die. But free.

> "Go tell it on the mountain,
> Over the hill and everywhere;
> Go tell it on the mountain,
> To let my people go...."

The fire came the first time when the good soldier-men in Washington and Moscow decided on mutual suicide. The Russians thought of victory in terms of population destruction. They shot at cities. Our people suffered more than Mr. Charley. We lived in the cities that were the targets. But so did the white liberals who were helping bring change.

The fire came a second time when militants burned remnants of Whitey's cities. Mr. Chancy was too busy with his war to be bothered then, but the fire came a third time when he finished and turned his attention inward. There was civil war between whites and blacks. Might may not make right, but it makes victory. White's Mate. A Fool's Mate. Black loses, and now tomorrow is yesterday.

The war killed most all the good folks. They lived where the bombs fell. The rednecks and the militants seem to be the only survivors. And now the rednecks, who waited so long for their chance, are "puttin' 'em back in their place." There are very few of us out here in the hills. We're hunted, and running, but *free*.

My son Al came to me this morning, while I was at the spring getting water for breakfast coffee. He asked when we could go home. Said he's getting tired of camping in a smelly cave. He misses Jamey, the son of the white couple who lived next door in St. Louis. At five he's too young to understand a child killed in war. Nor would he understand if I told him Jamey's father was one of the vigilantes who drove us south into these hills. He wouldn't understand, and I'm afraid to try an explanation. Because I don't understand either.

Met a man while I was hunting his morning. Gave me a rabbit he had extra, for which I was thankful. Said his name was Duncan X and he was trying to round up men for a freedom raid into the Bootheel. A lot of our people working down there, he said. Have to free them. I told him I'd like to help, but I have a family. Four kids, the oldest fifteen, and no wife. He looked at me like I was a monster and traitor, then wandered off through the woods, carrying his rifle with the safety off. He was wearing old Army camouflage fatigues. I soon lost sight of him, but I heard him singing for a long time.

> "Who's that yonder dressed in black?
> Let my people go,
> Must be a hypocrite turning back,
> Let my people go...."

What could I do? I hate the way things are as much as he, but there are the children to be cared for. I'm sick of the shooting and burning and

Song from a Forgotten Hill

dying. We're all Americans. Aren't we? Why do we have to hate so much? We've got a nation to rebuild.

After the wanderer left, I went up to my secret place to pray. It's a lonely, windy place atop a hill burned bald by an old fire. I usually feel close to God there, but not today. Lines from a joke I once heard one white man telling another ran through my mind. A Negro was hanging from a cliff, unable to save himself. He called for God's help and was told to have faith, to let go, and he would be saved. As he fell, a voice from the sky said, "Ah hates Nigras." I can't help thinking, sometimes, that he hates one of the races. He keeps us fighting on and on. Forever, it seems.

The hunters came while the kids and I were eating lunch. The hounds could be heard while they were still far off. I sent the children down the trail we picked when we first came, then took my rifle and went to see what was happening.

I watched from the underbrush as a dozen men with bloodhounds entered the clearing where I had spoken with Duncan X. They were hunting the organizer, but, from the hounds' behavior, they knew there had been two men in that clearing. They were trying to decide which trail to follow. I sighted on the leader's chest and prayed they wouldn't make me shoot. The Lord must have heard that one. They set off along Duncan's trail. I sighed with relief, but felt more guilty than ever. I hoped he could outrun the pack.

I watched the clearing for a long time after they left, afraid some would turn back to the second trail. Their sort didn't appreciate mine running free. In their own way, they were as afraid as I. Who could blame them? When you treat men the way they do, you have to worry about being hit back. Then everyone's afraid, and fear breeds hate. And hate leads to bloodshed.

I waited, and after a while I followed their trail. They were moving southeast, toward the Bootheel. I turned back after being satisfied of our safety. Trotting, I went after the children. They were waiting quietly in the hiding place we had chosen when we first came into these hills. Little Al thought it a marvelous game of hide and seek, but the others, who were old enough to understand what was happening, were frightened.

"Are they gone?" Lois asked, her brown eyes wide with fright. She was the oldest, and could understand something of our situation. She remembered life before the fire came, and knew the hatreds hatched in the incubator of war.

"They're gone," I sighed. "I want you to say a prayer for Duncan tonight, before you go to bed. He's a fool, but he *is* one of our people. Come on. Let's go have supper."

As we were nearing the cave, far away, we heard the *pop-pop-pop* of rifles. I winced. Lois looked at me accusingly. The shooting was in the south. If it was Duncan and his pursuers, then the man was running a circle. "You kids start supper," I said. "I'm going up the mountain for a while." I looked at Lois. She stared back, still silently accusing. I turned and left. There was no point in explaining. She was a militant in her own fashion, and never understood when I did try. As well talk to a stone.

I went up the bald hill, to the little cross I've put there, and prayed. I wondered if God was listening. He'd been terribly unresponsive the past few years. A preacher, just before the war broke, told me the millennium was at hand. I was patiently skeptical at the time, but now it looked as if the man was right. The Lord was unlocking the seven seals and I felt I was living on the Plain of Armageddon. For all I tried putting my trust in God, I felt reservations. He was no longer the loving God of the New Testament. He was the fiery deity who wreaked havoc throughout the Old. Sad.

There were shots again as I came down to the cave. Still far away, but now around to the southwest. Lois had heard them too. When I reached our home-in-exile, she silently offered the rifle. I shook my head. She bit her lip viciously and turned away, saying nothing. The silence hurt more than bitter accusation. We were drifting apart, she and I.

We had a good supper. After a stew made of the rabbit Duncan had given me, I opened a can of peaches and gave the kids a treat. It was usually a holiday when we opened canned goods. Little Al wanted to know which one. Before I could reply, Lois said, "It's the day Judas sold a good man for his own peace."

Song from a Forgotten Hill

That hurt, but I didn't pick up the argument. Instead, I took out my old notebook and went outside. As the sun set, I wrote down the day's events, just as I had done since we had come to the cave. After a while, Lois came out to apologize. I said I understood, but I didn't, really, no more than she.

I wrote for an hour, until it was almost too dark to see the paper. The kids came and went, to the spring and back, to the wood pile and back, getting ready for bed and the night. I did not really notice them. I was thinking about Lois, about her growing militancy and her words of accusation. I did not want the kids to sink into the same morass of hatred which had already claimed so many. Neither did I want them to think me a "Tom." I did not think myself a "Tom," but Duncan X, and those who believed as he did, said those who went into slavery also denied it. I began to feel a great sadness. Was there no reasonable alternative to hatred and fighting? There was slavery, of course, but that was not an alternative. It must all be a cosmic jest, or a chess game. Would the Ivory and Ebony play to the last piece? Would God, or the gods, then declare a draw? Sad.

In my preoccupation, I did not see the running man coming up the hill. He was almost on me before I noticed him. A fall of loose rock warned me when he was about twenty feet away. I jumped up and started to go after the rifle. Then I recognized him. Duncan X. Panting, staggering, his clothing torn, blood oozing from a dozen gashes. His pack was gone, and his canteen belt, but he still carried the rifle. I waited till he came close.

"Mon, you gotta hep me," he said. The fear in his voice was the same I had heard before the kids and I left the mess in St. Louis. "Mon, they gon' kill me!"

"What happened?"

"Dogs...dogs caught me. Killed 'em, all but one. Mon, they chewed me bad."

"Come inside. We've got a first-aid kit. Lois!"

She came out, looked at Duncan's wounds, and threw her hands to her cheeks.

"Clean up those gashes," I said. "Bandage him if we've got anything."

"Mon, they gon' kill me!" The loud, confident rebel of the morning was gone. He was a hundred and twenty years of scared nigger, running from a lynch mob. When the ropes came out, and the hounds and the guns, he was every black man who had ever run from redneck "justice." He was afraid, and running, probably a dead man, and didn't know why.

"Go ahead. Fix him up," I told Lois. "Heat up some of that stew."

She looked at me strangely, questioningly, making no move. I took the rifle from Duncan's hands, though he tried to stop me. He clung to that weapon like a drowning man to a log. It was the only salvation he knew. It was the only salvation anyone seemed to know these days. Lois watched me take the gun, then took Duncan's hand and led him into the cave. I watched her go, wondering what it was like to be an adult at fifteen.

As the moon came up, I walked back the way Duncan had come. I heard the hound baying, not more than a mile away. Hard. I didn't like things this way, but my decision had been made for me.

I chose my position carefully, behind a large log at the edge of a clearing. They were not long in coming.

The hunters had chosen to leash their remaining hound, keeping him where he could be protected. And there were only nine men. If Duncan had gotten the other three they wanted him worse than ever. They might not quit till they were all dead, or had their "buck" swinging from a tree. I knew sadness again.

I put the first shot between the hound's eyes. He yelped once, leaping toward the moon. I emptied the clip among running men, but hit no one. They reacted quickly. Rifles and shotguns boomed, peppering the woods around me. I ran, trying to keep low. Without that hound they would have a hard time following.

The shooting stopped a moment later. They realized they were wasting ammunition, trying to murder an empty forest.

I returned to the cave. Lois had fed Duncan, and patched him, and had put him in my bed. He was sleeping, though fitfully, like a man with bad dreams.

Song from a Forgotten Hill

"What'd you do?" she asked, at once frightened of and for me.

"Shot their dog. They won't be tracking Duncan or me without him."

"Oh."

"Stoke up the fire a little, will you? I want to do some writing while I'm watching. Then get to bed. It's been a bad day."

"But Duncan…"

"I'll look after him. You just go on to bed."

She went. I wrote for a while, then leaned back to think. Eventually, I dozed off. A couple hours must have passed.

I started awake. There were sounds outside the cave. The fire had died to coals. Carefully, I reached for the water pitcher and used it to drown the remains. A figure moved across the cave mouth, outlined by the moonlight. White man! His skin shone in the light. I took the rifle from the table and fell into a prone position. I waited while they talked it over out there. They seemed certain their quarry was inside. I didn't know how they had found the cave—blind luck, probably—but once here, they knew they had their man. I remembered having seen Duncan's fatigue jacket outside, a dead giveaway. I cursed myself for being fool enough to expect them to stop after losing their hound.

They didn't bother with a warning or to-do about surrender. They came in the cave, trying to sneak up on Duncan. I started shooting. The .30-.06 roared like a cannon in the confinement of the cave. The muzzle flashes splashed white faces with orange light.

I never was much good at killing, not in Vietnam, not here. They were less than twenty feet away, but I only hit one, in the arm. They got out before I could get another.

The shooting woke the kids. Lois slipped up beside me where I lay in the cave mouth, asking what had happened.

"Never mind!" I snapped. "You get the kids out the hole in back. Go up to the hiding place. I'll meet you later."

"Aren't you coming?"

"Lois, neither Duncan nor I can get through that passage. It's too tight. Now get."

As if to punctuate my argument, the rednecks opened up. It was like a regular war, like I saw in Vietnam. They were all over the slope. Bullets whined and pinged as they bounced from one cave wall to another. Lois left, dragging the younger kids down the small tunnel which opened on the far side of the hill.

Duncan crawled up beside me. "Right side fo' me," he said. "How many?"

"Eight. Nine if you count the one I wounded. Didn't think they'd find us after I shot their dog."

"Mon, them honkies half dog themselves. One day you gon' learn."

We shot at muzzle flashes. Funny. Of all the stuff I had in the cave, ammunition was the one thing not in short supply. And me a peaceful man.

"Hey, Duncan," someone downslope shouted, *"who's* that up there with you?"

"Who's that?" I asked, whispering.

"Jake Kinslow. Him an' me met befo'."

"Hey, Duncan boy," Kinslow shouted, "you better come out before you get your friend in trouble. Whoever you are, mister, this ain't none of your nevermind. We got no argument with you. We just want that rabble-rousing, baby-raping nigger in there with you."

I looked at Duncan. His teeth gleamed as he grinned. "I shacked with his daughter befo' the war. He gon' get even now."

To hide my reaction, I turned and snapped a shot in the direction of Jake's voice. There was a cry. I was surprised.

"Jake, I'm hit!" someone screamed. "God, my leg, my leg!"

Laughing, Duncan reached over and punched my shoulder. "Seven," he said.

"Mister," Jake shouted, "we're gonna hang that nigger. You don't get out, we might hang you too. We got no cause to be after you yet."

Yet. Meaning they were going to be if I didn't get out of their way. But how could I, even if I wanted to? They had put me in a position where I had no choice.

Time passed. We exchanged shots, but the firing dropped off. The moon eventually rose to where it was shining directly into the cave. I

Song from a Forgotten Hill

glanced at my watch, miraculously still working. Eleven. It had been a long, strange day, and still wasn't over.

A scream downslope drew my attention. I recognized it. Lois!

They dragged her into the moonlight, where I could see her. Jake shouted, "You up there! You see what we've caught hanging around, spying? Know what we're gonna do? Same thing Duncan did to *my* daughter, unless you come out."

I growled deep in my throat. "Let her go!" I shouted. I rose and started out, but Duncan tripped me and dragged me back.

"We'll let her go when we get Duncan!" Kinslow shouted. "Meanwhile, we're gonna have some fun."

I tried to get a clear shot at the man holding Lois, but he stayed behind her, no matter how much she struggled. Duncan dragged me back again. "They're going to rape her!" I snarled. "Let me go!"

"Mon," he said, grinning wickedly, "they gon' rape her anyway. They's honkies. Gon' kill us an' rape her anyway."

"No!" I suddenly shouted, coming to a sudden decision. He had an expression of surprise on his face when I hit him with the gunbarrel. It faded as he fell. "You!" I shouted down the hill. "Jake! Let the girl go! I'll throw Duncan out to you!"

"No! Don't do it!" Lois screamed. "They'll kill you anyway!"

"Throw him out first!" Kinslow yelled.

"Let her go!"

"Tell you what. We'll bring her up and trade you."

I thought for a moment. "All right. But just one man." They were quiet for a while. Lois kept screaming for me to stop, till they gagged her, but I couldn't throw my daughter to them to save someone like Duncan. "All right, mister," Jake called, "I'm coming up. You bring that nigger out. No tricks. Pretty girl gets it if there are."

I saw movement below, near the edge of the trees. Lois, being dragged by a white man. She was kicking and scratching, but he ignored her. They came up the hill. When I judged they were close enough, I lifted Duncan and went out. He was half-conscious, just enough to stand with my help, not enough to understand what was happening.

Jake stopped about five feet away. He held a pistol to the side of Lois' head. He grinned. "Okay, boy. We trade."

"Let her go."

He moved slightly behind my daughter. He grinned again. "Dumb nigger!" he whispered, then dove behind rocks toward which he had been moving.

The rifles barked all around the cave. I felt bullets hit Duncan. One caught me in the thigh, spinning me away, back into the cavern. As I fell, I saw Lois stagger and try for the cave, but Kinslow fired around the rock.

"Only one of you in there now, black boy," he laughed. "And we're gonna get you. Gonna have a real old-fashioned hanging."

I suppose they are. That was twenty minutes ago. I'm writing this by moonlight, as they creep closer. The bullets are coming in a steady rain, ricocheting throughout the cavern. One will get me any minute. The King of Ivory wins another match. Sad.

I forgot. All the good ones were dead. I trusted bad ones. If God is in a better mood later, I guess I'll have all eternity to think about it. Hatred. It's sad.

"Go tell it on the mountain,
Over the hill and everywhere;
Go tell it on the mountain,
To let my people go—"

And Dragons in the Sky

In this frenetic, quick-shift, go, drop-your-friends-possessions-roots-loyalties like throwaway containers age, heroes, legends, archetypal figures are disposable: as brilliant and ephemeral as the butterflies of Old Earth. One day some researcher may wrest from Nature a golden, universe-changing secret, some brave ship's commander may shatter the moment's enemy, be a hero, legend for a fleeting hour—and fade to dust with Sumer and Akkad. Who remembers on the seventh day? Who remembers Jupp von Drachau finding those Sangaree? Mention his name. Blank stares reply. Or someone may say, "He's too old," meaning too long gone. A whole year, Confederation.

I think of heroes and legends as, toolcase in hand, I wander toward the gate of Carson's Blake City spaceport, wearing a name a size too small—latest in a list of dozens—the clothing of a liquids transfer systems tech—which work I loathe—and, within me, the nerves of an instel radio. A small, dying pain surrounds a knot behind my right ear. Each slow step drives spikes of agony into the bones of my legs. They've been lengthened three inches, hastily. My stomach itches where twenty pounds have been taken off, hastily again. This is a hurry-up job.

But, then, aren't they all? There's no time, these days, for carefully executed operations. Everything is rushed. Nothing is permanent, there are no fixed points on which to anchor. Life is like the flash floods of Sierran rivers in thaw time, roaring and cascading past too swiftly for any part to be seized and intimately known. But wait! In the river of life apassing, there *are* a few fixed rocks, two long-lived legends that're heavy on my mind. Like boulders in Sierran streams, they're all but hidden in the turbulence of our times, but they endure, go forever on.

There has to be something for me. *I want!* I cry, but what I don't know. I've been trying to find it through all my years with the Bureau.

Ahead, I spot my small, brown, mustached Oriental partner, Mouse. Making no sign, I turn in the gate behind him. We don't know each other this time.

I wish there were something solid to grasp, to *know*. Everything moves so fast… Only in legends…

There is Star's End; there are the High Seiners. Sheer mystery is Star's End, fortress planet beyond the galactic rim, with automatic, invincible weapons to kill anyone foolish enough to go near—without a shred of why. In the lulls, the deep, fearful lulls when there's nothing to say, nothing being said, we moderns seize Star's End as strange country to explore, explain, to extinguish the dreadful silence—we're intrigued, perhaps, by the godlike power there, destructive as that of ancient, Earth-time deities. Or we turn to the High Seiners, the Starfishers.

We should know them. They're human. Star's End is just a dead metal machine's voice babbling unknown tongues. Yet, in their humanness, the High Seiners are the greater, more frightening mystery. Destruction is familiar, though to encompass its purpose is sometimes impossible. The quiet, fixed culture of the Seiners we comprehend not at all, though we yearn for it, hate them for their blissful stasis: their changelessness oddly twists our souls.

But such thoughts fade. Work comes first. I enter the terminal, great plastic, glass, and steel cavern with doors opening on other worlds. Light crowds it. We need light these days, fearful as we are of entropic night. (I wanted to be a poet once. An instructor assigned me a paean to Night. I lost my want then. Too many dark images crowded my mind.) People are here in their multitudes, about the familiar business of terminals.

And Dragons in the Sky

Several men in odd, plain High Seiners' garb wait behind a distant table. My new employers.

Mouse passes small and brownly with a wink—why that name I don't know. He looks more like a weasel.

I study faces in the crowd, mostly see bewilderment, determination, malaise. I'm after the nonchalant ones. The competition is here somewhere. The Bureau has no copyright on interest in Starfish. "Uhn!"

"Excuse me?"

I turn. A small blue nun has paused, thinking I've spoken. "Pardon. Just thinking out loud." The Ulantonid wobbles off, leaving me wondering why all modern Christians are aliens. But it fades. I return to that face.

Yes, Marya Strehltsweiter—one name I remember—though she has changed too. Darker: skin, hair, eyes, darker, and heavier. But she can't disguise her ways of moving, speaking, listening. A poor actress, unusual in her race. She's Sangaree, who have passed as human for ages—who, also, are almost always murdered on discovery. Marya has talent. She stays alive.

She sees me looking. Eyebrows raise a millimeter, questioningly, then consternation briefly, before a smile. She knows me, remembers the last time we crossed swords—I think of a place in Angel City on the Broken Wings, of lifting the papers Von Drachau needed to nail the Sangaree. Perhaps, she's thinking, this'll be *her* game. She nods ever so slightly.

Other faces tease my memory, though I think they serve no governments. Corporation agents, perhaps, or McGraws. Considering what we're after, I'll not be surprised if there are more agents, than job-hungry techs here.

The crowd. I now see it as a whole, much smaller than expected. Maybe two hundred. The Seiners advertised for a thousand. Hard to find techs romantic, or hungry, enough to plunge into an alien human society for a year.

Speculation dissolves. The Starfishers are checking us in. I shuffle into line four places behind Mouse, wondering why he's so shaky. He's always shaky.

"Mr. Niven." A whisper, warm rubbing my arm. I look down into eyes dark as Sangaree gunmetal coins.

"Pardon, ma'am? BenRabi. Moyshe benRabi."

"How quaint." She smiles a gunmetal smile. My bed she has shared, and would share, I know—and, in the end, she'd drink my blood. "And the Rat, eh?" Meaning Mouse. "So many people want to bleed for a little Seiner money. Orbit in an hour. See you." More gunmetal smiling as she takes her gunmetal-hard body toward the *Ladies*.

The nervousness begins, as it always does before I jump in the lion's den. Or dragon's lair. They say, to the uninitiated, the Starfish appear as dragons a hundred miles long…

Before liftoff, a briefing. The officer-in-charge is brutally honest. "We don't want you," he says, "we need you. You'll mock us as anachronisms. Oh, yes," to a lone headshake. "You're here hunting the myth of the Starfishers, or to spy, but you'll find neither romance nor information—just hard work and strangeness. We won't ease you into our culture. You're here only so we can meet our harvest contracts." I suffer a premonition, a feeling this man has more than harvests on his mind. Plainly, through his words, I sense disappointment, a touch of hatred for landsmen. They have a wounded ship out there, badly mauled—I'm not sure I believe that—which needs a thousand techs to salvage, and they are only getting two hundred.

He pauses, fumbles in pockets—a *pocketed, cloth* jacket—produces an odd little instrument. Only after it's lit and belching noxious clouds do I recognize it. A pipe! I shudder. Romantic techs, I see, are wondering what greater horrors lurk ahead. Good psychology, the pipe. The Seiner is easing us in after all, preparing us for bigger shocks to come.

"Among you," he says after his pause grows squirming long, "are spies. So many interests want a Starfish herd." He smiles, but it quickly fades to grimness. "You'll learn nothing. Till your contracts end, you'll see nothing but the guts of ships—and only when you work. You'll not come in contact with those who have the information you're after. You, who'd steal our livelihood and culture, be warned. We're a nation, a law unto ourselves. We hold to old ways, still execute for espionage and treason."

And Dragons in the Sky

While the pause for effect lasts, I think of the many times Confederation has tried to bring the Seiners into the fold, to impress upon them "enlightened" justice. They always fail, yet annexation remains a major government goal.

A nervous stir runs through the room. The briefing officer meets pairs of eyes one by one. The romantics are finding their legend toothed and clawed. The disquiet grows. Executions. You don't *execute* people any more.

Soon we're herded aboard a shuttle—first landsmen for the fleets in generations—that is obviously no commercial lighter, just stark functionalism and steel painted gray. We're lifting blind, I see. Weedlike clumps of wiring hang where viewscreens have been removed—no chances are they taking.

The knot behind my ear, the nondispersable parts of the tracer, seizes me with iron, spiked fingers. I've been "switched on" by the Bureau. I stagger. The thin, pale Starfisher girl seating us asks, "Are you ill?" On her face, shocking me more than talk of execution, is a look of true concern, not bland, commercially dispensed stewardess's care.

I want fires across my mind, as it so often does. "Yes." Dropping into my seat, "A touch of migraine." But I can never discover what I need.

Her eyes widen a fraction. She'll report this. But, somewhere in my medical file, a tendency toward migraine is noted to cover the pain of the tracer. I am susceptible, though it hasn't bothered me in years. There are pills. Why, I ask myself again, do they have to use an imperfect device? Of course, it's all we've got, the only way to track them to the herd. Completely nonmetal, the tracer is the only undetectable device available.

I want is in my mind. The Bureau has supported my years of search, knowing I'm searching (Psych doesn't miss much), knows it's showing a good return on investment (the sane make poor agents, axmen, or whatever). Years, and I still have no intimation of the absence in my soul.

The vessel shivers. We're on the way to the orbiting Starfisher. Three rows ahead, Mouse shakes. He's terrified by space travel.

"The Rat's chicken." She's beside me. I didn't see her sit down. "Sorry to startle you. Maria Elana Gonzalez, atmosphere systems, distribution." Gunmetal smile.

I want. What? "Moyshe benRabi." In case she has forgotten. We exchange nothings all the way to the Starfisher, too wary to probe for clues to one another's missions.

I'm forgetting she's Sangaree, that once I used her to find and kill a lot of her people. I don't feel guilty, either—not that I hate Sangaree, as is common. In my mood of the moment she doesn't count. Nothing does. I'm the uninvolved, uncommitted, unemotional modern man. I'm concerned more with Mouse than the steel-souled death beside me.

According to our pasts on file, our paths have never crossed. But this is our fourth team job and, though he's always afraid, he's a good partner—especially when the roughhouse begins. He's the only person I know who has killed a man (except the Sangaree lady who, being Sangaree, doesn't qualify as a person). Killing isn't uncommon these days, but the personal touch has been eliminated—ergo, the shock of "execution." Anyone can punch a button, hurl a missile to obliterate a ship of a thousand souls. There is no lack of nice remote space battles (against Sangaree, McGraw pirates, in the marquee-and-reprisal antics of governments, in raids and overnight wars), but to do in a man face-to-face, with knife or gun…it's just too personal. We don't like to get close to people, even to kill.

I'm afraid. I'm getting close to, growing fond of, Mouse. We work together too much. Bad for our detachment. The Bureau promised no more jobs together last time, but then came this hurry-up, top-men job. Always the rush. Somehow, sometime, one of us will get hurt. We're so much safer as islands in motion (Brownian), pausing for interaction, moving on before roots can take, be ripped up, leave painful wounds.

There's a clang through the shuttle, rousing me. We've nosed into the mother ship like piglet to sow's belly. The pale, helpful girl leads us into the starship, to a common room where notables wait.

They're unceremonious. One says, "I'm Eduard Chouteau, Ship's Commander. You're aboard Number Three Service Ship from *Danion*,

And Dragons in the Sky

a harvestship of Payne's fleet. You're to replace people *Danion* lost in a shark attack. We don't like outsiders, but we'll try to make your stay comfortable. We've got to keep *Danion* alive until we receive replacements from our schools..." I have the feeling he isn't telling all Starfisher motives.

Most everyone, via the romantic entertainment media, knows of the Seiner schools, the crèches within asteroids of deep space where Starfishers hide their children. They are nursery schools, boarding schools, military academies, technical colleges, safehouses where children can grow up unexposed to disasters of *Danion*'s sort. Unlike landsmen, though, Seiners send their children to professional parents out of love. We do so to be rid of cargo that may slow us in shooting the rapids of life.

"Lights," says the Ship's Commander. They fade. Central to the common, a spatial hologram appears. "Those aren't our stars. The ship *is* ours. *Danion*." Something focuses, something like octopuses entwining—no, like a city sewage system with buildings and earth removed, vast tangles of tubing with here and there a cube, a cone, a ball, with occasional sheets of silverness, or great nets floating, between arms of piping, raggedly bearded with hundreds, thousands of antennae. In theory, a deep space ship needs not be contained, needs have no specific shape, yet this is the first such I've ever encountered. I realize I've discovered an unsuspected rigidity of human thought. The needle-shaped ship has been with us since space travel was but a dream.

My surprise is shared. A stir runs through the common. But now I'm suffering another surprise.

Mouse and I once studied the Seiner from Carson's surface. She's a typical interstellar vessel. A ship of her class approaches the harvestship in the hologram. The surprise is relative size. The starship is a needle falling into an ocean of scrap. The harvestship must be thirty miles in cross-section.

Light returns, drowning the hologram. Around me are open mouths. We thought we were *aboard* a harvestship. I begin, with distress, to realize how little prepared I am to go among these people, how little the Bureau has told me. A more than usual job-beginning nervousness sets in. Until now, with change the order in my fast-paced universe, I've assumed I can handle the strange, the unknown—but this space-borne mobile, it's *too* alien. True alien handiwork suddenly seems less foreign, less frightful. It's the size. Nothing human should be so *big*.

"This's all you'll know of *Danion*," says the Ship's Commander, "of her exterior. Her guts you'll know well. We'll get our money's worth from you there."

And they will. Fifteen hours a day, teamed with Seiner technicians, we landsmen will labor to keep *Danion* alive and harvesting. Scarce four hundred of us will manage the work of a thousand—and, in our free time, we'll repair the shark attack damage responsible for the original casualties. Daily, we'll work to exhaustion, then stagger to our bunks too weary even to think about spying...

But there're problems first, a time of distress two days after departure. The ship drops from hyper. I, and everyone, assume we've arrived. We gather in the common room, a custom of travelers, somehow expecting viewscreens and a look at our new home. Shortly, however, the First Lieutenant appears.

"Please return to your quarters," he says. He seems paler than the usual Starfisher. "We're ambushing Confederation Navy ships following us from Carson's."

I'm dumbstruck. The Navy shouldn't move in yet. Nor should Seiners so casually turn on pursuers—not, at least, on *my* Navy. I look around. The few angry faces I label "competition dismayed." Across the room, Mouse appears bewildered. The Sangaree woman is in a rage, face red, fists clenched.

The First Lieutenant fields a few questions before retreating, all with a single explanation. "We've entered a hydrogen stream, taken station with a fleet. Starfish noise is being broadcast from scoutships. We often do this to cover the withdrawal of our vessels forced to enter 'civilized space.'" He leaves us thinking.

We go too, Mouse and I glumly wondering if we're now expendable.

The general alarm sounds. Engagement is imminent. I hope the admiral (I'm considering my own survival, not his comfort) recognizes

And Dragons in the Sky

the trap and gets out. I'm hoping the Seiners don't do angry, rash things afterward.

I've hardly strapped in. The vessel rocks. Departing missiles. I'm amazed. She's got batteries heavier than her appearance suggests.

I took this job expecting the total boredom of unchange, nul-novelty, but find surprises come almost too fast to assimilate.

The all-clear sounds shortly, and with it a buzz from my cabin door. It opens. A crewman asks, "Mr. benRabi? Come with us, please." He's polite, oh, polite as the spider inviting the fly. His teeth seem all white sharp and pointy. Behind him are ratings with angry guns. Yes, I'll go with him.

As I join him in the passage, another door opens with a characteristic squeal. Yes. A group is collecting Mouse. Done already, I think, and by space gypsies centuries behind the times. How?

"Ah," says the Ship's Commander as we enter his office, "Commander Igarashi, Commander McClennon."

My eyebrows rise. I didn't know Mouse's name, but Igarashi it might be. He's got me nailed, though McClennon I haven't used in fifteen years. "Please be seated."

I sit, glance at Mouse. He, too, is stunned.

"You're wondering about your Navy friends? Decided discretion was the better part. Admiral Beckhart must be perturbed." He chuckles. "But that's not why you're here. It's those tracers you've got built in."

This startles me. He's talking plural. I thought I was the only one with a unit, and Mouse was along for the ride. Mouse, it seems, thought the same. Wheels within wheels, and I should've guessed. It's the Bureau's way.

"*All* biological, eh? Interesting development. Passed our detectors easily. But we're a paranoid people—and think of everything." Smugness. "We've watched the hyper bands since liftoff, had you pegged in hours. Dr. DuMaurier..."

Hands seize me. The doctor examines me quickly, numbs my neck and the side of my head with an aerosol anesthetic. He produces an antique lase-scalpel.

The Ship's Commander says, "This'll be fast and painless. We'll pull the ambergris nodes…and sell them back to the Navy next auction, I think." He chuckles again. I smile. There's a curious justice in it. Mouse and I, and others, are aboard in hopes of locating the great night-beasts which produce just that little item.

Ambergris, the High Seiner calls it. My studies say ambergris is a "morbid secretion" of Old Earth whales, very valuable. Others, landsmen, call the material star's amber, spacegold, skydiamond, any of many names. It's the wealth of our age. In the old tongues its name is hard, pithy. It's the solid wastes of Starfish—crap, but crap without which interstellar civilization, as it exists, could not be. There would be no fast star-to-star communication.

In a way I don't understand (having no knowledge of the physics), a tachyon flow is generated in a gap between as ambergris node and a Bilao crystal anode. These are the only materials that will do. Neither can be synthesized. Bilao crystal, mined on Sierra, is many times cheaper than ambergris. The tachyon stream is formed into a coherent beam which computers impress and aim at a receiver. Each tachyon carries an impressed hologramatic portrait of the whole message. The receiver need catch but a few. Thus distance, diffusion, beam spread, small aiming errors are overcome.

Every planet in The Arm, of six races and countless governments (the Sangaree not included) is part of an instel net: military, government or commercial. The demand for ambergris far exceeds the supply. Such a vast market can never be saturated.

Communication is the foundation of civilization. There are trillions of beings in The Arm, thousands of planets, millions of ships, all wanting instel—and all the Seiner fleets produce less than a hundred thousand nodes each year. No wonder the vultures gather.

Vultures. Mouse and I are vultures—no, rapacious birds, falcons hurled aloft to bring down game information. We're to locate a herd, tell Navy where, let it be seized for Confederation. A better ownership than the Seiners', who sell to anyone meeting their price. They're too democratic, from Confederation's viewpoint. Often, under their system, the stones go to belligerent, imperialistic governments or unscrupulous corporations.

And Dragons in the Sky

We're here to stop that. Uh-huh. Sometimes you tell yourself tall ones, else you ask questions, worrying no-matters like *right* and *wrong*.

My soul, slithering past morality shyly, merely mumbles *I want*. There is pain in it I can't withstand. I must find my Grail, and soon, or abandon this secret quest. I've seen men so, in grim places on beautiful worlds, zombies with humanness gone, defeated by the universe, time, and all-too-rapid change, the little ones in madhouses, the big ones masters of corporations or governments in which people are the cattle of machines. Not for me, no... My soul howls at an invisible moon.

"One down." The doctor tosses the node-anode piece to the Ship's Commander. I feel no pain. I'm glad he interrupts the thoughts. I'm on the edge of a scream. He turns to Mouse.

"We don't like spies," says the Ship's Commander. *We*. Always these people say *we*. The worm within me squirms. This man touches my need. I try to seize something, to *know*, but like a wet catfish it easily wriggles from my grasp. "But *Danion's* dying. We love her. We'll keep you alive, keep our contracts, work you till you drop, till *Danion* can live without you, then we'll send you away. Please be no more trouble than you've been. We need you desperately, but we'll not be pushed too far. Return to your quarters. We'll get underway soon, for home."

I rise, touching the small bandage behind my ear. There is no pain, but its presence makes me think of bigger cuts on my body and soul.

Mouse is done. We walk glumly along a passage, unescorted. There is nothing to say, so we're silent. Finally, as we near my cabin, he asks, "What now?"

I shrug. We're partners, neither senior, but I've been hoping he would decide. "Go for the ride, I guess. We have a year. Can they keep their guard up forever?"

Beyond Mouse I see the Sangaree lady. She smiles and waves. There's a hint of gloating in her manner. She somehow helped betray us, probably by pointing out which men were Navy agents.

Mouse catches it too. "Should've killed her on the Broken Wings," he mutters. He's shaking. His brown face wrinkles nastily. "Maybe this time."

I shake my head. "Not here, not now. We've got enough trouble already."

Mouse has never liked her. (I shouldn't, but I haven't his singular gift of hatred. Everyone, everything is too transient for more than mild aversion.) He frequently needs restraint. "She'd better move fast when we hit dirt." I hope our year here will temper his feelings, but fear it won't. His hatred's beyond the usual. I think someone close was a Sangaree stardust addict ("the dream that burns, the joy that kills," the poet Czyzewski said as he was dying). His assignments, he says, are all counter-Sangaree. Those I've shared, he prosecuted with fanatic zeal.

The Sangaree. Who, what are they? Like the Seiners and Star's End, another legendary force, but satanic, one we seldom mention. Like the savage in the night before his fire, we withhold the name of the demon for fear of invoking his presence. After centuries of sullen, subdued conflict, we know little about them. They are humanoid, pass for human, even produce mule offspring on human women. They come from afar, planet unknown. Their numbers are limited, supposedly because their women conceive only under their native sun.

A particle from that sun, long ago, buzzed through space, atmosphere, flesh, ricocheted through a chromosome, rearranged DNA, obliquely fathered a race of brigands. All the worst characteristics of Mongol, Viking, Caribbean pirate, Mafiosi, Chinese Tong hatchetman, name it, are stamped on Sangaree genes. For themselves they produce little. They raid, they steal, they deal in drugs and slaves and guns—anything profitable (in their own view, they do nothing wrong). They are cunning, hard to find, operate as shadow-masters of native syndicates complex as Minoan labyrinths—all as government agents. Crime is their racial industry.

They are considered a nuisance, prosecuted at opportunity—except by Man. In us the Sangaree inspire irrational hatred, deadly retaliation—I think because in them we see mirrored the demons lurking on the borders of our own benighted souls. Sangaree are what we would

And Dragons in the Sky

be if freed from social restraint. Thus Jupp von Drachau's bloody action after Mouse and I located Sangaree headquarters for their human operations. Their privateers he destroyed, their drug farms and refineries, the laboratories where they force-grew pleasure slaves to the fantasy specifications of wealthy, evil men.

"I hope we find their world before I die," Mouse says. I feel a twinge of jealousy. Mouse has his Grail. It's a cup of blood and hatred, but I envy him his wholeness. Would that hate were simple enough for me.

We reach the harvestship. In the pressure of work I forget my screaming need. It haunts me only at night, or when I encounter the Sangaree woman, inevitable because air ducts and liquids pipes follow the same service passages. Then I'm ripped from my peace for, invariably, she'll taunt Mouse (we work together for the convenience of Security Department), and the wholeness of being that permits him a predictable response reminds me of my own incompleteness.

"Well, Rat," she may say, "killed anybody lately? Lots of non-Confeds here. Why not me? Or don't you have the guts?" She knows he has, but thinks she can take him. She's sure he's a strike-from-behind man, but he's much more. Mouse wants to demonstrate, but he fiercely represses temptation. She's playing some game. We want the stakes and rules before getting in. She's no actress. Her easy confidence gives her away.

During the passing months I learn of Starfish. Once they were just a wonderful concept. Now, with my contract half complete, I know that there are many forms of "life" in the hydrogen streams, though it's life difficult to comprehend, consisting more in fields of force than in common matter. A grandfather Starfish two hundred miles long and a million years old contains fewer atoms than a human adult, most unbound by molecular energies. They are more foci upon which forces are anchored, gravity and subtle electromagnetic forces which permeate the twists and folds of time and space surrounding a Starfish "body." Within his vacuole universe, the creature supposedly exists as solidly real as we. What the Seiners sense with their instruments is but a fraction of the beast, like a shark's fin seen cutting the surface of an Old Earth ocean.

They feed on hydrogen and the other elements in the fusion chain. Once I asked a Seiner why they don't gather at stars. He said they can't remain integrate in the field stresses about masses much greater than a harvestship, nor can they "digest" matter more complex than the water molecule.

Within a Starfish, surrounded by awesome fields and spread across all their many dimensions, is a fire violent as the heart of a sun. Atoms, primarily hydrogen, are fed in, fast-shuffled through dimensions and a fusion chain, are mixed with antimatter from another universe in which they simultaneously exist; there is annihilation. The energies they bind with dimensional shifts are truly fearsome.

Physics? I don't know. Beside this, the goings-on in a supernova are kindergarten stuff. I understand only that some wastes are evacuated as the ambergris nodes used in instel transmitters.

The greatest, most unsettling surprise to date comes when I discover this is no man-cattle relationship, it's a partnership. Starfish are intelligent and, via machinery whose sophistication we landsmen never suspected, Seiner techs maintain constant mental contact with members of the herds. Starfish produce ambergris, but demand a service in return: protection.

For they're not alone out here. Like oceans, the hydrogen streams teem with life—some "carnivorous." The Starfish have a natural enemy which, at the coming of Man, threatened to end their species. "Sharks," the Seiners call them, after habits cruel as of those sea-killers of Old Earth. They're smaller than Starfish and hunt in packs like wolves and men.

Both species hyper short distances.

Most herds are shadowed by shark packs which, at opportunity, cut a beast from the herd. The Starfish aren't defenseless—they burp up balls of gut-fire and fling them about like granddaddy nuclear bombs, but with sharks so fast and the burping so slow, they seldom get more than a single shot. The packs recently grew tremendously, why unknown. Herds dwindled, unable to cope. Man arrived.

And Dragons in the Sky

The Starfish touched the minds of the early Seiners, explored them, contacted them, made the Bargain. (Sometimes they touch *my* mind, I think, though my imagination may play me tricks. In my dreams I see great swimming space as if with unhuman eyes. Each time I dream, I wake with a screaming migraine.) The Starfish would produce quantities of ambergris in return for protection.

Human guns serve, and missiles. Sharks' binding forces are easily disrupted—then they are feasts for *their* attendant scavengers.

But sharks, in their slow fashion, are intelligent. They now associate high casualties with ships about the prey. An old fear became fact the day sharks turned on *Danion*. Now they hit harvestships before approaching a herd. So it's war—Seiners won't take attack stoically—a war to be lost. The Seiners are too few, the sharks too many, and the slow thought of the enemy seems the only hope.

The pale Seiner who explained this knew more, but when he was about to tell, suddenly fled. They often do. I'm the visible hand of another ancient foe: landsmen.

He was speaking of a need for more powerful weapons when he broke off, left me with a cold premonition. Something grim's happening. I've felt it since coming aboard. This is no ordinary harvest. *Danion* has been under drive for months, sometimes in hyper, which isn't ordinarily done. Near Starfish, a harvestship maneuvers only on "minddrive" (I've heard the term but once—the Seiner wouldn't explain). Other drives harm the beasts.

Seven months have passed. Yesterday the Sangaree woman almost reached Mouse. Whatever her game, it's in its final moves. She's pushing hard. Wish I could figure her, but there's no understanding a Sangaree mind.

The engines are two weeks dead. Wherever we were bound, we arrived. I know little. The Seiners are more closemouthed than ever, speak only when they must.

Nervousness and fear haunt the ship. I hear great shark packs are gathering. I sometimes see weary Seiners from our constantly busy service ships, wonder if they are fighting those packs, or are at something else. Though we landsmen are permitted little knowledge of it, there is a great race on. In some desperate gamble, the Fishers are trying to finish something before the sharks finally throw themselves against us. My ignorance grows trying.

It's evening. Mouse and I are playing chess. Despite ourselves, we grow increasingly close. We're forced together. The Sangaree woman is one of the few who will speak. Others avoid us, fearing guilt by association.

My game's bad. I'm piqued. The *I want*, so long played down in my soul, has burst upon me again, louder than ever, mocking, saying I'm at the threshold but too dense to recognize my discovery.

"I can't hold off much longer," Mouse says, capturing a pawn. "Next time she shows, or the next, I'll bend her."

Moving to protect my queen, "We're almost in. Five months. Don't ruin it."

With a quick hand he slaughters a knight. "Platitudes coming?" I glance at his expressionless face, back to the board. I see disaster.

"Yield." Another pattern of disaster grows clear. I know what she's doing, and how. Unthinking, I stand abruptly. "We may have to!"

"Eh?"

"Bend her. Just figured how she's doing it. Assume she's got a tracer, broadcasting random bleeps…"

"Got you. Easy for the Sangaree to triangulate on, but a worm in her guts *Danion* might never pin down. Let's not bend her, let's chop it out." Coldly, that, with anticipation of pain inflicted. He returns chessmen to their box, takes a wicked, homemade knife from beneath his mattress, says, "Let's go."

I have a hundred reasons for not, for his going alone, for many alternatives, but am able to articulate none. It's time she was stalemated.

We're halfway to her cabin when a notion strikes. "Suppose she's got us bugged." We assume the Seiners listen, but this is the first I think of spying by a third party.

And Dragons in the Sky

"Then she'll expect us." He shrugs. "Better think about it." While he is at it, a squad of Seiners appears.

"Looks like the job gets done for us." They stop at her door.

"They're not thinking!" Mouse is shaking, excited and afraid.

My heart begins a flamenco beat. The Seiners push through the door. As Mouse said, they aren't thinking. Two fall before they get out of sight, dropped by what's waiting there for Mouse and me. Loud reports (later: gunpowder pistols, homemade). Some grunts, a scream. The remaining two men are inside.

"Come on!"

I don't know what he has in mind, but I follow. In the door low he goes, pauses to lift a weapon from a dying Seiner. As I do the same, I see the Sangaree woman beyond him, back to us, struggling with the last Fisher. She disarms him. Her hand darts past his guard, smashes his windpipe.

My grunt tells her of our presence.

"Slowly," says Mouse as she turns. "I'd hate to shoot." Hope is thick in his voice.

For once she does as told, has no instant, sharp reply. As she faces us, her distress is very evident. But it fades into her oppressive smile. "Too late. The last signal's already sent. They'll be here soon…"

Underlining her words, strident alarms hoot. Shortly, *Danion* shivers—service ships launching, I think. "I'll go on station," I say. "Watch her till the masters-at-arms show." I start for Damage Control Central.

How fast news travels! By the time I arrive, the duty section is abuzz about the appearance of fifty Sangaree ships. Frightened landsmen are certain these are our last hours. I don't comprehend till I overhear Seiners out-admiraling Payne himself. They're certain we'll fight.

I shudder.

The Sangaree maneuver in the darkness beyond these walls. Outnumbered service ships race toward them. I wonder if Payne will call for help from other fleets—no, he won't know where they are. Security. Unanswerable questions dash across my mind, the biggest, still: what do I want?

The attack that comes isn't Sangaree. Sharks, distressed by the new arrival, strike in all directions. News filters in from Operations, some good, some bad. The Sangaree are having a hard time. The sharks are concentrating on *Danion*.

In the sea of nothing our ships are killing, being killed by sharks. The Sangaree fight an enemy undiscoverable while, foolishly, trying to move to a position of vantage vis-a-vis the fleet.

Danion shivers constantly, all weapons in action. In the heart of the great mobile we wait, wait, wait for a shudder and alarms to announce the sharks have scored. There is fear aplenty, and courage brewing. For once there is no tension between landsman and Seiner. We are brothers before an unprejudiced Death.

And, though I note it not, my soul is quite content.

Danion reels. Sirens hoot. Officers shout. A damage-control team piles aboard an electric truck and hurries to aid technicians in the affected area. Behind, here, the mood turns quickly grim. Though we feel so little, the damage is tremendous there. Two thousand persons, ten percent of *Danion*'s population, perished in a moment—an oppressive weight indeed.

And here I sit, awaiting my dying turn.

Somewhere offstage, the Sangaree decide they've had enough, leave us their ghostly foe.

"Suits," says the bleak-faced Seiner directing D.C. operations. He sees the end. From lockers come spacesuits one by one. I slip into mine, remembering I've never worn one except in fun, or way back during midshipman training. I think of Mouse, not yet here, and wonder what has become of him.

Danion screams. She whirls beneath me and I fall. Suit servos hum and force me to my feet. The lights pale, die, return as stored power's injected. In my heart I know we're dead. The sharks have gotten our power and drives. The end.

Someone is yelling my name. "What?" I reply. I'm too scared to listen closely, hear only that my team is going out. I jump at the truck. Seiner hands pull me aboard.

And Dragons in the Sky

Twenty minutes later, in an odd part of the ship devoted to nuclear plant, my team captain sets me to sealing ruptured piping. Here whole passageways are open; occasionally I glimpse a starless night. I think nothing of it for a long while. Too busy am I, doing the work of a Seiner.

Only hours later, when the pipes no longer bleed, when I spy a vacuum-ruined corpse tangled in a mass of wiring dark against an outer glow, do I pause. Space. This is what I'm not supposed to see. I must look. I walk to the hole, see nothing but the tangle of harvestship.

I stand there frozen, disbelieving, I don't know how long. No stars. Where can we be that there are no stars?

The ship is revolving slowly. Something gradually appears, the source of the glow on *Danion*'s hull. I recognize it. The galaxy, edge on, as seen from outside. My premonitions return to haunt me. Far, I see another harvestship coruscating under shark attack. My own has shuddered to several while I've worked. But my eyes hurry on, to a coin-sized brightness in the direction of spin.

Self-illuminated, no sun. Beyond the galactic rim. My heart stutters, my fear redoubles. There is only one place…

Star's End.

What are the Seiners doing?

Something breaks, something blossoms across the night. Fire. Fire like a dying star. A harvestship is burning in a flame only a multidimensional shark could ignite. They're getting more cunning, hitting us with antimatter gases. My grief is like a physical blow. In the corner of my mind, a strange voice asks, as a Fisher would, if the death does good for the fleet. Are sharks there dying too?

Star's End. My eyes return. All my myths have hemmed me in. I serve the most pleasant, am trapped between the wicked and ugly—I have no doubts the Sangaree will soon return. It is not in their nature to quit when the stakes are so high.

The permanencies of my universe are here awarring, and doubtless one will fall… I fear it.

I comprehend why the Seiners have come. As all who seek Star's End do, they want the fortress world's fabulous guns. For centuries opportunists have tried to master this planet. Who owns its timeless weapons is dictator to The Arm. No defense of today could stand against Star's End's power. This is the salvation for which the Seiners faintly hope. What I don't see is how they hope to penetrate the planet's defenses. Battle fleets have failed.

A touch. A voice comes by conduction. "Let's go. *Danion's* hit inboard of us." In the words I imagine great sadness, but none of the fear I feel. I follow the man, rejoin my team. We return to D.C. Central, through locks, through regions of ship ruined as by weapons of war. Hard to believe it is done by a creature I can't even see.

They've prepared a room for us to relax in, safe enough to shed our suits—nothing there, except people, that sharks can harm. I see Mouse, freshly wounded.

"Should've bent her," he says. "Waited me out. Now she's up to deviltry."

I look at his arm. It's mangled. His face is drawn, but doesn't complain. She must have really surprised him. "Thing like a hatchet," he says.

Unless that arm is quickly tended, he'll lose it. I find an officer, ask for a doctor, get told he's on his way. I think of the Sangaree woman.

I've had a feeling for her, I realize, a strange, miscegenous desire (I've had feelings for many people, though I've long lied myself into not caring). My emotions kept me from letting Mouse do what should have been done—and now I pay. Before me, blood of a friend; in my mind, a gunmetal smile.

"I'll take care of it."

From the tool crib I draw a laser cutting torch, no questions. The attendant assumes I need it. Outside D.C. Central I open an access plate and make the adjustments taught me in Navy schools. I have an unwieldy gun. I borrow an electric scooter.

She will be somewhere where she thinks she can take out the crew without damaging the ship. To her mind, something involving air. Hydroponics? No. Central blowers. From there, by cutting off air or introducing chemicals, she can neutralize most of us.

And Dragons in the Sky

I arrive, see I've reasoned well. Dead men guard the door. Beyond is a vast place, as it must be to serve a ship so huge. Somewhere in this mechanical jungle she waits...

Time so swiftly passes. A half hour departs and still I'm creeping among Brobdingnagian machines. *Danion* still shivers, but the battle is so old it no longer forces itself on the consciousness. I'm tired. I've been up for twenty hours. Finally I spy the mighty consol from which *Danion*'s lungs are controlled.

I crawl, I climb, I find myself a perch on a high catwalk from which most all the board's visible. I see only empty seats where technicians once manipulated our air, a couple of corpses. She's well armed.

From somewhere she appears, as if spontaneously generated. My eyes have wandered. I lift my weapon and aim, but...

"Maria... Marya..." It rips itself from me. She has been closer to me than most women—I never met my mother.

Her head comes up in startled play, searching. Suddenly there is an explosion of that mocking smile. "Why Moyshe, what are you doing here?" She's looking for me, eyes narrow over the smile, hand on her gun a-twitching.

"You're trying to destroy us."

She steps over a dead Seiner. "Moyshe!" Accusing. "Not you. You'd be repatriated."

The lie's as tall as a mile. After the Broken Wings and Von Drachau's raid, she'll have my guts on her morning toast. She crosses my aim repeatedly, but I won't end it. I can't. My aim falls.

In moving I give myself away. The gunmetal smile is replaced by clashing-sabers laughter. Her weapon jumps up.

To this I can react. The blast reddens metal where I crouched. I'm in the open, running. I fire wild, get behind some great machine. Her shouts mock—I catch no words—and beams lick about my covert.

I'm terrified. I've swum too deep. I've feared this since need drove me to the Bureau. Now I'll die.

She's too confident of my ineptness. Something within me breaks; I realize there *is* something in which I can believe, something to grasp, to serve. I grin, laugh at my laughing soul. The Grail. We've found it. We. This ship, this I, we're part of a *We...*

In all marvelous stupidity I step into the open. The woman is so startled she hesitates. Against the conditioning of my pyramid of years, I shoot first.

I'm standing over her when Fishers arrive. I have tears. I've always wondered about that—Mouse cries as though the dead one were his brother, or more, for we value brothers little these days. One takes the cutting torch. Another asks, "Moyshe benRabi?" He knows, of course. They've been watching. Ship's security doesn't fold because a battle is on. These, I discover, were coming to do what I've done. They received orders concerning me while on their way.

"Yes."

"Fellow with the headaches?"

I nod.

"Follow me, please."

I do, though looking back at Maria. Now she is dead, she isn't just "the Sangaree woman." She is Maria, Marya, a woman I may have loved some odd, unexplainable way. Perhaps I've had a deathwish.

I follow, and somewhere along the line note we're entering forbidden territory, Operations Sector, where landsmen dare not go. Nervous, I look around. It's quieter, more remote than the rest of the ship. The people we pass seem more aloof than the technicians to whom I'm accustomed. They must be. They are the men and women will think us beyond defeat—maybe.

We enter a vast room filled with damaged machinery. Here there has been death aplenty; casualties still wait on a dozen stretchers. My guide leads me to a man. "BenRabi," he says, departs.

This room is much like a ship's bridge, though larger, and the machinery unfamiliar. I see people on reclining couches, heads hidden in great helmets. Technicians grumble over them and damaged gear. A spatial display globe lurks blackly in a corner. Centered in it are seven golden balls, harvestships. Golden needles are service ships, maneuvering against sharks portrayed as scarlet fish. Tiny golden dragons at

And Dragons in the Sky

the periphery mark what must be distant Starfish. No Sangaree are to be seen.

"Mr. benRabi!" I realize the man is after my attention.

"Why dragons?"

He stops an angry word. "Image from our minds, archetypal. You'll see."

"I don't understand."

He ignores me. "The drives are dead, except minddrive. For that we need power from the Fish. But sharks have burned out most of our mind-techs." He points to the nearest stretcher. The face of a girl, a child just out of crèche, smiles in vacant madness. "We haven't standbys to replace them, so we're drawing marginal sensitives from the crew. You're subject to migraines?"

I nod. I'm reeling. What strange thing...

"We want you to go into rapport with a Fish."

Fear. Memories of terrible, haunting dreams, of the pain resulting. "I can't!"

"Oh?" This man has eyes that reach for my soul—which cowers, though it knows not what to fear.

"I don't know *how*." Somehow, this feels lame.

"You don't need to. You just hook up. The Fish will push the power through to the helmet. You're just a receiver."

"But I'm tired. I've been awake for..."

"So is everybody." He gestures impatiently. A couple comes. "Put him in Number Three." They nod. Departing, I hear, "That the last one?" wearily.

I want to protest, but get no chance. The techs put me on the couch. Ah, well. I've undoubtedly faced worse for the Bureau.

One tech is a woman reminiscent of the professional mother of my childhood. She is gray-haired, cherry-faced, chatters comfortably while strapping my arms to the couch's. She points out grip-switches beneath my fingers, does my legs.

The other, a quiet man, efficiently prepares my head for the helmet. He rubs me with an unscented paste, covers my hair with a thing like a hairnet. My scalp protests a thousand little stings that quickly fade. "Lift, please." I do. The helmet devours my head. I'm blind.

A green ogre with dirty claws shoves his hand into my guts, grabs, yanks. My heart plays battledrums. Words from Czyzewski's *The Old Gods:* "...who sang the darkful deep, and dragons in the sky." My body's sweat-wet. Surely the contacts won't work.

In my ears, a voice. "Ready, Mr. benRabi." A sweet-voiced woman, ancient trick for calming—which works. "Depress the right grip-switch one click."

I do. Fear returns. I've lost all sensation, I float, see, hear, smell, feel nothing.

"That's not bad, is it?" The voice of the professional mother again. I remember that plump old woman's lap and arms and love (but we must all depart that nest), the comfort she gave when I feared... "When you're ready, depress the switch another click, then release it. To withdraw, pull *up* on the left switch."

I depress the switch.

My dreams return awake, space swimming, the galaxy wrong in color, Star's End strangely bright. Things move. I remember the display tank. This is like being at the heart of that. Service ships are glimmering needles (invisible to ordinary sight), harvestships glowing balls of wire, sharks red fish-shapes. Far, Starfish are golden Chinese dragons, drifting lazily closer.

My terror fades as if a hand is pushing it back...

Gently warm, a hint of voice trickles into my soul. "I do it. Starfish, Chub." There's a wind-chimes tinkle of laughter. "Watch. I show me."

A small dragon soars from the distant herd, does a ponderous end-over-end roll. Shortly, "Old Ones don't like. Dangerous. But we winning, new friend. Sharks running. Most destroyed."

The creature's joy is obvious. He has the right. The sharks are abandoning the fleet.

My terror is still great, but the night creature holds it back, infecting me with his excitement. Time passes. He learns the ways of my mind. He could play me like a musical instrument if he wanted.

And Dragons in the Sky

"First battle won," he says when I'm under control, "but another fight come."

"What?" I speak in return with my mind.

"Ships-that-kill, bad ones, return."

"How do you know?"

"No way to show, tell. But come, hyper now. Your people prepare."

I go silent. So does he. I take in the wonders about me, the rippling movement of sharks far out, the ponderous approach of dragons, the shimmering maneuvers of service ships, preparing for another fight. The galaxy hangs over all like a hole in the night. Nearby, Star's End sits, waiting.

"Coming," says my dragon. My attention turns. Glimmering ships appear against the galaxy. Sangaree. Down in my backbrain, behind my ears, there is a gentle tickle. "Power."

Sangaree ships radiate from the arrival zone in lines like octopus legs, form a hemisphere. They intend to englove us. Far, the sharks mill uncertainly, retreat.

A light-ball flares among the Sangaree. A Fisher mine has scored. But it makes no difference. This battle we can't win. The service ships number but ten, all wounded, and even the most hale harvestship has lost power and drives. Minddrive and stored power just aren't enough.

The Sangaree maneuver closer, but there's no firing. My dragon says they're treating with Payne for surrender—a herd's no good without a fleet.

The herd drifts closer, almost onto the Sangaree. They'll join this battle, but cautiously because sharks still watch from afar.

"Fight soon."

The Sangaree fire on the service ships, our most expendable vessels. They'll force us to submit.

The slow, stately dance of enmity ends. The Sangaree move fast, service ships evade, missiles are everywhere like hurrying wasps. Beam-fire weaves beautiful webs of death. My terror is replaced by depression. I see no way to win.

Far, a Starfish approaches a Sangaree. Dangerous. The ship's weapons can easily destroy him—the ship stops firing.

"We do shark-thing," echoes in my mind, "but more power. We stop fleet fast if no guns." Another Sangaree falls silent. A Starfish burps gut-fire. The ball hurtles through space, so slowly seeming—Sangaree burning.

The hemisphere closes about us. The open side, toward Star's End, grows rapidly smaller. The diameter shrinks, two harvestships unleash fire of fantastic magnitude, yet scarcely enough to neutralize the growing attack.

The Starfish mind-bum another Sangaree, turn to run. They've waited too long. Their central fires are seen. Chub's sadness touches my mind as a dragon dies.

The Sangaree globe closes. Like a squeezing fist, they tighten up, pile up toward Star's End. Their attack grows terrible. They begin pushing—and I see their goal, the confused sharks milling against the galaxy. I suppose they think we'll give up before enduring that again.

"It works well," my mindvoice says. "Is hard to think thoughts in bad commander. Sangaree heads twisted." The Sangaree are thickly massed now, pushing hard. The sharks are more agitated. The Starfish are cruising their way, ready to cover if we retreat.

The trickle in the root of my brain waxes, becomes a flaming torrent. It hurts, my God; it hurts! Burning, the power surges through me. I'm scarcely able to observe.

Then the harvestships surge *toward* the Sangaree, all weapons firing—I think with no aim, just to hurl all destruction possible. The Sangaree push back—but waver, waver.

In pain, I sweep the night. Sangaree ships burn, service ships the same. A harvestship stops shooting. The Sangaree begin knocking it apart—they've lost all patience. I suffer another sadness, my own, for those were my people.

The Sangaree withdraw—not retreating, but pushed. We may not last long, but our ferocity is, for the moment, greater than theirs.

Something screams across my mind. It's a mad voice babbling, shrieking fear, incoherencies. I sense little sense, but warning touches me, terror. Phantoms taunt, grotesqueries as of the worst medieval

And Dragons in the Sky

imagination gather in space before me, gargoyles and gorgons, Boschian nightmares writhing, fangs and talons and fire. They shriek, "Go away, or die!" Insanity. They're not real. I'm trapped in the thoughts of a mad mind... I scream.

Nightmare is after me like a drug dream (it's like descriptions of stardust deprivation), burning now, with salamanders. I must escape this haunted place. Again, I scream. The madness deeply holds my mind.

Then the warm feeling comes, gently calms my soul, soothes my fear, pushes the terror and madness away. My dragon from the stars... He tells me, "We succeed. Maybe win." Then, darkly, "Fear is Star's End mind-thing. Planet is mad machine. Mad machine use madness weapons.

"She!"

Shielded by his touch, I turn to Star's End. The Sangaree are silhouetted against the right planet. The face of the world is diseased behind them, spotted blackly, covered with sudden clouds.

I see we are no longer advancing. Indeed, the planet is receding. We're running full speed, dispersing. I know that, if we could, we'd hyper. But we can't on minddrive. Nor can the Sangaree while they're combat-locked. A hundred miles closer than we, they're scattering, breaking lock—too late! The mad machine's weapons arrive.

"Close mind! Get out!" my dragon shrieks. "Not need power now." I understand because of the earlier nightmares—Star's End's are weapons of a terrible kind, of the mind. I stop looking—though I have no eyes to close here—lift the switch beneath my left hand.

I feel the helmet now, the couch, and loss. I miss my dragon, and, in missing him, I understand Starfishers a little better, why they enjoy being so far from the worlds of men. This Fish-Fisher thing is a whole new experiential frontier... My body is wet with sweat, I'm shivering cold. The room is silent. Where are my techs? Am I alone? My head is a thundering migraine. Rational thought is impossible. I want free of the straps that bind my limbs.

Danion staggers, staggers, staggers. I hear screams—I'm not alone! Loose things racket around; I suffer momentary visions of beasts of hell.

Terror grips me anew. The Star's End weapons have arrived, and I'm pinned here, helpless...

Slowly, slowly, it fades. The screams die (some, I think, were my own), are gradually replaced by excited chatter—I can distinguish no words. My head is tearing itself apart. I was a kid the last time it was this bad. I shout. Someone finally notices me. The helmet comes off, a syringe stabs my neck. Tingles spread. The migraine begins to pass.

The room is cloaked in gloom. Stored power is almost gone, I guess. A drain, the fighting. But the faces I see are joyous—with the exception of those gruesomely vacant few of mind-techs who didn't get out in time.

"We've won!" says the motherish half of my tech-team. "Star's End killed them." Not all, I suspect, though I say nothing. Some broke lock, and will carry a grudge.

"And four harvestships," says a sad-faced man passing.

A Pyrrhic victory. We won, but there is nothing to celebrate. Our joy dies.

I'm ready for collapse, yet hours pass before I rest. First, I search for Mouse, find him in D.C. Central, unconscious on a stretcher, his arm crudely bandaged and splinted. Then it's back to my team, patching pipes. There is so much to do, just to keep *Danion* alive. But power we eventually restore, life support we repair, drives we jury-rig. It's not too hard. The damage is more to people than plant (over half the crew is gone). The surviving service ships are recovered. A watch for sharks is set, but those nightmares have gone to places of easier hunting.

There is no time for mourning, so fierce is the battle for life. We save *Danion,* but abandon the Star's End project. The war with sharks may well be lost.

Months pass. Something dread approaches: time to return to Carson's.

It is five months since *I want* drank of the blood of my soul. Five peaceful months. I belong, finally—but I'm afraid to ask to stay. For weeks I worry asking, decide, undecide. I'm so terribly afraid of being turned down; and a little afraid of being accepted.

And Dragons in the Sky

Even the days are gone now. We're down to the hours, and still I haven't asked, still I haven't found the courage to seize what I need. I think of crèche days, of story time, of heroes who were never undecided, never afraid—all from the past. There is no room for heroes in the kaleidoscope universe of today. (Strange. I'm suddenly certain that was one of the things I've sought: heroism, to be a hero. The Broken Wings was as close as I came… But that conjures visions of Maria.)

The ship for Carson's departs in two hours. What can I do? I know what I should, but still I fear committal, rejection. I don't want to leave, but what if staying is a mistake? The questions I ask myself would fill a book. Finally, with just an hour remaining, I seek Mouse.

He never has doubts, no matter how much he fears—paranoia has its rewards. Maybe he can help.

We've seen little of one another since the battle. I've spent most of my time in Operations Sector, still forbidden him (I'm being used as a mind-tech—are they expecting I'll stay? Or is it just because they're forced by circumstances?), so he is bright when I arrive. "Hey, how about chess while we're waiting?" he asks. He is addicted. "Nobody else will play." He is still an outcast.

Maybe a game will relax me. I nod. He's very excited, shaking a little. I hardly notice. Over opening moves, I say to broach my problem. "Mouse, I want to stay…"

He looks at me strangely, as if with mixed emotions, as if he expected this, but was hoping for something else. "Let's talk about it after the game. Drink? It'll unwind you."

A man about to undergo acceleration and temporary null-gravity shouldn't, but I nod. He goes to a cabinet, gets a bottle of something pre-mixed. While he's getting glasses, I look around. Everything that is Mouse is gone, except the chess set. So nice to be sure. My gear is packed, but I still haven't sent it to the service ship…

A glass breaks. Mouse curses, gathers the pieces, curses again as he cuts himself. Wish he'd quit using his bad hand… I see why. With his good he's pushing gooey stuff into and over Security's bug—we hunted it up one day after Star's End, when we wanted to talk. He brings the drinks, returns to the game.

It's a slow one. He studies each move so carefully. I down several drinks, grow relaxed, turn off the troublesome part of my mind. I get involved. I'm holding my own. Unusual. He's far the better player, but he seems remote, disturbed. Time swiftly passes.

Sudden, rapid moves. My queen goes, then, "Checkmate?" The alcohol no longer helps. This defeat just adds to a growing depression, a small symbol of my big-time losing. A moment later, while boxing the pieces (he fumbles with his bad hand), he says, "I kept this out, hoping we'd play on the way back. You want to stay?"

"Yes."

"That's why I'm here." He turns. I see the fumbling wasn't purposeless. In his good hand is a Fisher weapon. I groan.

"You should've figured, Moyshe. Wheels within wheels." (Maybe I did down deep, and came to Mouse for an easy answer.) "Psych figured you'd fall, figured you'd get where I couldn't. So they sent you out as a remote data-collecting device—and I'm your keeper. *That* is the worm gnawing around the core of all the rotten plans." This is a long speech for Mouse. He's doing something more than trying to explain—maybe he doesn't like what he's doing. "We're friends, so let's play it gentle, eh?"

Yes, gentle. As in chess, he outskills me here. I'm the half of the team who always does the "soft," people stuff. He does the "hard." He may like me, but he will, and easily can, kill me if I don't cooperate. I look at his face. There's pain there. There's something he wants to tell me—maybe, just maybe, he doesn't want to go himself. I'd best not push if he's under stress. He'll overreact. My shoulders slump forward. I surrender. Back to being a chip in the stream.

Dread voice through *Danion,* godlike, calling us to the departure station for pay-off and check-out. Mouse pockets his weapon. "Sorry, Moyshe."

"I understand." But I don't, of course.

And Dragons in the Sky

He nods at the door. We go. I give him no trouble all the way, even when opportunity occurs. I'm sure I could do something in the crowd there. But I've surrendered all. No home. Guess I'll never have one. Back to being a chip in a universe like Sierran rivers raging. Back to the beginning.

No home…

"Mr. benRabi?" Here's a man coming through the press, my bags in his hands. "You left these."

I know this man. He's Security, the fellow who first took me into Operations Sector. He steps between Mouse and me. Landsmen mill excitedly around us, talking excitedly of home, rushing to the paymaster when their names are called. I don't really notice in my shock.

"The gun, please?" There are several of them now, all around. Mouse surrenders his weapon meekly. "I told Beckhart it wouldn't work." He looks shattered.

"We'll have to hold you."

There's a stir among the landsmen, a confused shout, screams. A Seiner twists past me, falling, an expression of incredible surprise on the unburned half of his face.

Now there's screaming, running, Security men plunging into the crowd.

"Wheels within wheels, and this was mine," Mouse says. "I thought Beckhart would have a fail-safer aboard." (Fail-safer. Trade term for a fanatic sent on a mission, unknown to the mission, to assassinate agents about to defect or be captured. Didn't know we used them any more. Sure didn't think Mouse and I were that important.) "Sorry, Moyshe. I couldn't tell you. Had to have you thinking I meant what I was doing." Did he? Or was he just bending with the breeze? "Had to spot him before we went over. Otherwise…" He shrugs, then smiles. So do I. I'll believe him.

There're more shots, then the Seiners catch their man—now we're home free.

Home, after all—and with a friend.

Appointment in Samarkand

The world's oldest man sat at a table in a hovel beside the river, in the heart of the city's slums. Before him: a half-empty can of cold chili, an onion cut in slivers, an empty bottle once filled with dreams (California Port), and cloves of garlic. The old man, feeling the effects of the wine, leaned back in a rickety chair, drawing deeply on the remnants of a cheap cigar.

A knock at his door.

The old man was startled. He snorted as only an oldster can, popped a clove of garlic into his mouth, chewed as he made his way to the door. Opened, it revealed a stranger clad in black.

"Yes?" the old man snapped, his fetid mouth but inches from the stranger's face. "What is it? What is it?"

"Ah!" the dark stranger gasped, staggering back. "Never mind! I'll come back later. Remembered an appointment in Samarkand."

The oldest man cackled as the stranger fled.

For the umpteenth time.

Sunrise

1

Kim the Piper, pale and thin, walked the silent streets of a judgement morning—a morning which was, of course, no morning at all but merely the beginning of another day-called period etched on an endless night. Never in all his eighteen hundred years, nor she in her ten thousand, had Edgeward City seen sunrise breaking the darkness besieging her protective dome. Blackworld was a one-face planet, lifeless and boiling on Brightside, frozen on Darkside, where were built the cities of men.

City of men, Kim told himself as he reached Dome Street, which encircled the City just inside the massive glassteel shield. The Star Fathers had made one small error in creating the world. They'd left it with a little spin. It rotated once every twenty-five thousand years, a mile a year, nearly fifteen feet each day. In a sacrilegious moment, Kim questioned the omnipotence of the Star Fathers. They'd been sloppy planet builders, not taking into account the long-term effects of the world's spin.

Ancient books placed Edgeward City near the western terminator, in a vest, steep-walled meteor crater behind the Thunder Mountains. That morning, as Kim climbed stairs to an observation chamber thirty feet up, inside the glassteel of the dome itself, the eastern terminator lay fifty miles away, about to break over the White Mountains which hugged the crater's eastern lip. A first real dawn, and doom, was creeping steadily closer.

Kim entered the chamber, seated himself in an ancient chair, wondered at the needy for observation. There was so very little to see. Night, forever on. Stars immobile, untwinkling; frozen constellations. A hint of dark landscape, poorly illuminated by the stars. A dull red glow at the foot of the driftwall (which kept dust from the crater wall from engulfing the base of the dome) where the conical and hemispherical tractor and presser fields of the meteor screens were generated. A ghost image of the White Mountains, starlight reflected off fields of oxygen and nitrogen snow.

There was a hint of corruscation outlining the peaks of the mountains, barely discernable, gaseous matter and stripped ions fleeing to Darkside from the sun-burned plains beyond, reflecting the sun's electro-magnetic field and particular radiations. The matter solidified again this side of the mountains. Gradually, over the decades as sunrise drew nearer, the white snowfields darkened, the dust against the driftwell deepened…

The conical tractor field glowed pinkly, the pressor hemisphere glared into golden flame, the City shuddered on its foundations, grumbled. "Meteor," Kim whispered to himself. "Big one." High in the night above the City somewhere the meteor's course was changed, directed away from the dome. Kim saw it, white hot from the heat energy gained during the sudden change, smash into the crater wall some miles away. The explosion was almost atomic in proportions. Dust boiled up, the City shivered, glowing bits of shattered rock streaked toward the White Mountains like a thousand tiny rockets.

"Magnificent!" he whispered. For the first time in a year, he was glad to be alive. Lately, he had been thinking much of voluntary termination, but this vindicated his reluctance. There was always one more new thing to be seen, if one could endure the overpowering boredom between happenings. Two new things, perhaps.

He was nearly blinded by the sudden spear of light exploding upward from somewhere in the White Mountains. Like a long and dissipating

Sunrise

arm of fire, it reached toward the City. "Flame tongue." He was awed. It was the first time he had seen this most spectacular of Blackworld's few weather phenomena, the result of the sun's rays falling suddenly on a patch of gas snow, converting it from the solid to gaseous states in microseconds. Sunlight reflected off the dust carried upward by the expanding vapors made the flame tongue.

Kim considered both manifestations with something like religious awe. They were omens, harbingers of the fiery doom the sun promised the City.

So said the Disciple of the Sun Cultists, whose word was presently law, both religious and temporal (conveniently ignoring the fact that the meteors were present only because Blackworld had entered their cometary orbits as they came in from deep space, as happened every nine hundred years; and sunrise was an event expected for millenia). Edgeward was the last of the great dome cities of Blackworld, farthest from the sun when the world was created (or colonized, as a small, atheist faction would have it), last to be destroyed as the world turned, her agony prolonged because, according to Sun Cult dogma, the Sun God had known she was the city to sink deepest into iniquity. For her wickedness and belief in the heresy of the Star Fathers, the jealous god would slay her with spears of light. One day soon the sun would rise above the White Mountains, The tractor and pressor screens would be as nothing before the sudden storm of radiant energies. The top of the dome would melt, the City's atmospheric temperature would soar three thousand degrees, and molten glassteel would be hurled into a burning sky.

So said the Disciple of the Sun, and Kim knew most of it was true. He had watched the destruction of The City of Night fifteen hundred years earlier, and had talked to men who had seen Darkside Landing die...

He sighed, tried to turn his thoughts to more pleasant subjects, could not. Well, thank the Star Fathers, the end, when it finally came would be swift. A lance of sunlight, a boom, and the structures of Edgeward City would like waxen images melt into a vast and bubbling pool—a lake of fire. The Disciple made much of that lake of fire.

A few structures would remain standing—skeletal grotesqueries with melting temperatures above those induced by Blackworld's fierce little pre-nova sun.

Another shudder ran through the dome's foundations. Meteor? He saw no evidence. Probably caused by tectonic activity in the White Mountains. Perhaps there should be some changes in old names. The Thunder Mountains were now silent and white with gas snows while the White Mountains were dirty and rumbling with the expansion effects of the sun's heat. Once it had been the other way around.

The clicking open of the chamber door drew Kim's mind from the sword extended over Edgeward City. But he did not turn. This was his private place, the place where an immortal could escape the crowds of anciently familiar faces, the place where he could be alone with his thoughts. He would recognize no intrusions.

"Kim?" Soft, feminine, a voice he knew well, a voice which was part of the laughter and tears of his recent past, a voice not entirely unexpected. A voice from the days—before the rise of the Disciple—when a Piper had been allowed to pipe, and a Dancer to dance. Illian Gey, a Dancer. Still a mortal, only twenty, undecided as to when she would begin taking the drugs—as if they mattered now. He and she had nearly been a couple once, when joy and entertainment had been unforbidden.

"Kim?" There was pleading in her voice this time, a soft little cry for support. "Did you hear? The Disciple sentenced my brother to the fire."

He had no need to look to picture her face as it must be, surrounded by disheveled hair, her eye- and cheek-paints smeared by hands and tears. Thus she had appeared an hour earlier when, at the Temple, the Disciple had ordered the stake for her brother, guilty of trying to flee the doomed City. Kim had watched Illian from across the chamber. He remembered the sudden pallor, the sudden shriek, the struggle with Heaven's Guard...

"Kim?" This time there was desperation.

"I know," he replied, still not turning. "I saw a flame tongue this morning. My first."

Sunrise

"How nice for you." Her sarcasm overrode her sorrow. Soon she would be angry. Kim smiled at the night before him.

"What're we going to do?" she asked. "My father won't help. You're all I have."

"I'll watch the execution, perhaps," Kim replied. "I've never seen one. I should before the end. One vision of all things..."

"You hate him!"

Smiling again, Kim said, "And not without reason. What did Walther the Dancer deny Kim the Musician, without cause?"

"Dancers don't couple with Musicians!" she retorted. But her words had that ring of rote Kim remembered all too well. She had said those words before, and had denied them by her actions until her brother and father had threatened to stop her dancing—all pointless now, with the Disciple in power, entertainment denied, and sunrise but days away.

"Nor do devil worshippers, sun worshippers, cultists rule the City," he replied. "If *that* tradition can be broken, how little meaning have the customs of Artists?"

"He didn't do anything!"

"He denied me you." Kim wished she would go away now. Her sorrow and self-pity had been replaced by anger. Fine. He had given all he was willing. Now let her take her problem to her own kind.

"That's not what I meant. His crime. All he did was try to leave the City, to join the Nomads. They're a people who'd appreciate him. He committed no crime."

Kim frowned. This was growing tedious. Yet he answered her, "But he did. He tried to deny the Sun God retribution for his unbelief. As the Disciple said, he has to be given to the flames early, lest he escape punishment. It's simple, Illian. Surely even you can understand." His frown deepened. He had spoken her name, He had vowed never to do so again.

He did not believe his words. Sun Cultists were mad mortals, their religion insane. Enough, Illian, go away. He had no time for the frenzied affairs of mortals.

No time? He had had ages of leisure, ages of boredom, Edgeward City was automated to the nth degree. What work there was was play, with waiting lists hundreds of names long. Art was the reason most people lived. Music, sculpture, painting, dancing, writing, and each immortal Artist had an eternity in which to do nothing but polish his art.

Had, Kim reminded himself. No more. The sun was close. Works centuries in the creation were being savagely whipped to completion. His own *Dying Star* a vast, epic overture two centuries in the composition, had been claiming all his attention of late. Working under pressure, he had almost regained the urgency of Man the Mortal. Until he had gone this morning to see Illian's brother's judgement…

"Kim, I need help."

His anger grew. Would she not leave? He had already tolerated more than he would have from anyone else. "Go to your Dancers!" he snapped as he turned in his seat. "Or your mortals."

He stopped. Looking at her was a mistake. Behind him, she was a disembodied voice. Now she was Illian, the woman with whom he had almost coupled. A woman he loved still, though he refused to admit it, even to himself. To look at her was to see her, in dimension up into the past, to the happy days and beyond, and all along the line downward to the present misery.

"They say Musicians can be crueler than priests," she murmured.

Harsh words, marshalled at his lips, were stifled. Her point told. He stared at her there, silhouetted against the lights of the City behind and below her, a woman-shape without the features painted in.

"There's nothing I can do," he said at last, "so there's nothing I'll try to do. Your brother, like most mortals, is a fool. There's no escape." Inside, although he would not admit it, this disturbed him. "I've no love for the Sun Cult, yet I'll die here in the City where I was born and have lived. To join the Nomads and become Homeless…that would be worse, I think."

She moved up beside his chair. The light through the glassteel behind her did little to illuminate her. "Are you sure *he's* the fool?" she asked softly. Kim shivered. Her voice… So many memories… "Father says we have a week. Seven days, then sunrise—" the word came out like a curse which had to be forced—"will come through the Teeth—" she pointed to a pair of tall, conical mountains with a deep cleft between

Sunrise

them, clearly defined by the coruscation—"and hit the dome. Don't you want to live?"

After a moment of silence, Kim replied, "Yes. But not in a Nomad tractor."

"Isn't that better than being dead?"

"No." Did he really believe that? He wanted to think about it, but she gave him no time.

"There's a city…"

"Illian, Illian, don't be silly. Rumors, legends. Barrow-Beneath-the-Mountain? That's nonsense. And you know it. The Nomads haven't the art. They're mortals. They don't live long enough to build cities. And, even if the fairy tale were true, the sun will reach the Thunder Mountains before the end of the century. Here or there, where would my death be more important?"

2

Illian stamped the floor beside him, looked down angrily. Part of the anger, she realized, was because he refused to look at her again. "Why? Why're immortals determined to die? Why won't you save yourselves?" She knew one answer, though it was hard to accept. The immortality drug. One paid in lost emotion and initiative for the banishment of death. Some of the oldest immortals had grown lethargic almost to the point of catatonia—there was so little to *do* with all the time gained. Which, when considered with the imminent death of the City, was why she had not as yet taken the drugs. She felt that if she must die, she should do so as a whole human.

But, she admitted to herself, if the sun were no threat, she would have taken the drugs. Twenty years old was a perfect age to be forever, for a women. Looking into the night above Kim's head, she tried to picture the extinction of death (she could not accept the afterlives of the Sun Cult or the Church of the Star Fathers). Not even stars to break the eternal darkness—if even that could be experienced.

She was suddenly aware that he was trying to answer her questions. "This is the last city on a graveyard world. What future have we? What cosmic difference if we die now, next year, or next century? We're an old race, Illian, pale and tired. There're no frontiers anymore. To lie down, to rest, to steal a few moments of peace, these are the only things that interest us. There's no reason to live. You, your brother, your mortal friends, you're anachronisms, throwbacks, relics from a time so far in the past that, were you not human, you'd be considered rare artifacts. Take the drugs. You'll soon understand." He paused, sighed wearily. "You've heard my thoughts. May I be alone?" He turned his eyes back to the landscape outside, leaned back in his chair, closed his eyes.

Pique. "We're the anachronisms?" she asked softly, staring down, almost laughing. "Us? Throwbacks? Kim, that's funny. You're what? Ten, twenty centuries older than me? You Old Ones are the ones who want to die…" Suddenly she was frightened, terribly frightened. She did not want to die.

Didn't he remember the death of The City of Night, fifteen hundred years ago, and the destruction of Darkside Landing a century before that? Did he want that for himself? Wasn't he afraid too? Why were the Old Ones so little interested in surviving? Because they were so old death was unreal? Many were older than Kim and had watched their world dying for millennia. Perhaps it was because the drugs left them no will.

Something caught her eye. "Oh, look!"

"Now what?" Kim grumbled. But he opened his eyes. "Oh. Another flame tongue."

She'd not noticed it. "No, no," pointing, "there by the driftwall."

"A Nomad tractor," he said. "So? They're not uncommon."

"Well, what's it doing there?"

She could have slapped him for his unconcern. He just shrugged, said, "I don't know. Wasn't there a while ago," and closed his eyes again.

She stamped her foot again, anger rising because she could not understand his lack of emotion. While he had been courting her, she had been so flattered at receiving the attentions of an immortal that she had overlooked his flatness. But now she saw him for what he was. Just a

Sunrise

name, ambulatory. Hardly a person, different from other Musicians only in his choice of instrument. A nothing.

The flame tongue faded, the Nomad tractor flickered into invisibility. It occurred to her that the tractor might be there to pick up refugees. The Nomads were descendants of refugees from other domes. Suddenly excited, she revealed the true reason she had come. "Kim, I've got to know the key-code for the gate locks." He was old enough to remember. No one had gone out of the City for centuries, and the verbal opening code was almost forgotten, but Kim knew it. If only her brother had not tried to open them by trial and error...

Kim's head, almost invisible in the renewed darkness, shook slowly. He lifted his pipe to his lips, ran up and down a scale, then began playing experimentally. She recognized a passage from his *Dying Star*. A flat, gloomy work, like Kim himself, and as lifeless. She doubted it would be proclaimed a masterwork, for, of all Musicians, Kim was the only one who did not know he had no talent.

He offered no hope—for the moment. She turned, eased out the door, left him to contemplate the City's last days of night.

Illian Gey was a sad young woman striding angrily, returning home. The young of Edgeward City, except those of the Sun Cult, were all sad or angry—cultists were merely mad. It was something youth was born to, something they outgrew when they began taking immortality capsules. For the drug, like most, exacted a price. It polished off the edges and corners, wore the hollows, of a user's emotions. It pulled the teeth of curiosity and clipped the claws of the competitive drive. In the eyes of Illian, it left one less than human.

She slowed, considering the immortals' lack of passion in the face of sunrise. Above, serpents of light wriggled across the inner surface of the dome, masking the forever darkness beyond. Like intellect, she thought, which helped mask the forever darkness beyond life. Let either flicker for an instant and the endless black gulf rolled quickly in upon one.

She feared death. Was terrified. Though dawn had approached as inexorably, she had not feared before the rise of the Sun Cult. There had been no need, men had evaded death for millennia. It was an accidental thing, involving only the incautious. It was no personal danger, no, never, for there were the drugs and, certainly, *she'd* never be careless. And when sunrise drew near, one could go live with the Nomads.

She had not anticipated the difficulty of escaping the City. Nor had she expected the rise of the Sun Cult. Suddenly, death was at hand.

She shivered as she walked The Street of a Thousand mirrors where her reflection was presented in a thousand distortions, like her self-image on a thousand different days. This, she thought, was Edgeward City's one truly great work of art. Here the Artist's message was simplicity itself, you cannot know all your own faces.

She neared home. Music came forth, and laughter. Her friends, mortal Artists, mocking death the unreal. They could not believe that doom crouched behind the White Mountains. It would leap upon them, and they would die not believing.

She passed a man of the Sun Cult who made no secret of watching her house. Stanwin, a childhood friend of Walther's. How did he dare appear here, after the morning's trial? She wanted to scream, to claw—no, no sense following Walther's deadly lead. Stanwin would report her if given reason. A child, trying to hurt in return for the hurt of rejection…

She entered the house and a dozen gay couples surrounded her, grew silent in the face of her depression. She looked at their faces, saw disbelief—and the underlying fear and resignation. Were they beaten? After only one defeat? Or did they truly disbelieve? Why the laughter? Forced cheer to banish thoughts of night?

Pale laughter forcedly resumed.

"Illian?"

She turned. Markel Gay, a cousin. Not a favorite. The sort who would've been a cultist had he been allowed to run things. A man of mechanations, totally self-centered, often unconsciously cruel, uncaring if aware. "He'd scarcely talk to me."

"Hard feeling still?"

She nodded. "And he doesn't care. None of them do. It's the drug."

Sunrise

"Yes." He was a handsome young man, easily able to project an unreal "rightness" that made people want him to have his way. Illian sometimes wished he wasn't a relative. She knew him well enough to see the monster behind the public mask. But fear had begun to crack that mask. "Can we talk?"

In those three words, Illian knew, he expressed his contempt for the partiers' intellect. Leave them. They were unworthy of inclusion. Sometimes she hated Markel. At that moment she wondered if she was a cut above the partiers only because she was a link with Kim and the key-code.

"Father's bedroom. It's the only room not filled."

They went.

"There's a notion that's been in my head all morning," said Markel. "Hand me a life capsule."

She took one from a container on a table near her, tossed it.

"These can be opened." He demonstrated, pulling the halves apart and dumping immortality drug onto her palm. "Suppose we replace Kim's drug with powdered sugar? Five days without won't hurt him, and should release his emotions."

"And?" She did not like the risks, Yet the alternative was to do as Kim did—sit and wait.

"He'll get scared. Scared enough, maybe, to want out. Can you get into his room?"

"Yes." Unless his door key-code had changed, Unlikely. Immortals changed nothing. She bit her lower lip, feeling guilty. As with Kim, the love spark within her died hard.

"Oh," she said, remembering, "there's a cultist across the street. Watching us."

"I know. Stanwin. I'll take care of him." She moved away, suddenly frightened. That look on his face... But she had to listen. He was leader, now that Walther was gone. She distracted herself by saying, "There's a Nomad tractor outside the east gate, by the driftwall."

Markel mulled this over before saying, "Good. What kind?"

"I don't know. Big, though, like some of the mining machines in the museum."

"Could carry a lot of people, Wait a few minutes while I take care of Stanwin. Then go to Kim's." He left.

Illian dropped to her father's bed, wondered if she was doing right. To keep the drug from Kim was dangerous. If the concentration in his tissues grew too small, he would begin aging again. Rapidly. He could die.

But everyone would die soon if something weren't done! The fear came on like a tall breaker, crushing... So terrible to know one's allotted time and have to sit counting the minutes... She had to do something, anything, to keep from thinking. Kim. The capsules. A hope. A hope that endangered someone else; better than nothing...

The logical, survival, and moral parts of her mind fought, and, as they will, yielded a compromise favorable to herself. She'd change the capsules and risk Kim, but would stay close to see that nothing bad happened. Just because of an old feeling for an immortal Musician.

She got powdered sugar from the kitchen, made hasty explanations to curious partiers who watched her go out with uncertain frowns.

Stanwin wasn't in the street.

Kim's apartment. She knocked. No answer. She spoke the words that opened his door. As expected, they were unchanged. She found his capsules, replaced the drug of the dozen in the container.

She was shaking when she finished, again uncertain of the rightness of it. But fear knew no morality, paid no service to scruples.

She had to get out before he returned. Her presence would be too suspicious...

The door opened as she approached it.

3

Kim was uneasy as he walked The Street of a Thousand Mirrors. Here and there he paused to examine his distorted image, as if he might find the cause of his malaise hidden in his reflection. It was getting worse fast. Now there were nightmares—how long since he had dreamed? So

Sunrise

many centuries he had lost count. Since the destruction of The City of Night. Destruction. Perhaps that was it. The discomfiture had begun with Illian's visit, and had grown steadily since.

He glanced toward the east end of the street, saw nothing but dome, blackness overlaid by squirming serpents of light. The same above.

The City shuddered underfoot. Another omen. They were increasingly common, caused by almost constant tectonic activity in the thawing White Mountains.

There were executions, too. A dozen in the past four days as the Disciple made certain his Sun God went uncheated Mortals of all stripes were growing increasingly frightened—Illian among them.

Illian. He'd found her in his apartment, terrified, and she'd fallen into his arms weeping, begging him to help her brother. He'd been defensive, thinking she was after the key-code again, yet had been touched by her concern for Walther. Of course, nothing could save the man, but her emotions were impressive (familial bonds were tenuous among immortals—Kim had a sister he'd not seen in centuries). Today he fought a vague guilt—in addition to the ghosts of other unfamiliar emotions—at not being able to help Illian.

He paused, piped a tentative arpeggio for *Dying Star*. It sounded sour. The entire work was sour. In a fit of frustration, last night, he'd thrown away two decades' work, begun an entire movement anew. Illian had been there—she was at his apartment often, which disturbed him not a little—and had been shocked.

He stared at himself in a mirror, portrayed with a head shrunken by two-thirds. What had happened to the easy comfort of his life? He knew death would claim him sometime, despite the drugs, and had thought his peace was made—until the past few days he'd never worried about his final event. His head seemed bigger now, with sudden room for all the fears of mortal man.

Mortal man. Ages had passed since he'd become immortal. And now he felt as he had before taking the first capsules. And he was tired, feeling old. Did a known hour of death do that? He'd noticed no distress in his fellows.

He piped another arpeggio. Better. Perhaps he should return to work. He had forty-six hours to complete *Dying Star*... He hurled the pipe at a mirror. Neither was damagsd, but his heart was broken. He'd suddenly and clearly seen his creation for what it was. Hackwork. He was no composer. Anyone honest could have told him *Dying Star,* grand as it was in conception, was mediocre. Bad. Passage moved into passage jerkily; some of the movements, if orchestrated, would prove sheer cacophony. He remembered the forced smiles and shaking heads he wasn't supposed to see, that he hadn't noticed even when looking, and realized how patronizingly he had been treated. He could pipe another's music, but could create nothing significant himself. His heart was shattered. In self-realization he was left with nothing, save, perhaps, a pale anger.

Suddenly, there was no more solace in music. He felt alone, abandoned. A mere technician. Less than a machine, for a machine could perform and never make a mistake. Less than a machine.

He had been bound to Music Hall for premier and final performances, to hear the epitaph compositions of friends; but, no, not now, they might laugh. In these last few hours, with no future to concern them, they could freely laugh at the little incompetent with his simple pipe—the only instrument he could master. No, he could not face that. He must go home. Illian would be there. Poor, sad Illian. They could comfort one another. Too bad that only imminent death had been able to bring them together.

As he walked, he met several people he knew. They smiled pleasantly and bowed and made small talk and asked if he had seen Regev's superb *Requiem—A Sonata in B flat Major,* and he had to say no, he'd been working, and they all went away with little shakes of the head, hiding condescension behind modest little smiles, Meaningless smiles, mocking smiles for the village idiot. They went about their business, smiling as if the sun would never rise.

What was wrong? The more time passed, the more he thought mortally, and the older he felt, His emotions, too long dull, were raging like storms. Soon, if they continued to grow, they would be explosive as sunrise.

Sunrise

Sunrise. For the first time in memory, it frightened him. Just a mild fear, nothing to set him running like a mortal, but a fear all the same. Until that moment, sunrise had been just another event in the orderly progression of his life. More important than most, true, because of its magnitude… Suddenly, he panicked. He ran for the safe, warm womb of home.

Illian was out. Where was she? The panic grew. She was all he had. He gulped an immortality capsule and glass of water, rushed back into the street. Her house. She must be there. He ran again, and ignored the amazed glances of fellow immortals. Some were shocked.

His lungs were bags of fire when he reached the street where she lived. No athlete, he was unaccustomed to such activity—still, he shouldn't have been so tired. He was growing old while regaining the wild emotionalism of his youth.

A mortal in Sun Cult dress lounged opposite Illian's tiny house. The boy's eyebrows rose slightly. Kim ignored him, knocked.

Her father answered. His face clouded, angry as ever an immortal's grew. "Go away," he said.

Kim's fear evaporated. A new emotion formed. A hard, cold emotion. It grew in him like a sword—a two-edged sword, he quickly saw. And didn't care.

"Where's Illian?"

"Go away, Musician." Contempt dripped from his last word. Dancers saw Musicians as an evil necessary to their art, but of no importance in the general scheme. Musicians thought Dancers mere leeches…

The sword within grew hard and long. Eighteen hundred years long, Kim thought. "Move aside, Dancer." He surprised himself with the hardness of his voice. And Illian's father, Kim found his expression a delight. But the man would not move. Kim swung.

It was a clumsy blow, delivered with no forethought and no idea of target. It hit the man's chest. He gasped, staggered back. Kim moved forward for another. Here, on this man, he could vent all his anger, all his frustrations, could show all Edgeward City he was not a dull child to be patronized…

"Kim!"

He stopped. Illian, distraught, got between them, flashed him an angry look, then maneuvered her bewildered father into another room, Soon she returned, more collected.

"What's the matter? You're acting like a savage."

He wanted to say something pithy, something shocking, but when he started, his distress poured out: the fear, loneliness, sorrow, love, hurt. Especially the fear. It grew rapidly, approaching real terror. He wanted to, had to get away...

"We can, Kim, we can," Illian whispered. She glanced at the door to her father's bedroom. "You know the key-code, remember? We can get out..."

And all his earlier arguments against that raced mockingly across his mind. Nomad life no longer seemed so terrible, Barrow-Beneath-the-mountain was an incredible legend no more. "Outside?" he murmured, aware of yet another fear. "Outside? I haven't been outside for...since The City of Night..."

4

Illian rose, went to the door, opened it a crack, peeped into the street. As she feared, the watcher was gone. A small knife of terror pinked her heart.

She'd call Markel. He'd know what to do. "Excuse me a minute, Kim." He nodded. But his face said he'd rather she didn't. Fear. She had never seen its like in an immortal.

She entered her bedroom hoping her father would stay out of the way, made the call. "Markel? He's here, I think he's ready."

Questions.

"The watcher's gone," she replied.

"They'll be suspicious," said his faint voice. "You'd better hide till we're ready."

"Where?"

Sunrise

"Hydroponics plant. Meet me in thirty hours at the west gate dressing station."

"My father..." He cut her off. An old argument. There were too few suits, and, anyway, the old man wouldn't go. Illian broke the connection. Despite Markel's logic, she hated leaving her father to die. She glanced at the time, forty-two hours to sunrise. She and Kim must hide for thirty. Bad, bad. Men hunting men to kill when death for all was less than two days away...

Why hadn't she done her father's capsules the same as Kim's? She started in horror. She could have saved him, if only she'd thought... Tears came with self-accusation, but there was no time...

She had to hurry. No telling when the cultists would arrive with questions she dared not answer. Quickly she added personal items to a bagful already gathered. One small bag, all of her life she would carry into the new world.

She'd not learn about vacuum damage until too late.

"Kim," she said on returning to the sitting room, "we've got to run. The cultists will be looking for us."

He seemed startled; surprised the Disciple's people might be interested in him. Then he nodded wearily. "The gates. All right, Illian, you win, I'll open them, I can't stay here."

He seemed so old, so tired. His capsules. He would have to start the drug again soon. "Let's go to your apartment," she suggested. "You'll want some things." Especially capsules. *Murderess*! a voice screamed inside. Through inattentiveness she was killing her father, and for her own survival, possibly, Kim.

5

Kim gulped his daily pill. Eight hours till meeting time, at the fall of Edgeward City's last official night. In twenty hours the true, long night would end. Just twenty hours the City would live, and the people were still unconcerned, He could not now comprehend his own past disinterest.

He was so frightened by sunrise, now, that he had been unable to sleep since going into hiding, although weary to collapse.

Illian stirred under his right arm, woke. "You let me sleep too long," she complained. "You have to rest too."

He shook his head, surveyed the quietly busy machines of the hydroponics plant. "Couldn't." He couldn't say that thoughts of his own mediocrity, along with fear, had made sleep impossible.

She took his pipe from him, pushed his head down onto her bag of belongings. "Try." He felt her lips against his forehead.

And then she was shaking him. "Time," she said. "There was a patrol through, but they weren't looking very hard. Come on. It's time." Her words were taut. A sudden tenseness of his own made it a sharing. Time. Half an hour till the meeting. Twelve and a half till sunrise. Close. Time was suddenly a torrent, rushing past, time that had been an ally for eighteen centuries, time he'd thought would never run out.

It was a short walk to the rendezvous, the ancient "dressing station" at the west gate. There the suits for outside work were stored, unused for generations. Sudden new fear. Suppose none were operable? Suppose the cultists had destroyed them?

There were too many fears already. The new suffered anonymity in the crowd. His prime fear of the moment was Sun Cultists. Surely, they would be searching…

They were. Three patrols crossed their path along the way. But each they avoided easily. The searchers were not very concerned about escapes. Kim soon saw why. At least a dozen cultists held the gate. No problem, Kim told himself. A man in suit, with a suit's servos and protection, could easily walk through them.

There were eight people at the dressing station, Markel and two mortal men, two mortal women, and three cultists. The cultists had been bound and gagged and tossed in a corner like yesterday's forgotten underwear.

"Ah, Illian," said Markel. "I was beginning to worry. You'd better get your suits on." He and the others were in the process of dressing.

Sunrise

Two suits lay on a table. Kim glanced at them, at Markel. "These all?" He saw no others.

"The others weren't functional," Markel said blithely. He gestured at a darkness-hidden pile. An arm here, a leg there. The non-functionality had been helped along. No one would follow to bring them back to the City.

Kim looked at the pair again. He felt a little twinge of uncertainty, of new fear. The larger suit, obviously his, was not functional either. Fifteen hundred years had passed, but Kim knew a weak suit when he saw one. It would, where little cracks appeared at seams, break open as the gate lock decompressed.

"The suit's no good." And he knew he should have kept silent. Though Markel hid it quickly, he had smiled. A suspicion formed. Kim stepped to the table, looked closer. The cracks were no cracks at all. They were tiny cuts. A clumsy, though sinister, attempt. He looked at each of the others, at all the frightened young Dancers—especially Illian. He reserved judgement.

"What's the key-code?" Markel asked. It sounded casual. Kim felt it was anything but.

"Listen when I open the gate," said Kim. Through narrowed eyes, he studied the mortals. Markel was dressing as if nothing was to happen. The others were tense, frightened—except Illian.

"I guess I will," said Markel. He turned with a wicked smile. "Do hurry, Illian."

"The suit's no good," Kim repeated, "Damaged." Into that one word went all the hatred that had built during the past few days. Markel's eyes widened a fraction. "I'll need another." That steely sword he'd felt growing at Illian's made itself felt anew, harder and sharper than ever, obliterating a rising fear.

"There aren't any," Markel replied. "If you refuse this; you'll have to tell me the key-code." There was a hint of condescension, of mockery behind his words. He looked away, unable to meet Kim's angry eyes.

Perhaps Markel meant the cuts to be seen. Perhaps he meant to bluff Kim into staying behind. Perhaps...

Kim's fear suddenly returned. It came in a huge wave, left beads of perspiration standing out on his forehead and throat, then went, left the sword within him tempered.

No, Markel probably hadn't intended a murder. There was zero personal violence in Edgeward City. Was.

"Markel…" said Illian. Her voice was like a distant child's cry. Kim saw she had realized what her cousin was doing.

Markel smiled. "Won't you tell us the key-code? For Illian's sake?"

The rage came suddenly, explosively. Kim jumped at Markel, swung his pipe at the man's astonished face. Violence had returned to Edgeward City (the Disciple's executions were, of course, sanctioned by law). Markel staggered, grunting in surprise, raised his hands to protect his eyes. Kim hit him again. Again. The pipe bent in his hands. He struck repeatedly, repaying days of fear, anger, and frustration.

Markel was no villain. Night was, darkness, death, the oblivion of mediocrity—one's self being a nothing before all these things. Markel was no villain, yet Kim used him as one. Kim made him an enemy with a face. He let the rage roar through him and enjoyed it. Markel fell to his knees, shielding his head with his arms, Kim kicked, and a part of him stood separate, amazed by his savagery. So great, his fear and frustration. Markel collapsed, panting, nose bleeding.

A light touch at his arm. He looked down into Illian's frightened face. The pleading in her eyes shattered the mad anger. The others were staring at him, stunned. He regained some calmness—though it was exterior only. His mind, his body, were riot with the juices and emotions of battle.

He stripped Markel before Illian's frightened eyes, donned the man's suit himself. "He meant to kill me." And, although it was true, even to him it sounded a weak excuse for the madness he had shown. *He tried to kill me…tried to kill me…* That expression, worn by Markel now crawling for a corner of darkness to be alone with his fear and pain; how long would it haunt him?

"Let's go. Just push through the guards at the gate."

Sunrise

6

While he practised self-mortification of the mind, the Nomad tractor whined and growled around him, an ancient iron leviathan clawing through shadows up the sides of the Thunder Mountains. Illian and the mortals were scattered about the passenger chamber, silent, though in the passing hours they seemed to have forgiven him his outburst.

The tractor whined louder, slowed, backed, turned, came to a stop. A lean, cadaverous, smiling young man thrust his head through the pilot room hatch. "We're at the top. Fifteen minutes. Anyone want to look?" One by one, the mortals shook their heads. Kim thought a moment, remembering The City of Night—perhaps seeing the truth might lay Markel's ghost.

He went forward, surprised that Illian changed her mind and followed. They were given seats where they could watch through polarized glass, in the safety of a long-shadowed pass thirty miles from Edgeward City.

Spears of light already probed through slots in the wall of the White Mountains, passed above Edgeward and her deep crater, and caressed the snow-clad flanks of the Thunder Mountains, as the world slowly turned, the heads and shafts of the spears crept nearer the City... That which came through the Teeth reached the crater ringwall. Ten minutes.

The White Mountains were outlined by a brilliance almost eye-searing. Beyond, the pre-nova white dwarf consumed itself in incandescent fury, blasting its only daughter. Here, gas, steam, dust, boiled up from a worse-than-lunar, mad landscape. Sunbeams played among the gasses and dust, setting them aflame with reflected light—flame tongues on a grand scale, like a fire among forests of insane rock spires. The Thunder Mountains were thunderous once more. Heat expansion caused a constant grumbling beneath the tractor.

Illian, face averted from visions of a world gone mad, whispered, "I'm not a Dancer anymore, Kim. You're not a Musician..."

Her way of saying the past was dead and there was a future they could build upon their might-have-beens. She had forgiven him. His heartbeat increased. He shivered. His hand found hers in the darkness.

The first of Edgeward City's screens flared brilliantly as it was touched by a storm of solar radiation, died as it burned itself out. The second quickly followed. The City lay open to the flood of charged particles. Five minutes.

"You should hate me," he said softly. "Markel…"

"Please," she murmured. "I can't. Let it be. We've got forever to forget."

Silence, except for the grumbling of the mountains. The Nomad crewmen watched the City with ghoulish interest. They were the mortals of their society, knew the destruction of cities only through the stories of their fathers.

Forever. The Nomads had given them capsules already. Kim smiled. Forever. He and Illian. One small success for the incompetent little Musician. Forever. Around the world running with the Nomads, always one step ahead of the demon sun, until it finally went nova in its efforts to kill the lice on the corpse of its child.

Perhaps there would be an escape from that, too.

No minutes.

Sun God's spear touched the top of the City's dome.

The Devil's Tooth

1

A man with long arms and legs, thin waist and barrel chest, a long hatchet face, clothed in knee-length kilt and a true-steel sword scabbarded across his back, stopped carving the small wooden doll that had been in his hands for hours and became as motionless as the weathered old idols beside the dusty road. He could have been a statue himself but for lacking the dull greyness of skin.

The man's cold eyes, bright as the violet sky, watched a three-inch gallowglass beetle venture near, its imposing mandibles clacking ravenously. Its antennae twitched toward him, sensing meat, then toward its fellows, hundreds of thousands strong, crossing the road in a dark, glistening river a hundred yards wide and miles long, heading south in an unbroken flow. If so tiny a monster had a mind, this one must have spent that moment of antennae-dancing trying to decide whether to rejoin its fellows or investigate the attracting aroma of flesh. The decision was: feast first.

The man's hand scarcely moved, yet the true-steel knife with which he had been whittling transfixed the hungry beetle. A wan smile tugged at the already uptilted corners of his mouth. White teeth sparkled for a moment. A flick of the wrist and one less insect blocked his path.

Violet eyes rose beneath coppery brows, studying the cluster of squalid ochre buildings huddled between two small hills a few miles southwest, the city to which he was bound but which remained unattainable until the beetles were passed.

His eyes fell to the earth again. A half-dozen large pale blue executioner ants, which always hung about the edges of gallowglass armies, were marching toward the still living knife-stricken insect. They surrounded it with military efficiency, carefully avoiding the poisonous mandibles, and quickly closed in. Audible, chitinous snip! snip! in the right places, and the gallowglass ceased writhing. There came a brief waft of sour odor; the executioners' victory scent.

A new party of ants hurried from the purple-black, shining grass beside the road. These were smaller, dully-colored, slaves of the executioners. They began opening the exoskeleton of the gallowglass and chopping its muscle tissue into portable pieces. The blue executioners, which were equipped with poisons much more deadly than those of the beetles, formed a skirmish line between man and insect corpse.

The man smiled again, with respect, and a touch of smugness. He had not tried to recover his knife because he had expected the deadly ants.

His name was Fastenrath-by-the-Sword and, in this final age of Earth when no one dared stand alone, he was that rarest kind of man: a lone wandering free-sword. He came from a town called Sidikih in Draugenstarke country, born of an unwed woman scarcely a decade older than himself, Judi-with-the-Bells-on.

Again, Fastenrath examined the upstream end of the insect horde. Far up the low hill, in an area stripped to bare earth, he saw the glistening backs of the last beetles. Soon he could proceed along the dusty yellow road, to his appointment in Kristengrin. His eyes darted to the sun, to check the time. It was ancient, that sun; bloated, its dull red face blemished by a dozen leprous black sunspots. It hung overhead like a vast, bloody balloon, apparently close enough to touch, nearly ready to collapse in upon itself. It was ancient and tired, like the Earth it sullenly warmed.

The Devil's Tooth

There would be time to reach his destination before sundown, unless he miscalculated the beetles' speed. Leaning far forward, he both recovered his true-steel knife and re-read the legend on the stone he sat upon: three miles to the Kristengrin gates. But how much further to the house among many that he sought, on the corner of Metal Street and Music Lane, where artists and artisans mixed? All he had was that address, and a name; the name of a man of many memories. The possessor of that name might have the answer to the question that nagged at his brain since he first heard of a now forgotten land called Moon.

His first knowledge of that land came from a crumbling manuscript scribed in Old High Lothman that he found in the hands of a skeleton occupying the blackest depths of a crypt that superstition had saved from thieves, until he had come. He had squinted in the light of his hand-held torch, deciphering the ancient script which hinted at strange things and used words that had no counterparts in modern tongues, and just when he was in the grip of intrigue, the page ended. Fastenrath reached for the manuscript, anxious to turn the page and resolve the mysteries the first page hinted at. To his greatest frustration, the millenia undisturbed bones and manuscript alike powdered at his touch. Now to find his answers he had to seek the knowledge of this learned one, who some said was immortal and knew all and some said was a sorceror with three mirrors that one each saw into the past and present and future. There was only one thing about him that offered no difference of opinion; that he was evil and parted with his knowledge only at high prices. This Fastenrath was willing to face, for he suffered a curiosity unfashionable for his time and would not sleep well until that strange word that rolled strangely off his tongue was given meaning: Moon.

The gallowglass beetles had almost passed, down to the stragglers. Soon he could move on, but in the meantime he would work some more on the piece of hardwood he had been whittling.

The gathering shadows of evening were bizarre, distorted; shifting like the play of light and darkness at the bottom of an underwater garden. Kristengrin was not pleasant without sunlight. It was not a pleasant city at any time. Dark and Deadly were its names. But there was little pleasure anywhere in the world anymore. The dark and deadly lurked everywhere.

Fastenrath-by-the-Sword walked the shadowed streets boldly, silently, seldom letting his eyes probe the clots of darkness around him. His air of casual self-confidence was his best protection.

And there was that long-bladed, gold-damascened, shining true-steel sword hanging across his back, over his brown leather shirt, and the true-steel knife on his hip, over his ragged kilt, also with gold-inlaid spells of omnipotence. But he did not entirely trust the protection of the magic in those blades. After all, they had done little enough to save the man he had slain to obtain them.

Sounds of toenails on worn flagstones. A rat scuttled out of his path. Then came a wolf-like growl.

A large, hairless dog with blood-red eyes was challenging his passage. His orange boot flickered forward with casual swiftness. The dog could only whine once the metal toe had crushed its windpipe. Fastenrath stepped around the thrashing body.

He reached the crossing of Metal and Music, considered a moment, then selected the large, dark blood house behind the wall on the southeast corner. The windows were unlit, but it looked like the place he had heard described. There dwelt the man.

He smiled. The soft feet that had been following him did not resume their stalk when he started toward the house. In fact, his choice elicited a startled gasp.

There was no knocker on the gate, but it stood open a crack, as if in invitation. That in itself was a warning. Peeping through, Fastenrath saw a strange garden; quiet, peaceful, and deadly. Just behind the gate grew a dancing sabers, a sword-leafed plant that would stab at anything warm, and which carried an anti-coagulant drug on the hard tips of its leaves.

Beyond the dancing sabers stood a skull-bell tree with its white, skull-shaped blossoms twirling in the evening breeze. The fruit of that tree, pleasing to the eye and nose, if eaten, caused an instant paralysis. As he watched, a rodent tested a fallen fruit, shuddered, twitched, froze.

The Devil's Tooth

Hair-fine rootlets rose from the earth and sank into the unfortunate animal, drawing nourishment.

There were other dark plants, all adapted to depleted soil conditions. The dancing sabers enriched the earth around it with blood, the skull-bell with corpses. And yonder butterfly tree, with the gaudy, scented butterfly blossoms, lured unsuspecting lepidoptra, trapped their feet in sticky gums, and planted its seeds in their living bodies, which were later allowed to fall to earth.

A strange, deadly garden, but no more deadly than the world at large; just more concentrated. Fastenrath-by-the-Sword surveyed it, trying to determine a safe path to the house.

Did he really want to continue his quest, into this place? He looked up, at the scattered red dots forming a bloody belt in the sky. The ancient manuscript had posed a mystery, saying that those crimson droplets came from Moon. Moon? Where, or what, had the place been? Curiosity, which had already earned him more scars than he cared to count, demanded that he find the answer. The search could not be abandoned now, not after a month of inquiry which had done no more than yield an address, and the name Valdur of Kristengrin. Valdur would know, he had been told. Valdur knew everything. He was Valdur the Eye.

The doorbell was a serpent's head with open jaws that formed the handles of a small bellows. Unusual. Fastenrath examined it for several minutes, making certain it was no trap. He squeezed the handles, was startled by a honking cry from behind the door. It echoed, as if the room within were vast and empty.

Nothing happened. After a reasonable wait he slapped the serpent's ruby eyes. Another honk died away with mocking echoes. Then came a shuffling sound. And the heavy bronze door swung slowly inward. Fastenrath found himself staring into cold, glowing blue eyes. He could see nothing else, just those disembodied eyes.

His own eyes adjusted to the greater darkness. He made out the form of a man bundled in heavy robes, distinguishable only because they were of a darkness even deeper than that which seemed to flow from the interior of the house. The face in the cowl, too, was black, glossy like polished ebony. He could not make out the features, save those remarkable blue eyes.

"Valdur the Eye?" he asked.

"I am he," said the dark one.

"I have a question."

"Of course. None come for any other reason. You can pay?"

"Perhaps. I have yet to hear the price."

"And I the question."

Fastenrath took a breath, and had a strange thought: what if he really were talking to a hole shaped like a man, so dark and substanceless was he. A rent in darkness, with two blue candles shining in what appeared to be a cowl. He shook off the dreadful notion and stated his inquiry, "What, or where, is, or was, Moon? This thing I must know to banish the demon curiosity."

The voice called through the man-shaped hole with a bemused tone. "A strange question in these times. What do you know of it already?"

"That it may be a far country, a fallen empire. There was a manuscript in a Lothman tomb, ancient beyond reckoning, that crumbled as I finished the first page."

"You are a man of attainments. Those who read the Lothman are not common. A true seeker I see you to be, so you will have your answer."

"Ah?"

The shadow figure moved slightly, nodding. "But still there is the matter of price."

"My ears remain open."

"In the west there is a city called Warasdin, on the River Bryne, near a sea. And west of the city is a mountain, Arcelin, overlooking both city and sea. People there say it is the tallest mountain in the world, though you and I know otherwise."

"Ah. And?"

"Atop the mountain is a monastery. It is occupied by the last devotees of the most ancient religion in the world. It is called the Monastery of the Moon."

"This is my answer? Moon is a monastery?"

The Devil's Tooth

"No. I merely lay grounds for discussing price. Inside the central cathedral—which was once the heart of a great city and empire that antedated the Lothman by a millennium of millennia—stands a statue of a god. There is a large, fang-shaped ruby in the statue's mouth. The Devil's Tooth."

"And you want this ruby?"

"In exchange for your answer."

"I have heard of Warasdin. A dark city dying and evil."

"Everything is dying. It is in the nature of a created universe that all things shall die in time. And all creation is innately evil."

"Perhaps. I will collect your jewel."

The heavy bronze door began to close slowly, as if loath to shut out the night. Fastenrath shivered, disturbed by the implied nature of the interior of Valdur's home, darkness thick as treacle. His curiosity was sparked. How did the man, if man he was, live in such a place? He fought that curiosity, intuitively knowing that to enter the house was to leave the rest of the world forever.

The curiosity, the curiosity, something would have to be done about it. Someday he would have a magician exorcise it, lest it be the death of him. This dark earth with its billion deadly traps had no room for the inquisitive. Curiosity was an atavism, survival of an age when the world was friendlier and sticking one's nose in was not a contra-survival trait.

He turned, surveyed the sinister garden, picked a path among the deadly plants. But, as he started to leave, the door groaned open behind him and Valdur's ghostly voice said, "A moment."

Fastenrath turned. "Yes?"

"I'd beg a favor. That you deliver a package to a colleague in Warasdin." Dark from the darkness, a robed arm reached out, a glossy black hand proffered a small brown packet tightly wrapped in some thin skin. Fastenrath tried not to consider from whence that skin had come.

"A colleague?"

"One called Ghul. Deal carefully with him. He has the soul of a spider, though his word is good." Valdur quickly described the home of his correspondent, added, "Arrive at sundown. Ghul will give you honest shelter. But beware once you leave his house. Warasdiners take pleasure in the Wild Hunt."

"A tale I have heard told," Fastenrath nodded indifferently, though inwardly the fact revolted him. The Wild Hunt was the hunting of men for sport and, considering the reputation of Warasdin, for dark usage. "As for my answer?"

"When next we meet, you will have had your answer," the ebony, featureless face assured mysteriously. Then the door groaned shut. Fastenrath considered a moment, fingering the skin-wrapped package, finding the wrapper smoother and thinner than pig-skin. He shrugged, then took his first step toward the distant Monastery of the Moon.

Fastenrath-by-the-sword paused on the last low ridge lying between himself and Warasdin. His eyes, tracing the ill-marked trail before him, found a metal and silica-leafed forest downhill to the right of the road. Tree trunks stood like dark glass sculptures. The wind set up a song like the tinkling of wind-chimes. His thoughts raced back over all the long roads of his memories and lingered over a tavern conversation of years before. He had heard a tale then, about the deadly woodland view ahead. This, he knew, was the Tinsel Forest; twisted willows hung with razored leaves. Its deadliness would be obvious to a fool, but the road that skirted it did not take passers close enough to cause a real problem. So Fastenrath was at a loss to surmise the real danger, and that half-remembered tavern-tale tugged at his memory like a mouse trying to ring a temple bell. What was it? What was it?

He looked around. A hundred yards below, to the left of the road, stood a lone weeping pine. Out of season, the tree could not drip the poison that killed on contact. He strode thither, kicked a dog-sized skeleton out of the shade, sat down and leaned against the trunk and stared at the strange forest while he searched his memory. He would not move on till he knew the form of his danger.

The Devil's Tooth

For a long space of time, nothing came, and he roughly carved the hard block, shaping it more and more into a small, rotund human form, all the while trying to recall the threat imposed by the Tinsel Forest. Occasionally he looked up and yonder where the sharp edges of glass leaves and iron trees reflected the reds and purples in the light of the dying sun. Not until he heard the sound of distant singing rise above the accompaniment of the tinkling music of wind-danced leaves did Fastenrath cease his slow, careful carving and recall the peril that lay at hand.

Within that forest lived an immortal and, as usual, immortality was predicated on death. The undying female who lurked in the Tinsel Forest—somehow protected from the flesh rending foliage—was a dryad; death in a most attractive package. He pocketed his doll, rose, strode down the road, kept his eyes off the forest.

The voice sang out sweetly. Despite himself, Fastenrath looked for the source, saw naked female flesh flickering behind the deadly leaves. Danger! He turned his eyes away, chanted a Lothman marching tune to drown temptation, and lengthened his stride. Women were another of his weaknesses. The creature in the woods sang back to him, pursued him down the boundary of the lethal forest. Hers was a siren call, almost irresistible, yet by hurrying, and occasionally pricking his palm with the knife of true-steel, he succeeded in passing the beautiful snare.

Past one danger, he looked ahead to the next: Warasdin brooding beyond the Bryne, a grey city crumbling, where old men behind moldering walls amused themselves with evil while waiting out the last of the world's days. There, once upon a time, Yeshudi the Wise had held court, and from the city had ruled the ruins of the Lothman Empire. But now the city was fallen, physically and morally, the victim of no enemy but Time, and had become a lurking place for all the darkness haunting the human soul.

Fastenrath found his eyes caught by the upward sweep of the mountain behind the city; up, up, to where ancient structures perched like a broken crown atop its bald head. The Monastery of the Moon, his goal, atop Mount Arcelin. He closed his violet eyes and shivered.

He picked a path to the river carefully, for this was a country where dragon's teeth grew in great profusion. The grass-related plant lay hidden in sandy places until triggered by a footfall. Then long, toothlike spikes shot up to stab feet. At the least, the plant drew blood nourishment. If its victim were not quick, the poisons on the spikes would cause unconsciousness and collapse, allowing more spikes the opportunity to kill.

The sun was moving westward, a bloated, blood colored fruit marred by sunspots like black wormholes. How long till the end, he wondered. In his lifetime? It dropped behind that marred mount and left a thick violet twilight that deepened rapidly toward indigo. Fastenrath reached the river bank wondering if there would be any tomorrow.

The ferryman was a surly, misshapen fellow, as much gorilla as man, who wore a cunning expression and more than once tried to sidle behind his fare. Fastenrath did not turn his back till he was safely across the river.

Darkness came, indigo evening giving way to night with no noteworthy display. The first stars appeared. A belt of tiny asteroids stretched like falling blood droplets across the sky, hurrying to some rendezvous beyond the western horizon. Fastenrath began walking the last mile.

Something passed overhead, high up, like a shadow against the blood drops. In shape it resembled a bat, yet was larger than any Fastenrath had ever seen. But this was a strange land with unfamiliar horrors, and its night beasts might be quite unusual. Nothing in this world was cause for surprise. It trailed a muted chuckle.

The fallen gates and moldering walls of Warasdin loomed ahead. He trotted forward eager to be out of the night, yet moved with more than normal caution. Remembered rumors and travelers' tales weighed upon his mind, sending chills along his spine.

Yet nothing stirred behind the shattered gates, which sometime in the deep past had been opened by force and never repaired. The dark city streets were empty. Not even the usual rodents moved about. He did not like it. Normal city night-dangers being absent implied much greater perils. He thumped his purse, wondering. Should he deliver Valdur's package? His thin fingers strayed upward to the hilt of the sword hung

The Devil's Tooth

over his shoulder; to make certain that his coppery hair was firmly held by his headband, out of his eyes.

Playing confident, as in Kristengrin, he strode into the city, followed streets between ranks of crumbling buildings, moving toward the shadowy black silhouette of the structure that fulfilled Valdur's description of Ghul's abode. But he could not muster the bravado to stray from the deeper shadows.

Something was deadly wrong. The smells of death, decay, and evil surrounded him.

But no dangers he found.

Ghul's door was ancient wood, rotted, worm-eaten. It looked past due collapse. All the grey city round was overripe. An ordinary brass knocker hung to one side. He used it.

The door quickly opened as if—and surely he had—the little cripple there had been waiting. "Yes?"

"Ghul?"

"Indeed."

"I have a package from Valdur of…"

"Yes, yes, I've been waiting. Do come in." The dwarfed, misshapen man (his right arm and side were withered into near-immobility) stepped aside.

Fastenrath paused, wondering if he dared enter.

"Safety here," said the dwarf, around a chuckle. "Warasdin is honorable about one thing: guest right. I owe you for the delivery. All my power will stand between you and disaster as long as you remain in my house. Outside, I promise nothing."

Fastenrath thought a moment. Yes, the fat little merchant he had met on the road yesterday, and with whom he had shared a fire last night, had spoken of Warasdin's guest-right. And Valdur had said Ghul would keep his word. He stepped into a chamber where spiders had for generations made their homes undisturbed. Little Ghul himself looked like a creature that should properly be lurking in the corners of webs.

The dwarf had red eyes and drooping, heavy mustachios—facial hair was rare these days—that looked like mandibles. "A moment," said

Ghul, and hustled off, opening the package from Kristengrin as he went. Somewhere, shortly, he began shouting and soon he was back, saying, "A meal is being set out. If you'll follow me?"

Fastenrath was led to a room where a table had been hastily set so fast that he wondered about Ghul's unseen servants. Hearing strange, unpleasant noises, he decided to ask no questions.

"Take a seat, take a seat," said Ghul, offering a choice of two. "Here's hot food, fresh from the kitchen, the finest in all Warasdin."

Warily, Fastenrath took a seat. The dwarf scrambled into the other, snatched a fork with his good hand, began. Around a mouthful he asked, "Well. Another of Valdur's thieves, eh? The Devil's Tooth again?"

Fastenrath started slightly as he lifted his first forkful, but made no comment.

"Yes, I see it, it's the Devil's Tooth again. They come and they come to steal it, to sate Valdur's lust for life, and they never go home." Was there a malicious glee behind the dwarf's bland expression? Fastenrath could not be sure. Shadows had gathered like cobwebs about him, a cloak to hide expressions.

"Yes, they come and they come, and they go up Arcelin to steal Valdur's immortality, and we never see them again. And the Tooth remains in the Devil's mouth. Warasdin has its reputation," and here the dwarf paused, as if waiting for confirmation, "but they don't come back from Arcelin to tell damning tales." He stopped, though Fastenrath felt there was something more he had been about to say.

Still the wanderer did not speak. He ate, watched Ghul through narrowed eyes, and waited.

"The Devil's Tooth. You know what it is?" Ghul waited for an answer, visibly irked by Fastenrath's endless unresponsiveness. Finally, he went on, "It's not just a jewel, it's a cusp; not just a bauble in a stone idol but a channel and broadcast point for all the power of life that keeps the monks alive eons beyond their time. For as long as there has been a mountain called Arcelin they have been there, and they'll remain till the death of the sun or the theft of the Tooth, a deed that has been tried

The Devil's Tooth

hundreds of times since Valdur first began to covet immortality." Ghul fell silent, stared into his empty mug, awaited comment.

When it became apparent that again none was forthcoming, he continued, "The Tooth is Life. Valdur is ancient beyond your reckoning, but the monks are to him as a grandfather to a new-born babe. And even his extended span will soon end—unless he can seize some greater talisman than he owns. The Tooth…"

Fastenrath questioned a lust for immortality in a world so dark and obviously doomed. He shook his head. There were too many questions. His curiosity threatened him with passage through the gates of hell. "It's been a weary journey, and dangerous."

"Ah, to be sure," said Ghul, sparklingly, as if glad of a change of subjects. "A safe, comfortable room should be ready by now. Follow me."

Fastenrath followed through dusty halls draped with tapestries bearing Ghul's crest: a giant bloodhawk standing with feet on the backs of a pair of huge spiders. Moments later and a floor higher, he was standing inside the door of a bedroom—as grey and dusty and moldering as the rest of the house—waiting for Ghul's chatter to end. Finally the dwarf tired of his unresponsive audience, said, "The guest-rule is inviolable," and hurried away. Displeased by the grim little smile he had last seen, Fastenrath braced the door shut and checked the walls for hidden means of entry. He found nothing.

After dousing the lamp, he lay on the bed for a long time, hands behind his longish head, staring out the room's single small window. The blood-drop asteroids still chased one another across the night. They were quite like himself, he thought, always in pursuit but never quite overtaking their quarry.

The question of aspiration had begun to bother him. Where was he going? What did he want? Why? His progression from bastard child to orphan to beggar and thief, to wanderer and adventurer, had seemed to suit him for many years, but now the life had begun to pale. His three years in service to Frey Levchescu of Gormflaith, when he had been taught so much—the reading, writing, and speaking of many languages, kindness, art appreciation, and the belief that every man should be an artist (the Frey had started him carving dolls of blocks of wood)—and had learned so little, had spoiled the joys of aimlessness for him. Perhaps it was Levchescu's fault, perhaps his own. In any case, that period had been the only in his life when he had really *belonged*. And he had destroyed that. Perhaps his problem was guilt. Like a fanged and clawed animal brought from the wild as a kitten, there had come a day when he had turned on his benefactor, for the sake of possessing a true-steel sword and dagger pair with magical gold damascening. Whatever the cause, now his life was pale.

The Frey had almost pressed him into a new mold.

Now, always, his adventures began with questions. Damn Levchescu for starting that! He was no scholar, no wandering truth-seeker and do-gooder like the Frey. He was a wanderer, a sword-for-hire, a thief. He did not want to be a student, a slave of his own curiosity. He wanted to return to the life he had always lived.

Yet here he was, in a black, lethal corner of the world, about to hazard a darkness and death, and all for a worthless bit of knowledge!

Gradually, he grew angrier, both with himself and Frey Levchescu, until a single large tear slipped from the corner of one large violet eye and trailed hotly down over his angular cheekbone. Then he sealed out the vision of the perverse, hurtling blood drops in the sky, rolled onto his stomach, and forced himself into a troubled, shallow sleep.

2

While tightening the belt of his kilt and settling the sword more comfortably across his shoulder, he listened. The ancient house was silent. He listened again before opening the door, then, after a deep breath, slipped out.

The halls were dark, lighted only by small lamps at great intervals which did little to conquer the shadows. They were navigating lights, no more. Fastenrath started off with his right hand held high, near his sword.

The Devil's Tooth

No opposition did he meet, and all his caution seemed wasted. Through the house and downstairs he went, to the door he had entered by, and saw no one, heard nothing. Perhaps Ghul did not care if he left.

Relieved, he lifted the bar from the door. A lean smile played across his thin lips. So much for the horrors of Warasdin.

"Ghul!" the door screamed, from no mouth that Fastenrath could detect, "Ghul!" The cry echoed through the decayed halls, "Ghul-ghul-ghul-ghul."

Fastenrath broke the rigidness which had seized him when the door first screamed. He dashed out, picked the street that he thought led to the gate, and trotted off. A mile separated him from that safety.

There were shouts in the house behind him, laughter, and Ghul's voice raised in exultation. They had been waiting for him to leave. Fastenrath caught the words, "Blue hounds." He lengthened his stride and silently, angrily cursed himself for being a fool. Would it all end this pointlessly?

Elsewhere, at that moment, bells began ringing. He glanced back. High in the truncated tower of another mansion, men were a-scurry, gesturing toward him. Their cruel laughter came lightly on the breeze, maniacally gleeful.

The Wild Hunt was on. All Warasdin had been waiting for him.

Levchescu had brought him to this. What subtle revenge.

Somewhere, something bayed long and dolefully, with a lust for blood, like the cry of a banshee. Those were the voices of the blue hounds, dogs bred for hunting men.

He was on a long, straight avenue with a quarter mile to go when first he saw the hounds, as far behind as he had to go to reach freedom. And his human pursuers were behind the hounds, some afoot, some in sedan chairs. Two sedans vied for the lead, one of which had curtains emblazoned with the crest Fastenrath had seen on the hangings at Ghul's home.

The hounds were closing fast, though not running all out. They moved at a fast lope, certain of their prey. But Fastenrath, with huge chest and long legs, was a born runner. He suddenly stretched himself in a wind-sprint that took him along almost as fast as the hounds, fast enough to take him out the shattered gates a step ahead of snapping teeth. There, momentarily safe, he slowed to a brisk walk, panting, feeling he had somehow cheated fate.

For the blue hounds had stopped, waiting for instructions from their slower masters. Then Fastenrath, too, stopped and spat in the direction of the tall, lean, whippetlike hunters. All travelers' tales he had heard said that the hounds never left the city.

But Ghul and his followers were close now, and presented another danger. Fastenrath gulped air and began to trot up Arcelin, toward the Monastery of the Moon. If the place was as terrible as Ghul had claimed, there would be no pursuit.

After climbing a half mile of naked slope, Fastenrath paused at the edge of a thick stand of skull bells. Looking back, he saw men and hounds milling behind Warasdin's gate. An argument seemed to be in progress, perhaps over whether or not he ought to be pursued, or, more probably, to whom the right of pursuit belonged. He shrugged, entered the deadly wood, carefully avoided a bone-strewn patch of sand which obviously harbored dragon's teeth. A flock of small, stupid birds had visited the wood lately, to eat the fruit of the skull bells. Feathers and tiny bones littered the forest floor. Carrion-eating insects were thick, picking at the decaying flesh, and in their turn were being trapped and eaten by bat's wings, a breed of pitcher plant which exuded a carrion smell. The plant had wings like a bat's, night black, which closed over the mouth of the pitcher.

A place of danger and death, that wood, but safe enough for a careful man. He need only beware the dragon's teeth and have the good sense not to eat skull bell fruit.

Fastenrath made it through easily and sat down on the bank of a shallow gully above. There he took out his true-steel knife and a block of wood, whittled while he studied the Monastery of the Moon still high above. A partially fallen wall lay scattered down a hundred yards of slope toward him. Something grey to white lay scattered among the stones. Behind the wall stood a half dozen buildings in poor repair. All but one were small grey stone things. The larger structure was time-worn gothic,

The Devil's Tooth

all the frills scrubbed away by age. The gargoyles had become blind, featureless, lump-headed monsters, fading in their endless vigil. The monastery as a whole could have room for no more than two dozen monks. He whittled, and wondered how those monks supported themselves. He saw no fields, nor chattel, nor orchards, unless they were on the seaward side of Arcelin.

He sat there for twenty minutes, the doll almost unconsciously taking shape in his hands as he tried to reason out how that innocuous-looking structure could contain all the horror Ghul had proposed the night before. Not that he disbelieved the dwarf. Masks of innocence often hid the faces of the world's blackest terrors.

Terror. Surely nothing else lay ahead. He began to question his presence on Arcelin, to question the driving curiosity that had taken him first to Valdur the Eye, then to Ghul, and now here. It was going to get him killed. Ghul had hinted darkly when speaking of the Monastery. If Warasdiners feared the place...

There was a gruff bark, a shuffling, and a yelp of pain in the wood behind him. Someone growled a curse at the clumsiness of blue hounds.

Fastenrath leapt to his feet, silently cursing himself for assuming the Warasdiners would not pursue him this far up the mountain. Now his decision was being forced upon him. He would have to go on. Down the bank of the gully he scrambled, and up the far side with a yelp and a bound high into the air that carried him to naked rock ten feet from his jumping point.

There he paused to suck the poison from the puncture where the dragon's teeth spike had pierced his left palm. Only his quick leap had saved his feet and, perhaps, his life. He looked at the flood of little brown spikes washing against the rock. He could jump over or pick a path through. He decided on the latter course, knowing that a second patch might be triggered if he leapt to the sand beyond the limits of the patch he knew.

Carefully he moved, placing his orange boots between spikes until he reached the limits of the dragon's teeth. Yes, another patch nestled against this.

Behind him, in the wood, his pursuers drew noisily closer. He triggered the second patch with a stone. It was the last. Once through he could run.

Halfway between the wood and tumbled stone monastery wall he paused. Sounds from the cathedral, the larger building, had reached him: a distant, deep, weird chanting. He listened, pulled his hair back out of his eyes, for the first time considered the white and grey detritus scattered among the rocks from the shattered wall.

Bones! Thousands and tens of thousands of bones. Human, it seemed, all stripped of flesh, the larger ones cracked as if something had been after the marrow. The thousand broken skulls leered at him with empty eye-sockets, their broken jaws spoke—not with words for none were needed—of peril above.

Fastenrath once more thought of abandoning his quest. For these were not just dead men decayed where they had fallen. These had been butchered and eaten and their bones tossed away when the flesh was gone.

He glanced back. Nothing could be seen, but his enemies were making noise near the verge of the wood. There was no escape downward. They could intercept him in all directions. So up the mountain he continued, into the field of stones and bones, avoiding several patches of dragon's teeth—he had never seen that deadly plant so ubiquitous—and, from the cover of a large block of stone, in the company of skulls, watched his pursuers come from the wood and cross the gully.

Ghul had won some argument below. His was the only sedan chair coming up, carried by four armed men. Bowmen with arrows ready walked before and behind the chair, calling encouragement to the hounds. Only two of these were in evidence and they, after taking one look up the mountain, began to drop to the rear.

The gaudy sedan chair came winding up among the patches of dragon's teeth with all the stateliness of a coronation processional. Ghul's ugly face peeped out once, grinning evilly. Fastenrath, on all fours, scurried toward the monastery wall. A shout informed him that he had been seen.

The Devil's Tooth

Angrily, he asked himself why the dwarf was so persistent. Ah. Perhaps because of his eyes. It would not be the first time someone had coveted his strange violet eyes.

He paused just inside the shattered wall and looked back. The chanting in the cathedral went on, chillingly, like an invocation of some unspeakable god. Ghul's men were drawing close to the bone field now and the cripple leaned from behind his curtains to exhort them onward. The six refused to approach the monastery any closer. The two blue hounds had begun slinking down the mountain like whipped pups.

Ghul's porters dropped the sedan to earth and stepped back. Ghul held the curtains aside, shouted angered orders, but the six hunters cowed and did not obey. Fastenrath watched his enemy and carried on a silent argument with the guilt-ghost of the kind old man he had slain a year before. The chanting in the cathedral at his back went endlessly on, utterly depressing in its sameness.

The curtains of Ghul's sedan snapped shut and his shame-faced men stood in expectation. Nothing happened for a spell and Fastenrath nearly lost interest. Then a sudden agonized shriek rose from the sedan that snapped Fastenrath to attention. The curtains were being fluttered and buffetted as though the occupant were having some sort of a fit. Then, after another shriek, those curtains burst open and a huge red bloodhawk hurtled out, took flight, and climbed into the sky. It ascended staggeringly because one wing was deformed to a point where it was only barely of use. Fastenrath goggled.

The six footmen did not seem startled by events. But one was forced to leap out of the path of the bird and, unable to watch where he was going, set foot in a patch of dragon's teeth. And tripped. His still living body was pierced by hundreds of spikes, profusely providing scarlet sustenance for the subterranean plant.

Fastenrath watched the hawk, noted that it always wheeled the same direction above, always favoring the bad wing.

The tenor of the chant from the cathedral changed. It became excited and seemed to be approaching culmination. Fastenrath slipped off his rock, bounded down a safe path he had already selected, and concealed himself in a shadow lying thick between a wall and a fallen pillar. Squatting, sword across his lap, he watched the door of the cathedral.

As were the five hunters. They stood with terror on their faces, as if petrified, staring up the mountain.

One by one, the monks of the monastery came forth. Tall, taller even than Fastenrath-by-the-Sword, and so thin that their heavy brown robes seemed supported by stick frames, were they. They bent forward slightly as they walked so it seemed that their weight was supported by the long, thin, carven black staffs they bore in their left hands. Their progress was slow, as if hasty movement was dangerous.

One of the men of Warasdin moaned, ran. A monk's staff came up, pointed down the slope, and the man stopped moving. He fell. The others remained frozen by terror.

There were seven of those iniquitous priests. They paused just where Fastenrath had entered the monastery, considering the Warasdiners. Staffs rose, men below fell. Eagerly, then, the priests hurried forward.

And, suddenly, Fastenrath was painfully aware of whom it was that had gnawed and broken all those bones below the wall. Why did immortality always cost so horribly? It depended on cannibalism here; vampirism on the part of that dryad beyond the river Bryne. In other places, at other times, he had encountered other creatures equally depraved, all plunged into degradation and horror because of their lust to escape the claws of the great inescapable. Valdur the Eye, of Kristengrin, was trying to obtain the Devil's Tooth with full awareness that it would lead him along the same dark path being followed by these seven brown-clad priests. Was death that terrible?

The priests. They were now gathered like thin vultures among the Warasdiners, cackling shrilly to one another in an unknown tongue. What better time to enter the cathedral and snatch the Tooth from the Devil's jaw? For he had decided that it would give him a strong bargaining position when he tried to get back out.

Staying low, darting from cover to cover, with his true-steel sword in hand for the first time since starting this adventure, Fastenrath hurried

The Devil's Tooth

toward the gothic arch of the cathedral door. Were there more priests inside? He hoped not.

A shadow passed. He threw himself against a block of stone, looked up. The huge, deformed bloodhawk was diving, its wings folded, but not at him. Its talons hit the cowl of one of the priests, ripped the robe away, and sent the priest tumbling. A wailing stick figure that seemed hardly a man at all, naked, rose and staggered several steps, fell again, and moaned. Ray sunlight, even of this bloated, dying sun, was too much for him. The other priests forgot their prey, gathered round their brother, chattered shrilly while they shielded him with their shadows.

And then the bloodhawk was coming down the sky again, wobbling in flight as staffs came up to point threateningly. As it neared the priests it seemed to decide that further attack was too dangerous. It broke its plunge and hurried off toward Warasdin. Fastenrath wasted no more time watching. He sprinted into the cathedral, looked for the idol. It was not easy to overlook.

The huge black Buddha-fat, many-armed and ugly thing squatted in the shadows at the far end of the nave, the Tooth in its mouth burning a sullen red with a life of its own. It looked as though it had been freshly dipped in blood. In all the vastness of the place Fastenrath saw nothing else of note. Time had ruined everything not made of stone.

He hurried toward the stone monster thinking surely it had been patterned after nothing that had ever lived. No one, nothing stood in his way. He reached it, climbed into its lap, cocked his arm back for a smashing blow with the pommel of his sword. The Tooth looked like it would pop right out.

Shrill voices raised angrily, preceded by long shadows across the cathedral door. Murmuring a curse, Fastenrath leaped from the Devil's lap and scrambled behind the idol. There he found a narrow crack opening on a hollow interior. He used it immediately. Only a man as thin as himself, or one of the priests, could have done so.

He found himself inside a tiny chamber containing a desk and chair carved of the idol's stone. There were eye-level peepholes for a seated man which looked out through the Devil's mouth. The red light of the Tooth filtered through them. Here, he decided, priests of the past had given the Devil a voice, using the desk to support a heavy book from which they read responses to a litany. The desk held such a book now, an ancient, dust-encrusted thing.

Through the peepholes Fastenrath watched the seven thin priests make their entry, two carrying the one who had fallen, the other four carrying two of the stricken Warasdiners. They came down the nave, laid their fallen comrade and victims before the idol, began chanting pleadingly. Idly, Fastenrath wondered if they remembered the importance of the Tooth, or if they thought its power was that of the god the idol represented. He turned away when sacrificial knives came out to carve up a gory offering. Blood they caught in cups and splashed on the Tooth. Fastenrath could have sworn that it hummed softly after the soaking.

He shifted his attention to the book, which he opened as delicately as possible. But it was not the fragile thing he had expected. Its contents were engraved on incredibly thin sheets of an unfamiliar silvery metal and the crumbling expected was limited to the binding, which appeared to have been changed many times. The writing within, on wide pages, existed in three narrow columns per page, Fastenrath had little difficulty reading what appeared to be the most recent version, which was in Old High Lothman, still used as a liturgical tongue though it was tens of thousands of years old.

It was a holy book of a not unusual sort, a copy of a copy of a copy that began with the beginning and recounted the events of millenia on every page. But the viewpoint was unfamiliar, as was much of the earliest mythology. Fastenrath oh'd and ah'd silently, and soon lost himself in chronicles of times and nations ancient beyond anything he had ever before encountered. He nearly forgot the chanting priests, almost gave himself away when he happened on the long-sought answer to his question concerning "Moon." Only years of self-discipline damped an explosion of joy.

Moon, he discovered, was no far and forgotten country, but a celestial orb like the sun; one which millenia past had come too near the earth and had been torn apart by tidal forces in its crust. The earth, too,

The Devil's Tooth

had suffered terribly. The manuscript mentioned upheavals Fastenrath was sure had to be grossly exaggerated: nations and continents had been utterly destroyed, mountain ranges had risen and fallen, whole new lands had emerged from beneath the sea. Very few men had survived.

All this was covered on a single page, then abandoned as the forgotten historian went on to describe other disasters attributable to his dark god.

Fastenrath became aware that shadows were gathering thickly in the nave, as if it were growing late, and that the six hale priests had departed with the meatier portions of their sacrifices. The seventh priest still lay before the idol, motionless, apparently dead. Time to move.

But first there was a question he must answer to his own satisfaction. Did he owe Valdur of Kristengrin a service for this serendipitous answer to his question about Moon? Had the man foreseen this? Perhaps. Rumor had it that Valdur the Eye saw everything, even, at times, the future.

A little squeaking mouse of suspicion scampered through the back hallways of his mind, a suspicion that had first arisen while he had been listening to Ghul's monologue the night before. Was Valdur already an immortal of sorts, buying exposure to the power of the Devil's Tooth by sending victims to the seven dark priests? Ghul, it seemed, had suggested the possibility.

He would steal the Devil's Tooth. It should be raped away from the human monsters who dwelt here. The question was, could he, or should he, keep it from Valdur the Eye? He was morally certain that he should not be responsible for removing the horror of Arcelin to Kristengrin.

No. He decided. No Tooth for Valdur.

He must move out. The priests might be back soon, and the longer he lingered the more he risked discovery. After binding the old holy book across his back so he could carry it and still have free hands—it would be of tremendous value in certain markets—he left the idol's interior, slipped around its flank, stepped over the stricken priest, climbed over the pile of gore and human parts which had been placed in the god's lap, clung to the idol's lower lip with one hand while he drew his sword with the other. He dealt the glowing ruby a blow with the pommel.

It barely wiggled. He struck again, again, seven times in all before the thing broke loose, fell, and came to rest on the idol's tongue.

Then came a shriek of horror as he was about to sheath his blade. He whirled, found the injured priest risen from the altar, his skull-face a sallow mask of fear, his hands reaching like a pair of giant spiders. Fastenrath seized the Tooth from the idol's tongue as cold, claw-like hands closed on his throat. The sword was too long to operate at close quarters, so he dropped it purposely as he fell into the gore, the priest atop him. His wind was going fast as he struggled with the amazingly strong skeletal figure whose fingers crimped his wind-pipes. Using the Tooth as a dagger, he stabbed and stabbed and stabbed. The world began to grow black. Unconsciousness was closing in.

The Tooth hummed in his hand as he struck with it, pulling as if desirous of more blood. The priest's shrieks took on a new and even more desperate note, slowly dying away, and Fastenrath was certain there would be more than one corpse left in the idol's lap.

Something had begun to happen to him just as he was on the verge of blacking out. New strength was flowing up his arm. He suddenly felt able to fight thousands. He clawed the priest's hand free of his throat with one hand while continuing to stab with the Tooth. At long last his attacker suffered a series of spasms, relaxed. Fastenrath's stomach churned sickly. For a certainty he knew that the Tooth had raped the man's strength and soul and transferred his vital forces to himself. He felt ages younger. Was this the path to immortality, the will-o'-the-wisp so many pursued?

Sounds of excitement and anger reached his ears. The other priests, aroused by the uproar, were returning to the cathedral. He had to run. Could he avoid the power of their staffs and the horror of death on their altar?

He grabbed his sword, sheathed it, thrust the Tooth into his purse, and sprinted down the nave and out the cathedral door. Shouts followed. The other priests had seen him.

He immediately went down on his hands and knees, scrambling along trying to keep fallen blocks between them and himself. The tenor of their outcry changed, from outrage to terror. They had sensed the

The Devil's Tooth

theft of the Tooth. He was raping away their immortality. And their shouts were drawing closer, though they still could not see him where he crept. Fear, not a familiar passion, made him quiver and sweat. Soon they would cut off his retreat.

A shadow passed near him and Fastenrath looked up, seeing something slanting down the purple sky of twilight. It struck the nearest priest, soared up, circled for altitude; circled left because one wing did not function well. The sudden reappearance of the bloodhawk Ghul caused massive confusion among the already upset priests.

No less confused, but grateful for the diversion, Fastenrath scrambled out of the monastery into the boneyard before the fallen wall.

Down came the bloodhawk again, shrieking, but this time it did not make a direct attack. Instead, it dropped something round and the size of a clenched fist. Fastenrath watched it tumble down, heard it hit stone with a tinkle of breakage, saw sudden clouds of gas flare up, saw the priests begin staggering and coughing in the vapor. The bloodhawk squealed triumphantly. Fastenrath resumed running, keeping low, one eye always on the sky.

What cunning plan, he wondered, had Ghul put into motion? He certainly had one or he would not have returned with the globe of gas. And unquestionably there was some selfish reason for Ghul coming to the aid of the violet-eyed adventurer and seeker.

Then he knew. Below the bonefield, shadowed in the twilight, were many armed men and sedan chairs; likely all the lords of Warasdin and their retainers. So. An alliance of thieves come up after the immortality in his purse.

Out of the pan, into the fire. How had he ever come to this pass? That Frey Levchescu...

Ghul wheeled above him, shrieking triumphantly. How long before the bloodhawk came down to pinpoint his position for the lords on the ground?

The twilight thickened. Fastenrath, clinging to the deepest shadows, moved to his left in an effort to slip around the Warasdiners' right flank, anchored where the skull bell wood came nearest the monastery.

But the bloodhawk spotted him, circled overhead, shrieked. Below, men moved to prevent his escape. When he turned to go in the other direction the bloodhawk shrieked again and again men moved to intercept. And, emboldened by Ghul's victory over the monks, the men on the ground began moving uphill through the bone field, the ends of their line swinging to encircle. Fastenrath considered retreating into the monastery and trying to escape down the seaward side of the mountain, but he soon saw that Ghul's attack on the monks had served a double purpose. The gas that had defeated the priests also made withdrawal impossible for him. So this was the end to which his inconquerable curiosity had brought him. Wishing he had a bow, he drew his sword. Perhaps if he charged suddenly they would be surprised enough to kill him quickly, rather than at leisure later in Warasdin.

Another something appeared in the gathering night of the sky, coming from the seaward side of Arcelin. It appeared to be the same creature he had seen after crossing the River Bryne the previous evening; the laughing bat-thing. With a much clearer view this time, he saw its great black wings and polished-ebony body. Valdur, surely, here to reap his profit.

As the bat-thing wheeled past the bloodhawk, circling right in counter to the instability imposed by the crippled wing, Fastenrath stared and wondered. The bat flickered back and forth as agilely as its smaller relatives, sailed along the line of armed men approaching. There were cries of fear. Someone shouted something about vampires. The line broke. Men ran down the slopes so carelessly that they did not beware of dragon's teeth. There were shrieks of agony as the dark traps sprung. The outcry shattered the nerves of those who had not as yet broken. Before long the slope below Fastenrath was naked of all human life.

Above, the bloodhawk screamed angrily and clumsily flapped after the laughing bat-thing. It seemed unafraid. The bat scrambled for altitude, the bloodhawk struggling upward close behind. The darkness of falling night was by then almost complete. Under its cover Fastenrath moved down Arcelin as fast as he dared, more cautiously than the Warasdiners, but fast. His immediate goal was the skull bell wood. There the victor of the aerial battle would have great difficulty reaching him.

The Devil's Tooth

He attained the wood without difficulty or mishap, as often as not avoiding the dragon's teeth by circling the dead men who marked the patches. The traps were otherwise hard to see by the wan blood-light of the Moon-droplets racing above. He wished the great reflecting body of Moon was still extant, in all the glory described in the book tied to his back.

The battle above, it became obvious, would come to no fast conclusion, for both were-creatures continued shrieking endless challenges above the night. Fastenrath could occasionally spot one or the other as its vast wings obscured a star or hurtling fragment of Moon.

A thought came to him. He took the Devil's Tooth from his pouch. Yes, it cast sufficient light for his needs. Moving ahead with great care, he made his way through the thousand snares of the wood, taking a good two hours reaching its lower verge.

3

Fastenrath crouched in a cluster of sawgrass, least of the dangers of Arcelin, and studied the gates of Warasdin. Excited and fearful men, restraining a pack of blue hounds, waited there with torches, crowding close together as if to reassure one another against the night. Their talk was low, frightened, reached Fastenrath only as a constant low grumble. He could imagine what they were discussing: the chances of being killed by one snare or another as weighed against the certainty of immortality if only they were able to capture the Devil's Tooth.

Renewed shrieks broke out above. Dimly, Fastenrath saw a bat shape hurtle overhead pursued by a limping bloodhawk. So that battle endured still. No wonder the Warasdiners yet waited within their gates. They would not venture out till Ghul had a certain victory.

Fastenrath considered. His hopes of survival lay in getting out of the area quickly, and in not leaving a trail indicating whence he had gone. Yet he was a remarkable man physically and would be remembered wherever he passed. Bad. And he needed to be rid of the Devil's

Tooth soon, before it got a firm hold on him. (The thought of giving up the immortality it promised already hurt a little, yet he knew that there would always be those, like the thousands whose bones littered the slopes of Arcelin, who would hunt him as long as he possessed the Tooth.) It had to be put away somewhere where it would be unattainable. Such a place had come to him as he passed through the skull bells, though he was more hesitant to risk its dangers than he had been to face those of the Monastery of the Moon.

But first he must escape the environs of Warasdin, had to reach and cross the River Bryne, which meant crossing miles of open fields without light. To use the glow of the Tooth would mean revealing himself to both those who waited at Warasdin's gates and the embattled creatures in the sky. By daylight he could make the crossing in half an hour. By night it was possible he wouldn't make it at all.

He dropped to his hands and knees and began creeping along, using his long true-steel blade to probe for danger. In the back of his mind lurked the names of all the strangely adapted night-creatures that might waylay him. In this age no sane man risked the night alone. But, hopefully, all the uproar of the evening would have frightened the night-haunters away. The dangers he met were those of the earth, primarily the ubiquitous dragon's teeth. Many times his probing blade rang softly to the strike of upthrusting spikes.

Near dawn, and with a half mile still separating him from the ferry, Fastenrath paused. There had been silence above and behind him for a long time now, as if the battle in the air had stopped. Yet he had heard no cry of victory nor any scream of defeat. It occurred to him that, perhaps because they had been unable to fight to any conclusion, Ghul and Valdur could have come to some accommodation. A frightening possibility. Perhaps they now lurked above on silent wings, stalking. Involuntarily he glanced at the sky. There was nothing to see.

There was dawnlight sufficient to sketch in Warasdin's grey distant walls by the time Fastenrath reached and pounded upon the ferryman's door. He got no answer. Angry at being thwarted this late in the game, he dealt the door a savage kick. Unlocked, it opened easily.

The Devil's Tooth

The ferryman had crossed his last river. He lay sprawled across his filthy cot, his throat ripped out. But there was no blood to be seen anywhere. Vampire. Fastenrath immediately pictured a great bat-thing coming during the night, sating a wicked thirst while sealing one avenue of escape. So. They would see.

Outside again. Yes, as he had expected, the ferryboat had been sunk. But its bronze guiding chain still hung in a long curve above the turgid water. Fastenrath looked about him, wondering if a guard had been posted. Ah, yes, he saw the fellow now. But he would never give an alarm.

The night-creatures had not all been idle. Something huge, slimy, and hungry had come from the river and returned, leaving bones, clothes, weapons, alarm horn, and bits of flesh scattered near the watchman's hiding place a hundred yards upstream from the ferryman's home. As he made certain that his weapons, the ancient book, and the contents of his purse would not be lost in the crossing, Fastenrath prayed that the creature had had enough to eat.

Hanging like a sloth he inched out along the chain, finally dropped to earth on the far bank after what had seemed an eternity of exposure. He wrung out his kilt where it had dragged in the water, then rubbed at his legs, where the chain had caused abrasions, to ease the sting.

He considered Warasdin. Nothing seemed to be happening there. Then he turned toward the vale whence he had come yesterday. Very faintly, he thought he heard the dryad of the Tinsel Forest singing. He started off at a trot.

A half hour later he had reached his immediate goal, a low hummock topped by a bit of bald rock just off the trail, close beside the deadly Tinsel Forest. From up the vale a short distance he could hear the singing of the dryad. She had not as yet noticed him, apparently expecting travelers from the opposite direction. Well. He took a seat on the boulder, tried to decide whether he should read the religious book or should carve again at his doll. He decided on the latter. It wouldn't command his attention to the point where he would forget to watch for danger. And it might become useful later. Frey Levchescu may have taught him something of value after all.

Frey Levchescu. His thoughts returned to that charming, chubby, foolish old man, to those brief three years during which the blind (metaphorically) old teacher had tried to shape an image of his own idealism in already hardened clay. For the first time Fastenrath caught glimmerings of the true motives behind the old man's having taken him in. Without having come into contact with Ghul and Valdur, he might never have made the discovery. But the Frey had been seeking an immortality of his own, by stamping his values on the heart and mind of a pupil. It wasn't a cruel form of immortality, yet, in its way, it was as selfish as the methods selected by the rival magicians.

His eyes sought the decrepit sun. What form did his own search for foreverness take? With present death so constantly flaunted by that scarlet, leprous orb, every man sought some way to stamp his memory upon every moment. Was this the cause of his own early wanderlust? A need to carve his immortality with a blade? With a stolen blade?

The old guilt returned. Frey Levchescu had never treated him other than well. Perhaps the inner man was now trying to repay the crime of the outer and this was the cause of the curiosity that kept pulling him into impossible adventures. Sure, he owed the Frey something, for Levchescu had given him much more than a pair of extremely rare true-steel magical blades. He stared at his hands.

Under his expert touch the image of a fat baby grew quickly more humanoid. The sun rose above the eastern hills and bathed the vale with its bloody light. Suddenly Fastenrath turned to discover the source of a long shadow that had come stretching down toward him. It was cast by the fat merchant with whom he had spent the night a few days earlier. He was leading his slow fat burro, heavily laden, toward Warasdin. Merchants, of all people, had little to fear at the hands of their own kind. Even the worst bandits and murderers and magicians treated them with a respect bordering on the religious. They did not need to fear traveling alone if they were wise in the traps of nature.

The fat man was moving at an unseemly pace, possibly from gallowglass beetles. Fastenrath did not like that possibility. Gallowglass beetles could bar his path when flight was critical. He began to consider

The Devil's Tooth

revisions of his plan, but inasmuch as the original plan had not taken clear form it was hard to make sensible changes. Yet there was the glimmer of a plan, a foolish one perhaps, and a river of marching beetles could well ruin his chances.

The distant dryad's voice rose in a sudden song of exultation. Fastenrath watched the fat merchant stop as if instantly petrified. He pitied the man—he had shown him kindness when it was unnecessary—but made no move to go to his aid. He needed all his will to fight the song of the dryad himself.

The merchant was unable to fight it successfully, perhaps because he was unaccustomed to facing dangers from human sources. It was not long before he started walking toward the source.

A sudden outbreak of excited speech behind and below him caught his attention. Ah. He smiled. Here came armed men from Warasdin, with blue hounds. Ghul and Valdur were sure to be somewhere nearby. Though he disliked seeing the merchant condemned, there could have been no better time for his demise.

A shadow passed Fastenrath's resting place. Above him he discovered a giant bloodhawk soaring on one good and one crippled wing. Nearby, a black bat-thing which defied visual examination was having extreme difficulty operating in sunlight. Both were dropping down toward him, one cutting his path to the ridge top, the other escape across the vale to his right. The Warasdiners were hurrying to prevent any escape in the direction of the river. No sane man would willingly enter the Tinsel Forest, so that route was left clear.

Fastenrath rose, surveyed the land one last time, carefully arranged a mental photograph, then burst into a hard run. Far down the vale he had pictured the glistening purple flood of encroaching insects. Animals—predators and prey alike—were scattering quickly. From the width of the coming flood, Fastenrath judged it would prove the biggest army of gallowglasses he had ever seen. The presence of that deadly flow could prove beneficial after all, he reasoned as his plan became a bit clearer, complete with the revisions necessitated by the beetles. He could only hope those insects would not enter the Forest, as that might spoil the plan after all, and he would have enough to reckon with when his swift legs had brought him to those boundaries.

This he took in the instant before he broke into his speedy retreat, doll and knife in hand. Ghul and Valdur shrieked in the voices of the shapes they wore and adjusted their flight to cut him off. He was pretending to try for the top of the hill, but when Ghul was almost upon him he stopped, took two careful steps to his left, and was in the Tinsel Forest, amongst the razor-edged, metal and silica leaves. Those leaves tinkled maddeningly around him, reflected a thousand shades and hues of reds and purples. Behind him, Ghul flew into a loud rage. At the very least he and Valdur would have to resume human shapes before they dared pursuit. If they dared at all.

Fastenrath was no more than a dozen careful steps into the Forest when he encountered the dryad, a beautiful nude, just then lifting her bloody mouth from the throat of the fat merchant. Her satiated eyes were a dull blue, glazed, and took nearly a minute to fully focus on him. She was blonde, lithe, and lovely, and it was easy to see how a man could fall into her deadly hands even if she were unarmed with songs of compulsion.

Carefully Fastenrath sat down facing her, crossed his lank legs, and exchanged stares over the corpse. He prayed that her lusts were sated. Here, as with the Devil's Tooth, was another ancient experiment in immortality; one that had yielded the woman endless life but at the cost of almost everything else that was human. Was life really so dear?

Warily, but without fear, the woman watched as he resumed carving his doll. He was a quick worker when he concentrated, able to fulfill a pattern with the deft speed that comes of long practice. Her blue eyes never left his moving hands. She seemed mesmerized by his creation. She was beauty, he, art. And between them lay a warm corpse with an arm slowly moving as dead muscles contracted.

There were shrieks and thrashings beyond the edge of the weird Forest. The shape-changing process was, apparently, extremely painful. Fastenrath smiled grimly, hoping he had time.

Red sunlight broke through the tinkling leaves overhead, got caught amidst the golden hair of the woman, hung there like splashes of blood.

The Devil's Tooth

She was unaware of her own grimness, completely innocent of either good or evil, childlike in her rapture with his carving. It was curious that such innocence and deadliness should be found in one being. Yet many of the ancient immortals were like that, Fastenrath knew. They did not remember what they had been, did not understand what they had become, had even lost much of their ability to reason. Most interacted with the world in rote manner dictated by long ages of experience, not by using the minds that had developed the immortality processes. In some ways they had regressed to the purely animal plane.

He finished the doll, looked into her eyes once more while holding it up for display. A small, childish flash of greedy hope crossed her face. He offered the doll. She stared at him in disbelief, slowly extending a hand, then grabbed, held the doll in closely folded hands while studying it, crushed it to her breasts and crooned softly. Fastenrath sighed in relief. He had guessed right when he had decided to try playing on her long-denied attribute of Mother. She might not remember babies, but her instincts did.

Minutes passed. Eventually something moving tinkled the leaves behind him. He shivered. The moment of decision was almost at hand. He thrust a hand into his purse, brought forth the Tooth, slowly extended it toward the woman.

Her eyes rose from the doll, saw the glowing ruby, widened with a childish interest. It was a pretty bauble, that could not be denied. Slowly, uncertainly, she reached for it.

Then she was crushing both doll and ruby to her breasts, one in each hand. While she was thus bemused, Fastenrath rose carefully and made his cautious way deeper into the Forest. Despite all his care, his bare arms and legs became badly lacerated; his shirt, kilt, and boots were slashed to ribbons by the leaves. At least they did not actively oppose his passage as would have been the case if the woman had considered him an enemy.

He soon found a suitable hiding place, and from it continued to observe the woman. She continued crooning to her doll and ruby. He congratulated himself on the success of his ploy. It was a long chance he had taken, betting his life on the naivete and denied instincts of this unhuman creature.

He had been successful up till then, but he wasn't out of his difficulties yet. Key parts of his plan were still to unfold and could easily go wrong.

Already there was a feeling of terrible loss and a growing temptation. Could he wait his plan out, recover the Tooth from the dryad when it was complete, and with its promise of immortality escape her anger? The Tooth had gotten a hold on him, such power it had to shape and warp the mind. He shuddered with horror at his own thoughts. He had seen and done many black things during his years—the murder of Frey Levchescu weighed ever more heavily on his mind—but this temptation was almost too much for reason. His one taste of the Tooth's power, when he had slain the priest, had become as haunting and attractive as a draught of Night's Dream, a spicy narcotic wine made of the de-poisoned juices of skull bell fruit. He felt both fear and horror of the Tooth even while his mind kept trying to find ways to steal it back. A temptation altogether too attractive, this immortality.

Events helped defeat the devils of his mind. The sounds he had heard before ridding himself of the Tooth now came from quite near the enthralled dryad, approaching. Ghul appeared, stared down at the corpse, at the woman, at the treasures in her hands. He glanced behind him, perhaps to ascertain the nearness of his unwanted partner. Fastenrath smiled. He could see what was in Ghul's mind. He was considering seizing the jewel, hiding it, and allowing Valdur to think that it was still in Fastenrath's possession.

The dwarf took the first step, snatched the Tooth.

The dryad looked up, surprised, then sprang with the suddenness of a cat. The tinkling of the Forest changed from a soft merry note to an angry one. The branches of the metal trees began to stir. The woman's nails went for Ghul's eyes, her teeth for his throat, and she had both in a death-grip before he could utter his first startled cry. Fastenrath watched unsmiling. The dwarf would struggle a bit, but he was as good as dead. With teeth in his throat he could neither call for help nor utter

The Devil's Tooth

the words of a defensive spell. The trap was nicely sprung; Ghul's greed had brought him to a form of suicide. Fastenrath's estimates of the woman's behavior had come off even better than he had hoped.

As Ghul twitched his last, one dying hand vainly clutching that of the merchant already dead, Valdur of Kristengrin stepped into the tiny clearing. Man and clothes, though the latter had been savaged by angry leaves, were so deeply black that Fastenrath's eyes kept slipping off to more substantial objects. Looking at Valdur was like staring into a hole in nothingness.

Chuckling, Valdur snatched the Tooth from dying Ghul's hand and ran.

The dryad rose angrily, but too late to attack. Fastenrath cursed softly. He had brought the Tooth here because he had thought it would be unattainable once in her care.

The woman sang something. Valdur froze for an instant, then resumed his flight. The woman sang again. All around the man the Tinsel Forest, already writhing, sprang into insanely lashing life, the razor-edged leaves and steely-whip branches reaching for his body. Stripes of scarlet began to mar his perfect blackness. One of his arms seemed nearly severed. He shrieked, dropped the Tooth from a hand that could no longer grip, and hurled himself at the last writhing barrier to his freedom. He made it through.

Fastenrath cursed again. Valdur had escaped. The trap had worked less than perfectly. But, at least, the Tooth would now be even more unattainable than it had been in the Monastery of the Moon, though Valdur would know its new location and would continue trying to get it.

The woman recovered her new bauble, returned to the clearing and resumed crooning. Fastenrath tried to make out the subject being discussed by the excited voices arguing beyond the Forest edge. At last he got it. Valdur was demanding, unsuccessfully, that Ghul's retainers break him a path through the dangerous leaves. Moving with the utmost caution, Fastenrath eased away from the dryad and his hiding place and made for the uphill end of the Forest. Leaves continued cutting him, but not maliciously. He endured.

He stepped from the Forest an hour later, just above where the flood of gallowglass beetles washed against its flank and turned away, moving toward the River Bryne. No enemies did he see anywhere, and even were they near, he had come out of the Forest on the opposite side of the vast living river of beetles. Likely, seeing themselves foiled, they were already on their way to Warasdin, grey and brooding in the distance.

A man's skeleton lay in the gallowglass stream. He wondered if it could be Valdur, struck down by Ghul's angry retainers. But that seemed to be too much to hope. More likely it was that of a man who had angered the sorcerer. Fastenrath shrugged, smiled crookedly. Well, enough of wizardry for a while. He was off to find a buyer for the ancient book.

And to lay at peace the ghost which would otherwise haunt him all his life. He set his course for Gormflaith.

In the Wind

1

It's quiet up there, riding the ups and downs over Ginnunga Gap. Even in combat there's no slightest clamor, only a faint scratch and whoosh of strikers tapping igniters and rockets smoking away. The rest of the time, just a sleepy whisper of air caressing your canopy. On patrol it's hard to stay alert and wary.

If the aurora hadn't been so wild behind the hunched backs of the Harridans, painting glaciers and snowfields in ropes of varicolored fire, sequinning snow-catches in the weathered natural castles of the Gap with momentary reflections, I might have dozed at the stick the morning I became von Drachau's wingman. The windwhales were herding in the mountains, thinking migration, and we were flying five or six missions per day. The strain was almost unbearable.

But the auroral display kept me alert. It was the strongest I'd ever seen. A ferocious magnetic storm was developing. Lightning grumbled between the Harridans' copper peaks, sometimes even speared down and danced among the spires in the Gap. We'd all be grounded soon. The rising winds, cold but moisture-heavy, promised weather even whales couldn't ride.

Winter was about to break out of the north, furiously, a winter of a Great Migration. Planets, moons and sun were right, oracles and omens predicting imminent Armageddon. Twelve years had ticked into the ashcan of time. All the whale species again were herding. Soon the fighting would be hard and hopeless.

There are four species of windwhale on the planet Camelot, the most numerous being the Harkness whale, which migrates from its north arctic and north temperate feeding ranges to equatorial mating grounds every other year. Before beginning their migration they, as do all whales, form herds—which, because the beasts are total omnivores, utterly strip the earth in their passage south. The lesser species, in both size and numbers, are Okumura's First, which mates each three winters, Rosenberg's, mating every fourth, and the rare Okumura's Second, which travels only once every six years. Unfortunately...

It takes no mathematical genius to see the factors of twelve. And every twelve years the migrations do coincide. In the Great Migrations the massed whales leave tens of thousands of square kilometers of devastation in their wake, devastation from which, because of following lesser migrations, the routes barely recover before the next Great Migration. Erosion is phenomenal. The monsters, subject to no natural control other than that apparently exacted by creatures we called mantas, were destroying the continent on which our employers operated.

Ubichi Corporation had been on Camelot twenty-five years. The original exploitation force, though equipped to face the world's physical peculiarities, hadn't been prepared for whale migrations. They'd been lost to a man, whale supper, because the Corporation's pre-exploitation studies had been so cursory. Next Great Migration another team, though they'd dug in, hadn't fared much better. Ubichi still hadn't done its scientific investigation. In fact, its only action was a determination that the whales had to go.

Simple enough, viewed from a board room at Geneva. But practical implementation was a nightmare under Camelot's technically stifling conditions. And the mantas recomplicated everything.

My flight leader's wagging wings directed my attention south. From a hill a dozen kilometers down the cable came flashing light, Clonninger

In The Wind

Station reporting safe arrival of a convoy from Derry. For the next few hours we'd have to be especially alert.

It would take the zeppelins that long to beat north against the wind, and all the while they would be vulnerable to mantas from over the Gap. Mantas, as far as we could see at the time, couldn't tell the difference between dirigibles and whales. More air cover should be coming up...

Von Drachau came to Jaeger Gruppe XIII (Corporation Armed Action Command's unsubtle title for our Hunter Wing, which they used as a dump for problem employees) with that convoy, reassigned from JG IV, a unit still engaged in an insane effort to annihilate the Sickle Islands whale herds by means of glider attacks carried out over forty-five kilometers of quiet seas. We'd all heard of him (most JG XIII personnel had come from the Sickle Islands operation), the clumsiest, or luckiest incompetent, pilot flying for Ubichi. While scoring only four kills he'd been bolted down seven times—and had survived without a scratch. He was the son of Jupp von Drachau, the Confederation Navy officer who had directed the planet-busting strike against the Sangaree homeworld, a brash, sometimes pompous, always self-important nineteen year old who thought that the flame of his father's success should illuminate him equally—and yet resented even a mention of the man. He was a dilettante, come to Camelot only to fly. Unlike the rest of us, Old Earthers struggling to buy out of the poverty bequeathed us by prodigal ancestors, he had no driving need to give performance for pay.

An admonition immediately in order: I'm not here to praise von Drachau, but to bury him. To let him bury himself. Aerial combat fans, who have never seen Camelot, who have read only corporate propaganda, have made of him a contemporary "hero," a flying do-no-wrong competitor for the pewter crown already contested by such antiques as von Richtoffen, Hartmann and Galland. Yet these Archaicists can't, because they need one, make a platinum bar from a turd, nor a socio-psychological fulfillment from a scatterbrain kid...*

Most of the stories about him are apocryphal accretions generated to give him depth in his later, "heroic" aspect. Time and storytellers increase his stature, as they have that of Norse gods, who might've been people who lived in preliterate times. For those who knew him (and no one is closer than a wingman), though some of us might like to believe the legends, he was just a selfish, headstrong, tantrum-throwing manchild—albeit a fighter of supernatural ability. In the three months he spent with us, during the Great Migration, his peculiar talents and shortcomings made of him a creature larger than life. Unpleasant a person as he was, he became *the* phenom pilot.

> *This paragraph is an editorial insertion from a private letter by Salvador del Gado. Dogfight believes it clarifies del Gado's personal feelings toward his former wingman. His tale, taken separately, while unsympathetic, strives for an objectivity free of his real jealousies. It is significant that he mentions Hartmann and Galland together with von Richtoffen; undoubtedly they, as he when compared with von Drachau, were flyers better than the Red Knight, yet they, and del Gado, lack the essential charisma of the flying immortals. Also, von Richtoffen and von Drachau died at the stick; Hartmann and Galland went on to more prosaic things, becoming administrators, commanders of the Luftwaffe. Indications are that del Gado's fate with Ubichi Corporation's Armed Action Command will be much the same.
>
> —Dogfight

2

The signals from Clonninger came before dawn, while only two small moons and the aurora lighted the sky. But sunrise followed quickly. By the time the convoy neared Beadle Station (us), Camelot's erratic, blotchy-faced sun had cleared the eastern horizon. The reserve squadron began catapulting into the Gap's frenetic drafts. The four of us on close patrol descended toward the dirigibles.

In The Wind

The lightning in the Harridans had grown into a Ypres cannonade. A net of jagged blue laced together the tips of the copper towers in the Gap. An elephant stampede of angry clouds rumbled above the mountains. The winds approached the edge of being too vicious for flight.

Flashing light from ground control, searchlight fingers stabbing north and east, pulsating. Mantas sighted. We waggle-winged acknowledgment, turned for the Gap and updrafts. My eyes had been on the verge of rebellion, demanding sleep, but in the possibility of combat weariness temporarily faded.

Black specks were coming south low against the daytime verdigris of the Gap, a male-female pair in search of a whale. It was obvious how they'd been named. Anyone familiar with Old Earth's sea creatures could see a remarkable resemblance to the manta ray—though these had ten meter bodies, fifteen meter wingspans, and ten meter tails tipped by devil's spades of rudders. From a distance they appeared black, but at attack range could be seen as deep, uneven green on top and lighter, near olive beneath. They had ferocious habits.

More signals from the ground. Reserve ships would take the mantas. Again we turned, overflew the convoy.

It was the biggest ever sent north, fifteen dirigibles, one fifty meters and larger, dragging the line from Clonninger at half kilometer intervals, riding long reaches of running cable as their sailmen struggled to tack them into a facing wind. The tall glasteel pylons supporting the cable track were ruby towers linked by a single silver strand of spider silk running straight to Clonninger's hills.

We circled wide and slow at two thousand meters, gradually dropping lower. When we got down to five hundred we were replaced by a flight from the reserve squadron while we scooted to the Gap for an updraft. Below us ground crews pumped extra hydrogen to the barrage balloons, lifting Beadle's vast protective net another hundred meters so the convoy could slide beneath. Switchmen and winchmen hustled about with glass and plastic tools in a dance of confusion. We didn't have facilities for receiving more than a half dozen zeppelins—though these, fighting the wind, might come up slowly enough to be handled.

More signals. More manta activity over the Gap, the reserve squadron's squabble turning into a brawl. The rest of my squadron had come back from the Harridans at a run, a dozen mantas in pursuit. Later I learned our ships had found a small windwhale herd and while one flight busied their mantas the other had destroyed the whales. Then, ammunition gone, they ran for home, arriving just in time to complicate traffic problems.

I didn't get time to worry it. The mantas, incompletely fed, spotted the convoy. They don't distinguish between whale and balloon. They went for the zeppelins.

What followed becomes dulled in memory, so swiftly did it happen and so little attention did I have to spare. The air filled with mantas and lightning, gliders, smoking rockets, explosions. The brawl spread till every ship in the wing was involved. Armorers and catapult crews worked to exhaustion trying to keep everything up. Ground batteries seared one another with backblast keeping a rocket screen between the mantas and stalled convoy—which couldn't warp in while the entrance to the defense net was tied up by fighting craft (a problem unforeseen but later corrected by the addition of emergency entryways). They winched their running cables in to short stay and waited it out. Ground people managed to get barrage balloons with tangle tails out to make the mantas' flying difficult.

Several of the dirigibles fought back. Stupid, I thought. Their lifting gas was hydrogen, screamingly dangerous. To arm them seemed an exercise in self-destruction. So it proved. Most of our casualties came when a ship loaded with ground troops blew up, leaking gas ignited by its own rockets. One hundred eighty-three men burned or fell to their deaths. Losses to mantas were six pilots and the twelve man crew of a freighter.

3

Von Drachau made his entry into JG XIII history just as I dropped from my sailship to the packed earth parking apron. His zepp was the first in and, having vented gas, had been towed to the apron to clear the

In The Wind

docking winches. I'd done three sorties during the fighting, after the six of regular patrol. I'd seen my wingman crash into a dragline pylon, was exhausted, and possessed by an utterly foul mood. Von Drachau hit dirt long-haired, unkempt, and complaining, and I was there to greet him. "What do you want to be when you grow up, von Drachau?"

Not original, but it caught him off guard. He was used to criticism by administrators, but pilots avoid antagonism. One never knows when a past slight might mean hesitation at the trigger ring and failure to blow a manta off one's tail. Von Drachau's hatchet face opened and closed, goldfish-like, and one skeletal hand came up to an accusatory point, but he couldn't come back.

We'd had no real contact during the Sickle Islands campaign. Considering his self-involvement, I doubted he knew who I was—and didn't care if he did. I stepped past and greeted acquaintances from my old squadron, made promises to get together to reminisce, then retreated to barracks. If there were any justice at all, I'd get five or six hours for surviving the morning.

I managed four, a record for the week, then received a summons to the office of Commander McClennon, a retired Navy man exiled to command of JG XIII because he'd been so outspoken about Corporation policy.

(The policy that irked us all, and which was the root of countless difficulties, was Ubichi's secret purpose on Camelot. Ubichi deals in unique commodities. It was sure that Camelot operations were recovering one such, but fewer than a hundred of a half million employees knew what. The rest were there just to keep the windwhales from interfering. Even we mercenaries from Old Earth didn't like fighting for a total unknown.)

Commander McClennon's outer office was packed, old faces from the wing and new from the convoy. Shortly, McClennon appeared and announced that the wing had been assigned some gliders with new armaments, low velocity glass barrel gas pressure cannon, pod of four in the nose of a ship designed to carry the weapon system…immediate interest. Hitherto we'd flown sport gliders jury-rigged to carry crude rockets, the effectiveness of which lay in the cyanide shell surrounding the warhead.

Reliability, poor; accuracy, erratic. A pilot was nearly as likely to kill himself as a whale.

But what could you do when you couldn't use the smallest scrap of metal? Even a silver filling could kill you there. The wildly oscillating and unpredictable magnetic ambience could induce sudden, violent electrical charges. The only metal risked inside Camelot's van Allens was that in the lighters running to and from the surface station at the south magnetic pole, where few lines of force were cut and magnetic weather was reasonably predictable.

Fifty thousand years ago the system passed through the warped space surrounding a black hole. Theory says that's the reason for its eccentricities, but I wonder. Maybe it explains why all bodies in the system have magnetic fields offset from the body centers, the distance off an apparent function of size, mass and rate of rotation, but it doesn't tell me why the fields exist (planetary magnetism is uncommon), nor why they pulsate randomly.

But I digress, and into areas where I have no competence. I should explain what physicists don't understand? We were in the Commander's office and he was selecting pilots for the new ships. Everyone wanted one. Chances for survival appeared that much better.

McClennon's assignments seemed indisputable, the best flyers to the new craft, four flights of four, though those left with old ships were disappointed.

I suffered disappointment myself. A blockbuster dropped at the end, after I'd resigned myself to continuing in an old craft.

"Von Drachau, Horst-Johann," said McClennon, peering at his roster through antique spectacles, one of his affectations, "attack pilot. Del Gado, Salvador Martin, wingman."

Me? With von Drachau? I'd thought the old man liked me, thought he had a good opinion of my ability…why'd he want to waste me? Von Drachau's wingman? Murder.

I was so stunned I couldn't yell *let me out!*

"Familiarization begins this afternoon, on Strip Three. First flight checkouts in the morning." A few more words, tired exhortations to do

In The Wind

our best, all that crap that's been poured on men at the front from day one, then dismissal. Puzzled and upset, I started for the door.

"Del Gado. Von Drachau." The executive officer. "Stay a minute. The Commander wants to talk to you."

4

My puzzlement thickened as we entered McClennon's inner office, a Victorian-appointed, crowded yet comfortable room I hadn't seen since I'd paid my first day respects. There were bits of a stamp collection scattered, a desk becluttered, presentation holographs of Navy officers that seemed familiar, another of a woman of the pale thin martyr type, a model of a High Seiner spaceship looking like it'd been cobbled together from plastic tubing and children's blocks. McClennon had been the Naval officer responsible for bringing the Seiners into Confederation in time for the Three Races War. His retirement had been a protest against the way the annexation was handled. Upset as I was I had little attention for surroundings, nor cared what made the Old Man tick.

Once alone with us, he became a man who failed to fit my conception of a commanding officer. His face, which usually seemed about to slide off his skulbones with the weight of responsibility, spread a warm smile. "Johnny!" He thrust a wrinkled hand at von Drachau.

He knew the kid?

My new partner's reaction was a surprise, too. He seemed awed and deferential as he extended his own hand. "Uncle Tom."

McClennon turned. "I've known Johnny since the night he wet himself on my dress blacks just before the Grand Admiral's Ball. Good old days at Luna Command, before the last war." He chuckled. Von Drachau blushed. And I frowned in renewed surprise. I hadn't known von Drachau well, but had never seen or heard anything to suggest he was capable of being impressed by anyone but himself.

"His father and I were Academy classmates. Then served in the same ships before I went into intelligence. Later we worked together in operations against the Sangaree."

Von Drachau didn't sit down till invited. Even though McClennon, in those few minutes, exposed more of himself than anyone in the wing had hitherto seen, I was more interested in the kid. His respectful, almost cowed attitude was completely out of character.

"Johnny," said McClennon, leaning back behind his desk and slowly turning a drink in his hand, "you don't come with recommendations. Not positive, anyway. We going to go through that up here?"

Von Drachau stared at the carpet, shrugged, reminded me of myself as a seven year old called to explain some specially noxious misdeed to my creche-father. It became increasingly obvious that McClennon was a man with whom von Drachau was unwilling to play games. I'd heard gruesome stories of his behavior with the CO JG IV.

"You've heard the lecture already, so I won't give it. I do understand, a bit. Anyway, discipline here, compared to Derry or the Islands, is almost nonexistent. Do your job and you won't have it bad. But don't push. I won't let you endanger lives. Something to think about. This morning's scrap left me with extra pilots. I can ground people who irritate me. Could be a blow to a man who loved flying."

Von Drachau locked gazes with the Commander. Rebellion stirred but he only nodded.

McClennon turned again. "You don't like this assignment." Not a question. My face must've been a giveaway. "Suicidal, you think? You were in JG IV a while. Heard all about Johnny. But you don't know him. I do, well enough to say he's got potential—if we can get him to realize aerial fighting's a team game. By which I mean his first consideration must be bringing himself, his wingman, and his ship home intact." Von Drachau grew red. He'd not only lost seven sailships during the Sickle Islands offensive, he'd lost three wingmen. Dead. "It's hard to remember you're part of a team while attacking. You know that yourself, del Gado. So be patient. Help me make something out of Johnny."

I tried to control my face, failed.

In The Wind

"Why me, eh? Because you're the best flyer I've got. You can stay with him if anyone can.

"I know, favoritism. I'm taking special care. And that's wrong. You're correct, right down the line. But I can't help myself. Don't think you could either, in my position. Enough explanation. That's the way it's going to be. If you can't handle it, let me know. I'll find someone who can, or I'll ground him. One thing I mean to do: send him home alive." Von Drachau vainly tried to conceal his embarrassment and anger. I felt for him. Wouldn't like being talked about that way myself—though McClennon was doing the right thing, putting his motives on display, up front, so there'd be no surprises later on, and establishing for von Drachau the parameters allowed him. The Commander was an Old Earther himself, and on that battleground had learned that honesty is a weapon as powerful as any in the arsenal of deceit.

"I'll try," I replied, though with silent reservations. I'd have to do some handy self-examination before I bought the whole trick bag.

"That's all I ask. You can go, then. Johnny and I have some catching up to do."

I returned to barracks in a daze. There I received condolences from squadron mates motivated, I suppose, by relief at having escaped the draft themselves.

Tired though I was, I couldn't sleep till I'd thought everything through.

In the end, of course, I decided the Old Man had earned a favor. (This's a digression from von Drachau's story except insofar as it reflects the thoughts that led me to help bring into being the one really outstanding story in Ubichi's Camelot operation.) McClennon was an almost archetypically remote, secretive, Odin/Christ figure, an embastioned lion quietly licking private wounds in the citadel of his office, sharing his pain and privation with no one. But personal facts that had come flitting on the wings of rumor made it certain he was a rare old gentleman who'd paid his dues and asked little in return. He'd bought off for hundreds of Old Earthers, usually by pulling wires to Service connections. And, assuming the stories are true, the price he paid to bring the Starfishers into Confederation, at a time when they held the sole means by which the Three Races War could be won, was the destruction of a deep relationship with the only woman he'd ever loved, the pale Seiner girl whose holo portrait sat like an icon on his desk. Treason and betrayal. Earthman who spoke with forked tongue. She might've been the mother of the son he was trying to find in Horst-Johann. But his Isaac never came back from the altar of the needs of the race. Yes, he'd paid his dues, and at usurous rates.

He had something coming. I'd give him the chance he wanted for the boy... Somewhere during those hours my Old Earther's pragmatism lapsed. Old Number One, survival, took a temporary vacation.

It felt good.

5

Getting along with von Drachau didn't prove as difficult as expected. During the following week I was the cause of more friction than he. I kept reacting to the image of the man rumor and prejudice had built in my mind, not to the man in whose presence I was. He was much less arrogant and abrasive than I'd heard—though gritty with the usual outworlder's contempt for the driving need to accomplish characteristic of Old Earthers. But I'd become accustomed to that, even understood. Outworlders had never endured the hopelessness and privation of life on the motherworld. They'd never understand what buying off really meant. Nor did any care to learn.

There're just two kinds of people on Old Earth, butchers and bovines. No one starves, no one freezes, but those are the only positives of life in the Social Insurance warrens. Twenty billion unemployed sardines. The high point of many lives is a visit to Confederation Zone (old Switzerland), where government and corporations maintain their on-planet offices and estates and allow small bands of citizens to come nose the candy store window and look at the lifestyle of the outworlds... then send them home with apathy overcome by renewed desperation.

In The Wind

All Old Earth is a slum/ghetto surrounding one small, stoutly defended bastion of wealth and privilege. That says it all, except that getting out is harder than from any historical ghetto.

It's not really what Old Earth outworlders think of when they dust off the racial warm heart and talk about the mother-world. What they're thinking of is Luna Command, Old Earth's moon and the seat of Confederation government. All they have for Old Earth itself is a little shame-faced under-the-table welfare money…bitter. The only resource left is human life, the cheapest of all. The outworlds have little use for Terrans save for work like that on Camelot. So bitter. I shouldn't be. I've bought off. Not my problem anymore.

Horst (his preference) and I got on well, quickly advanced to first names. After familiarizing ourselves with the new equipment, we returned to regular patrols. Horst scattered no grit in the machinery. He performed his tasks-within-mission with clockwork precision, never straying beyond the borders of discipline.

He confessed, as we paused at the lip of Ginnunga Gap one morning, while walking to the catapults for launch, that he feared being grounded more than losing individuality to military conformity. Flying was the only thing his father hadn't programmed for him (the Commander had gotten him started), and he'd become totally enamored of the sport. Signing on with Ubichi had been the only way to stick with it after his father had managed his appointment to Academy; he'd refused, and been banished from paternal grace. He *had* to fly. Without that he'd have nothing. The Commander, he added, had meant what he said.

I think that was the first time I realized a man could be raised outworld and still be deprived. We Old Earthers take a perverse, chauvinistic pride in our poverty and persecution—like, as the Commander once observed, Jews of Marrakech. (An allusion I spent months dredging: he'd read some obscure and ancient writers.) Our goals are so wholly materialistic that we can scarcely comprehend poverty of the spirit. That von Drachau, with wealth and social position, could feel he had less than I, was a stunning notion.

For him flying was an end, for me a means. Though I enjoyed it, each time I sat at catapult head credit signs danced in my head; so much base, plus per mission and per kill. If I did well I'd salvage some family, too. Horst's pay meant nothing. He wasted it fast as it came—I think to show contempt for the wealth from which he sprang. Though that had been honest money, prize and coup money from his father's successes against the Sangaree.

Steam pressure drove a glasteel piston along forty meters of glasteel cylinder; twenty seconds behind von Drachau I catapulted into the ink of the Gap and began feeling for the ups. For brief instants I could see him outlined against the aurora, flashing in and out of vision as he searched and circled. I spied him climbing, immediately turned to catch the same riser. Behind me came the rest of the squadron. Up we went in a spiral like moths playing tag in the night while reaching for the moons. Von Drachau found altitude and slipped from the up. I followed. At three thousand meters, with moonlight and aurora, it wasn't hard to see him. The four craft of my flight circled at ninety degree points while the rest of the squadron went north across the Gap. We'd slowly drop a thousand meters, then catch another up to the top. We'd stay in the air two hours (or we ran out of ammunition), then go down for an hour break. Five missions minimum.

First launch came an hour before dawn, long before the night fighters went down. Mornings were crowded. But by sunrise we seemed terribly alone while we circled down or climbed, watched the Gap for whales leaving the Harridans or the mantas that'd grown so numerous.

Daytimes almost every ship concentrated on keeping the whales north of the Gap. That grew more difficult as the density of their population neared the migratory. It'd be a while yet, maybe a month, but numbers and instinct would eventually overcome the fear our weapons had instilled. I couldn't believe we'd be able to stop them. The smaller herds of the 'tween years, yes, but not the lemming rivers that would come with winter. A Corporation imbued with any human charity would've been busy sealing mines and evacuating personnel. But Ubichi had none. In terms of financial costs, equipment losses, it was cheaper to fight,

In The Wind

sacrificing inexpensive lives to salvage material made almost priceless by interstellar shipment.

6

Signals from the ground, a searchlight fingering the earth and flashing three times rapidly. Rim sentries had spotted a whale in the direction the finger pointed. Von Drachau and I were front. We began circling down.

We'd dropped just five hundred meters when he wag-winged visual contact. I saw nothing but the darkness that almost always clogged the canyon. As wide as Old Earth's Grand Canyon and three times as deep, it was well lighted only around noon.

That was the first time I noticed his phenomenal vision. In following months he was to amaze me repeatedly. I honestly believe I was the better pilot, capable of outflying any manta, but his ability to find targets made him the better combat flyer.

The moment I wagged back he broke circle and dove. I'd've circled lower. If the whale was down in the Gap itself that might mean a three thousand meter fall. Pulling out would overstrain one's wings. Sailpianes, even the jackboot jobs we flew, are fragile machines never intended for stunt flying.

But I was wingman, responsible for protecting the attack pilot's rear. I winged over and followed, maintaining a constant five hundred meters between us. Light and shadow from clouds and mountains played over his ship, alternately lighting and darkening the personal devices he'd painted on. A death's-head grinned and winked...

I spied the whale. It was working directly toward Beadle. Size and coloring of the gasbag (oblate spheroid sixty meters long, patched in shades from pink to scarlet and spotted with odd other colors at organ sites) indicated a juvenile of the Harkness species, that with the greatest potential for destruction. Triangular vanes protruding ten meters from muscle rings on the bag twitched and quivered as the monster strove to maintain a steady course. Atop it in a thin Mohawk swath swayed a copse of treelike organs believed to serve both plantlike and animal digestive and metabolic functions. Some may have been sensory. Beneath it sensory tentacles trailed, stirring fretfully like dreaming snakes on the head of Medusa. If any found food (and anything organic was provender for a Harkness), it'd anchor itself immediately. Hundreds more tentacles would descend and begin lifting edibles to mouths in a tiny head-body tight against the underside of the gasbag. There'd be a drizzling organic rainfall as the monster dumped ballast/waste. Migrating whale herds could devastate great swaths of countryside. Fortunately for Ubichi's operations, the mating seasons were infrequent.

The Harkness swelled ahead. Horst would be fingering his trigger ring, worrying his sights. I stopped watching for mantas and adjusted my dive so Horst wouldn't be in line when I fired...

Flashing lights, hasty, almost panicky. I read, then glanced out right and up, spied the manta pair. From high above the Harridans they arrowed toward the whale, tips and trailing edges of their wings rippling as they adjusted dive to each vagary of canyon air. But they were a kilometer above and would be no worry till we'd completed our pass. And the other two ships of our flight would be after them, to engage while Horst and I completed the primary mission.

The relationship between mantas and whales had never, to that time, been clearly defined. The mantas seemed to feed among the growths on whale backs, to attach themselves in mated pairs to particular adults, which they fiercely defended, and upon which they were apparently dependent. But nothing seemed to come the other way. The whales utterly ignored them, even as food. Whales ignored everything in the air, though, enduring our attacks as if they weren't happening. If not for the mantas, the extermination program would've been a cakewalk.

But mantas fought at every encounter, almost as if they knew what we were doing. A year earlier they'd been little problem. Then we'd been sending single flights after lone wandering whales, but as migratory pressures built the manta population had increased till

In The Wind

we were forced to fight three or four battles to each whale attack—of which maybe one in twenty resulted in a confirmed kill. Frustrating business, especially since self-defense distracted so from our primary mission.

Luckily, the mantas had only one inefficient, if spectacular, weapon, the lightning they hurled.

That fool von Drachau dropped flaps to give himself more firing time. Because I began overtaking him, I had to follow suit. My glider shuddered, groaned, and an ominous snap came from my right wing. But nothing fell apart.

Fog formed before Horst's craft, whipped back. He'd begun firing. His shells painted a tight bright pattern in the forest on the whale's back. Stupidly, I shifted aim to the same target. Von Drachau pulled out, flaps suddenly up, used his momentum to hurl himself up toward the diving manta pair, putting them in a pincer.

A jagged bite of lightning flashed toward von Drachau. I cursed. We'd plunged into a trap. Mantas had been feeding in the shelter of the whale's back organs. They were coming up to fight.

I'd begun firing an instant before the flash, putting my shells in behind Horst's. Before the water vapor from my cannon gas fogged my canopy I saw explosions digging into the gasbag. I started to stick back and fire at the mantas, but saw telltale ripples of blue fire beneath the yellow of my shells. The bag was going to blow.

When the hydrogen went there'd be one hell of an explosion. Following Horst meant suicide.

The prime purpose of the explosives was to drive cyanide fragments into whale flesh, but sometimes, as then, a too tight pattern breached the main bag—and hydrogen is as dangerous on Camelot as elsewhere.

I took my only option, dove. With luck the whale's mass would shadow me from the initial blast.

It did. But the tip of my right wing, that'd made such a grim noise earlier, brushed one of the monster's sensory tentacles. The jerk snapped it at the root. I found myself spinning down.

I rode it a while, both because I was stunned (I'd never been downed before, accidentally or otherwise) and because I wanted the craft to protect me from downblast.

The sun had risen sufficiently to illuminate the tips of the spires in the gap. They wheeled, jerked, reached up like angry claws, drawing rapidly closer. Despite the ongoing explosion, already shaking me, blistering the paint on my fuselage, I had to get out.

Canopy cooperated. In the old gliders they'd been notoriously sticky, costing many lives. This popped easily. I closed my eyes and jumped, jerking my ripcord as I did. Heat didn't bother me. My remaining wing took a cut at me, a last effort of fate to erase my life-tape, then the chute jerked my shoulders. I began to sway.

It was cold and lonely up there, and there was nothing I could do. I was no longer master of my fate. You would have to be an Old Earther near buying off to really feel the impact of that. Panicky, I peered up at the southern rim of the Gap—and saw what I'd hoped to see, the rescue balloon already on its way. It was a hot air job that rode safety lines payed out from winches at the edge. If I could be salvaged, it'd be managed. I patted my chest pockets to make sure I had my flares.

Only then did I rock my chute away so I could see what'd happened to von Drachau.

He was into it with three mantas, one badly wounded (the survivor of the pair from the Harkness—the other had died in the explosion). He got the wounded one and did a flap trick to turn inside the others. His shells went into the belly of one. It folded and fell. Then the rest of our flight was pursuing the survivor toward the Harridans.

I worried as burning pieces of whale fell past. Suppose one hit my chute?

But none did. I landed in snow deep in the Gap, after a cruel slide down an almost vertical rock face, then set out my first flare. While I tried to stay warm, I thought about von Drachau.

I'd gone along with his attack because I'd had neither choice, nor time to think, nor any way to caution him. But that precipitous assault had been the sort that'd earned him his reputation. And it'd cost again. Me.

In The Wind

Didn't make me feel any better to realize I'd been as stupid in my target selection.

A rational, unimpetuous attack would've gone in level with the whale, from behind, running along its side. Thus Horst could've stayed out of sight of the mantas riding it, and I could've avoided the explosion resulting from a tight fire pattern in the thin flesh of the back. Shells laid along the whale's flanks would've spread enough cyanide to insure a kill.

Part my fault, but when the rescue balloon arrived I was so mad at Horst I couldn't talk.

7

Von Drachau met the rescue balloon, more concerned and contrite than I'd've credited. I piled out steaming, with every intention of denting his head, but he ran to me like a happy puppy, bubbling apologies, saying he'd never had a chance at a whale…righteous outrage became grumpiness. He was only nineteen, emotionally ten.

There were reports to be filed but I was in no mood. I headed for barracks and something alcoholic.

Von Drachau followed. "Sal," he said with beer in his mustache, "I mean it. I'm sorry. Wish I could look at it like you. Like this's just a job…"

"Uhm." I made a grudging peace. "So can it." But he kept on. Something was biting him, something he wanted coaxed out.

"The mantas," he said. "What do we know about them?"

"They get in the way."

"Why? Territorial imperative? Sal, I been thinking. Was today a setup? If people was working the other side, they couldn't've set a better trap. In the old ships both of us would've gone down."

"Watch your imagination, kid. Things're different in the Islands, but not that different. We've run into feeding mantas before. You just attacked from the wrong angle." I tossed off my third double. The Gap bottom cold began leaking from my bones. I felt a bit more charitable. But not enough to discuss idiot theories of manta intelligence.

We already knew many odd forms of intelligence. Outworlders have a curious sensitivity to it, a near reverence puzzling to Old Earthers. They go around looking for it, especially in adversity. Like savages imputing powers to storms and stones, they can't accept disasters at face value. There has to be a malignant mover.

"I guess you're right," he said. But his doubt was plain. He *wanted* to believe we were fighting a war, not exterminating noxious animals.

Got me thinking, though. Curious how persistent the rumor was, even though there was no evidence to support it. But a lot of young people (sic!—I was twenty-eight) are credulous. A pilot, dogfighting a manta pair, might come away with the notion. They're foxy. But intelligence, to me, means communication and cooperation. Mantas managed a little of each, but only among mates. When several pairs got involved in a squabble with us, we often won by maneuvering pairs into interfering with one another.

The matter dropped and, after a few more drinks, was forgotten. And banished utterly when we were summoned to the Commander's office.

The interview was predictable. McClennon was determined to ground von Drachau. I don't know why I defended him. Labor united against management, maybe. Guess Horst wasn't used to having a friend at court. When we left he thanked me, but seemed puzzled, seemed to be wrestling something inside.

Never did find out what, for sure—Old Earthers are tight-lipped, but von Drachau had the best of us beaten—but there was a marked improvement in his attitude. By the end of the month he was on speaking terms with everyone, even men he'd grossly alienated at JG IV.

That month I also witnessed a dramatic improvement in Horst's shooting. His kills in the Sickle Islands had been almost accidental. Changing from rockets to cannons seemed to bring out his talent. He scored kill after kill, attacking with a reckless abandon (but always with a care to keep me well positioned). He'd scream in on a manta, drop flaps suddenly, put himself into a stall just beyond the range of the manta's bolt, then flaps up and fall beneath the monster when he'd drawn it, nose up and trigger a burst into its belly. Meanwhile, I would fend off the other till he was free. My kill score mounted, too.

In The Wind

His was astonishing. Our first four weeks together he downed thirty-six mantas. I downed fourteen, and two whales. I'd had fifty-seven and twelve for four years' work when he arrived, best in the wing. It was obvious that, if he stayed alive, he'd soon pass not only me but Aultmann Zeisler, the CO JG I, a ten year veteran with ninety-one manta kills.

Horst did have an advantage we older pilots hadn't. Target availability. Before, except during the lesser migrations, the wing had been lucky to make a dozen sightings per month. Now we piled kills at an incredible rate.

Piled, but the tilt of the mountain remained against us. Already stations farther south were reporting sightings of small herds that had gotten past us.

It was coming to the point where we were kept busy by mantas. Opportunities to strike against whales grew rare. When the main migratory wave broke we'd be swamped.

Everyone knew it. But Derry, despite sending reinforcements, seemed oblivious to the gravity of the situation. Or didn't care. A sour tale began the rounds. The Corporation had written us off. The whales would remove us from the debit ledger. That facilities at Clonninger and stations farther down the cable were being expanded to handle our withdrawal didn't dent the rumors. We Old Earthers always look on the bleak side.

In early winter, after a severe snowstorm, as we were digging out, we encountered a frightening phenomenon. Cooperation among large numbers of mantas.

8

It came with sunrise. Horst and I were in the air, among two dozen new fighters. The wing had been reinforced to triple strength, one hundred fifty gliders and a dozen armed zeppelins, but those of us up were all the ground personnel had been able to dig out and launch.

Signals from ground. Against the aurora and white of the Harridans I had no trouble spotting the Harkness whales, full adults, leaving a branch canyon opposite Beadle. Close to a hundred, I guessed, the biggest lot yet to assault the Gap. We went to meet them, one squadron circling down. My own squadron, now made up of men who'd shown exceptional skill against mantas, stayed high to cover. We no longer bothered with whales, served only as cover for the other squadron.

I watched for mantas. Had no trouble finding them. They came boiling 'round the flank of an ivory mountain, cloud of black on cliff of white, a mob like bats leaving a cave at sunset. Hundreds of them.

My heart sank. It'd be thick, grim, and there was no point even thinking about attack formations. All a man could do was keep away and grab a shot at opportunity. But we'd take losses. One couldn't watch every way at once.

A few mantas peeled off and dove for the ships attacking the whales. The bulk came on, following a line that'd cross the base.

We met. There were gliders, mantas, shells and lightning bolts thicker than I'd ever seen. Time stood still. Mantas passed before me, I pulled trigger rings. Horst's death's-head devices whipped across my vision. Sometimes parts of gliders or mantas went tumbling by. Lower and lower we dropped, both sides trading altitude for speed.

Nose up. Manta belly before me, meters away. Jerk the rings. Fog across the canopy face, but no explosions against dark flesh. We struggled to avoid collision, passed so close we staggered one another with our slipstreams. For a moment I stared into two of the four eyes mounted round the thing's bullet head. They seemed to drive an electric line of hatred deep into my brain. For an instant I believed the intelligence hypothesis. Then shuddered as I sticked down and began a rabbit run for home, to replace my ammunition.

A dozen mantas came after me. Horst, alone, went after them. I later learned that, throwing his craft about with complete abandon, he knocked nine of those twelve down before his own ammunition ran out. It was an almost implausible performance, though one that need not be dwelt upon. It's one of the mainstays of his legend, his first ten-kill day, and every student of the fighting on Camelot knows of it.

The runway still had a half meter of snow on it. The three mantas followed me in, ignoring the counterfire of our ground batteries. I was so

In The Wind

worried about evading their bolts that I went in poorly, one wing down, and ended up spinning into a deep drift. As a consequence I spent two hours grounded.

What I missed was sheer hell. The mantas, as if according to some plan, clamped down on our landing and launching gates, taking their toll while our craft were at their most vulnerable. In the early going some tried to blast through the overhead netting. That only cost them lives. Our ground batteries ate them up. Then they tried the barrage balloons, to no better effect.

Then the whales arrived. We'd been able to do nothing to stop them, so busy had the mantas kept us. They, sensing food beneath the net, began trying to break in. Our ground batteries fired into the dangling forests of their tentacles, wrecking those but doing little damage to the beasts themselves. Gigantic creaks and groans came from the net anchor points.

For pilots and ground crews there was little to do but prepare for a launch when circumstances permitted. I got my ship out, rearmed, and dragged to catapult head. Then for a time I stood observer, using binoculars to watch those of our craft still up.

In all, the deaths of a hundred fourteen mantas (four mine, ten Horst's) and twenty-two whales were confirmed for the first two hours of fighting. But we would've gone under without help from down the cable.

When the desperation of our position became obvious the Commander signalled Clonninger. Its sailcraft came north, jumped the mantas from above. They broke siege. We launched, cats hurling ships into the Gap as fast as steam could be built. Horst and I went in the first wave.

Help had come just in time. The whales had managed several small breaches in the netting and were pushing tentacles through after our ground people.

Even with help the situation remained desperate. I didn't think it'd take long for the mantas, of which more had come across, to clamp down again. When they did it'd only be a matter of time till the whales wrecked the net. I pictured the base destroyed, littered with bones.

Before we launched, the Commander, ancient with the strain, spoke with each pilot. Don't know what he said to the others, but I imagine it was much what he told me: if I judged the battle lost, to run south rather than return here. The sailcraft had to be salvaged for future fighting. If we were overrun the fighting would move to Clonninger.

And in my ear a few words about taking care of von Drachau. I said I would.

But we survived. I won't say we won because even though we managed to break the attack, we ourselves were decimated. JG XIII's effectiveness was ruined for the next week. For days we could barely manage regular patrols. Had we been hit again we'd've been obliterated.

That week McClennon three times requested permission to evacuate nonessential ground troops, received three refusals. Still, it seemed pointless for us to stay when our blocking screen had been riddled. Small herds were passing daily. Clonninger was under as much pressure as we and had more trouble handling it. Their defenses weren't meant to stand against whales. Their sailplanes often had to flee. Ground personnel crouched in deep bunkers and prayed the whales weren't so hungry they'd dig them out.

Whale numbers north of the Harridans were estimated at ten thousand and mantas at ten to twenty. Not vast, but overwhelming in concentration. Populations for the whole continent were about double those, with the only other concentrations in the Sickle Islands. By the end of that week our experts believed a third of the Harridan whales had slipped past us. We'd downed about ten percent of those trying and about twenty-five percent of the mantas.

9

A fog of despair enveloped Beadle. Derry had informed McClennon that there'd be no more reinforcements. They were needed further south. Permission to withdraw? Denied again. We had only one hundred twelve effective sailcraft. Ammunition was short. And the main blow was yet to fall.

It's hard to capture the dulled sense of doom that clung so thick. It wasn't a verbal or a visible thing, though faces steadily lengthened. There

In The Wind

was no defeatist talk. The men kept their thoughts to themselves—but couldn't help expressing them through actions, by digging deeper shelters, in a lack of crisp efficiency. Things less definable. Most hadn't looked for desperate stands when they signed on. And Camelot hadn't prepared them to face one. Till recently they'd experienced only a lazy, vacation sort of action, loafing and laughter with a faint bouquet of battle.

One evening Horst and I stood watching lightning shoot among the near pure copper peaks of the Harridans. "D'you ever look one in the eye?" he asked.

Memory of the manta I'd missed. I shuddered, nodded.

"And you don't believe they're intelligent?"

"I don't care. A burst in the guts is all that matters. That's cash money, genius or retard."

"Your conscience doesn't bother you?"

Something was bothering him, though I couldn't understand why. He wouldn't worry bending human beings, so why aliens? Especially when the pay's right and you're the son of a man who'd become rich by doing the same? But his reluctance wasn't unique. So many people consider alien intelligence sacred—without any rational basis. It's a crippling emotional weakness that has wormed its way into Confederation law. You can't exploit a world with intelligent natives…

But conscience may've had nothing to do with it. Seems, in hindsight, his reluctance might've been a rationalized facet of his revolt against his father and authority.

Understandably, Ubichi was sensitive to speculations about manta intelligence. Severe fines were laid on men caught discussing the possibility—which, human nature being what it is, made the talk more persistent. Several pilots, Horst included, had appealed to McClennon. He'd been sympathetic, but what could he have done?

And I kept wondering why anyone cared. I agreed with the Corporation. That may have been a defect in me.*

*If this thought truly occurred to del Gado at the time, it clearly made no lasting moral impression. News buffs will remember that *he was one of several Ubichi mercenaries named in Confederation genocide indictments stemming from illegal exploitation on Bonaventure, though he was not convicted.*

—Dogfight

As soon as we recovered from attack, for morale purposes we launched our last offensive, a pre-emptive strike against a developing manta concentration. Everything, including armed zeppelins, went. The mission was partially successful. Kept another attack from hitting Beadle for a week, but it cost. None of the airships returned. Morale sagged instead of rising. We'd planned to use the zepps in our withdrawal—if ever authorized.

In line of seniority I took command of my squadron after a manta made the position available. But I remained von Drachau's wingman. That made him less impetuous. Still addicted to the flying, he avoided offending a man who could ground him. I was tempted. His eye was still deadly, but his concern over the intelligence of mantas had begun affecting his performance.

At first it was a barely noticeable hesitance in attack that more than once left blistered paint on his ship. With his timing a hair off he sometimes stalled close enough for a manta's bolt to caress his craft. My admonitions had little effect. His flying continued to deteriorate.

And still I couldn't understand.

His performance improved dramatically six days after our strike into the Harridans, a day when he had no time to think, when the wing's survival was on the line and maximum effort was a must. (He always performed best under pressure. He never could explain how he'd brushed those nine mantas off me that day. He'd torn through them with the cold efficiency of a military robot, but later couldn't remember. It was as if another personality had taken control. I saw him go through three such

In The Wind

possessions and he couldn't remember after any.) It was a battle in which we all flew inspired—and earned a Pyrrhic victory...the back of the wing was broken, but again Beadle survived.

The mantas came at dawn, as before, and brought a whale herd with them. There'd been snow, but this time a hard night's work had cleared the catapults and sailships. We were up and waiting. They walked—or flew—into it. And kept coming. And kept coming.

And by weight of numbers drove us to ground. And once we'd lost the air the whales moved in.

McClennon again called for aid from Clonninger. It came. We broke out. And soon were forced to ground again. The mantas refused to be dismayed. A river came across the Gap to replace losses.

Clonninger signalled us for help. From Beadle we watched endless columns of whales, varicolored as species mixed, move down the dragline south. We could do nothing. Clonninger was on its own.

McClennon ordered a hot air balloon loaded with phosphorous bombs, sent it out and blew it amidst the mantas crowding our launch gate. Horst and I jumped into their smoke. That entire mission we ignored mantas and concentrated on the whales, who seemed likely to destroy the net. Before ammunition ran out we forced them to rejoin the migration. But the mantas didn't leave till dark.

Our ground batteries ran out of rockets. Half our ships were destroyed or permanently grounded. From frostbite as much as manta action (the day's high was −23° C.), a third of our people became casualties. Fourteen pilots found permanent homes in the bottom of Ginnunga Gap. Rescue balloons couldn't go after them.

Paradoxically, permission to withdraw came just before we lost contact with Clonninger.

We began our wound-licking retreat at midnight, scabby remnants of squadrons launching into the ink of the Gap, grabbing the ups, then slanting down toward Clonninger. Balloons began dragging the line.

Clonninger was what we'd feared for Beadle: churned earth and bones ethereally grim by dawn light. The whales had broken its defenses without difficulty. Appetites whetted, they'd moved on. From three thousand meters the borders of the earth-brown river of devastation seemed to sweep the horizons. The silvery drag cable sketched a bright centerline for that death-path.

We were patrolling when the first airships came south. The skies were utterly empty, the ground naked, silence total. Once snow covered the route only memory would mark recent events...

Days passed. The Clonninger story repeated itself down the cable, station after station, though occasionally we found salvageable survivors or equipment. Operations seemed ended for our ground units. But for us pilots it went on. We followed the line till we overtook straggler whales, returned to work.

As the migration approached Derry corporate defenses stiffened. Though we'd lost contact, it seemed our function at the Gap had been to buy time. True, as I later learned. A string of Beadle-like fortress-bases were thrown across the northern and Sickle Islands routes. But even they weren't strong enough. As the mantas learned (even I found myself accepting the intelligence proposition), they became more proficient at besieging and destroying bases. The whales grew less fearful, more driven by their mating urge. Mantas would herd them to a base; they'd wreck it despite the most furious defense. Both whales and mantas abandoned fear, ignored their own losses.

JG XIII was out of the main action, of course, but we persevered—if only because we knew we'd never get off planet if Derry fell. But we flew with little enthusiasm. Each additional destroyed base or mine (whatever Ubichi was after had to be unearthed) reassured us of the inevitability of failure.

When a man goes mercenary in hopes of buying off, he undergoes special training. Most have a paramilitary orientation. (I use "mercenary" loosely.) Historical studies puzzled me. Why had men so often fought on when defeat was inevitable? Why had they in fact given more of themselves in a hopeless cause? I was living it then and still didn't understand. JG XIII performed miracles with what it had, slaughtered whales and mantas by the hundreds, and that after everyone had abandoned hope...

In The Wind

Horst reached the one fifty mark. I reached one hundred twenty. Almost every surviving pilot surpassed fifty kills. There were just thirty-three of us left.

11

On the spur of the moment one day, based on two considerations, I made my first command decision: good winds during patrol and a grave shortage of supplies. For a month the wing had been living and fighting off the remnants of stations destroyed by migrating whales. Rations were a single pale meal each day. Our remaining ammunition was all with us on patrol.

When I began this I meant to tell about myself and Horst-Johann von Drachau. Glancing back, I see I've sketched a story of myself and JG XIII. Still, it's almost impossible to extricate the forms—especially since there's so little concrete to say about the man. My attempts to characterize him fail, so robotlike was he even with me. Mostly I've speculated, drawn on rumor and used what I learned from Commander McClennon. The few times Horst opened at all he didn't reveal much, usually only expressing an increasing concern about the mantas. Without my speculations he'd read like an excerpt from a service file.

The above is an admonition to myself: don't digress into the heroism and privation of the month the wing operated independently. That wasn't a story about von Drachau. He endured it without comment. Yet sleeping in crude wooden shelters and eating downed manta without complaining might say something about the man behind the facade, or something about changes that had occurred there. Hard to say. He may've ignored privation simply because it didn't impinge on his personal problems.

We were in the air, making the last patrol we could reasonably mount. I had command. In a wild moment, inspired by good ups and winds, I decided to try breaking through to Derry territory. Without knowing how far it'd be to the nearest extant station—we hadn't seen outsiders since borrowing the Clonninger squadrons. That Derry still held I could guess only from the fact that we were still to its north and in contact with mantas and whales.

The inspiration hit, I wag-winged *follow me* and went into a long shallow glide. Derry itself lay over two hundred kilometers away, a long fly possible only if we flitted from up to up. Much longer flights had been made—though not against opposition.

It took twelve hours and cost eight sailcraft, but we made it. It was an ace day for everyone. There seemed to be a Horst-like despair about the mantas that left them sluggish in action. We littered the barren earth with their corpses. Horst, with seven kills, had our lowest score. Because I was behind him all the while I noticed he wasn't trying, shot only when a pilot was endangered. This had been growing during the month. He was as sluggish as the mantas.

Our appearance at Derry generated mixed reactions. Employees got a big lift, perhaps because our survival presented an example. But management seemed unsettled, especially by our kill claims, our complaints, and the fact that there were survivors they were obligated to rescue. All they wanted was to hold on and keep the mines working. But aid to JG XIII became an instant cause *célèbre*. It was obvious there'd be employee rebellion if our survivors were written off.

I spent days being grilled, the price of arrogating command. The others were supposed to remain quarantined for debriefing, but evaded their watchers. They did the public relations job. Someone spread the tales that were the base for von Drachau's legend.

I tried to stop that, but to do so was beating my head against a wall. Those people in the shrinking Derry holding needed a hero—even if they had to make him up, to fill in, pad, chop off rough corners so he'd meet their needs. It developed quickly. I wonder how Horst would've reacted had he been around for deep exposure. I think it might've broken his shell, but would've gone to his head too. Well, no matter now.

Myself, I'd nominate Commander McClennon as the real hero of JG XIII. His was the determination and spirit that brought us through. But he was an administrator.

In The Wind

Much could be told about our stay at Derry, which lasted through winter and spring, till long after the manta processes of intellection ponderously ground to the conclusion that we humans couldn't be smashed and eaten this time. The fighting, of course, continued, and would till Confederation intervened, but it stayed at a modest level. They stopped coming to us. Morale soared. Yet things were really no better. The mating whales still cut us off from the south polar spaceport.

But the tale is dedicated to Horst-Johann von Drachau. It lasts only another week.

12

Once free of interrogation, I began preparing the wing to return to action. For years I'd been geared to fighting; administration wasn't easy. I grew short-tempered, began hunting excuses to evade responsibility. Cursed myself for making the decision that'd brought me inside—even though that'd meant volunteer crews taking zepps north with stores.

An early official action was an interview with Horst. He came to my cubby-office sullen and dispirited, but cheered up when I said, "I'm taking you off attack. You'll be my wingman."

"Good."

"It means that much?"

"What?"

"This stuff about manta intelligence."

"Yeah. But you wouldn't understand, Sal. Nobody does."

I began my "what difference does it make?" speech. He interrupted.

"You know I can't explain. It's something like this: we're not fighting a war. In war you try to demonstrate superiority of arms, to convince the other side it's cheaper to submit. We're trying for extermination here. Like with the Sangaree."

The Sangaree. The race his father had destroyed. "No big loss."

"Wrong. They were nasty, but posed no real threat. They could've been handled with a treaty. We had the power."

"No tears were shed…"

"Wrong again. But the gut reaction isn't over. You wait. When men like my father and Admiral Beckhart and Commander McClennon and the other militarists who control Luna Command fade away, you'll start seeing a reaction…a whole race, Sal, a whole culture, independently evolved, with all it might've taught us…"

It had to be rationalization, something he'd built for himself to mask a deeper unhappiness. "McClennon? You don't approve of him?"

"Well, yeah, he's all right. I guess. But even when he disagreed, he went along. In fact, my father never could've found the Sangaree homeworld without him. If he'd revolted then, instead of later when his actions turned and bit back…well, the Sangaree would be alive and he'd be off starfishing with Amy."

I couldn't get through. Neither could he. The speeches on the table were masks for deeper things. There's no way to talk about one thing and communicate something else. "Going along," I said. "What've you been doing? How about the kid who squawks but goes along because he wants to fly? That's what we're all doing here, Horst. Think I'd be here if I could buy off any other way? Life is compromise. No exceptions. And you're old enough to know it."*

Shouldn't've said that. But I was irritable, unconcerned about what he'd think. He stared a moment, then stalked out, considering his own compromises.

Two days later my ships were ordered up for the first time since our arrival. Command had had trouble deciding what to do with us. I think we weren't employed because the brass were afraid we were as good as we claimed, which meant (by the same illogical process that built legends around Horst and the wing) that our survival wasn't just a miracle, that we'd really been written off but had refused to die. Such accusations were going around and Command was sensitive to them.

We went up as air cover for the rescue convoy bringing our survivors in from up the cable. We wouldn't've been used if another unit had been available. But the mantas had a big push on, their last major and only night offensive.

In The Wind

*Del Gado may indeed have said something of the sort at the time, and have felt it, but again, once the pressure was off, he forgot. He has been bought off for years, yet remains with Ubichi's Armed Action Command. He must enjoy his work.

—Dogfight

Winds at Derry are sluggish, the ups are weak, and that night there was an overcast masking the moons. The aurora is insignificant that far south. Seeing was by lightning, a rough way to go.

We launched shortly after nightfall, spent almost an hour creeping to altitude, then clawed north above the cable. Flares were out to mark it, but those failed us when we passed the last outpost. After that it was twenty-five ships navigating by guesswork, maintaining contact by staying headache-making alert during lightning flashes.

But it was also relaxing. I was doing something I understood. The whisper of air over my canopy lulled me, washed the week's aggravations away.

Occasionally I checked my mirrors. Horst maintained perfect position on my right quarter. The others spread around in ragged formation, yielding compactness and precision to safety. The night threatened collisions.

We found the convoy one hundred twenty kilometers up the line, past midnight, running slowly into the breeze and flashing signals so we'd locate them. I dropped down, signalled back with a bioluminescent lantern, then clawed some altitude, put the men into wide patrol patterns. Everything went well through the night. The mantas weren't up in that sector.

Dawn brought them, about fifty in a flying circus they'd adopted from us. We condensed formation and began slugging it out.

They'd learned. They still operated in pairs, but no longer got in one another's way. And they strove to break our pairs to take advantage of numbers. But when a pair latched onto a sailplane it became their entire universe. We, however, shot at anything, whether or not it was a manta against which we were directly engaged.

They'd overadopted our tactics. I learned that within minutes. When someone got half a pair, the other would slide out of action and stay out till it found a single manta of opposite sex. Curious. (Shortly I'll comment on the findings of the government investigators, who dug far deeper than Ubichi's exobiologists. But one notion then current, just rumor as the sentience hypothesis became accepted, was that manta intelligence changed cyclically, as a function of the mating cycle.)

We held our own. All of us were alive because we were good. Dodging bolts was instinctual, getting shells into manta guts second nature. We lost only two craft, total. One pilot. Two thirds of the mantas went down.

Horst and I flew as if attached to ends of a metal bar. Book perfect. But the mantas forced us away from the main fray, as many as twenty concentrating on us. (I think they recognized our devices and decided to destroy us. If it were possible for humans to be known to mantas, they'd've been Horst and me I went into a robotlike mood like Horst's on his high-kill days. Manta after manta tumbled away. My shooting was flawless. Brief bursts, maybe a dozen shells, were all I used. I seldom missed.

As sometimes happened in such a brawl, Horst and I found our stations reversed. A savage maneuver that left my glider creaking put me in the wingman slot. During it Horst scored his hundred fifty-eighth kill, clearing a manta off my back. Far as I know that was the only time he fired.

The arrangement was fine with me. He was the better shot; let him clear the mess while I protected his back. We'd resume proper positions when a break in the fighting came.

A moment later Horst was in firing position beneath a female who'd expended her bolt (it then took several minutes to build a charge). He bored in, passed so close their wings nearly brushed. But he didn't fire. I took her out as I came up behind.

The eyes. Again I saw them closely. Puzzlement and pain(?) as she folded and fell...

In The Wind

Three times that scene repeated itself. Horst wouldn't shoot. Behind him I cursed, threatened, promised, feared. Tried to get shells into his targets, but missed. He maneuvered so I was in poor position on each pass.

Then the mantas broke. They'd lost. The rest of the squadron pursued, losing ground because the monsters were better equipped to grab altitude.

Horst went high. At first I didn't understand, just continued cursing. Then I saw a manta, an old male circling alone, and thought he'd gotten back in track, was going after a kill.

He wasn't. He circled in close and for a seeming eternity they flew wingtip to wingtip, eyeballing one another. Two creatures alone, unable to communicate. But something passed between them. Nobody believes me (since it doesn't fit the von Drachau legend), but I think they made a suicide pact.

Flash. Bolt. Horst's ship staggered, began smoking. The death's-head had disappeared from his fuselage. He started down.

I put everything in my magazines into that old male. The explosions tore him to shreds.

I caught Horst a thousand meters down, pulled up wingtip to wingtip. He still had control, but poorly. Smoke filled his cockpit. Little flames peeped out where his emblem had been. The canvas was ripping from his airframe. By hand signals I tried to get him to bail out.

He signalled he couldn't, that his canopy was stuck. Maybe it was, but when McClennon and I returned a month later, after the migration had passed south, I had no trouble lifting it away.

Maybe he wanted to die.

Or maybe it was because of his legs. When we collected his remains we found that the manta bolt had jagged through his cockpit and cooked his legs below the knees. There'd've been no saving him.

Yet he kept control most of the way down, losing it only in the last five hundred meters. He stalled, spun, dove. Then he recovered and managed a low angle crash. He rolled nose over tail, then burned. Finis. No more Horst-Johann.

I still don't understand.*

*Hawkins, you keep harping on the 'meaning' of Horst's death. Christ, man, that's my point: it had no meaning. In my terms. By those he utterly wasted his life; his voluntary termination didn't alter the military situation one iota. Even in terms your readers understand it had little meaning. They're vicarious fighters; their outlooks aren't much different than mine—except they want my skin for taking a bite from their sacred cow. Horst was a self-appointed Christ-figure. Only in martyr's terms does his death have meaning, and then only to those who believe any intelligence is holy, to be cherished, defended, and allowed to follow its own course utterly free of external influence. What he and his ilk fail to understand is that it's right down deep-streamed fundamental to the nature of our intelligence to interfere, overpower, exploit and obliterate. We did it to one another before First Expansion; we've done it to Toke, Ulantonid and Sangaree; we'll continue doing it. "In terms of accomplishment, yes, he bought something with his life, An injunction against Ubichi operations on Camelot. There's your meaning, but one that makes sense only in an ethical framework most people won't comprehend. Believe me, I've tried. But I'm incapable of seeing the universe and its contents in other than tool-cattle terms. Now have the balls to tell me I'm in the minority."

From a private letter by Salvador del Gado.
—Dogfight

13

According to the latest, the relationship between Manta and whale is far more complex than anyone at Ubichi ever guessed. (Guessed—Ubichi never cared. Irked even me that at the height of Corporate operations, Ubichi had only one exobiologist on planet—a virologist-bacteriologist charged with finding some disease with which to infect the whales. Even

In The Wind

I could appreciate the possible advantages in accumulation of knowledge.) At best, we thought, when the intelligence theory had gained common currency, the whales served as cattle for the mantas.

Not so, say Confederation's researchers. The mantas only *appear* to herd and control the whales. The whales are the true masters. The mantas are their equivalent of dogs, fleet-winged servants for the ponderous and poorly maneuverable. Their very slow growth of ability to cope with our aerial tactics wasn't a function of a cyclic increase in intelligence, it was a reflection of the difficulty the whales had projecting their defensive needs into our much faster and more maneuverable frame of reference. By means of severely limited control.

At the time it seemed a perfectly logical assumption that the mantas were upset with us because we were destroying their food sources. (They live on a mouse-sized parasite common amongst the forest of organs on a whale's back.) It seemed much more unlikely, even unreasonable, that the whales themselves were the ones upset and were sending mantas against us, because those were better able to cope, if a little too dull to do it well. The whales always carried out the attacks on our ground facilities, but we missed the hint there.

It seems the manta was originally domesticated to defend whales from a pterodactyl-like flying predator, one which mantas and whales had hunted almost to extinction by the time Ubichi arrived on Camelot. As humans and dogs once did with wolves. Until the government report we were only vaguely aware of the creatures. They never bothered us, so we didn't bother them.

The relationship between whales and mantas is an ancient one, one which domestication doesn't adequately describe. Nor does symbiosis, effectively. Evolution has forced upon both an incredibly complex and clumsy reproductive process that leaves them inextricably bound together.

In order to go into esterus the female manta must be exposed to prolonged equatorial temperatures. She mates in the air, in a dance as complex and strange as that of earthly bees, but only with her chosen mate. Somewhat like Terran marsupials, she soon gives birth to unformed young. But now it gets weird. The marsupial pouch (if such I may call it for argument's sake) is a specially developed semi-womb atop the back of a *male* whale. While instinct compels her to deposit her young there, the male whale envelopes the she-manta in a clutch of frondlike organs, which caress her body and leave a whitish dust—his "sperm." Once her young have been transferred, the female manta goes into a kind of travel-frenzy, like a bee flitting from flower to flower visiting all nearby whales. Any receptive female she visits will, with organs not unlike those of the male, stroke the "sperm" from her body.

Incredibly complicated and clumsy. And unromantic. But it works.

We never would've learned of it but for Horst—who, I think, had nothing of the sort in mind when he let that old manta bolt him down.

And that's about all there is to say. It's a puzzle story. Why did von Drachau do it? I don't know—or don't want to know—but I work under severe handicaps. I'm an Old Earther. I never had a father to play push-me pull-you with my life. I never learned to care much about anything outside myself. A meager loyalty to companions in action is the best I've ever mustered. But enough of excuses.

The fighting with mantas continued four years after Horst's death, through several lesser migrations that never reached the mating grounds. Then a government inquiry board finally stepped in—after Commander McClennon and Fleet Admiral von Drachau had spent three years knocking on doors at Luna Command (Ubichi's wealth has its power to blind). Their investigations still aren't complete, but it seems they'll rule Camelot permanently off limits. So Horst did buy something with his life. Had he not died, I doubt the Commander would've gotten angry enough to act.

That he did so doesn't entirely please me, of course. I inherited his position. Though I pulled down a handsome income as JG XIII's wing leader and on-going top killer, I loathed the administrative donkey work. Still, I admire the courage he showed.

I also admire Horst, despite his shortcomings, despite myself. But he wasn't a hero, no matter what people want to hear me say. He was a snot-nosed kid used to getting his own way who threw a suicidal tantrum when he saw there was no other way to achieve his ends.

In The Wind

And that's it, the rolling down of the socks to expose the feet of clay. Believe the stories or believe his wingman. It's all the same to me. I've got mine in and don't need your approval.*

> *Not true, in your editor's opinion. Especially in his private communications, del Gado seems very much interested in finding approval of things he has done. Perhaps he has a conscience after all. He certainly seems desperate to find justification for his life.*

—Dogfight

The Recruiter

Some people will do anything not to die, I thought as I stalked through calf-deep trash in one of the light canyons of St. Louis. Year: 3035. Mission: recruiting for Colonial service. Those are the polite words they use on paper or in the holonetnews. In reality, I was a one-unit press gang, a human brain riding a Navy-uniformed metal monstrosity responsible for collecting the scum of the slum of the universe for export to population-starved outworlds. Old Earth rectified her balance of payments deficit by selling warm bodies.

Walk drunkenly in your tin man suit, act like an offworld Spike fool enough to wander the valley of the shadow alone… Let them vent their envy and hatred of starmen on your tank of a body, then subdue a few and drag them to the Station where a lictor, with only your word to guarantee their criminality, will try, convict, and condemn them, and send them to the Colonial Draft. If they're good ones, not diseased or too far gone in psychotic rage against a universe that didn't see them born to the silver spoon, you'll earn a few retirement points. Enough of them, if you survive their attacks long enough, and you'll get yourself a real body, a good one, virgin-new, force-grown up from a clone-cell salvaged from your corpse. Welcome to the company store.

Why didn't they just feed the outworlds clones and let Old Earth go to hell? That's all these ground hogs want, to be left alone to die in their self-imposed misery and filth. Never mind population reduction and control of criminals and failing capacities. Never mind the mules, just load the wagon.

Some people will do anything not to die. I knew. That's why I rode the iron man through cement and waste paper jungles. Nothing's free. The masters in Luna Command want return on their investment. If an Old Earther got killed fighting McGraws or Sangaree on some nether frontier they usually let him die the death-without-resurrection and left him to lie where he had fallen. Neither the services nor the Old Earth planetary government cared to support the cost of shipment-for-funeral. But if you were lucky, your psych profile was right, and they caught you before your brain rotted, they sometimes kindled you and offered a bargain.

Men like me make deals with devils. The choice wore three faces after I died straightening the mess on Helga's World: I could go ahead and die; I could request salvage, which meant being ego-scrubbed and cyborged in as control brain of some googol-bit data system somewhere; I could earn a new body recruiting colonists for my homeworld. Old Earth would purchase my contract from the Corps.

Didn't take much thought. I remembered Old Earth and how, when I left its squalor and hopelessness, I swore nothing would make me return. I remembered the driving need to escape its eternal smog of despair that, in the face of a cultural agoraphobia that was almost psychotic in its rejection of the starworlds, had led me to enlist in the Marines. I remembered all the things I'd fled, I'd thought, forever—then opted for life with a whole personality. I'd been gone long enough to forget how bad it really was. Old Earth seemed better than death. Those Psychs knew how to choose.

The light canyon began showing promise as its walls closed in. My electronic ears detected whispers and scurryings. Not rats. My ancestors had somehow managed to rid the world of those. Probably ate them all during the chaos following the collapse of World Commonweal in

The Recruiter

Century Twenty-Three. They ate everything then, including each other. Could be dogs. They'd been reintroduced from offworld. But more likely potential recruits. The sort I hunted frequented tight and shadowy places. And their infra-red suggested people.

They seemed to come from everywhere and nowhere, from places you couldn't have hidden a roach and shadows thin as their Social Insurance cards. Children. One of those gangs that enlisted no one with hair below the neck, vicious as piranha in their collective rage against anyone and everything. There were at least twenty of them, the females more feral than the males. The latter just wanted to hurt me, the starman who—I could no longer remember the convoluted logic that even I had once accepted—was responsible for the pointlessness and hopelessness of Old Earth life. But the females went for the groin, to destroy the hook on which the offworld man hung his ego. Probably been exploiting some soul-abandoned hooker with it anyway...

I had the hardest time recruiting the children. They weren't yet people, weren't really as lost as a man or woman who had survived to maturity in that bleak environment. Though they didn't know or believe it, for them there was still hope. I hated taking that from them.

But they *hurt* me. And the recruiter body was programmed to react even when the brain wouldn't. Down in the chest cavity there was a little solid-state auto-pilot/mechanical conscience whose sole purpose was to make sure the fallible driver up top didn't blow a potential recruiting situation through some vagary of compassion. Its methods were simple. When I didn't get on the job soon enough to suit, it opened pain circuits. Then I felt what my attackers were doing as deeply as would any starman stupid enough to get himself in a similar situation.

They hurt me and I screamed; audio-tape agonies echoed off walls and down canyons generations along the path to ruin. A girl child made for my eyes with hammer and rusty finger of iron while pot-belly, starveling boys pinned my arms and legs in rubbish and rubble. I had to act. They meant I should die.

Servo strength surged in my limbs, voltage coursed my titanium skin. There were yips and shrieks and humble-jumble, the little killers jumped or were hurled off. The fingers of my right hand were my arsenal, stunner, needler, gas gun, pinky a dainty beamer that could slice recruits up thin as cold cuts and cook the blood into the slices. I sprayed a lot of gas, used the stunner on those observing, then the needler on a few trying to get away. In seconds I was the only upright form on that slash of shadow. "Twelve, thirteen," I counted. A nice baker's dozen. A lot of retirement points. The young ones were always worth more. Had more man hours left in them.

These would mean a substantial reduction in my remaining obligation—if I could get them to the Station without help-yelling. If I called a pickmeup, I'd have to share with the driver and defense-tech, and surrender most of my portion cost of fuel, maintenance, depreciation... Welcome to the company store.

One solution was to take only those I could lug, three or four, but greed now completely obscured compassion. Despite all the paper stall thrown up like flak in my flight path, I was so near retirement I could smell it. St. Louis had been good recruiting.

I roped them together and woke them up. I'd quick-march them in with all senses combat-ready. Snipers would haunt the trek. Recruiters were damned unpopular. Before departing I used the laser to fire the canyon-bottom detritus. That would protect my rear and draw the attentions of those gutty enough to be outside. The periodic canyon fires were big events in lives otherwise pale on random stimuli.

There is just one word which fits the condition in which the typical Old Earther exists: Poverty. Poverty of resources, of goods, of spirit, of morality, of intelligence, of courage. The brightest and richest and bravest got out generations ago; the moral were destroyed. The billions who remain are the descendants of those who hadn't the guts and off-your-ass to dump their welfare security and go where they could create something of their own. Rogues like myself turn up and opt out, commonly through the services, but we grow fewer in every generation. Old Earth is selectively breeding itself toward a whimpering Armageddon.

Station was a fortress I made steps ahead of a mob, with eleven resisting kids still trailing and one slow club-wielder worn as a stole.

The Recruiter

The door groaned shut behind us. Such hopelessness and despair filled their twenty-two little eyes. All would rather have died than face a real frontier. Old Earth was soul-desolation in human jungle, eye-deep in human-created horror, but to them it was secure, known, comfortable emotionally in its decay and deadliness, and required little of body or mind. The loathed starworlds would take care of tomorrow.

The door groaned shut and bodies smashed against it. It held long enough for me to herd my catch into a citadel room. Processing began immediately. Fingerprints, retinals, ID established. Move along now to the lictor. I'd seen it too many times before. The faces of the damned bore the resignation of Jobs by their God abandoned. I watched the relay of the mob breaking in to liberate them.

St. Louis hadn't been recruited much. In other zones the dullards knew better than to enter a door that gave. Station crew watched with greedy glee as a crowd surged in before the lictor's eyes breaking and entering. The trap closed. A little gas dropped gently in. They screamed, they trampled one another in an effort to force the door again. Futility. Chuckles behind me. This meant points for everyone.

"Your lucky day, Klaus," I heard. "Big bonus on prepubescents today. Four points per."

Had I had a forehead of flesh I would have frowned. Sounded like...

Whir. Communications printout coming in with our point credits as per now calculated at Recruiting Central in Geneva.

"Let's see... You lucky Spike. You made a killing, Klaus. You only got two points to go. Two lousy points. Man." Envy there. The man had been in recruiting two years longer than I. Wasn't hungry enough to work the streets and canyons. Takes a special kind to stay with it long enough to get out.

I thought about those bonus points again. Suspicious. I checked the holocomm following processing. As I feared. Downdeep, two levels, my plunder was running through Medical, not for a Med-check. They were being anasthetized and fed to a battery of surgical Frankensteins, solid-state all, that opened heads like muskmelons and scooped brains into support/travel tanks for shipment to commercial wholesalers. Down the line little bodies were being salvaged for transplantable parts. Must be a big brain order in from one of the cryocyborgic data processors.

Old Earth's got to stabilize that balance of trade.

Engineering had seen to it that there were no distracting glands in my body. Couldn't get into a really fine, shaking rage. It's hard to be mad when it's all in the mind, but I tried. I couldn't really stomach the brain snatching. But what could I do? We all do what we must to get what we need.

The choice was as simple as off-on. Stand by and not die, or revolt and join the children on the disassembly line, enroute to computer interface consoles somewhere in the outworlds.

Someone popped to my moral crisis. The bob portrait changed. The new scene showed a clone tank percolating in a remote corner of Medical. My soon to be brain-home, the prize for which I'd jackboot-Pied Pipered the children to their ego-deaths. It was ready for occupation. They kept the clones near so we could be reminded whenever we caught a dose of conscience.

I wondered what it would be like to *feel* again (pain was the only sensation my metal horse could relay), to *smell*. I hadn't smelled anything but imagination since I died. The thoughts calmed me a little, but not enough. The old tin man suit's monitors must have been playing quisling.

"Only two more points, Klaus," someone reminded. Trying to tell me not to blow it now. Tradition is, everyone helps the man who's short. For some reason the fellow with the best excuse for playing hoyle is the most likely to break. Maybe because they've been at it so long. It builds, like strontium-90 deposits in the bones. "Two points. God, I envy you."

When I thought about it, I envied me too. I could get out of the baby-stealing business almost any time. I just had to go catch a couple more. A week later I'd wake up a whole, free man, off Earth in Luna Command, credit in hand and passage to any frontier world available as soon as I learned to manage my new body.

Two points. Today one more kid would do, with points left over for friends. Friends? I hated them all, for what they were, mirrors in which

The Recruiter

I saw myself. They probably hated me. There'd be no reunions for this outfit. We were all predators devouring the weak.

I hated Old Earth and the cesspool of sub-humanity it had allowed itself to become. I wanted to pull cork and blow my fusion generator, myself, and the Station into the hell where we all belonged. I looked at that beautiful, virgin, scarfree young body in its clone tank and hated myself most of all.

Two points and it was mine.

I turned on a view of the hangers-round outside. Still a few children there. No one, not even Mr. Untouchable, Perfectly Just and Honest Lictor, would yell foul if I... Points for him, too, you see. The lictor was still in flesh, but he was *old*. Youth was the one way to reach him.

I looked at the clone body, looked at the street. Time to make a choice.

I did.

What choice was there, really?

Some people will do anything not to die.

The Seventh Fool

Cantanzaro sang as he walked along the road to Antonisen. Occasionally, he glanced back, smirked. The road remained an empty, meandering scar of brown on springtime's green. The Maniarchs of Kortanek hadn't yet picked up his scent.

Then he frowned. He had been compelled to flee without the Jewels of Regot.

He grinned again. The thousand gayly colored spires of Antonisen pricked the sky ahead. The man who had flummoxed Regot's pragmatist priests could, surely, make his fortune in a city ruled by a Council called The Seven Fools.

Springtime was spreading through Zarlenga like a happy disease. The Hundred Cities were opening like bright flowers. Travelers buzzed among them like bees. His reception at Antonisen's Harlequin Gate wasn't the least unfriendly.

Serendipity! he thought moments after penetrating the dusty streets. He had arrived just in time to witness one of Antonisen's fabled elections. A Fool had retired. Half the men of the city were vying for his Chair.

A clever man should be able to find an avenue to profit in that.

Antoniseners reasoned that, since government was evil but necessary, it ought, at least, to be entertaining. Those who wished to become

Councilors, therefore, had to convince the voters that they could provide the most amusing show.

There was a clown on every corner. Antoniseners were partial to humorists. The more inspired were winning votes with scandalous libels on the retired Fool's manhood.

Cantanzaro ventured from clown to clown, observing fingers and toes. Theft was the swiftest path to wealth. And in Antonisen it was the custom to flaunt one's fortune in the form of rings.

His natural impulse was to palm a few while shaking hands. But that, he noted, could be tricky business. Antoniseners seemed preternaturally sensitive to such maneuvers. Whenever a foreigner made a try—there were a good many in town for the election—the victim would shriek, a gang would fall on the thief, pummel him senseless, hoist him by the arms and legs, run him to a nearby low, shadowed archway, and chuck him in with a cry of "Hornbostel!"

Whatever it meant, Cantanzaro had no curiosity. He had had his encounters with the mysteries of the Hundred Cities before. Few had been pleasant.

He needed a better idea. And one came.

Cantanzaro seldom lacked for ideas, only for means.

He dug into his tattered purse. Still only four green-tinged copper alten of Kortanek, and one useless map.

So he sought a market with an antiquary. All Zarlenga was deep in the rubbish of its ten-thousand-year history. Every city had its junk men.

This one was typical, an old man whose place of business was a filthy blanket spread in the square, piled high with history's leavings. He probably went home to a palace. Zarlengans were suckers for anything ancient.

"Your wish, Grace?" The old man wrinkled his nose at Cantanzaro's shabbiness, but at election time one was rude to no man. That he himself was grubbier didn't faze the man. Poverty was part of his act too.

"A book."

"Ah. Yes. I've got a dozen. A hundred. Cook books, romances, histories, journals, magic by the right hand, magic by the left…"

The Seventh Fool

"It should be unreadable."

"Unreadable?" A live one, the merchant thought, rubbing his hands together. "Li Chi." He held up a scroll. "Got caught in the rain…"

"No. In a forgotten tongue." Cantanzaro smiled. The old man kept gawking at his ringless fingers.

"This, then. A genuine antiquity, recovered at great personal risk, by a tomb-miner working the Mountains of Dautenhain."

Cantanzaro considered the title. It was in no alphabet he knew. But he found the tomb-miner story doubtful. The tome was in too fine a shape. Stolen, likely. "Good enough." He tossed a copper, started off.

The merchant shrieked like a scalded cat. A dozen men closed in, already arguing over the quickest route to the nearest low black archway. Cantanzaro turned back, pretending bewilderment.

A half hour later he thundered, "But you admit you can't even read the thing?"

"Can't read anything." The old man went on to mourn about being cheated, robbed, losing money on the deal, but settled for Cantanzaro's remaining three alten.

The most desperate candidate, street talk said, was one Ablan Decraehe, son of a retired Fool who claimed the youth was a bad joke on legs.

While waiting to obtain audience with Decraehe, Cantanzaro worked his map into his scheme. It was a crude thing, but would do.

He had a low opinion of the intellect and morals of anyone who *wanted* to get into government. The best system, he thought, was that practiced in Immerlagen, where they seized a man off the street, carried him screaming to his inauguration at the Mayoral Palace. As soon as he showed signs of enjoying his post, the Aldermen had him stuffed and put into the City Museum.

"The book is the rare and famous Tales of Arabrant, of which great humorists have whispered for generations. A man of your stature has doubtless heard of it," Cantanzaro told Decraehe, a slim, snobbish man who affected an unnecessary monocle and would not have been caught dead entertaining a commoner outside election time. "The ultimate collection of humorous tales, some with such magic that men have been known to die laughing on hearing them. I heard you tell a censored version of 'The Bureaucrat's Revenge.'" It was the youth's obvious favorite and most successful story and the brightest spot in his leaden monologue. "I thought you'd be a man interested in the original."

Decraehe frowned suspiciously.

"It's always good to have a friend on the Council when one changes cities. One hand washes the other." He made the motions with slim, uncalloused fingers.

Cantanzaro had chosen his mark well. Decraehe was the sort who could admit no shortcoming, especially ignorance. "I've heard of it, of course." He tried to look conspiritorial. "How'd you come by a copy?"

Cantanzaro glanced around, leaned closer. Wishful thinking was doing his convincing. "Accidentally. Gambling with a thief. He left it as security for a debt. When I saw what I had, I hurried to Antonisen." A mark, he had long ago learned, often could be disarmed by an open admission of knavery. Forewarned, he would relax, sure he could not be had himself.

"Hardly proper, my dear fellow." Decraehe glanced meaningfully at a dark archway.

The things seemed to be everywhere.

This was the tricky part, getting past being robbed and chucked through the opening. Cantanzaro handed him the book.

"But...but..."

"Yes. It's in Old High Trebec. All the copies are. And the Brothers of Allgire guard the three known copies of translation dictionaries with unbreachable spells. But my victim...er, debtor, also knew what he had. And lately had come into knowledge of the whereabouts of a fourth dictionary." He produced the map. "He had taken this off a tomb-miner in the Mountains of Dautenhain, who mentioned the dictionary as he was dying."

"I see. What good does this do me?"

"For a fee I would recover that dictionary. Just enough to establish myself here."

The Seventh Fool

Decraehe frowned.

"The book is yours. A gift from a grateful immigrant. It's useless to me anyway. Being a foreigner, I'm ineligible for public office.

"Never understood why the Brothers worry about it getting out. The dictionary is the important thing. With that, a man could make himself *King* of Antonisen."

"Those mountains are four days away. Four there, four back, plus time to find and open the tomb. The election's in seven days." The claws of greed kept pulling Decraehe's face into off expressions.

"The tomb is found and open. Given a good horse and suitable incentive fee, traveling round the clock, I could deliver in five days."

"Why didn't you bring it?" Decraehe whined.

Cantanzaro tried to look amazed. "With the streets full of rogues who'd cut my throat for it? No, begging your pardon, I wanted a firm contract and gold in my purse before I took that risk."

"But if I paid you, what would keep you from running off with my money?"

"The honor of the contract. The value of Cantanzaro's word is known in a dozen cities. Also, you'd hold half the fee for payment on delivery. In fact, I'll leave the map. It's burned on the back of my brain anyway. Then, if I cheated, you could sell book and map, at a handsome profit, to someone willing to wait till next election. Moneywise, you can't lose."

Cantanzaro settled back in his chair, let the wheels turn. Decraehe would be thinking that he could have him chucked through the archway after relieving him of money.

"Twenty percent advance."

Cantanzaro smiled thinly. Decraehe had swallowed the whole six-legged horse. "Fifty. Against your certitude of becoming Chief Fool."

"But you'll have no time to spend it anyway…"

"A matter of principal. Of having equal amounts to lose. Just a hundred soli…"

"A hundred! Thief! What…"

"Against the certitude of becoming Chief Fool? A bargain at ten times the price. The payoffs from gamblers and thieves' markets would return that in a week. You must realize, a man of my station must establish himself properly in his new land."

"Twenty. Ten now and ten later."

"Ninety now and ninety later."

An hour later, with fifty gold soli practically ripping his belt off, Cantanzaro swung astride Decraehe's best horse. The would-be Fool had saddled the beast himself. With book held tightly in hand, he opened the courtyard gate.

An older man stumbled through. "Any way to greet your father, boy?" he grumbled. He scowled at Cantanzaro, at Decraehe, at the book. "What's this? My first edition Zavadil, that was stolen a month ago! Nursing a thieving viper in my own bosom…"

This Cantanzaro heard as he spurred through the gate, cursing the ill-fortune that dogged his steps. It happened every time, at the moment of triumph. Those old crones, the Fates, must have developed an abiding hatred for him.

Decraehe shrieked like an old woman. Antonisen poured into the streets. The warning swifteed ahead; Cantanzaro reached the Harlequin Gate only to find it already close. He swung into a side street, switched back and forth till he had gained a momentary lead, then eased up to the first inn he encountered. To the stableman he called, "Return this animal to the Ablan Decraehe immediately," and tossed a solus. The man's eyes grew huge. It was a small fortune to one of his station.

"Instantly, my lord."

Five minutes later, from a rooftop, Cantanzaro watched the protesting stableman being hustled to an archway. "Hornbostel! Hornbostel!" the crowd chanted.

Grinning, Cantanzaro waited till night, then went over the wall.

He kept on grinning till, in Venverloh, he tried spending one of his remaining forty-nine soli, all of which proved to be lead thinly surfaced with gold. The one checked by biting, which Decraehe had given for that purpose, had been the one he had tossed to the stable worker.

They had low black archways in Venverloh too.

Ponce

For me it started the day we got the new car. New in that we didn't have it before. It was a '62 Continental that the dude painted canary yellow (with a broom, it looked like) to get me to take it. It was our first. You got six kids, one trying to make the breakout in college, push a broom and moonlight as a watchman, and have a mama that's got to go to the kidney machine every three days and has diabetes besides, food stamps don't go very far, even if you can trade them off for something besides beans. We were proud of that car. Seven years we'd been saving pennies and nickels in a big lard can I got from the bakery. Once some kids broke in and got it, but that was early, when there was only a few dollars. We hid it good after that. Nobody ever found it.

First thing we did was go for a ride, cats and all. Sarah borrowed a camera from our downstairs neighbor, Wanda, and got some film with money she had, and we went to the zoo, then just rode around, showing it off.

People looked. That car was *ugly*. The kids all grinned and waved. The cats got sick and kept trying to get out.

We got home with some daylight and film left. Sarah wanted some pictures of the kids and car in front of the house. Blues maker. One rundown two family, flat, in the middle of a block where most of the buildings had been demolished, leaving a stony, bricky, weedy desert, littered with old tires and bedsprings that appeared overnight, like magic mushrooms. The few surviving flats rose like dirty, scattered teeth in an old man's mouth.

But the high of the car, of success, kept on. When Lania, our ten year old daughter, came up with another cat, found only she knew where, we hardly argued.

Then our boy Arivial, our youngest, came back with a dog. I put my foot down, but not hard enough. A lot of angry words, and some tears, and the dog had a home.

It wasn't the arguments that convinced me. It was that dog's eyes.

That was the strangest dog I ever seen. One of them little hairy ones, Scottie I think, black as night, bony as death, wanting to be friendly but nervous about it, like some white dude you've been working with for years who's friendly on company time but don't know how you want he should act when you meet him outside.

It was his eyes. You ever see a dog with blue eyes? Not blue like some blond white dude. Not like a kitten. Not like the sky, or turquoise, or anything light, but none of the darks either. A blue with depth. And, if you've ever looked at a dog's eyes, you know they're all color, kind of a brownish gold outside the pupil. Not these eyes. Outside the blue, that looked kind of deep and far away like the colored things inside the marbles kids call cateyes, they were clear as glass. My first thought was that he did have marbles for eyes. They were round and a little more forward on his head than most.

That whole dog was strange, but his eyes had a life of their own. Whenever I looked straight at them I felt like I was falling in, like I was watching a space show on Wanda's tv where Star Trek was coming to some planet. It scared me shitless.

I told Sarah maybe we better take him to the Humane Society, maybe something was wrong. Didn't want the kids to get bit. He didn't have no tags. She said we didn't have no money. Wouldn't till Friday, when the bakery check came, and that had to go for rent. Eighty bucks and we didn't even get hot water. Four rooms. It would have to wait. Maybe a long time. Next week was food stamps, then

Ponce

gas and electric, and cat and dog food, and clothes and shoes because school was starting and the younger ones were getting too big for last year's... It's hard sometimes, but I never been in no trouble. Neither have my kids, which makes me proud. It's harder for them. They're growing up with people who steal and cheat all the time. Only thing any of us ever did was sometimes get Sarah a carton of Kools with the food stamps.

Maybe Arivial could find some soda bottles, but that was always a hassle. The dude at the confectionary always thinks he stole them. We never buy no soda.

If you think I'm old fashioned, saving up to buy a car and not trying to break the system and raising my kinds the same, I guess you're right. That's the way I was raised. Times was different then.

Arivial named the dog Ponce. He didn't seem so spooky when you didn't look at his eyes. He settled right in, most of the time acted just like any other dog. He barked at strangers. He bounced around with happy whines any time anybody came home, especially Arivial from school. He really was Arivial's dog. He growled at me when I growled at the boy. Only three days after we picked him up, he bit a kid when some boys tried to steal Arivial's new shoes. I thought there would be some trouble, but nobody ever came around. Those boys must've been afraid of the trouble they'd get if they squawked.

Guess you get used to anything if it's around you all the time, like having less than most, or a dog with blue eyes. It's just there and, unless you trip over it, you don't much notice. Unless you're young and you've got time to look around. That's one problem for the kids today. They've got the time. We didn't when I was young. Too busy trying to stay fed. I worked all my life. Started picking cotton with my folks in Arkansas when I was barely big enough to walk. Only way I know. You get to my age, you're pretty set in your ways.

You've got to figure on what you're hungry for, too. My parents would've thought our flat a mansion. A man's big goal, them days, was to bring his wife to the city. Now Bobby, my oldest, was getting his foot on the next step up.

That Ponce was a smart pup. Wasn't a week before Arivial had him doing tricks. And there were some he figured for himself, like how to get out the screen door when it wasn't locked.

I came in from the bakery one night, to eat and get my watchman's uniform, and found Sarah all worried. Kids and cats and Ponce were all outside. The Lincoln was gone. I figured Bobby was off with his Mary Taylor again. I didn't see much of that car during the week. I hoped he wasn't wasting his book money.

Sarah said Arivial was talking to Ponce. I thought, so what? Everybody does. The cats too. But she said it was like they were talking serious, only Ponce just sat there real quiet and stared with those eyes. The boy had been telling her what Ponce had told him. She was afraid he wasn't playing pretend, that he really believed it. I said, well, I'll talk to him when I get a chance.

I was starting to be sorry that I let the kids have the pets. They cost too much even when we didn't get all the shots and tags. And I was sorry about the car, too, a little bit. Bobby wasn't home much anymore. He might get in trouble, might have a wreck, you know how you think.

It was a Sunday morning before church when I finally caught Arivial talking to Ponce the way that worried Sarah. You ever listen to a kid talking to a pet? When they don't know you're there? They get real serious, telling their problems. That dog, see, he don't tell no secrets, don't brush it off, don't make fun. He sits there and listens, and knows it's important, even if he don't understand. That's why kids need pets, I guess. A pet's always got the time.

That's what Arivial was doing, only it was going like half a conversation. The boy would say something, ask a question, wait a while, then ask one or two questions about the answers he seemed to have gotten. I don't remember what his problem was. It wasn't something a grownup would think important. After I listened a while, I went and sat by Arivial. He was surprised but Ponce wasn't. Ponce always seemed to know where everybody was. I scratched his ears.

I told Arivial I understood about Ponce, but his mother didn't, that him talking to the dog all the time scared her. Especially when he told

Ponce

her what Ponce said back. He said Ponce *did* talk to him, with his eyes, and why should he lie? I always told him not to lie.

I said he didn't have to, just don't tell your mother, it makes her unhappy. He butted me some buts, then said okay. No more talking to Ponce where she'd hear, no more telling her what he said.

All the time Ponce sat there looking at me with those eyes, making me feel guiltier and guiltier. I got the feeling he was trying to tell me something too, so I mostly looked away.

That took care of it for a week. Then it was Liana complaining. Don't know why she was upset. She was always talking to the cats. But I straightened that out, too. Then it was another of the kids, and another, till there was nobody left but me and Bobby, the two that was home the least. It got to be a puzzle. None of them bothered to explain, just to complain.

I finally got some time free, late in October, after Ponce had been with us two months. I took Arivial and Ponce to the park. You weren't supposed to let dogs run loose there, but I took a chance Ponce would behave like always and stay by Arivial. He did.

I had kind of a suspicion that I asked about then, and Arivial admitted that he'd known Ponce a while before he'd asked if the dog could stay with us. I nodded, smiled. Arivial told me how smart Ponce was, staying out of sight those days. I said yes. I never argued with how smart that dog was. He was the smartest I ever seen.

I asked what they talked about. School stuff, he said. Ponce could explain things better than his teacher. He made it fun. And there wasn't no dumb stuff, like history. I asked what kind of stuff. Mostly arithmetic, he said.

I was beginning to see why the others had been bothered. Arivial wasn't playing pretend at all. I asked why didn't he show me. He'd always been interested in arithmetic. Did real good at it in school. I'd played games with him before. That's what I expected then.

But what he scratched in the dirt with a stick looked like chicken tracks. I thought about Bobby's college books. This didn't look the same. But I really couldn't tell. I only went to school now and then when I was a kid, and only got my grade school equivalency now. I want to do high school, but there just isn't time.

I asked what it was. He said some fancy words I didn't know he knew, then said that Ponce didn't know our notation so he'd had to learn Ponce's. Took me a minute to figure out what he meant. Then I said, well, why didn't he use some of the older kids' books to learn? I was just going along, figuring he'd seen Bobby's books and was making up something that looked the same. He said he'd never thought about that.

There was peace around the house for a month. At least, nobody came to me complaining. Then Arivial brought home a note from his teacher.

It didn't say nothing but that Sarah should come in after school. She was so upset, so sure he was in trouble, that she wouldn't go. Arivial said he didn't know what it was about. Next day I took off early and went down.

His teacher and principal were both waiting. Liana had had that teacher last year. I didn't like her. She was the kind that thought you was against her if you taught your kid to brush his own teeth. But the principal was all right.

Wasn't no trouble, though. The principal did most of the talking. About where was Arivial learning arithmetic? The teacher just said she was awed. The principal said Arivial was doing high school work already, maybe higher. She thought he was a genius. Would I mind did they arrange for him to take some tests?

Then the teacher said that if he was a genius, he should get special training. I was surprised. I got in an unkind word when they asked did I know about Arivial's talent. Well, yes, I said, but I never said anything because of Liana last year. After that everybody told everybody how sorry they was, but by then I wasn't listening. I was thinking about Ponce.

I still didn't believe Arivial was really talking to him, but I worried that maybe he thought he was. Maybe the boy was a genius like they said, but what if he had to have Ponce to make it work? So he could believe in himself? I could fix it so he could study at home, but not so Ponce would live forever. Even if he was lucky and lasted maybe twelve years, there would be Arivial without him when he was twenty-one.

Ponce

Teacher and principal were saying was it all right did they let some people from the universities see Arivial. If he studied fancy arithmetic? Math, they said. He'd still have to study the regular stuff with the other kids. He wasn't no genius at everything. Sure, fine, I said, I'd be proud. But why were they so excited?

They said some things but I didn't listen. They weren't telling the truth. That was in their faces. They looked like old prospectors who had finally struck gold. Arivial was going to make them famous. I hedged then. Said everything was fine by me, sounded good, but I wanted to talk to Sarah and Arivial first.

I saw what could happen. Some good things could be done for Arivial, but it could be turned into a circus that would hurt him more. You hear about things like that in the news sometimes.

I just wanted to talk to Arivial. I knew what Sarah would say. She wouldn't want no part of it. She wanted her kids to be normal, as much like other kids as possible, to keep their heads down so to speak. She didn't realize that it was a new age, that some of the doors really were open a crack.

Arivial was waiting out front, scared to death. Sarah was waiting too, only upstairs, peeking out the blinds.

I told the boy what happened. At first he relaxed, then he got scared again when he realized people were going to make a fuss over him. He was always kind of quiet and private, and got embarrassed any time a stranger said something nice. He asked me did he have to take the tests and everything. I told him no, that was why I was talking to him, to see if he wanted to. I said the school wanted to get him some special teachers, and like that, until I was sure he knew what it was all about. Then I told him to make up his mind himself. Maybe he should talk to Ponce about it.

I don't know why I said that. I felt silly afterwards. He said yeah, that's what he'd do.

Later, almost bedtime, he came to the warehouse where I was watchman and whispered that he'd take the tests and things so he could study. He said Ponce thought it was a good idea, that he should learn as much as he could as fast as he could so he'd know how to say the things he really had to say, just in case something happened. I didn't understand, but I said okay, I'd come to school on my lunch hour and tell his teacher.

It went all right. After he got over being shy, Arivial liked the attention. And he got lots of it. The university people seemed like good folks, mostly, and they didn't get any newspaper or tv people coming around. His teacher and principal were disappointed about that, I think. Sarah got used to the idea, started getting proud. Only Bobby was a problem, and he wasn't a big one.

The old car kept breaking down and I wouldn't let him spend his college money to fix it. His romance died off because of that. Made him grouchy for a while, so he took it out on Arivial for getting into his books. He threatened to spank him or go join the Army, depending on who he was talking to. He got over it. By then Arivial had finished his books. He'd passed Bobby by.

The more he learned, the faster he went. Sometimes, when I could get away early, I went to school with him and talked to the university people. They used a lot of big words to do it, but what they said was that Arivial was starting to figure things out for himself. They could teach him something and he could almost, but not quite, tell them what came next.

What puzzled them was that he had his own system worked out and had to translate back and forth. They said he might be more than just a genius. The rate he was going, getting faster and faster, it wouldn't be long before they ran out of things to teach. They talked about sending away for teachers who knew more than they did. They were always all very excited.

Those nights I'd go home and stare at that blue-eyed dog and wonder. Somehow, he seemed the smaller miracle.

Summer came again. The university people wanted to take Arivial to California. He wanted to go, and to take Ponce. Sarah said no. She wasn't letting no ten year old son of hers go nowhere for three months with no honkey strangers. When she talked hard and bitter like that, I didn't argue. I knew she wasn't going to change her mind.

Ponce

So they brought the men from California to him. And a Dr. Conklin from back east, and even a man from Germany or someplace over there. I started getting real scared. They were spending more money than I made in a year, working two jobs, just to help my son learn math. I started thinking about things like Russian spies and the government locking Arivial up to protect him.

You can't keep secrets forever, especially when you got big-mouthed kids, a proud wife, and so many excited teachers. One day a radio man came to ask if he could interview Arivial on his station. Sarah got excited, I got more scared, the kids got jealous, and we all decided it was up to Arivial. I thought he could handle it. Being around all those college people, he'd changed. He was like a little boy with a grown man inside. When he was serious. Other times he was his own age. He loved baseball. Sometimes he complained about missing out on that when he studied.

His all-time hero was Lou Brock and he wanted to grow up and play left field for the Cardinals. He kept saying he'd be like Einstein afterwards, when he got old. That bothered me some. I thought maybe they were pushing too hard. Maybe he should take some time off. But he didn't want to. Math was fun too.

I worried all the time, seems like.

Acting like that grown man, he did good on the radio. He talked about Ponce, but he was smart. He told his truth, but did it so everybody thought he was jiving them. He did the same thing later, on the tv. People were never sure how to take him.

I went downtown with him for the tv thing, wearing my church clothes. I was more nervous than him. He wanted to take Ponce, but I said better not.

Sarah worried too, but she was also proud. Now she really had something to brag to her friends about. Me too, except I didn't start till somebody asked. Sort of embarrassed, you know. Me so ignorant and him so smart. But everybody kept telling me how great it was, even Mr. Kasselbaum at the bakery, who hardly ever came out of the office except to chew somebody out.

But it got to be too much, especially after, with help from this physicist, Dr. Conklin, Arivial wrote this article about hologrammatic numbers. He didn't know how to spell right or how to put the words down, but he knew the numbers. After that all kinds of people came to the house. We tried to be nice, but you couldn't get anything done. Just because my kid was smart didn't mean I should stop working, though Mr. Kasselbaum and the security company were good about me missing if I had to. And Sarah had the house and the kids had school, and Arivial was busier than anybody, trying to keep up with regular school, his special teachers, work on another article he wanted to write, Ponce, and all the people who wanted to talk to him.

It hurt some people's feelings and made some others mad, but we finally had to stop seeing anybody but family, friends, and the university people. Arivial kept telling me his new project was hard, that even Ponce had trouble explaining it because people still didn't have the concepts. Before they could really understand they would have to learn the hologrammatic notation.

Dr. Conklin tried to tell me about it. He said the new math would modify, prove, and expand some of Einstein's work. He was the translator, so to speak, the man who'd write it up so people could understand. He was having trouble, too, smart as he was. He said it was as much philosophy as physics and math, but when they got it straight it could be used to explain lots of things scientists had been having trouble with for years. I just kept nodding my head till he decided I was as smart as Arivial.

About that time Bobby found him a new girlfriend and had to have the car all the time. It was broke down more than it ran. Every time it died we had to wait and scrimp to get it fixed, plus saving up for licenses and insurance, that I never thought about when I bought it. That old thing was more trouble than it was worth. I would've sold it except for Bobby.

This Dr. Conklin wasn't only interested in Arivial. Sometimes he'd start talking about Nobel Prizes and look greedy, but I guess that's just the way people are.

Bobby kept the car fixed and started running around. This time he was so involved that he didn't care about anything else. I found out he

Ponce

was getting into his school money for gas and things. He wouldn't listen when I tried to talk to him.

Arivial and Dr. Conklin kept getting more and more excited. They were getting close. Though he didn't believe Arivial was really learning from Ponce, he kept telling the boy to spend time with him. Told me he figured any way a man got his mind working was all right, even talking to dogs. Only the output counted. I agreed some and didn't agree. You could push it too far.

The way they talked, they had their paper down to the final match. I got the feeling mobs of people were waiting to grab it. More and more people came to the house, though we kept telling them to go away.

There was something about it on the radio, the tv, or in the newspapers every day. Everybody was on about the ten year old who was opening a whole new view of the universe. Part of the paper got pirated and printed and scientists started fighting like dogs around a bitch in heat. Some said it was another breakthrough to understanding as important as Newton's or Einstein's. Some others said it was the biggest fraud since organized politics. On the tv, right after one of these men had his say, they would show Arivial talking about Ponce.

I still think I took that dog more serious than anybody but Arivial. Sometimes I would just sit and stare at him for an hour. And sometimes he'd open one eye and sort of smile, as much as a dog can. I thought about trying to talk to him, just to convince myself he was only a dog, but I never got around to it. Maybe I was scared I'd be wrong. If I was, that meant I had to think about a whole lot of other things, like how could a dog talk, how come he was so smart, how come he had blue eyes, and so on.

Sometimes I think about that anyway. Maybe it's just because I'm too ignorant to know better.

The car broke down again. Water pump. When I came home from the bakery, there was Bobby fixing it. I got mad. Really mad. He'd been spending all his money and time on the car and his girlfriend. Sarah said he'd started cutting classes. I really gave it to him.

He took it for a while because I don't get on him that much and, anyway, he knew he was wrong. But when I started talking about his girl he blew up. We never came closer to fighting. He jerked the last bolt into place, slammed the hood, wiped his hands, jumped in, roared away. For about ten feet.

Ponce managed just one surprised yip.

My god, Bobby said, jumping out, my god. Pop, I didn't mean... I'm sorry...

I hadn't seen him cry since he was eleven. Didn't see him too good this time. It was hard to see through my own tears. I went to the dog. Ponce, I said, Ponce... But there was nothing I could do. He was dead.

One by one the other kids turned up, and their friends, and Sarah and Wanda, and almost everybody in the neighborhood. A lot of the kids cried. They'd all liked Ponce. Nobody knew what to do.

All the time I was looking at those eyes. After a while the blue started fading. For a moment they were clear as colorless marbles, then they went dark. I thought I saw a lot of little lights swirling around in there, then they faded too. Might have been the street lights. They were just coming on. Then they were just plain dog's eyes.

Arivial was with Dr. Conklin, but he'd be coming home soon. We just kept standing around till a cop came by and asked what was going on. I told him. He remembered me and Ponce from tv. Told us not to block the street and went on. So I finally picked up Ponce and took him upstairs.

Arivial took it better than I expected, but he was hurt. Bad. He mostly stayed to himself for a few days, not doing anything but going to school and sometimes talking to Dr. Conklin. Conklin was upset too. Just another week, he kept saying, and they would've had it.

When Arivial got over it he went back to work. But he'd changed. He wasn't dumber, but he was a lot slower. It's been a year now and they're still trying to finish up. Arivial's showing the way, but without Ponce he can't get there except by inches.

The university people tried to convince him that he didn't need Ponce. It didn't work. Maybe it was all in his head, maybe it wasn't. I'm not sure. I don't think I ever will be.

Ponce

A couple weeks after Ponce died Arivial said something that still makes me wonder. He said Ponce wasn't really dead, that he just went back. It was only a dog that Bobby killed. Ponce would come home if he really needed him.

And maybe that would be true even if the dog's talking was all in his imagination.

Quiet Sea

With dawn a hundred doves unfurled their varicolored wings upon the quiet sea, fluttering nervously. The waves ran gentle now, but during the night the earth beneath the deep had groaned and shaken like a brunwhal in its death throes. Ahead lay deep blue water, cool Fenaja water from the arctic, but Rickli sensed no danger. They would reach the Pimental Bank before noon. Meanwhile, he would mend sail, ignoring the aches in his heart and leg, and daydream of mountains, forests, and snow. Maybe later, when they got ready to put the seines over the side and he would only be in the way, he would limp down to the galley and swap lies with the Shipwrecked Earthman and help sharpen scaling knives.

Such were the thoughts of Rickli Manlove at dawn on the Ninth of Eel in the year 866 of the local reckoning. The Shipwrecked Earthman prefered 3060. He had lost count of his months and days. After a few years he had given up trying.

Rickli, too, had given up. It had been a year since the Fenaja harpoon had shattered his knee. For months he had hoped, but, finally, he'd had to accept the truth: never again would he ride the bowsprit of a racing chaser and, with the salty spray stinging his eyes and soaking his beard, plant his harpoon in the glistening back of a fleeing brunwhal. Nor would he ever trade insults and harpoons with the cruel Fenaja.

Once the crew had named him Left Hand Sea Terror. Now he was only The Crippled Sailmaker. So it went. So it went. He bore the Fenaja no special malice. They had done what they'd had to do, as did Man. When the grunling weren't running, the blackfin were.

He wet a finger, held it up, sniffed, and considered the bow of the sails. The breeze was barely sufficient to keep way on. An inauspicious sign at dawn. The fleet could become becalmed. The Fenaja would be hard pressed to resist such temptation.

But there was no feeling of danger in the deep blue water. Perhaps the Fenaja were elsewhere.

Far over the quiet sea, shell horns winded. A chaser's mainsail fat-bellied in the breeze. Throughout the fleet youngsters scrambled into the rigging to watch. The brunwhal were the most valuable, and most cunning, creatures of the deep. The Children of the Sky used everything but the name.

The Shipwrecked Earthman had been amazed that they remembered their offworld origins after so many centuries. But many things had amazed him here, their survival most of all.

Rickli and the Earthman were almost friends, close enough that the Earthman had confided that he wasn't an Old Earther at all but a colonial from a world called Bronwen. The distinction seemed important to him.

They hadn't always been friendly. There had been a time, before the big fight off LaFata Bank, when Rickli had joined his peers in mocking the man for his incompetence. But a harpoon through the knee, the Earthman's ministrations, and a year of mending sail had given him a new perspective. The Earthman was no longer sailing his native sea, was almost as helpless as one of the bottom creatures the divers brought up and threw on deck. In the Earthman's water, Rickli suspected, he would be more helpless than was the Earthman here.

The youngsters drifted down from the rigging. Rickli chuckled. Even at the winding of the shells he had known there wasn't enough breeze for the chaser to overhaul the brunwhal. He carefully inserted his tools into their brunwhalhide case, reached for his carved cane of spearfish

Quiet Sea

ivory. The ship grew quiet around him. Soon there were no sounds but the soughing of the wind in the rigging, the sea whispering along the hull, and the creak of the vessel's planks and frame. Those sounds, in the deeps of the nightwatches, could leave a man terribly lonely. He added the thump of his cane as he hobbled aft.

There were times when Rickli cursed his leg for what it denied him, but as often he remembered that he was lucky to have it at all. Had it not been for the Shipwrecked Earthman, he might never have survived. As the augurs reminded them, when the grunling weren't running, the blackfin were.

"Thomas?" he called down into the galley.

"Here, Rickli." The man came to help him down the ladder.

Thomas Hakim, the Shipwrecked Earthman, was a small, dusky, dark-eyed man who had only recently developed the habit of wearing his hair long and tied back in a tail, though he still kept his beard carefully trimmed in a "space." It had taken years to break the habit of regular haircuts. On his ships, he had said, short hair had been mandatory.

The people of Quiet Sea all wore theirs long. Hair became rope and twine. On Quiet Sea all available resources were exploited.

"Looks like a peaceful crossing."

"Good. Good." The Earthman returned to his scaling knives. "A pity we can't make peace with the Fenaja."

It was, Rickli thought, one of the Earthman's favorite themes, one whose futility the man recognized. Natural competition made peace and cooperation impossible.

"The augurs say we'll do well here. No one's been to Pimental Bank for years. The sandweg should be tall."

The Earthman was ever a devil's advocate. "So? And what then? We build another ship. For what?"

Rickli chuckled, playing the game. "Why, so we can gather sandweg faster and build another ship sooner. Someday we'll have the biggest fleet on Quiet Sea."

"You already have it. One of those days you'll all listen to me, say the hell with it, and sail off the edge of the world."

"That's what I like about you, Thomas. Always a cheery outlook."

"Christ!" But he smiled. The manner was a pose, Rickli had learned after having been thrown into Hakim's constant company by the Fenaja harpoon. "What were the horns about?" Though he had been with the fleet for years, Hakim still couldn't read signals.

"Brunwhal. They didn't get him."

"So it goes."

"When the grunling aren't running, the blackfin are. You need any help?"

"No. I'm almost done. Nothing till the salting starts. Checkers?"

The game had made the Shipwrecked Earthman famous across Quiet Sea. Before his falling-star arrival, all games had had to do with the sea. Checkers had caught on as a simple alternative to tradition. Hakim had tried teaching other games as well, especially chess, but the Children of the Sky had rejected them as too complicated. Their culture, Hakim had told Rickli, was too tight and changeless, with never-varying, simple goals, to accept unnecessary complexity.

The Children, though, enjoyed it when he told fortunes with a now ragged deck of tarot cards, though the augurs frowned at his treading on their heels. The Earthman thought that it was the pictures which seized their attention, not the patter. Pictures were almost unknown on Quiet Sea.

With Hakim's aid, Rickli returned to the maindeck. They set up the board atop a cargo hatch. People not otherwise occupied came over to watch. They were the best players on board.

"So tell me about Outside," Rickli said after a few moves. Hakim never lost his zest for reminiscing. Rickli didn't believe a tenth of what he said, nor did anyone else, but his tales were always entertaining. Also, they distracted him from his game.

"Did I tell you about the Iron Legion and the war with Richard Hawksblood in the Shadowline on Blackworld?" Hakim scanned his listeners, responded to their headshakes with: "It started centuries ago, before the Ulantonid War, but the high game, the endgame, was played out on Blackworld…"

Quiet Sea

The crowd grew till Dymon Tipsword, captain of *Rifkin's Dream,* came round growling at people off their watch stations. It was one of the Earthman's best stories. He got into it so deeply that Rickli beat him three straight.

Despite his crankiness and inability to master the simplest skills of seamanship, the Earthman was well liked. Aboard *Rifkin's Dream,* at least as a storyteller, he had become an honored institution.

"Pale water!" a lookout shouted from the maintop.

"The bank," Rickli said. All aboard relaxed slightly. The Fenaja shunned shallow, warm water.

Hakim gathered the checkers. "Even in paradise there's work for the sinful," he muttered. Rickli had become accustomed to such cryptic remarks, remarks Hakim seldom explained.

For the hundredth time Rickli wondered what twist of fate had brought Thomas to Quiet Sea. Though Hakim willingly chattered about himself, he refused to explain how he had come to be in a small ship, alone, near this long-forgotten world, nor would he tell what had led him to crash. His sole recorded remark on the affair was an observation that he had been lucky to set down near the fleet.

Rickli remembered the day well. He had been a rigging boy then, a maintop boy, when the morning sky had shown sudden, short-lived, unknown stars, and it had been during his masthead watch, later, that the sky had opened up and a shooting star, throwing off blinding-bright fragments of itself, had come roaring down with thunders worse than those of any storm. The main body had hit the water beyond the horizon. A great column of steam had risen to mark the site.

The augurs, versed in the old lore, had turned the fleet that way, though the object had splashed down in Fenaja water.

Thousands of dead sea creatures had floated round a burned and twisted object wallowing deep in the waves. It had been huge, frighteningly so, and made of metal... That had brought awe into the eyes of everyone who had not yet made the pilgrimage to Landing, where the remains of the Ship still lay.

When the strange object had cooled enough to be touched, every person who could had set about scavenging metal, much of which had proven unworkable later. On Quiet Sea, where there was no land at all and smelters consisted of charcoal hearths in the galleys of ships where handfuls of bottom nodes, recovered by lucky divers, were worked, that much refined metal seemed an unbelievable fortune.

Then they had broken through the outer skin and had found the unconscious man hanging in the curious strapping. He had been a dark, angry little man whose features had borne the stamp of intense concentration and fear. Though fearful, the augurs had brought him out and had done their best to mend his health. In the meantime, his vessel had been looted. Many of the Children still wore bits of glass and plastic for jewelry.

In the early days there had been a communications problem. Hakim hadn't spoken a language anything like their own, which had evolved through the centuries into one whose primary concern was the sea, its colors, deeps, moods, denizens, and the ships that sailed upon it. There were language difficulties even between the older fleets, though the augurs did their best to discourage diversion.

The Earthman's ancestors, and Rickli's, hadn't spoken the same language as contemporaries on Old Earth. And Hakim's people had followed a far different road since then.

But he had been a fast study. Perhaps a hint of why could be found in his tales of adventures on many worlds.

Though it had been obvious he would be a long time becoming productive, every ship in the fleet had vied for possession of the castaway. The augurs had spread the news that he had come from the semi-mythical world of their origin. The Children of the Sky had been hungry for news and knowledge.

The competition had become so intense that the augurs, fearing violence, had ordered a lottery.

Rifkin's Dream had won.

And had never been sorry, though at first the young people, Rickli included, had resented his presence because he had been granted so much unearned privilege.

Quiet Sea

But when he had come to understand the tongue and culture, he had done his best to pull his weight. Often over Dymon Tipsword's objections. The captain had sensed from the first that his new man would never make a sailor.

Thomas Hakim had never seen a sailing ship before Quiet Sea. He could only admire the complex relationships between the maze of booms, yards, rigging, masts, and sails, not begin to understand. The youngsters, who had grown up on the ships, sometimes thought him retarded.

Where and when, the Earthman did what he could. He had settled into the galley because cooking was what, it proved, he best understood.

Signals sounded over the water as the lead vessels entered the shallows. Orders shouted by dozens of captains carried over the quiet sea, sometimes resulting in confusion. Sails came in with whines and shrieks of tackle. In places the Pimental was so shallow that the larger vessels might run aground. The Bank was rich, but had to be exploited carefully. One dared not risk losing the vessel that was one's only home.

Quiet Sea was a calm, peaceful, relatively friendly world which supported its human population comfortably, in almost Polynesian ease, but there were pragmatic realities to be faced even in Eden. Worst was the lack of living space. The ships were all they had, were difficult to build for lack of land, and were always populated to their supportive limits. Humanity being fecund, stringent measures were required to control population.

In Rickli's fleet this took its simplest form. Crews were segregated by sex. Male children were allowed to remain with their mothers only during their first two years. In other fleets other methods, often harsher methods, were employed, including drowning of unwanted newborns, the old and halt. No technology of contraception existed.

The sexual mores of the society had been hard on the Shipwrecked Earthman. His great goal, he had once told Rickli, was to make it possible to mate without breeding. He had shown Manlove one of his ideas, a sheath of finest grunling gut carefully scraped and cured. Rickli had understood the technical aspect, but not the emotional. He had simply remarked that the material could be put to better use as sausage casing.

The fleet began to disperse. Some, like *Rifkin's Dream,* would seine. Chasers would range out in search of brunwhal, which hugged the food-rich banks. Others would send divers below for shellfish, useful bottom plants, sand, and stone, the latter for potential ore, ballast use, and transport to the centuries-old project to create, at Landing, what Quiet Sea lacked naturally: dry land. Specialized vessels would harvest sandweg, a huge bottom plant that could be cut into lumber. The stands were rich on Pimental, often rising five meters above sea level.

Hakim and Rickli, with everyone else not otherwise occupied, helped clean and salt the catch.

"Mixed catch," said Rickli, puzzled, dragging a thrashing blackfin from a lively pile and stilling it with one quick jab of the butt of his knife.

Hakim took a smaller, more easily cleaned grunling. "Not a good sign," he agreed. When the species mixed in the shallows, it was because the blackfin felt threatened by something in the deeps. Blackfin preferred the cooler, deeper waters on the faces of the banks. The grunling preferred the warmer shallows. "Fenaja?"

"Probably not. There would've been some sign."

Dymon Tipsword, too, was concerned. He had a caution pennant bent to a halyard and run to the maintruck. Here and there, similar pennons ran to other mains.

"Whatever, we'll find out first," said Rickli. *Rifkin's Dream* was seining on the extreme left of the fleet, nearest the deep water.

"Probably just the temblor last night."

"Maybe." But a feeling of wrongness had begun growing on Rickli. Why hadn't there been any Fenaja sign during the crossing? They didn't attack often, but when ships entered their waters, they always came up to watch, their ugly, whiskered snouts trailing Vs on the surface as they dared the humans to start something. Sometimes they would lift their dun, scaly foreparts from the waves and croak insults learned from other men. But as long as there were no bone-tipped harpoons in sight, their intentions remained peaceful. Their attacks, generally, came in waters where one of their occasional, sudden, inexplicable population explosions had left the blackfin schools depleted.

Quiet Sea

The winchmen hauled a bulging net aboard, scattering the sand-covered deck with flopping fish. The youngsters, wearing brunwhalskin chaps and gloves, began heaving the smallest and females over the side. Neither grunling nor blackfin had dangerous teeth, but their scales could rasp the skin off a man with one caress. Dried blackfin hide was used to sand the decks. During fishing those decks were covered two centimeters deep with sand from ballast meant to absorb spilled blood and entrails.

"Uhn!" Hakim grunted. "There's your Fenaja."

Rickli stood, ignoring the sudden sharp pain in his knee. "Part of one." He hobbled forward, helped others pull the mangled corpse from the pile of fish. "Dymon!"

Tipsword came down from the helm, spent a long minute staring at the remains. "All right. Back to work. We've got a hold to fill. You three, put it back over the side. Its people will be looking for it." As activity resumed, the captain stalked back to his station. A new set of pennons ran to the main. The ship's armorer began making the round of battle stations, setting out harpoons, axes, swords.

Rickli resumed his seat, said nothing for a long time.

"What is it?" Hakim asked.

"Half the body had been eaten. It still had a broken harpoon in its hand."

Hand was a misnomer. From the Fenaja's forward end, near what might pass for shoulders were it accustomed to going upright, a specialized pair of tentacles grew; the ends of these had modified into three finger-length sub-tentacles. The quasi-intelligent creatures used them as a man used hands.

"Meaning he maybe died fighting something that was eating him?"

"Uhm." Naturally enough, the monsters of the legends and folklore of the Children of the Sky were all creatures from the deep and, though Hakim had never encountered a man who had seen one, the sea people believed in their existence as devoutly as their ancestors had believed in dragons and trolls.

The only known enemies of the Fenaja were human. But the Children of the Sky had little real knowledge of what lived at the bottom of the deeps. Their interest was the banks, an ecological cycle into which their ancestors had inserted themselves.

The seining, cleaning, and salting went on, though wary eyes kept glancing toward deep water. Yet the crew trusted Tipsword's judgment. Had he believed real danger existed, he would have had the nets hauled in and stored.

The tension bothered the Earthman. "Think I'll go get Esmeralda," he said, putting his knife aside.

Rickli nodded, reached for another blackfin. The thing the Earthman called Esmeralda had been one of the few possessions he had reclaimed after the looting of his ship. To Rickli it looked like an ornate mutation of a shipfitter's mallet, except that Hakim always handled it backwards. Manlove suspected it was some sort of Outside talisman. Hakim brought it out each time *Rifkin's Dream* sailed into danger, but Rickli had yet to see the man do anything with it.

Just as Thomas returned, flying fish began skipping across the sea. Tipsword judged their numbers and the length of their jumps, shouted, "Ship the nets! Forget the fish! Bring them in!"

It wasn't necessary to tell the cleaners and salters to clear the decks. Every man able began pitching fish over the side. New signals rose to the main; hornmen stood by.

The sea began boiling two hundred meters off the port bow.

"Cut it!" Tipsword thundered at the netmen. "Now! Move it!" Men shuddered. A good seine costs hundreds of man-hours to make. But, if they were lucky, they could come about and recover it later. Bladders made of brunwhal stomachs would keep it afloat. Someone began wielding an ax. The trouble horns screamed across the water. Nearby ships became furious with activity.

"Hard right rudder!" Tipsword ordered. "Stand by to shift sail."

The rigging boys were already aloft.

Rifkin's Dream was the long-dead shipbuilder Rifkin's attempt to combine the best of two types of rigging in one of the fleet's largest

Quiet Sea

vessels. She was square-rigged on her forward and topmainmasts, schooner-rigged on her main and mizzen. Sharp course changes could result in mass confusion.

There was little of that this time. Everyone was too frightened to make a mistake.

"Oh!" said Rickli. Nothing else would come.

"Jesus," said the Shipwrecked Earthman, softly. "What the hell is it?"

"Grossfenaja. The deepdark-devil."

Rifkin's Dream slowly heeled over as her rudder took hold and she took the wind on her beam. The stern slid sideways toward the thing rising from the deep. The nearest seining ship winded its own horns and cut its net lines too.

A shout from the masthead directed their attention forward. Half a kilometer ahead, another one was rising. Then another, off the port quarter.

"Never heard of anything like this!" Rickli shouted. The nearest beast was still surfacing, more and more tentacles slapping the water, some reaching for *Rifkin's Dream*. Dymon Tipsword shouted for the younger boys to get below.

"Must have been the earthquake," Hakim muttered. "Christ! Another one."

The main body of the nearest broke water. It was over sixty meters long and serpentine, like a fat Midgard serpent whose tail had turned into a kraken. The head was at the end opposite the main mass of tentacles, with just two five-meter Fenaja-type limbs nearby.

Regaining his composure, Rickli said, "Any of the other old monsters I would've believed, but this…"

The creature writhed in an effort to direct its head toward the ship, but it seemed Tipsword had acted in time and the vessel would slip away.

"Sandweg!" the forward lookout cried. A moment later he hurtled into the sea as the vessel plowed into a dense young stand, the tops of which hadn't yet broken water. The bows rose high, *Rifkin's Dream* shuddered, then lurched forward as her momentum snapped or uprooted the plants.

But she hadn't enough way on to carry her through. Her stern and rudder hung up. In moments she was dead in the water.

"Battle stations!" Tipsword bellowed. "You boys below, see if she's sprung any leaks. Spearsong, get a boat over. Winchmen, stand by to kedge her. Thomas, get coals from the galley."

Hakim ran. Rickli, trying to stay out of the way, wondered how their puny weapons, even fire, could stave off the predator. He glanced at the rest of the fleet. No help there. Panic and confusion were the supreme admirals of the moment. And running for shallower water seemed no real solution. The creature that had surfaced immediately ahead was already dragging itself through water just four meters deep. Speed seemed the only escape.

He noted a racked harpoon with an ornate grip of brunwhal ivory. His own, that the crew had given him when he had been Left Hand Sea Terror, best chaser spritman in the fleet. He hobbled over and exchanged it for his cane. There was comfort in the familiar grip. He would die with his old companion in hand.

The decks and tops seemed utter chaos, yet the frenetic activity had its purposes. But for the thing bearing down, it might have been the last moment before an ordinary Fenaja fight. There had been more panic and confusion at LaFata. Rickli stayed out of the way, gradually drifted forward.

The sword, ax, and harpoon men all seemed so young, just boys. Where were the longbeards, the grizzled old men who had manned the rail at LaFata? Dead, of course. Still there, consigned to the deep. Not many had been as lucky as he. Half this crew had transferred aboard after that battle.

"Jesus," he murmured, borrowing from the Shipwrecked Earthman. The thing's head was scarred with a mouth large enough to take a man or Fenaja at a gulp.

Twenty meters from *Dream*, it plunged beneath the water, torpedoing into the sandweg wrack left by the ship's passage. Rickli shouted a warning to Spearsong, but too late. The head rose and destroyed the longboat with a single snap of huge jaws. The foretentacles snatched men from the water.

The thing's rear smashed into the port side. The vessel jumped, shook, groaned in protest. Everyone went tumbling. Rigging boys rained

Quiet Sea

from above, smashing into deck or sea with terrified screams. Rickli lost the harpoon.

Tipsword thunderously ordered everyone back to the rail. Then a tentacle whipped over and snatched him away from the wheel. He went over the side, into the sea, hacking with a rare metal sword.

Though they numbered only twenty and were no thicker than a man's arm, the monster's rear tentacles seemed to fall in a deadly rain. Against them harpoons were useless. The sword and ax men managed to damage a few, but the beast seemed oblivious to pain. Its head reared high to starboard and observed critically while its tail worked murder to port.

Dead men speckled the sea. Tentacles began reaching through hatches and snaking out the boys below. Terrified, pathetic screams echoed below decks.

Rickli suddenly understood that they were fighting the wrong end. Its normal prey probably never realized that. He tried to tell someone, but with Dymon gone there was no one to make them listen. He glanced to starboard. The creature was casually nibbling on a boatman. He bent, picked up a harpoon, cast it.

His knee betrayed him. He collapsed on bloody sand, almost cried when the harpoon whispered past the thing's trunk, a meter below his target. He had to get closer.

It had to be out the bowsprit. From nowhere else could he be certain of being close enough to overcome his knee. He grabbed another harpoon and started.

There wasn't much thought in the journey, that seemed an endless pilgrimage to keep a rendezvous with death. There was pain such as he hadn't known since the Fenaja harpoon had struck. Tentacles whipped about with Rickli Manlove seemingly their special target. One seized him round the bad knee, pulled and squeezed, but fate placed a levelheaded axman nearby. He went on, crawling, dragging the re-injured leg. Something had gone in the knee. He had heard and felt it.

Three meters out the bowsprit, he collapsed, unable to go on.

Salt spray stung his eyes. Or was it tears? Failed again… He wasn't sure where he was, on a chaser racing after the humping brown back of a brunwhal, or lying half-dead after LaFata... His will returned. Then his strength. Just enough. He made it to the leadsman's platform, dragged himself upright, gripped his harpoon, threw.

And sagged in defeat. Low again. It buried itself deep, but a meter below the huge yellow eye for which he had aimed.

"Rickli! Rickli Manlove!" The Earthman's curious, harshly accented voice seemed to come from years and kilometers away. Slowly, he turned.

The Earthman stood at the foot of the bowsprit, harpoon in one hand, his talisman in the other. A tentacle had him round the waist.

Rickli reached a futile hand...

The Earthman put the harpoon in the air. It slapped his palm.

He felt familiar ivory, the old, comfortable grip of his high years.

He turned. He aimed. He cast.

He collapsed, but only after he had seen his old companion buried grip-deep in the yellow eye.

Rickli lay unconscious for days. He came round to find *Rifkin's Dream*, with help from other ships, trying to keep afloat during repairs to her hull and rigging. Some vessels worked the beast's remains. Masts crowded the battle site. Through them he could see a similar cluster in the distance.

The Shipwrecked Earthman lay beside him, drugged, his waist a mass of ripped skin and ugly bruises. His guts must have been churned good. His talisman remained gripped in his left hand.

"Good afternoon, Captain."

"Ilyana Wildhaber. What're you doing here?"

"Keeping this tub off the bottom." She was captain of *Replete*, a repair and stores vessel. "It's a jinx."

"Have Weatherhead change our station."

"There'll be changes. This made LaFata look like a christening party."

"Tell me."

Quiet Sea

"There were six of them. Several ships weren't as lucky as *Dream*. Three were dragged into the deep. Six more went down in the shallows. Two we'll refloat. Most everyone got involved."

"Guess there'll be work for a crippled sailmaker, then." Rickli's greatest fear was that the crew would vote him supernumerary, a fear that had begun while the Fenaja harpoon still quivered in his knee. No such vote had been taken in living memory, even against incorrigibles, but Rickli felt he was a child of fate. A malevolent fate.

"Didn't you hear? You're captain now."

"No."

"Yes. They voted. You'll replace Dymon. If you live."

Rickli at last found the nerve to look down. "A one-legged man?"

She shrugged. "Got to go. You lie still, don't get it infected. They'd take it off at the neck next time."

Rickli stared at the battered masts and rigging, pondering the odd course of fate. A harpoon man in good condition grew old in his job, usually perishing when age tricked him into fatal error. But as a sailmaker who could fight, he had with one cast of a harpoon won the hearts of a crew.

Such as it might be. His elevation might be a mockery. Losses had been heavy when he had made his throw.

Rijkin's Dream did not weigh anchor for six weeks and then moved only a kilometer. Rickli and the Earthman were both off their backs but not in good health. Hakim couldn't handle solid food.

Rickli drilled his crew mercilessly, trying to meld a scattering of veterans and dozens of transfers into a new ship's company.

"What do you think?" he asked the Earthman one day.

"They'll cope. They always do. Why worry?"

"I want them to look sharp. We're going on pilgrimage."

"Landing?" The Shipwrecked Earthman had never visited the site of Man's first touchdown on Quiet Sea. During his tenure individual ships or squadrons had felt the need and made the hadj, but *Rifkin's Dream* had sailed on, remaining with the fleet as it crawled from bank to bank. It had been twenty-five years since the vessel had gone.

"The whole fleet. We need the luck. Two disasters in one year… It's time."

Landing's special significance hadn't attained religious standing but some superstition had attached itself, encouraged by the augurs. To maintain their birthluck, all Children of the Sky were encouraged to visit the Ship every few years.

The reason, the Earthman had suggested, was so the augurs at the Ship could gather information from scattered sources, collate it, and disseminate it again.

The Earthman, Rickli reflected, had a lot of strange ideas about the Children of the Sky. He supposed that was the alien viewpoint. Whatever, Thomas was eager to reach Landing.

If anything, the encounter with Grossfenaja had ripened and mellowed their relationship. The Earthman now shared more of his alien thoughts.

While crossing the Finneran Bank, the traditional boundary between seas well-known and the frontier waters the fleet generally cruised, just a week's fast sail from Landing, Rickli said, "Thomas, you've never told us why you're here. Something must've brought you."

The sun had set an hour before. The bright jewels of the galaxy winked down as they began their migration toward dawn. *Rifkin's Dream* had settled into the long, lonely silence of night, whispering and creaking to herself, but telling few stories to listening ears. The passage of ships excited bioluminescent plankton in the shallows, scrawling pale stripes across the quiet sea. Hakim stared at the stars, at the constellation the sea people called the Spiderfish, for a long time.

"I don't know, Rickli," he said at last. "Why *does* a man leave home? I thought I knew then. Somehow, from here, it doesn't seem all that important."

"Was it so wicked a thing?" Rickli knew he had touched a nerve with the initial question. When Thomas stayed awake to watch the Spiderfish, he was feeling homesick. That much Rickli knew for sure about the Earthman.

Hakim frowned to him, his expression barely visible in the starlight. Afraid he had overstepped, Rickli turned to survey the running lights of nearby ships. Night sailing could be tricky.

Quiet Sea

"Some thought so. You wouldn't comprehend. The survival imperatives are different. Here, you all live in the same environment and culture." He pointed upward. "There's a fleet, the greatest of them all. Every ship is as far from its neighbor as we are from any of them. Some are big, some small, some strong, some weak. Like the fishes of the sea. Here, there're warm shallows where the living is easy and the fish get along, then the cold deeps, and in them things that get hungry, that sometimes surface, like Grossfenaja…"

Rickli wasn't sure he followed, unless the Earthman meant that some of his people preyed on others. "You mean like the pirate ship in the Saga of Wilga Stone-cipher?"

"Eh? Oh. Yes, I suppose so. In any case, men Outside sometimes go after other men the way chasers pursue brunwhal."

He went silent, continued staring at the Spiderfish.

Rickli knew he had pushed as far as he dared, yet couldn't resist asking, "Would you go back now? If you had the chance?"

Hakim studied him a moment, looked back to the sky, said nothing. Rickli shrugged, surveyed the fleet again.

Thomas had been thinking about it, he knew. The man couldn't help it, no more than he could help thinking about serving in chasers, despite LaFata. The Earthman was crippled too. It just wasn't anything as obvious as a missing leg. Perhaps it could be called a broken heartline home.

Landing, for those who had never seen it, appeared on the horizon as the most outstanding anomaly of the sea, a great hump rising from the water like the back of some mythologically huge brunwhal.

"That's the Ship," Rickli told the Shipwrecked Earthman, when the thing finally became visible from helm level. Excited crewmen had been scampering up and down the rigging for hours. But not Hakim. He had a positive terror of heights.

Strange, for a man who flew between the stars.

"Jesus, how'd they bring her down in one piece?"

"They didn't, really." Rickli scanned the fleet. By now, every vessel had hoisted at least one black sail. Some looked like the dark birds of death Hakim had called them. The chaser crews were getting impatient, waiting for Weatherhead's permission to begin their race to the ancient wreck. "That's why we're still here."

The vessel had been built at the close of Old Earth's Twenty-second Century, equipped with crude hyper generators, to take out certain political favorites before an anticipated collapse of civilization. Almost two kilometers long, she had never been meant to enter atmosphere. Rickli was unsure of the circumstances that had brought her to, and had forced her landing upon, Quiet Sea. Only the augurs knew. He cared only that it had been managed and that his ancestors had survived.

Thomas cared, mostly from curiosity, but could get no more from Rickli.

"Ask the augurs when we get there," Manlove kept telling him. "They'll spend a month talking to anyone willing to listen."

He thought he understood Thomas's interest. The Ship was the nearest a connection Outside as existed on Quiet Sea. A hopeless, centuries-out-of-date connection but certainly something more concrete than shared specieshood.

Outsiders, judging by Hakim, set great store by artifacts and possessions. The Earthman still, at times, mourned some small item lost when his ship had been looted.

Rickli had spread the word among the captains, but little had turned up. Everything convertible had long since been made into something useful.

Weatherhead released the chasers. With a strong following breeze they were soon dwindling in their race to the hump.

"You really miss it that much?" the Earthman asked.

Rickli smiled. "It shows? I think it's just not being able. It was my life, you know."

"I understand." Thomas glanced at the sky. "Those old-timers had guts. People out there nowadays, in their shoes, would just give up."

"It was a chosen crew. They knew they couldn't go back before they started."

"A definite advantage. None of us can, but few of us realize it." After a pause: "You know, I think what I miss most, more than land, is birds.

Quiet Sea

They were always a symbol of freedom." His expression became faraway. Rickli reached out and, for an instant, let his hand rest lightly on the Earthman's shoulder.

Thomas had told him a dozen times that his fellows would not be coming to rescue him. They had had no idea where to look.

It was almost dark when *Rifkin's Dream* dropped her stone anchors. In the morning she would move to one of the stone quays whiskering the dry land the Children of the Sky had built around their Ship.

"Seems to me," said the Earthman, gazing at the island that had taken centuries to create, "that it would've been easier to poulder. More land for less fill."

Rickli had to have it explained. Thomas told him about dikes and sub-sea-level land recovery.

"Suggest it to the augurs. They might be interested."

"I'm not sure I want to go anymore." Hakim nervously caressed his talisman. Since his narrow escape, he had kept it with him always.

Rickli smiled. Of course he would go, just as he himself would visit a chaser if invited. Every man tried to mend his heartlines.

"They've made a lot of headway since I was here last," Rickli said the following morning, as *Rifkin's Dream* warped in to a low stone pier. "They've doubled the land area. They didn't used to work that hard at it."

The Earthman observed without comment. Several vessels were already off-loading ballast to be added to the fill. The Ship itself was completely surrounded. Curious sea people were looking it over, some lining up at an open hatchway for an interior tour.

"Rickli, it sounds defeatist, but why bother? You seem to have adapted."

"We did without for centuries. It was just a dream thing. Ships would come on pilgrimage and everyone would bring a stone as a symbolic gift. They piled up. Then the augurs built a little sawmill on the pile. It made cutting sandweg so much easier that people started thinking it might be handy to have an island just for that. So they started bringing bigger loads of stone. Didn't push it, though, because they were used to doing things the old way. Then the augurs built a bigger sawmill, that handled about half the sandweg used in the fleets, and a smelter where they turned out almost a tonne of metal a month."

He took out the knife that, with the captaincy, he had inherited from Dymon Tipsword. "This's a genuine Wintermantel. Better than anything they make here, but it took the man a month, sometimes, to make one blade."

Hakim laughed sourly. "The glories of industrialization."

"It's so bad? Look there. Places where they can take a ship out of the water for repairs. And ways where they can build a ship in a tenth the time it takes at sea, with a quarter of the men."

"No. I'm a cynic. What're those buildings down there? Beyond the drydocks and shipyard."

"I don't know. They're new. Must be important, though. That's a lot of sandweg to hold out of ship construction."

"Uhm. Curious."

It wasn't till later that Rickli realized he had missed the specific that had caught the Earthman's eye. The buildings had glass windows. Hundreds of them, especially on top.

Partial starts on other buildings lay scattered over the manmade island. The augurs seemed to have a big program in mind. Rickli frowned. Providing the materials cost the fleets time and materials they could use themselves. He didn't understand. Unless there were rewards worth the cost, as with the sawmill and smelters.

Thomas didn't know what he wanted. Sometimes he would start for the pier, then would pace, then would return to wait till Rickli had fulfilled his duties. Then he would grow impatient again, only to repeat the cycle.

At last Rickli felt able to go. He left the ship to the duty section and, with Thomas's help, slowly advanced up the pier. He felt uncomfortable, naked, defenseless, so wide had the world expanded. And he felt dizzy. For the first time in a decade he was on footing that did not sway and roll with the restlessness of the sea.

"This isn't going to cut it," said Thomas. "I'm going to make those crutches."

Quiet Sea

They had argued about it before. Rickli didn't want them. But practicality began to alter his mindset.

"Where're you going?" he asked. Hakim was turning right, away from the rusty mountain of the Ship.

"I want to look at something." But they never reached the windowed buildings. Rickli's leg bothered him too much. At his request they paused to rest in the shade of an oddly designed hull in the last stages of construction.

The Earthman studied it, finally asked, "How much glass do they make here, Rickli?"

He shrugged. "Things have changed. Used to be just a little, from bottom sand, for special bottles and trinkets."

"Hand-blown?" Thomas ran his fingers over the smooth seamless hull.

"Never saw it done any other way." He, too, studied the strange vessel. So much metal had gone into its construction. Surely the augurs wouldn't be so wasteful. "Is something wrong?"

"I don't know. This isn't my native sea. But there's something odd here, something that makes me feel the way I did just before the Grossfenaja surfaced." He caressed his talisman, which protruded from the waistband of his trousers. Perhaps because he was in a suggestible mood, or because he was uncomfortable ashore, Rickli began to feel it too. "Let's go back to the ship. You make those crutches, and we'll poke around later."

"Crutches? Oh, yes." He helped Rickli up, saying, "Maybe you should think about a wooden leg."

"A *what?*"

By way of explanation, Thomas told him a decidedly fishy tale about an ancient seaman named Long John Silver. The idea intrigued Rickli. Though the notion wasn't unique, it hadn't occurred to him in relation to himself. He had encountered few men who'd had to cope with being an amputee. The state of medicine was such that few men ever survived such operations.

Returning, they encountered acquaintances from *Replete*, who, in good humor, offered to carry Rickli back to *Rifkin's Dream*, although the ship was out of their way. It seemed they hoped his luck would rub off. Though it hurt his pride, he accepted. His remaining leg hurt more.

As they moved down the pier, Hakim asked one of the women, "May I see your knife?" A shiny new fishknife protruded from her waistband.

Grinning, "Sure. The augurs are trading them for sandweg." Less cheerfully: "After Pimental, we're overstocked."

Rickli thought the Earthman would never stop turning the blade, examining its grip, thumbing its edge. Finally: "Rickli, can I see yours?"

The sailors, now puzzled, released him so he could hand Thomas the knife. It was one of only a dozen iron blades to be found aboard *Rifkin's Dream*. "Forged by Aulgur Wintermantel himself," he told the others. The smith, though a century dead, was still a legend.

The Earthman placed Rickli's knife back down on pier stone, suddenly swung the other so that their edges met sharply.

"Thomas!"

Ilyana's women growled angrily.

Hakim held the blades up for all to see. Rickli's had been deeply notched, the other nicked imperceptibly.

"A genuine Wintermantel?" the new blade's owner asked, her anger fading as she saw the quality of her knife. "Really?"

"Yes." Rickli was dumfounded. His edge should have damaged the other.

As the sailors drifted away, talking excitedly of further trades, Hakim said, "You may get an answer to the question you asked the other night." He didn't apologize for damaging the Wintermantel. He seemed terribly upset.

Rickli let it ride till they were comfortably back aboard, observing ship and Ship from the captain's station. The Earthman stared into the distance and caressed his talisman.

"What is it, Thomas? What's wrong?"

"I'm not sure. The knife. The finish on that hull. The glass-topped buildings. But especially the knife."

"Why? It was a good one."

"Exactly. Too good, don't care what the augurs have been doing, they couldn't have made that knife. That was a machined blade, an Outside

Quiet Sea

blade. The question is, did it come with the Ship?" After a glance toward the strange buildings, "I'm afraid of the answer."

Rickli made the intuitive leap. "You think the augurs are in touch with your people?"

"Not mine, Rickli. Not mine."

"Ah, so. The enemy. Your Fenaja."

Hakim took the talisman from his waistband, peered down its long axis.

"Grossfenaja." One word. But still he wouldn't elaborate.

"Your enemies are mine. Twice you've honored my life."

"So it goes," Hakim murmured to himself, the ancient acceptance of fate characteristic of Children of the Sky. "No. They're merciless. They'd destroy you all if I dragged you in. If they're really here."

Now Rickli said, "So it goes. If they're that kind of people, then they *should* be enemies."

"Stay out of it, Rickli. Stay out. I'll try to avoid them. Yes. That's best. If they don't know I'm here, they won't bother anybody. I'll just stay aboard till you put to sea again. I'll decide what to do when you're ready to cast off."

But the wills of Fate and the Shipwrecked Earthman weren't in concert. Shortly, Rickli said, "What's this?" indicating a group coming down the pier. "Ship augurs."

A youth ran up, announced, "Augurs Blackcraft and Homewood request permission to board, sir."

"Granted." To Thomas, "The top people. Must've heard about the Grossfenaja."

"Uhm." Hakim was not convinced.

The augurs were old, and some disabled. The lore mastery was reserved to those no longer able to cope with the sea. Though the whole party boarded, only Blackcraft and Homewood, male and female, approached the captain's station. Both eyed the Earthman.

"Greetings," said Homewood, her voice surprisingly youthful. "It's been long since Landing was honored by *Rifkin's Dream.*

"And longer since *Dream* was graced by the presence of an elder augur." Rickli decided he should try to put them on the defensive.

Their eyes kept drifting to Thomas.

"We hear some strange things have befallen in the interim." Blackcraft seemed strangely wary. "The years drift past, the ships come in, and sailors tell their tales. Some were hard to credit."

"No doubt. The young embellish with drama. A Saga grows from ordinary events."

"So it goes."

"Yet these tales seemed no rigging boy's daydream," said Homewood, looking directly at the Earthman.

"How can we judge the truth of sea stories?"

"Never mind the fencing, Rickli," said Hakim. To the augurs: "What do you want?"

"You're the Shipwrecked Earthman?"

"What do you want?"

"Are you the man called Thomas Hakim?"

"What do you want?"

"You must come with us."

"No," said Rickli. "Thomas is restricted to ship."

They were growing irritated. Blackcraft grumbled, "Captain, these are matters beyond you. And I remind you, you're no longer at sea."

"An oversight that can be corrected with a word."

"Tell your masters," said the Earthman, "that if they want me, they'll have to come see me themselves."

"Masters?"

"The Outsiders. The Sangaree. The people who sent you here. The people who have been giving you Outside goods in return for use of Landing. You probably think they've done well by you. But you've been cheated. Terribly. You don't know them, don't know what they are. Tell them that if they want Thomas Hakim, they'll have to meet him before the Children of the Sky. You'll learn."

They could see Thomas was immovable. Homewood bowed slightly. "So it goes." She and Blackwood rejoined their deputation. Soon one of the lesser augurs was hurrying up the pier.

Quiet Sea

"Ah." The Earthman chuckled nervously. "I was right. But I was only guessing."

"What's it all about, Thomas?" Rickli asked.

"My enemies are here. But they're not sure who I am." After a time: "You should have stayed out of it."

Rickli shrugged. "You're my friend. You were my right hand at Pimental." From the captain's equipment rack he took a shell-horn. "You're one of our own now." He blew recall.

Stunned silence settled over Landing. Then sea people were everywhere, running. Before the Earthman could protest, Rickli had had danger pennons run to the main and had instructed the armorer to fill the weapons racks. By ones, twos, and threes, crewmen came running aboard, battering the augurs in their haste to reach their stations.

"You're a fool, Rickli Manlove. This isn't your fight." But the Earthman wore a smile.

"Maybe. Stay out of the way till I get muster."

Other vessels, too, began readying weapons and sail. The chaos on Landing diminished as crews found their ways to their ships.

Through the confusion came a wedge of five tall men in outlandish clothing. Rickli stared. They were heavier than his people, more muscular. Even from a distance he could see that there was no humor in their faces.

"These are your enemies?" he asked.

"Some of them. Watch the little one. The one who seems the least. He's their leader, Gaab w'Telle. There're blood debts between us. I'll keep out of sight." He slipped down into the galley.

Rickli called his armorer.

The five came aboard as if they owned *Rifkin's Dream*. Their not having asked permission aggravated Rickli's predisposition to dislike them. The light one spoke with Homewood and Blackcraft, then came aft. All five had hard, dark eyes. Fenaja eyes.

"Where is he?" Telle asked. He glanced speculatively at Rickli's stump. Quiet as death, with an expression as grim, Thomas slipped from the galley, his talisman in hand. He nodded.

"Right behind you," Rickli replied.

They turned. The leader went pale. "You!"

"Of course. I take some killing. How's the universe been treating you, Telle? Not well, I hope."

"But..."

"As a writer once said, the reports of my death were exaggerated. You didn't send enough shooters."

So, thought Rickli, this was the man who had tried to kill Thomas. He signaled his armorer. Crewmen began selecting weapons.

Men of Quiet Sea almost never used weapons against one another. Rickli doubted his men could now. But maybe the Outsiders wouldn't recognize the bluff.

"I'll make sure this time. This's one operation you're not going to wreck." He didn't seem impressed by the martial display.

Thomas pointed his talisman.

The leader laughed. "Bluffing with a dead lasepistol, von Rhor? Six years old? Gotta. Take him."

One man took one step.

There was a dazzling flash. The man fell, steam twisting from a small black hole in his back.

Pandemonium. Crewmen scattered. The augurs fled to the bows. The tableau of confrontation remained a tense pocket of false calm amidst the confusion.

Telle and his men seemed stricken. And Thomas, too, as though he could neither believe what he had done nor that his weapon had actually functioned.

Rickli took his ivory-gripped harpoon from the captain's equipment rack. A great calm, like that of the last moment before the cast from a racing chaser's sprit, descended upon him. The sight of one man killing another had not shaken him as much as he thought it should. Maybe he would react later, after the tension had passed.

"Six years, Telle. Six years I've sailed the quiet sea, without a hope, yet cherishing this thing. My only regret had been that you were still alive, that I'd failed and you were still peddling your death dust.

Quiet Sea

"I don't expect to live through this. I tried to avoid it because it'll cost these good people. The augurs think you're benefactors; yet you're raising the drug right in their front yard. When I die, you'll carry the candle to light my way into Hell."

"Spoken like a true hero," Telle sneered. But most of his arrogance had faded.

"Rickli," said the Earthman. "A favor."

"Anything, Thomas."

"Have them stripped. Move the shooters forward."

"Thomas?" Telle asked. "What happened to Nicholas von Rhor?"

"Don't mean anything here, Telle. And just between us, that's not it either." The bodyguards moved away. "Actually, it's Soren Deatherage."

"The Hell Stars!"

"Yes."

Rickli did not understand the exchange, but the winds of hatred blowing between the men made it clear they had hurt one another deeply and often. Maybe Thomas would explain later. But he doubted it. He had learned more about Hakim in the past ten minutes than in all the years before.

Thomas handed his talisman to the armorer, began shedding his own clothing.

Rickli had never seen Thomas unclothed. Now he frowned. The Earthman was older than he had suspected. His body hair was heavily salted with grey.

"In the fleets we settle personal disputes by wrestling," said Hakim. "Man to man, Telle. I'll be thinking about what you did to my wife."

A smile ghosted across Telle's thin lips. "Then I'll remember Karamar and the Hell Stars." With a swiftness that stunned Rickli, he attacked.

Thomas was lighter, shorter. All the disadvantages seemed his. Yet he held his own.

He moved as suddenly as Telle, throwing an open-handed finger punch Rickli was unable to follow. Telle blocked with a forearm as he whipped past, flicked a kick at Hakim's groin. Thomas took it on his thigh, unleashed a kick of his own that connected with the back of Telle's pivotal knee as he turned. Telle went down. As he did, he caught Thomas's foot and dragged the smaller man with him. They rolled across the deck, kneeing, gouging, biting, then bounced up, and squared off. They traded feints and counterfeints, almost too subtle for Rickli to follow.

This, he thought, was another new facet of Hakim. The style of fighting was quick and deadly. He was glad Thomas hadn't lost his temper under the heavy needling of his first few years aboard. He might not be able to work ship, but he could kill.

The fighters came together in a flurry of punches and kicks. Then Hakim was on the deck, bleeding from one cheek. Telle circled him warily while Thomas awaited a chance to regain his feet.

Thomas seemed less practiced and clearly had less stamina than his opponent. Rickli worried.

Hakim suddenly seemed to do three things at once, reversing their positions. Now he circled cautiously while Telle awaited a chance to rise.

It went on and on, time weighing ever more heavily on the Earthman. He was getting slower. Telle began moving with more confidence.

The larger man suddenly moved in, forcing a contest of strength. For long minutes the two strained in one another's grasp; then there was a loud crack. Thomas gasped. His left arm went slack. Telle stepped back with a look of satisfaction—and Thomas loosed a kick that destroyed his knee as thoroughly as the Fenaja harpoon had destroyed Rickli's.

Telle went down with an expression of pained surprise.

Holding his broken arm with his good hand, Thomas circled, waiting to kick again.

Telle seized an ax from a nearby weapons rack, threw. Thomas dodged, but not fast enough. The blade opened a gash on the outside of his left thigh. He fell, his blood staining the deck. He tried to rise, groaned, fell back, dragged himself to the mizzenmast, placed his back to it.

Telle pulled a sword from the rack, crawled toward the Earthman.

"Thomas! Thomas Hakim!" The Shipwrecked Earth looked Rickli's way. Manlove threw the ivory-gripped harpoon.

It slapped Thomas's hand. He held on.

Quiet Sea

Crossing the Finneran Bank by night again, Rickli Manlove peered at the Spiderfish. Unnatural stars had been blooming there since before sundown. Thomas's people had come searching for their enemies. Hakim's message, sent on Telle's Landing equipment, had gotten through.

Quiet Sea would never be the same.

Rickli thought of Hakim's talisman, of the battle, and of Outside as Thomas had described it. *Rifkin's Dream* had departed Landing. He wondered if, knowing of those things, the augurs would have pulled the Earthman from the sea six years ago.

Too late now.

"So it goes," he murmured, surveying the running lights of the fleet. "When the grunling aren't running, the blackfin are."

Changes due or no, there was work to be done. Fish to be caught, sandweg to be harvested, Fenaja to be fought, stone to be transported to Landing. He had enough to concern him here on the quiet sea.

Darkwar

1

Three figures glided through an empty night street. Moonlight twinkled off the medals and tunic buttons of the tallest. There was a gentle tinkle as she moved. The smaller two made no sound at all. They were silth sisters, sorceresses, trained to the ways of the dark. The tall female, Kerath Hadon, knew that they trailed her only because she had asked them to do so.

A remote flash brightened the quiet street. Kerath glanced up. For a moment she saw only three moons. The smallest had an orbital motion perceptible to the eye.

Razor slashes of coherent light ripped the velvet sky, come and gone so fast she actually saw only afterimages. "Another strike at *Frostflyer* and *Dreamkeeper*," Kerath said.

Her companions said nothing. One may have nodded. These silth wasted no words. Kerath shivered. They spooked her. "Come. Let's get this done while we still have a few ships left."

A series of flashes illuminated the city, revealing crumbling old walls recently whitewashed in defiance of the doom overhanging the Meth homeworld, filling gothic aches with shadows, silhouetting distant onion domes. Kerath snarled, "Suslov is serious tonight. Here." She tapped a sagging door. It opened. A gray-whiskered male poked his muzzle into the rippling light, his eyes flashing golden.

"You?"

"Yes, it's me, Shadar. Wouldn't you know it? Is the High Lord here?"

"Waiting impatiently, Marshall. Off the street before you're seen."

Kerath pushed inside. Her shadows followed, two dark ghosts. Shadar led them through two rooms, to the foot of a stair. "Up there. Kerath? Marshall? Good luck."

"No luck involved, Shadar. Strictly fiat. But thank you." She touched his hand gently.

A moment later she stood in the doorway of a brightly lighted room. A half-dozen males with gray whiskers and ragged fur stared at her with tight eyes and tighter lips. Kerath flashed teeth. Folgar suspected. She stepped inside. "I thought this would be private, High Lord."

The eldest male flexed muscles still powerful despite gnawing age. "The circumstances suggested some unpleasant possibilities. You'll understand my urge to include reliable witnesses, Marshall." His teeth showed mockingly.

Kerath's ears tilted forward and down, the Meth equivalent of a sneer. The presence of his henchmen would do Folgar no good. "You and your packmates have destroyed the Meth, High Lord. The people are sick of alien ways, and even more sick of endless defeat." Kerath gestured toward the doorway. "The Meth might welcome the return of old ways."

A low rumble started deep in a half-dozen throats, an unconscious warning sound from males who saw their territories threatened. "Why are those silth witches here?" one demanded.

"Marshall?" Folgar asked. He concealed his emotions well for a male.

Kerath drew herself to her straightest. She knew she made an imposing figure, a hero of the Meth, well marked with medals and scars. She even wore the white cuff badge of Snow-No-More, a defeat that fewer than a hundred Meth had survived. "For three generations your all-male party has held the power, High Lord. What have you done with it? You have harried the silth. Slain their greatest. And you have made the Meth

Darkwar

into bumbling imitations of the humans you admire." She had rehearsed the message often, but her delivery was not going well. She did not *feel* it.

Folgar nodded. "To the point, Marshall. The Command had something in mind when they sent you."

Kerath would not be hurried. "You set aside the old ways, the old truths, the old knowledge. You made mock of millennia of tradition. You made the Meth a reflection of Man. Then you tried to usurp the humans. What has it profited you? What has it gained the Meth?"

Folgar stared stonily. His companions watched the silth warily, frightened, as if faced by something returned from the grave.

"Our worlds are lost. Our greatest warships are debris scattered among the stars. Our best fighters lie in iron coffins far in the bitter cold of the deep. We retain only that speck of space inside Biter's orbit. *Frostflyer* and *Dreamkeeper* are our last heavy ships. We have become prisoners upon our homeworld, awaiting the fall of a monstrous hammer. We are helpless to turn away the asteroid Suslov sends to shatter our world."

"He won't bring it all the way in," Folgar countered.

"He will if he must. I know Pyotr Suslov, High Lord. He doesn't bluff. But, of course, your contention is correct insofar as you know. You have been arranging a secret surrender."

Folgar's ears flicked in surprise.

"The Command knows." Kerath did not conceal her contempt. "Male treachery. It's always with us. You started this war, and now you mean to sell the Meth simply so you can retain power when the fighting stops."

"Now Marshall…"

"The Meth would drink your blood if they saw the Command's tapes of your communications with Suslov."

"Are you threatening me, Marshall?"

"This is the message from the Command. There will be no surrender. The Meth will die as they have always lived: without dishonor. If the asteroid cannot be turned, so be it. May the All forfend."

"Marshall—" Folgar's ears were back now, in fighting position.

"The Command will take appropriate steps if you have any further contact with Suslov."

"This is rebellion."

Kerath admitted it. "The Armed Force is the source of all power, Folgar. It no longer supports you. It is assuming direction of the war effort."

"Why are *they* with you?" Loathing and hatred edged Folgar's voice as he indicated the silth.

"We fought your way, the way that imitates humans. We failed. Now we turn to the ways of our foremothers."

The old males growled. A chair overturned. Someone dropped a bottle. The stink of male fear filled the room.

"Darkwar?" Folgar asked.

"Darkwar."

"But the old darkships were scrapped. Nor are there trained silth crews anymore."

Kerath revealed the points of her teeth. "Wrong on both counts. The silth have ships you never found. The legendary Ceremony darkships. And sisters who escaped your hunters. End of message from the Command."

Folgar growled, but there was a touch of fear in his defiance.

Kerath turned away. "Come," she told the silth.

Shadar awaited her at the foot of the stair. "You did well."

Kerath nodded. "I thought so."

"Good luck again, Marshall." Shadar touched her arm.

Kerath paused to hug the Meth who had sired her, before pushing into the street.

The sky was quiet. The orbital skirmish had ended. *Frostflyer* and *Dreamkeeper* still radiated the glow of active energy screens. They had survived again.

2

Kerath was uneasy in the company of the silth, though she concealed it well. Her adult life had run in tracks prescribed by Folgar's ilk. These

Darkwar

sorceresses were anachronisms, shadows of ideas long outdated. Facing down Folgar's scruffy pack was one thing; believing that the Command was doing right was another.

She pushed off a bulkhead, floated across the lighter's cabin, checked the harnesses of her companions. "Rendezvous with *Dreamkeeper* in fifteen minutes." They looked at her with fathomless eyes, saying nothing.

They were so young to be so spooky. They never spoke. That was unnerving. But they had to be good. Littermates, they had been chosen Mistresses of the Ships over any others of the surviving silth. It was said they were as filled with the dark strength as the great silth of old, when darkwar decided the destiny of the Meth.

Did the Command want those grim days to return from shadow? Folgar was a fool, yes, but he was right when he claimed the Meth were better off for having shed the yoke of the silth.

Docking alarm sounded. Overhead speakers relayed crisp instructions. The crew was trying to impress the oncoming Marshall.

Kerath needed no impressing. *Dreamkeeper* sprang from the same core of honor as she. The ship was a survivor.

She released her charges. "Follow me."

An honor guard waited aboard the warship. Kerath accepted their accolade but told the ship's commander, "Don't waste any more energy on protocol. My companions are cargo, and I don't need it."

"As you will, Marshall. Let me show you to your quarters."

"Have the other personnel arrived?"

The commander glanced back. The silth stalked them like wicked shadows. The boots of Kerath and the commander rang on the gray-painted steel decks. The two in black seemed to glide a whisker above the plating. "They're here. Have you noticed the quiet?"

"I noted a distinct lack of curiosity."

"The crew is staying out of the way. The first group distressed them. Now you bring Mistresses of the Ships. "They're frightened."

Kerath showed a glimpse of teeth. "They have cause, Commander. *I* wouldn't be here had I not been directed."

"When you were a whelp, did they tell you tales about the grauken?"

"Did they? My older brothers tried to convince our litter that he lived under our bed." The grauken was a shape-changing night monster fond of delicate young flesh, an archetype born during primitive winters, when desperate packs resorted to cannibalism to survive, luring or capturing the young of other packs.

"Seeing the silth aboard my ship gives me the feeling I'd have if I did find the grauken under my bed."

"I know," Kerath said. "How well I know."

"These are our guests' quarters," the commander said, halting before a door. He tapped. The door slid open a crack. "Sisters?" He indicated the two figures in black.

Kerath caught a glimpse of the cabin as the two entered. The darkness was barely broken by red light. Shapes in black sat motionless. A terrible bittersweet odor rolled out, offending Kerath's nostrils.

The door clumped shut.

"The grauken's den," the commander observed. "They're calling it that already. I hope the Command knows what it's doing."

"So do I, Commander. So do I. I don't think I could go on if I thought my efforts would facilitate a silth rebirth."

"Nor I. I suppose we must have faith that the Command can neutralize them once they have served their purpose."

"Are we ready to space?"

"Programmed for jump. *Frostflyer* should be moving up to cover our drive ports. Whenever you give the order, Marshall."

"Then show me my quarters. I'll shift uniforms and join you on the bridge."

3

"Ready on *Frostflyer*, Marshall."

"Ready here, Marshall," the ship's commander said.

Darkwar

Kerath stared into the situation display tank. The humans were shifting their dispositions. Suslov had noted *Frostflyer*'s change of station. "They anticipate a strike at the asteroid."

"As they would say, it's in the cards," the commander replied. "They would see that as our only remaining option."

"A weak one, though. If we reshape the collision orbit, they'll just warp another hunk of rock into the same groove."

"In that light, what we're doing here doesn't make much sense either."

"No. I suspect the Command just wants to scare them into backing off." Kerath studied the proposed track of the warship. It feinted toward the incoming asteroid, then curved out of the system. "It should work. They should be rushing one way while we jump the other."

"And then what?"

"It's hoped they'll assume we've been sent out as commerce raiders. If we shake loose, they'll concentrate on guarding their shipping lanes."

"That's the book?"

Kerath revealed a little tooth. "That's the book. Let's hope Pyotr Suslov buys it. Go when ready, Commander."

It looked book for awhile. But when *Frostflyer* and *Dreamkeeper* turned, human warships responded immediately. Kerath studied the tank. "Two main battles and a heavy chaser. Suslov hedged his bets." She turned suddenly, sensing a difference, a change of energy in the air.

Two silth had come onto the narrow balcony overlooking the fighting bridge: the two she had brought aboard. They remained out of the way, observing, but their chill filled the compartment.

"Coming up to first jump," the commander said. "And two. And one. And jump." The tank blanked. The fringes of the universe folded in. Bulkheads melted and crawled. Meth wavered like dancing flames. Kerath glanced at the silth. *They* remained rocks of blackness.

Real space clicked into place.

The tank began to assemble a portrait from data retrieved by the ship's exterior sensors. "*Frostflyer* is with us, right on station."

Kerath stared into the tank, watching starpoints wink into being, willing it not to show anything red.

"One counter. Two counter. Three counter. They stayed with us, Marshall."

"I see them, Commander. Next jump."

The stars changed thrice more. Three times the human trackers came through behind them. "They're good," Kerath observed. "Really good."

"Suggestions, Marshall?"

"They were ragged that go. The chaser was a half-minute late. Perhaps it's a cumulative error."

"We have only four jumps to shake them, Marshall."

"Continue, Commander."

Next jump the humans translated even more raggedly, arriving over a span of a full minute. Kerath sighed. Time to act. "Commander, Mission Officer to *Frostflyer*. Turn and attack after next drop. Lead them away. Head for home the long way."

The commander stared at her for several seconds before relaying the order.

The ships jumped, and dropped. *Frostflyer* charged toward where the humans were expected to appear. Kerath glared at the tank.

The first human ship appeared directly in *Frostflyer*'s path. The tank showed a great deal of weaponry action.

A second ship dropped. And then the first vanished.

"Ha!" a tech cried. "Got one!"

"Or it jumped out," Kerath whispered to herself, watching *Frostflyer* curve toward the newcomer.

The chaser arrived as the commander ordered the next jump. When translation was complete, Kerath suggested, "Hold the next jump. Let's see if they come through after us. Better to fight them here than around the target."

The commander observed, "It won't much matter now, will it? They've followed long enough to know we're not headed toward any commerce lane. If they bring in a fleet on our line of flight…"

Darkwar

"But it'll take days, or even weeks, to find us. That should be time enough."

Nothing appeared on *Dreamkeeper*'s backtrail. After waiting an hour, Kerath ordered the journey resumed.

Much, much later, as the ship cruised that section of space approximating its destination, she directed, "Secure to quarters, Commander. Standard watches. We'll begin searching after we've rested."

"Very well, Marshall."

The silth were at the hatchway when Kerath departed. She thought their eyes looked feverish in the subdued lighting. She nodded greeting and started to slip past.

A hand touched her elbow. She stopped as if she had encountered an iron bar. A whisper said, "The steel ship, *Frostflyer*, is no more. Two alien ships lighted its path into darkness. The third is injured. It limps back to its base. We tell you, that those with kin aboard *Frostflyer* might begin mourning in timely fashion."

"Yes. Thank you." Kerath shook off the staying hand and rushed to her quarters. For half an hour she sat rubbing fingers over her personal sidearm. The action had a calming effect.

She had ordered *Frostflyer*, half the fleet-in-being, half the surviving might of the Meth, to its death.

Her sleep was filled with terrible dreams, haunted by dry, withered old bitches flying on black wings. Last hope of the Meth. The Command had given its trust into the wrong hands.

4

"Coming up now, Commander."

Kerath and the ship's commander leaned over a vidtech's shoulders, peering into her screen. "Searchlights," the commander ordered.

Immediately something flashed out in the darkness. "There," Kerath gasped. "More light."

Several lights concentrated on the target. Gradually, parts became visible.

"Darkship," the commander breathed. "They really still exist. The Ceremony legend is true."

Kerath nodded, unable to avert her gaze from that ghost out of the far past, when disputes between silth sisterhoods were settled by combats between Mistresses of the Ships far in the black heart of space. The darkship didn't look like a ship at all, just a giant titanium girderwork dagger marked with mysterious symbols.

The darkship sprang from an era when sisterhoods formed associations human translators still confused with nations, corporations, and even families. The competition for control of the wealth of the stars had been savage, till silth-run merchants had encountered humans, with their contagious alien ways and unshakable disbelief. The ensuing confusion among the silth had allowed their overthrow, and hatred of their long tyranny had led to merciless slaughter, witchhunts that persisted yet, and over-reactive tilts toward the new human ideas.

"It needs a lot of repair," the commander observed.

"Supposed to be twelve of them," Kerath replied. "The legend is, they chose to meet and die a ritual death here rather than go home and submit to the will of the new order. We'll choose the best preserved."

The silth had other ideas. They wanted to locate specific ships.

"The spells of our foremothers guard them still," said the one who did the talking. "Only those two will be accessible to us."

Kerath frowned. That might mean troublesome delays. "You're the experts," she said, grudging them every extra minute.

Two days went into locating the right ships. They had drifted apart over the centuries. One of the two had sustained considerable damage.

Kerath worried. Suslov would be on the hunt. She did not want to waste time making repairs. The silth ignored her protests. They led their shadowy sisters out and went to work. There was nothing Kerath could do to hurry or help them, or to alter their perception of the way things should be done.

Darkwar

Kerath was sleeping when an orderly came with the commander's request that she join her on the bridge.

"Thought you'd want to see this, Marshall." The commander indicated a screen. "They've got one moving. There's not a hint of drive, but it's moving."

Kerath surveyed the detection boards. The commander was right. The darkship appeared only on visual and radar. She stared at the titanium dagger. It was receding toward distant stars. A vague glow surrounded it. "She's getting the feel of it. The old stories say they glowed too brightly to look at."

The commander nodded. Then she gasped, "Where did it go? Radar. Where is that target?"

"Gone, Commander. I'm not getting anything... Wait. Here it is. Nadir, thirty-five degrees, range fifteen."

Kerath exchanged glances with the commander. "Through the Up-and-Over," she murmured. "She's found her demons."

"So that's true too." The commander looked frightened. "Witches. You know, I didn't really believe this before."

Kerath stared at the empty screen. "I didn't either, Commander. Not down deep in my heart." She began to grow a little frightened too.

5

Fifth day on station. The second darkship had completed repairs. Both crews were outside learning to handle their ships. Kerath thought practice seemed unnecessary. "They appear to have been born to it," she said.

The commander growled, "They are, aren't they?"

Kerath's ears tilted slightly, expressing mild amusement. The silth claimed to possess the memories of all their foremothers. Watching these sisters ride their darkships, she was inclined to discard former doubts.

"Do they have names?" the commander asked.

"The silth? I don't know. I see. You can't keep them straight. Neither can I."

"One is faster than the other. I'd like some way to differentiate before we go into rehearsal."

Kerath's hackles rose slightly. She checked the time. In half an hour she would be out there herself, riding a darkship during the first mock attack. *Dreamkeeper* would play alien, its technicians searching for weaknesses Suslov could exploit.

Kerath was not sure why she was going out. An observer run was not essential to her mission. But she had been invited by the Mistresses of the Ships. Acceptance seemed politic.

Fear stalked her like a shadow that disappeared when she turned, like the grauken sliding out from under the far side of the bed as she bent down to look for it. The silth had reasons for being here that had nothing to do with saving the Meth homeworld. That would be incidental to their accomplishment of their true ambitions.

Seconds and minutes rolled past. Kerath watched the tank and screens and hoped they would forget her. Out there *she* would be the powerless minority, unable to call for help. She turned. "Commander, there's a hole in this thing. Darkships were meant to fight alone, against other darkships. They could smell each other in vacuum. But how will they find a human ship? How will they handle unexpected changes? This is going to be an attack by rote."

The commander nodded. "I was going to suggest we throw some kinks into the later maneuvers, to test their flexibility. Lack of flexibility broke them back when. They couldn't cope with the flood of novel ideas that came after meeting the humans. They couldn't shed roles programmed by their foremothers."

"I'll mention that to the silth."

"In a way, I feel sorry for them. Time has passed them by."

"Perhaps." Kerath glanced at the screen. A darkship was docking. "They didn't forget me. Wish me luck."

The Mistress of the Ship met her in docking bay. She had brought her darkship inside. It floated free, ignoring *Dreamkeeper*'s artificial gravity.

Darkwar

Fresh, updated symbols had been painted on the titanium beams. A variety of new mystical hardware had been installed. Overall, the darkship looked new.

Kerath opened a locker to secure an eva suit.

"No, Marshall. No artifacts. You alone, naked."

Kerath bared her teeth. "No."

"We wish you to partake of the silth experience. We wish you to meet those-who-dwell."

"That's your problem. If you really want me to make the fly, do it on my terms."

"No."

"Compromise?" Kerath thought the female's eyes flared for an instant. Silth did not compromise. "I want my clothing and my communicator."

"Clothing is neither dignity nor worth, Marshall."

"Then shed yours, silth."

The female's eyes flared. "Very well. Set your communicator to receive only. We wish you to concentrate on the experience, not what to report."

"Agreed."

The Mistress glided away. Kerath followed. The silth was angry. She stepped heavily enough to be heard.

The Mistress led her to the axis of the titanium dagger. "Stand here. This is the traditional Place of the Mother in combats to determine the fates of sisterhoods in blood feud. Fear not. A dome of power will shield you from the breath of the All." The silth left her and took her own station at the tip of the longest arm of the cross. Riding the point of the dagger, Kerath thought.

"Marshall?" Another silth held out a silver bowl filled with an amber liquid. Kerath had seen the sisters sip from similar bowls before each of their trips outside. Shakily, she took the bowl and drank.

"More," the sister said.

Kerath drank.

"More... Enough. Yes. I think that's enough."

Kerath felt lightheaded. Her eyeballs felt prickly.

The silth took the bowl to each of the stations, then assumed her own place at the tip of one of the dagger's arms.

Kerath became aware of microscopic points of light around her. She caught hints of similar phenomena surrounding the other females. The phenomena grew more pronounced as *Dreamkeeper* evacuated the atmosphere from the bay.

The bay door opened. Naked stars stared in. Kerath felt only a slight moment of chill; then the golden points redoubled in intensity.

The darkship turned, pointed toward the stars—then stabbed toward them at screaming speed. Kerath felt no inertial drag. She turned and saw the rectangular lighted bay shrink with incredible rapidity. This was impossible. Even more impossible, her fur rippled as if in a strong wind.

Dreamkeeper shrank to a point and vanished.

She was alone among the stars, standing in space. She could not see the darkship. Her companions were golden columns that looked more like distant star clusters than nearby phenomena. She was alone, and frightened as she had never been frightened before. Something burned in her veins. Her head spun. Her eyes would not track. The amber drink? Strange, colored things crawled round the edge of her vision.

Had they poisoned her? No. They had drunk from the same bowl. Suddenly it became clear, a whole different view of the darkful deep between the stars; a view of a chill filled with color and life. Life? Life was impossible out here...

A swarm of a million bright little deltoid darts drifted toward her, slowly shifting color from yellow through red and back again, in perfect unison. They sensed the darkship suddenly. As one they turned white, flipped around, and streaked away. They moved almost faster than the eye could track.

There were little things, big things, even bigger things. Some crowded the darkship, curious. Some remained indifferent. Some fled. A few cruised with the ship, seeming to pull it along. Those were the demons of legend, Kerath decided. The demons the silth summoned and commanded to carry their darkships through the Up-and-Over.

Darkwar

In her wonder she forgot her fear. "Oh!" Fear returned a dozenfold. But why? It was nothing. Just a dust cloud obscuring a few stars. Wasn't it?

The stars rotated around her. Vaguely, she sensed the approach of the second darkship. The creatures of color shuddered and made way, slithering over and around one another like a nest of serpents. Four columns of witchfire took station to Kerath's right. The entire second ship began to glow. Ahead of Kerath, her Mistress of the Ship caught fire. The stars began to rock. Moving again, Kerath thought. The things of color—those-who-dwell, in silth parlance—scattered. So fast!

The universe turned inside out. Horrible things clawed and howled at her. "Up-and-Over!" she screamed. The silth had conjured them into the Up-and-Over, where the darkship dagger hurtled faster than light. She screamed again as *Dreamkeeper*'s lights appeared for a second, so close she could almost touch them.

And she screamed once more as the darkship returned to the Up-and-Over.

Drifting. Shaking. *Dreamkeeper* a few light-seconds away. A voice in her ear. It was several seconds before she could concentrate on the message. "Impressive, Marshall, but abort the drill. I say again, abort the drill. We have unfriendly company. Get aboard fast."

Get aboard? How was the Mistress of the Ship to know? No! She couldn't. But she found her feet moving of their own volition, carrying her forward. The commander kept chattering in her ear, telling her how close the enemy was. In half a minute she was at the tip of the dagger. Her shielding melded with that of the silth. "Enemy ship, Mistress," she gasped. "Only a light-minute away, right on a line with our sun. We have to get back aboard *Dreamkeeper*."

The Mistress bobbed her head, asked a few questions. Then she said, "Back to your position."

The return trek seemed far longer. She finished it with a bad feeling gnawing her gut.

6

The darkship began to glow. Round it those-who-dwell scattered. They seemed suddenly two-dimensional, bright paper cutouts imbued with panic, flickering toward silent stars. Only the silth's driver creatures remained, stretching and straining as they dragged the darkship.

Kerath glanced upward. A chill seized her. That dark dust-cloud thing hovered overhead, obscuring different constellations.

The darkships became a pair of fiery daggers hurtling toward nowhere. The universe twisted and folded and opened its evil belly and gave birth to a horde of silently screaming horrors. They had gone into the Up-and-Over. Kerath screamed back. They weren't supposed to do this.

Normal space exploded around her. She caught a half-second glimpse of a human warship, long and lean and deadly, its riders already running free. *Dreamkeeper* had been spotted!

Cold blackness enveloped her. She could not see her sisters on the darkship. She felt their fear, felt the Mistress waver. The stench of death stung her nostrils. Something that felt like the damp at the bottom of a grave crawled over her protective shielding. In her mind she heard the first of a thousand death cries...

Twist. Fold. The Up-and-Over. A distinct feeling of hard deceleration a twinge of fear. Something was wrong with the Mistress. The darkship was out of control. *Dreamkeeper* was swelling ahead, docking bay ablaze with light. "Too fast!" Kerath cried. "Slow down!" Her ears folded forward. She sank to all fours, sure she was about to die.

What a waste, to end it all here. *Dreamkeeper* would be crippled, and the Meth could no longer manage major repairs. She had failed, and would not live to see the final consequences.

She was right and she was wrong. The darkship continued its deceleration, lowering its daggertip slowly. In a flicker the warship swelled, rose...they were going to make it! They were going to slide beneath it.

Darkwar

The shock of an earthquake hit her. The titanium girderwork ripped, tore, screamed in the silence of the big chill. Kerath clung to the metal. The stars twirled. And then they went out.

She awakened in her quarters. The ship's commander appeared almost immediately, her face grave. "I told you one of them was slow."

"How bad was it?"

"The darkship was a total loss. An arm torn off. One of the silth is dead. *Dreamkeeper* lost a main vent stack. It's not serious as long as we don't have to face heavy particle beam fire."

"One darkship left to complete the mission. Maybe we should abort."

"I don't think so."

"Commander?"

"You'd have to see the human ship to understand." The commander paced, made several false starts before saying, "The old darkwar legends understate. I say send the fast one in and hope the humans get her before she gets all of them. She might have impact enough to encourage a negotiated peace."

"I don't understand, Commander."

"You haven't seen that ship. There may be futures worse than surrender. Would the silth be forgiving if they returned to power?"

"No."

"When you visit the human ship, remember that you're looking at enemies of the silth. The ancient mothers confined darkwar to their high duels in deep space, but it *could* be used against a world. The Command made a grave mistake. The silth offered a straw to grasp, and they grabbed it without looking for the trap. These are new, young Mistresses of the Ships, probably bred and trained for a mission like this. The silth claim to see the future. If they really do, then they would have foreseen desperate times and would have prepared Mistresses like these. If just one survived, with her ship, the silth would win their gamble. They would return."

"You're uncommonly emotional today, Commander."

"I saw the enemy ship. See it yourself. All else will follow."

She had nightmares every time she slept. The human ship had been that grim. The dead had looked as though they had been torn apart from within, or as though they had tortured themselves to death slowly. Just what the silth would wish on their enemies. A lot of Meth would go the same way if the silth had their day.

Kerath studied the rehearsal runs of the surviving darkship. The Mistress of the Ship was superb. She never gave *Dreamkeeper*'s weapons people time to track, train, and fire. And unlike her failed sister, she had no trouble handling the Up-and-Over in rapid sequence. She was a creature without soul, a reflection of the popular view of what silth were.

Kerath studied the silth while they were aboard. They were cold creatures, but her taste of the amber drink, of flying with the darkship, had sensitized her to subtle nuances. Even the failed Mistress was frightened of the other.

Days rolled away. Kerath was tugged this way and that. It would be so simple to abort the mission, equally easy to loose the darkwar and blind herself to the harvest that must follow. Or equally difficult. Either way, she would live in infamy in the legends of the Meth, as she who was afraid to save the race, or as she who had destroyed everything gained in generations free of the silth. She saw no middle road—unless Suslov's gunners got lucky.

Dreamkeeper, last of the great warships of the Meth, was creeping toward home system. Whose dream would it preserve?

7

Kerath turned her back on screens and tank. "Scan on the asteroid?"

"In the groove, Marshall. Three days until it's too late to divert."

She turned to see if the silth had sent an observer. They had: the talker. From a place of power and honor she had fallen to go-between. Kerath almost pitied her. She had suffered that decline herself after Snow-No-More, until the Command had needed her for another suicidal operation.

Darkwar

"Tight beam to the Command. Full report. Request update and instructions." She went to the silth. "Could your people divert the asteroid past the point where it's no longer possible for technology to do so?"

The silth looked at her with empty eyes. "No."

"Thank you." So. There was very little time to decide. The darkship strike had to be launched soon if there was to be time left for reshaping the asteroid's orbit. But for now she could only await the Command's reaction to what had happened in the deep.

She fell asleep and dreamed worse nightmares than ever before. The commander awakened her.

"Reply from the Command. Proceed with mission."

"That's all?"

"That's it."

"No shock? Commander, would the silth have collaborators there?"

The commander eyed the screens. "I've wondered about that since I visited the human ship. I think so. I can't picture the Command jumping into anything blind."

"My own impression. That means I'm more a pawn than I thought. Perhaps I was supposed to be converted."

"Have you decided? I'll follow your orders even if they contradict the Command's apparent intent."

"Thank you. I won't be long." Kerath moved away. She wanted to pace, but there wasn't room. She chewed a claw and searched for a middle road.

She had little choice about the strike itself. It had to go on. The question was how to ensure that the silth did not survive. She checked the observer from the corner of her eye. The silth was watching intently. This would be delicate. Timing would be critical. "Commander, are we in enemy detection?"

"I don't believe so, Marshall. They would have reacted."

Of course. Suslov would want to finish *Dreamkeeper*, definitely as a symbolic move, possibly to retaliate for ships recently lost.

She turned slightly and examined enemy positions estimated from data squirted in with Command's message. "Prepare to launch the strike."

The silth turned and glided out.

"Commander, tight beam to Suslov's flagship. I want the Admiral himself. Quickly."

"This will reveal our position, Marshall."

"So be it. Quickly, now. Quickly." Kerath grabbed a young male. "Go stand by the hatch. Watch for the silth." She turned. "I want the docking bay on screen. What's holding that link, Commander?"

"Have to find a target first, Marshall."

"Don't waste time." Kerath faced the screens. Someone had keyed into an eye cell overlooking the entrance to silth quarters. Kerath watched the observer enter.

She could not remain still. Somehow, movement was so soothing.

Ping!

"We have a beam lock on a human ship, Marshall."

"It had better be the right one," Kerath murmured. The silth were leaving their quarters. All seven turned toward the docking bay. Kerath released a long sigh.

"...Corps Marshall Kerath Hadon for Vice Admiral Pyotr Suslov, personal access only urgent," the commander loudly said as if volume could make up for her difficulty in speaking the alien language.

Suslov's rumpled face appeared with gratifying swiftness. "Kerath. I thought I smelled your touch in that breakout." He exposed his teeth. She reminded herself that humans considered that a pleasantry. "Why haven't they hung you out yet? Calling to surrender? It's almost too late."

"I want to offer you the opportunity you gave me before Snow-No-More. I hope you have more sense than I had."

"Really? You're going to hurt me with one ship?"

"One ship like nothing in human experience, Pyotr Suslov. Conscience forces me to advise you to depart."

The sentry called, "She's coming back, Marshall."

"Pyotr Suslov. Key darkwar your Meth history tapes. Out. Secure, Commander." She faced the screen relaying events in the docking bay. The silth were aboard their darkship. The titanium dagger floated away from the docking grappels. Camera and screen were unable to relay

Darkwar

the true intensity of the golden nimbus surrounding the darkship, but Kerath felt its power in some remote recess of being still touched by the amber fluid.

She went to meet the silth. "Darkship ready?"

"Yes." The female's voice was hollow. Failure had emptied her.

"The enemy have a saying, sister. They also serve who stand and wait." The attempt at comfort fell flat. For silth there were no shadow gradients between success and failure. Kerath gestured. "Launch the darkship, Commander."

The commander hit an alarm. It honked throughout the vast warship. "Commencing darkship strike. All personnel take combat stations."

The docking bay screen relayed the cry of klaxons warning of decompression under way. The titanium dagger rotated until its blade faced the bay door.

"Decompression complete, Commander."

"Open the bay door."

Everything went so slowly. Every detail registered on Kerath, even the tiny groan of scraping metal, conducted through the fabric of the ship, as the bay door moved.

It was just a third of the way open when the darkship surged out into the night. On visual, the darkship dwindled rapidly. Such a tiny thing to be so deadly, not a thousandth the mass of *Dreamkeeper*. Kerath faced the tank. Detection had the darkship moving away fast. "She's in a hurry," Kerath whispered to the commander.

"Maybe she enjoys her work."

Four red alien blips were moving toward *Dreamkeeper*. Kerath beckoned the silth observer. "You'll have a better perspective from down here."

She had racked her brain trying to figure how the darkship would locate its targets without radio. She now understood. The Mistress of the Ship had mind-to-mind contact with her unshipped sister on *Dreamkeeper*'s bridge. That was why the silth had taken her into space. They had meant her to become their contact until the slow sister's unshipping made her redundant. Mind to mind. More silth sorcery. No capability surprised Kerath now, not since she had seen the dead ship.

The observer descended to the operations deck. She did nothing to support or refute Kerath's suspicion or to acknowledge her aid.

"Up-and-Over," a tech announced.

8

"Four," the silth whispered.

That was the last of the outbound hunters. *Dreamkeeper* was safe for the moment.

What state was Suslov in, after losing contact with four heavy warships? How would she respond in similar circumstances?

She would get the hell out. But she was Meth, and she knew about darkwar from old legends. Suslov would examine his Meth historical data and scoff. Being human, he was sure to delay too long.

"Up-and-Over."

A moment later, the silth murmured, "Five. She is well named."

"What?" Kerath was startled by the gratuitous remark.

"She Walks in Glory."

"Ah. Commander, it'll be a while. I feel the need to roam. I'm on pager three if I'm needed."

"Very well, Marshall."

She stopped at her quarters briefly, collected her sidearm, then went on to a weapons observation bubble high on *Dreamkeeper*'s humped back. She chased the weaponry technicians out and stood there staring at the stars. A part of her yearned for another darkship experience. A part sobbed for the sentients dying down near the sun of the Meth.

Colored cutouts flickered at the edge of her vision, legacy of the amber drink. The silth sisters must see them all the time. She forgot *Dreamkeeper* and tried to bring those-who-dwell into focus. Success opened her to a trickle of screams from down near the homeworld.

The cutouts faded. She was not silth. She faced the cold, colorless stars, the stars she loved, the stars that would be lost to the Meth if she made one misstep traversing her middle road.

Darkwar

She took one deep breath for courage and started the long walk back to the fighting bridge.

"Status?" she demanded as she entered.

"Fourteen gone, Marshall," the commander replied in a tight voice. "The silth says the darkship suffered slight damage by catching the edge of a particle beam. Suslov seems to have developed an attack profile. He'll get her if she doesn't control her silth arrogance."

"Fifteen."

"Tell her not to underestimate the alien, silth," Kerath said.

"Marshall, here's an anomaly," the commander said.

Kerath stepped over to study the tank. "He's jumping out," she whispered, excited. "Those look like long jump lines. He's running, Commander."

"He'll come back."

Kerath controlled her emotions. "Of course. But maybe he'll be more amenable when he does."

"The High Lord will be pleased."

"Sarcasm, Commander? The High Lord lives numbered days. His clique are walking worm food." Including her sire, she thought. Poor Shadar, doomed though he was but a servant.

"There goes the last squadron, Marshall. Can the silth follow them?"

"No. Commander, in the next few minutes I'll need absolute obedience. Yes?" She turned to the silth's touch.

"She's hit, Marshall. The last attack. One of her bath was killed."

"Bath?"

"The females who help. Bath. She will have difficulty returning."

Bless the All, Kerath thought. "Medical team and damage control people to docking bay, Commander."

"Thank you," the silth said. The words seemed to rip themselves from her hidden self.

"Up-and-Over," a detection technician called.

Kerath drew her handgun and shot the startled silth through the heart. "Order here!" she shouted, as panic hit the bridge. "Order. Full battle alert, Commander. I want that darkship under fire the instant it reappears. Somebody get rid of this body. Send a security party to arrest the other two silth."

The commander executed orders in a daze. "What are you doing, Marshall?"

"Ensuring the failure of the silth design. The All favored us by taking one of her crew. She will have less control. Less ability to resist the vacuum. By firing upon her I prevent her from coming aboard, reaching safety, and finding a replacement bath. Maybe I'll destroy her. Maybe not."

"She'll attack us."

"She can't send the cloud against us. She can't destroy *Dreamkeeper* without destroying herself."

The commander looked puzzled. "Can't she Up-and-Over home and let one of the orbital tugs pick her up?"

"She doesn't know where home is, Commander, not without somebody here to tell her. To reach homeworld she first has to get orbital data from us and translate it into something understandable by those-who-dwell. To survive she has to come here and has to get inside. I don't intend to let her."

The commander nodded. After a few seconds she said, "But you would have done this even if she were returning healthy."

"Yes. I sought a middle road between surrender and a return of the silth. This was the best I could do."

"They'll make a villain of you."

"They would in any case. That's why they sent a loser of battles who always came home a hero. This time they gave me one they thought I couldn't win no matter what."

"Darkship is here, Marshall. Headed for docking bay."

Kerath nodded.

"Commence firing," the commander directed.

Darkwar

9

Swords of fire flailed the dark. The darkship reeled, slid sideways. Something in Kerath's backbrain buzzed. She saw the darkship as a glowing, tumbling cross. One arm flew off, chased by a golden shape grabbing wildly at nothing. The silth bath's deathwail burned through the core of her mind.

You traitor.

Kerath wobbled under the impact of the mental blow.

You have betrayed your sisters.

The Mistress of the Ship! She couldn't be alive. Nothing could come through that fury... *I am not silth!* she cried back.

The darkship straightened up and turned its daggertip to *Dreamkeeper*. Bright paper cutouts swirled around it. A black cloud slithered across the stars behind it. Panicky, Kerath shouted, "Commander, destroy that damned ship!"

"I'm trying, Marshall. I'm trying." Terror haunted the commander's eyes.

"Then jump, dammit. It's a short jump to Biter orbit. Leave her out here."

The commander stabbed a finger at the jump operators. "Program it."

Kerath stared at the screens, transfixed. The darkship was coming in, accelerating, a screaming, flaming sword. A skeleton rode its tip, jaws opened wide, blood trailing from its fangs. A hungry darkness coiled behind its hollow eyes. The silth was insane. She meant to board by ramming!

Alarms sounded. Collision alarms, never heard except during drills. "Jump, Commander. Dammit, jump anywhere."

The darkship kept accelerating.

Jump alarms shrilled a five-second warning—just as the darkship reached *Dreamkeeper*'s fat guppy belly.

The warship began to twist with the impact. Torn metal shrieked. Breech alarms wailed. Kerath watched the burning blade drive deeper and deeper into the great vessel's belly. "No," she breathed. The silth had lost control and come in far too hard.

A tendril of the black cloud touched the ship.

Then *Dreamkeeper* finally jumped, carrying the darkship with it, still boring into its guts.

Crew people added their screams to those of the alarms, responding to the instant of cloud-touch. On the fighting bridge they clawed their scalps and smashed their foreheads against their consoles. Below, where the darkship's momentum still drove it deeper into *Dreamkeeper*'s belly, it was worse. They were clawing at their eyes.

Dreamkeeper rolled out of jump. Kerath glanced at the readouts. Orbit around homeworld. Almost perfect… Only then did she realize that the blackness had barely caressed her. The silth drink had prepared her for that, too.

The comm boards began lighting up, announcing incoming traffic. Kerath ignored them. She listened. No sound came from below. The darkship had come to rest. "Commander!" She swung hard. "Snap out of it." She exaggerated. "We're in a decaying orbit."

The glaze left the commander's eyes. She scanned the bridge. "Internal pressure is down, but the collision doors have maintained integrity. Help me shake these people out of it. We've got to get moving. The ship is in a bad way." She surveyed the available data again. "We will be lucky to save it."

"We'll save it, Commander. We have no choice. We have to shunt that asteroid."

"That's the Command channel screaming over there."

"To hell with Command. We don't have time for them."

Getting the bridge crew back to work was not difficult, but there was trouble down in the collision area. Half the crew there was dead. The rest had to be restrained for their own protection. Officers culled every department for extra bodies.

Darkwar

Kerath went down, donned an eva suit, and combed the wreckage for the Mistress of the Ship. She refused to be satisfied until she found a mass of torn, raw meat and fur in tatters of black near the head of the column of scrap that had been a darkship.

An hour passed before Kerath was sure that *Dreamkeeper* would survive—if nothing else went sour. She returned to the bridge and collapsed into the first seat she found vacant.

The Command was still trying to get through. By now, they would have studied the damage optically from the surface. They could guess that the darkship had rammed. They would be thinking up cruel replies to her middle-road venture.

Detection showed a number of small vessels closing in—coming to look *Dreamkeeper* over, of course, maybe to put a representative of the Command aboard.

She did not much care now.

"Route that Command call to this board, please," she said. "I might as well face them now."

"Sure you want to deal with them?" the commander asked. "I can…"

"There's no getting out of it." Kerath stabbed a button.

A weathered old female appeared on screen, growling and snarling. Kerath allowed the storm to run its course. When it slackened, and she could pull the main thread from the skein of complaints, she decided that the Command was more interested in the fate of the silth than in Kerath Hadon or *Dreamkeeper*.

"Here's our silth insider," Kerath whispered to the commander.

"The Supreme Commander. I suppose it had to be."

Kerath was exhausted, but she had enough anger and outrage left to respond. She depressed the send key and shouted a line spoken by a victorious pup to conclude a popular story told to small Meth. "The grauken is dead."

The Commander revealed her teeth. She was amused. She keyed into the Command net herself. "Command, this is *Dreamkeeper*. Confirm that last from mission officer Kerath. The grauken is dead." Off comm, she added, "They can't court martial everybody."

Kerath leaned back, closed her eyes, and said, "Secure outside comm. Commander, we'll let them wonder what we meant. The grauken is dead. I wriggled away again." She had found the middle road.

But middle roads went nowhere. They just bought time. Suslov would return. The silth would persist. But there was time now, precious time, to buttress the bridge she had begun to build.

Enemy Territory

Tuesday, 14 April

"They do it after every war. We're not unique." There goes Mickey with the old bullhoolie. Naturally, Tommy powders back a yeahbut.

"Yeah, but not like they done us. They should've saved trouble and gassed us."

So Mickey blazes him with an irrelevancy. "Hell, during the Hundred Years' War the English sometimes didn't even bring their troops home. Just left them in France."

Round the table. "Goddamned company man." "Nah. He's just stupid." "Stuff it, Mickey."

"Whyn't you guys shut up and play cards?" Corky says. He is winning.

Don't think I got no imagination. That's the kind of names they gave us. Mickey. Tommy. Billy. Joey. Nicky. Child names hung on the killers of the 454th Special Commando. We invented our own last names. They don't matter now. We can't get confused anymore. Since the Defile we've only had two doubles: Freddie Hoarfrost and Freddie Lightning, Willie Greensnakes and Willie Fear. Of course, here at Center we mix with the survivors of all the other special commandoes:

elephant men, ape men, spider men, frog men, what have you. It's a regular human zoo.

Major Willie Fear says, "I was a goddamned battalion commander. Don't that mean nothing? What're they trying to do to me?" He talks fast when he's mad. I can barely write down what he's saying.

Mickey says, "They locked up Billy Thunderballs again," by way of hinting that Major Willie should tone it down. General Billy commanded the whole Special Commando. He spends more time in Building Four than out. Can't keep his mouth shut. He scares the crap out of the desk jockies up the line.

No matter how you feel, inside the band or out, we got us a real question here. What do you do with us after we finish our job? Take 454 Codo. I mean, we're smart enough, and our parents were human, but how the hell do spider monkeys fit into civilian life? We've got one talent. Soldiering. Anything else we taught ourselves. Half the people outside are scared of us. The other half want to make pets out of us.

Some guys find themselves do-gooder sponsors. They figure anything is better than Center. They go out, and they all come back. A monkey can be a monkey. A man gets his pride up sooner or later.

There aren't no pretty alternatives. We were genetically engineered, raised, and schooled to be soldiers. What else can we be? What a lot of guys can't figure is why they didn't keep us on. The Service didn't fold because the war ended.

They're scared of us, that's why. They put up with us when they needed us, but… Well, they don't need us any more. They want to sweep us under the rug now. We're different.

Don't get me wrong. It's not something really pushy. Most people don't realize what they're doing. But the fear is there. You can smell it when you're out with the Normals. The quick, surprised rise of the eyebrows when they run into you, the stiffness of speech, the withdrawal… You can see it if you look. Most of us pretend real hard. Some of us even fool ourselves.

Center isn't a prison. They say. It's a "Readjustment Interface." We can come and go when we want. We can leave forever. And can come back

Enemy Territory

when it gets too rough outside. Center will be here as long as we need it. They promised. After all, without us the war wouldn't be over yet.

So how come the news is full of speeches by guys who want to close Center?

We're dead if the budget cuts start. We don't have a lobby. Anybody who cares about us is right here in Center already.

All the arguing is old stuff. It's been the same so long it's like a liturgy. I should make cards for them. They could hold the right one up at the right time and save their jawbones.

Sunday, 19 April

"I'm going to torque over and see Harry. Anybody want to go?" No. Hospital gives them the drooling grey creeps. Hardly anybody goes anymore.

You step off the elevator. To right and left the ward stretches toward infinity. No rooms. No partitions. Just beds as far as you can see, a line against each wall and two down the middle, toe to toe. A few tired, sad-eyed Normal nurses try to keep up. They are good ladies. They believe. They agree we're getting shafted. Some of them have people here. Hospital treats Normal vets too. They come in as beds open up. Every bed is used.

They were racing wheelchairs today. A marathon, apparently. They came from my right, faded to my left. More chairs sped the other direction in the far aisle. The staff ignored them. They ignore anything that helps the guys get by.

There are twenty-eight levels to Hospital, each exactly like all the others.

The unwritten law there is, don't give staff no grief. They're dedicated people. They're about the only Normals who treat Specials like people.

Still... Still. Patients are patients. Some are cranky and unreasonable.

A surge of racers whipped past. I ducked into a break in the flow and skipped down the aisle.

"Look out, runt!" An elephant man in a tank-sized chariot came roaring toward me. I dodged, snagged his chair, hitched a ride. He laughed, called me a parasite, slowed a little when we reached the monkey man section.

He wasn't really an elephant, any more than I'm a monkey. He was just engineered big and strong. His kind usually go on all fours because of the weight they carry. I am cat size, with elongated arms, legs, fingers, and toes. Spider monkey without a tail. Big eyes, to see good at night. Extra good hearing and smell. We were engineered to become infiltrators, scouts, snipers, attackers of points inaccessible to Normal troops. Like fastnesses in stony badlands…Stony badlands…

"Hey, Sammy!" Harry's face lighted up. "How's the boy?"

"Same old shit, Sarge." Harry was my platoon sergeant in the Defile.

Harry stuck out the wrist stump of his one remaining arm. He is in Hospital for life. All he has left is one foot. A man can't do much with that. But Harry tries.

"What's the matter, Sammy? You don't look so good." Nothing gets Harry down. He's one of those people who's by damned going to enjoy life or die trying.

"Guess it's starting to get to me, Sarge."

"You think too much, Sammy. Always did. Relax. Enjoy."

"Sarge, that's damned hard when you look at this." There are five thousand men just on his floor, all of them permanently disabled. That's why the other guys don't come anymore. It's hard to be cheerful in surroundings so grim.

"You got to censor your outlook, Sammy. Concentrate on the good times. Look at me. I got plenty to cry about if I want to be a whiner."

Yeah. Good old Harry. Sometimes he's so Pollyanna he drives you up the wall.

"Been thinking, Sammy."

"Sounds dangerous, Sarge."

"Yeah, sure. Look. We've got to get the band out of Center."

"There ain't nothing out there for us, Sarge. They should've kept us in Service."

"But they didn't, Sammy. So we go on. We've got to worry about tomorrow, not yesterday's should have beens."

Enemy Territory

"The future is enemy territory."

"Hum. That's profound, Sammy. Not like you. Enemy territory, eh? And we've seen so much that we're gunshy. So we turn Center into a bunker and sit tight? Sammy, it's not going to go away. You gotta do something besides keep your head down."

"Like what?"

"Like find something we can do better than Normals. You tell Major Willie I said that. Then break up the damned card games and woe-is-me sessions and get to work, same as if you were preparing a mission. Figure out what to do, then by damned do it."

"Like we did in the Defile, eh?"

Harry's face clouded. "Could end that way, Sammy. But even that was better than rotting like an old tree that fell down and nobody cared."

"Sarge... Harry..."

"Try it, Sammy. For me. Right?"

"For the band, Sarge. All right."

I thought about it going back to barracks. It just depressed me. I told the Major what Harry said. He suggested we sleep on it.

Wednesday, 22 April: Two Years Ago Today

It was all slow motion. Shadows drifting among the rocks. Glimpses of monkeylike figures slipping from cover to cover by the light of three moons. Somewhere ahead, a sound, a swelling rumble. Freeze!

An atmosphere fighter streaked overhead, a glowing blue diamond with a needle nose. Its growl faded into the distance. Zoof! Zoof! Zoof! Three more belched from the Defile ahead.

We scrambled forward, froze again. A second flight followed the first. Scramble. A third flight. Scramble. A fourth. There was a brief, blinding flash in the distance behind us. A sky battle was shaping up over the diversionary attack on the Eben pocket.

"Move them up, Sammy," the sergeant said. "That ain't going to last."

It didn't. Their flyers were the best, aces all. They'd been sent to Dorphat to fight a last stand or tide-turning battle. That night they seized the air for their own.

Neither attack from the air or from orbit could silence their subterranean base because it couldn't be properly located. We were headed in to wipe it the hard way.

Rustle, rustle, among the shadows of steeplelike rocks. Even the best of us couldn't avoid making noise.

Never had we fought in stranger, wilder country. It was a grownup cousin of Bryce Canyon, hammered into a hundred kilometer wide gap in a gargantuan cordillera. The Defile. A home for devils. Scorching by day, frosty by night.

Zoof. Zoof. More fighters went up. The sergeant whispered to his throat mike: "Anybody spot their launch gate?" A chorus of negatives on platoon tac. Too far away.

Rustle. Rustle. Four hundred odd little men crept forward… Flash! Somebody missed a sentry. We'd been spotted. Flash! Flash!

My earplug speaker went crazy. Everybody asked questions at once. The Major shut them up, demanded proper reports. Forward again, under fire from a hundred weapons.

We were expected.

Mortar bombs fell to the right of my platoon. I waved the squad forward. An enemy position lay dead ahead. Grenades arced through the air. The shooting stopped.

Their first line gave way. The mortars stopped talking while their crews dropped back. Obviously old hands. Probably veterans on a par with the flyers. The ambush was calculated to reveal our mettle.

Boom-boom-boom-zing-whine. Ricocheting shrapnel howled all around us. It was nasty in those rocks.

Thump-Thump-thump. Friendly mortars talked back. One weapons company of ape men were along to support us. We were too small to handle heavy weapons ourselves.

Enemy Territory

Harry dropped down beside me. "It's rotten, Sammy. The Major's asking if we can pull back." Someone moaned a dozen meters behind us. "How're your boys?"

"Okay. So far."

Sudden radio chatter. A counterattack coming in. A rolling barrage crept past us. The lock spires did a *danse macabre* in the flicker of weapons and explosions. They were delicate structures. Many of them fell. We squeezed into cracks, fired at glimpses of silver-blue shapes. "What was that shit about they've used up all their crack troops?" I asked an unanswering night.

There was a lot of noise to our left. It was hand to hand over there. Harry poked me, said, "We're wheeling left to help Charlie Company."

Mortar bombs rained down. I kept the squad low. "Whoa!" Enemy squad ahead. Massed fire. The opposition vanished. In my ear, "Pull back. Third platoon, pull back. Original positions."

We were too late. Charlie Company was beyond help.

"Where's the air cover?" Harry grumbled. "We're supposed to get air support if we get in a firefight."

It was a great game. Couldn't get air support without clearing the Defile, and couldn't clear the Defile without air support.

"Here they come again!"

Aim-fire. Aim-fire. I froze in a shadow while a big body lumbered past, shot it in the back.

"Tighten it up! Tighten it up!" The Major was on the all-channel. Training and experience overcame dismay. The second attack faded. Platoon leaders and company commanders consulted. I checked the time. Holy! ... It was almost morning.

The sergeant poked me. "We're pulling out whether Division likes it or not. Major's asking for emergency evac."

I assembled the squad. I had two wounded and one dead. "Have to leave him. Carry those two." We scrambled and trudged a panicky two kilometers. The sky began to lighten. My earplug squeaked. Harry growled. "Rearguard says they're coming."

A hurricane of mortar bombs. Weapons company didn't answer it. They were scattered all over hell, running away. Senseless rhythm. Aim-fire. Aim-fire. The sun crept over the horizon. We had to hide before it cooked us.

454 Codo was surrounded. The mortar attack let up only because the other side ran out of bombs. I checked the squad. Four more dead. Two missing. Two wounded. One would die without quick evacuation. Willie Hoarfrost and I were the only healthy soldiers left. Willie was trying to help Harry. Harry had caught a bomb in his lap. He had a tourniquet on each arm and one on a leg. "Not much hope there, Willie."

"Don't hurt to try, Corporal."

The sun climbed higher. The temperature soared. Breathing became painful. Even in the shade the heat was maddening. The other side laid low, letting the sun work for them. They had their suits and nearby base.

Stubborn Harry wouldn't die. He came round once, grinned, whispered, "I didn't duck fast enough." I gave him a knockout shot. I couldn't stand his smiling.

High noon. The Major spoke on the all-channel. He sounded crazy. "Everybody gather round me. To my beacon. Forget the perimeter. Boys, the war is over. Belimar surrendered four days ago."

Was there cheering? No. Plenty of cussing and nobody believing, though.

Four days ago? Ours and a hundred simultaneous strikes, all over Dorphat, were a waste? Half a million men, mostly Specials, committed after there was no more point? What the hell? Communications lag? That's the kind of screwup that makes a soldier hate everybody on top.

The Major said, "Lay down your weapons. They're going to give us a hand."

"Like shit," somebody replied.

"Do what you're told, soldier. Or I'll shoot you myself."

That was the day suspicion was born. The rumors started as soon as the fighting stopped.

Enemy Territory

Sunday, 26 April

My thirty-second birthday today. Wish I could share it with Harry, but I just can't stand the hopeless look he gets when I tell him I haven't found anything yet. Damn it, we need a war.

I was in the mine for fourteen years. God knows how long it went on before I arrived. Why did it have to end?

Four hundred men died in those godforsaken rocks… For what? Center? Maybe we were on the wrong side. It was those guys that helped after the shooting stopped, not ours. Harry owes them a life.

Screw it. Some birthday. Might as well sack out.

I must have screamed. The Major shook me. I cracked an eyelid. "Dreaming about it again?" he asked.

"Yeah." We all do.

"Been thinking," he said over supper. "Harry has the right idea."

"'Bout time somebody admitted it."

"Sammy…"

"But we've been over it a hundred times."

"So we keep on."

"Would they let us go?"

"Hell, why not? Most of them would love to get rid of us."

"By burying us."

"Don't go General Billy on me. They let him out yesterday. He's already stirring the pot again. He's more trouble than any normal. He gives the nuts all the ammo they can use. If he don't stop claiming the Board of Inquiry is a coverup, somebody's going to run out of patience."

"We'd make good burglars." The Major glared at me. "Just a thought."

"Corporals don't think. It's dangerous."

"Security work? Go mercenary?"

"Cram that. It ought to be something where we can stick together. And where we can stay out of the Normals' way. But not no bloody damned freebooting. You sound like one of the General's idiots."

On cue, Mickey stuck his head in the door. "Major? Might be trouble. General did something again. There's a thousand MPs out there looking for him."

"So?"

I said, "Ease up."

"Yeah. I'm just tired of Billy Thunderballs. He's going to kill us, you know."

"Better check it out."

"Yeah."

We went outside. Mickey hadn't exaggerated. The grounds were lousy with MPs. All Normals, and some damned arrogant. The Major was in a mood to turn the General in till he talked to an MP lieutenant. That idiot almost got his head broke.

Back in the barracks, the Major said, "The reactionaries are taking over."

"They aren't all like that."

"One is one too many, Sammy. I'm going to find the General. There's something going on. Ain't no call for a whole police brigade to move in on us."

The invasion wasn't limited to Center. They'd put teams into the city, shutting down transportation and communications. That *was* a little too much effort to spend harassing one pain in the ass General.

We've got to get out of here. Before this kind of crap gets worse.

Wouldn't you know silly Mickey would have an idea? One that sounds only half bad?

"Sammy," he said, softlike, not wanting the others to hear and maybe mock him, "I maybe got something." He showed me a city paper. The classified. Us brains never thought to pick up a hard-print and look through the want ads. He had one circled:

> VETERANS: *Combat or Military Police. Major police command has immediate openings in all entry-level police MOS. Excellent salary and fringes. Performance bonuses, hazard pay. Accelerated*

Enemy Territory

advancement to qualified personnel. Contact North American Interest Section, Old Earth Chancery, Inglespoort, 31-28-2211

"Police work? On Old Earth? They won't get a lot of takers?"

"It's the kind of thing we could do, isn't it?"

"Maybe." Funny. Old Earth doesn't intimidate me the way it does most Normals. "Be going back into action, if the stories are true. But would they take Specials?"

"I called. They said come on over and sign up. The guy I talked to sounded excited."

"Read me that number." I called, asked questions Mickey hadn't, wrote down answers. They had a variety of openings and no apparent prejudice against Specials. It sounded too good to be true.

I thought about it a while, decided they would give us duties nobody else would take. Well, we were used to that. That's why we were created. "It might be a ticket out, Mickey. Rough or not. I'm going to talk to Harry before I take it to the Major. He's got a better head for stuff than me."

Monday, 27 April

Couldn't see Harry till this morning. MPs kept us buttoned. Couldn't get out. The Major didn't get in. I left right after breakfast, before he came back.

Harry lit up like always. He really gleamed after he took a second look. "You finally got something."

'Yeah. Not great, but maybe the best we'll ever do." I showed him the ad and told him what the Chancery had to say.

"Fits the character of the outfit," he said. "Puts us in an us-against-everybody spot. Like always."

"What I was worrying about was, we'd need to put a team together. Ape men. Elephant men. The works. It'd be like full time war again." They say the safest spot on Old Earth is just a whisker less deadly than the most dangerous. Police there are nothing but moving targets. The whole world is an armed ghetto with a big hatred for anybody who wants to tame it. I added, "I think they'd sign up everybody in Center if they could get them."

"Sign up?"

"They want a six year first contract."

"What's the Major think?"

"I don't know. Curfew caught him outside last night."

"Curfew? The General again? What'd he do now?"

"I don't know. I guess he just won't learn."

"Tell the Major I said give this a good look." The Major trusts Harry's judgment.

Something went bad wrong during Major Willie's visit with the General. He was in a lousy mood. He did agree that the police thing was maybe the best we could do.

"One problem," he said. "General Billy." He handed me a wad of papers.

They unfolded into a three page copy of an official document copied from a copy of a copy. It was a precis of an interim report from the Dorphat Board of Inquiry. It said that, despite a lack of hard evidence, it was probable that high level officers on the scene had conspired to delay the announcement of the armistice. The delay had resulted in almost two hundred thousand friendly casualties. And there was more. Support for some of General Billy's wildest accusations.

The thing was a top-secret bomb and somebody had started it ticking by turning it loose. "How'd he get ahold of this?"

The Major shrugged. "The problem is, he's going to go public."

"That's why we're up to our ears in MPs?"

"They're trying to stop him. Somebody way up is nervous. Somebody with enough clout to deploy a police brigade so he can cover his ass."

"What do we do?"

"Probably too late to do anything, Sammy. We're in for it. A lot of guys are damned mad. One stupid mistake will blow this place apart."

The MPs didn't find General Billy. They didn't keep him from connecting with the media. He hit the evening network news.

Enemy Territory

There was a little trouble when MPs tried to arrest one of the General's aides. They got too enthusiastic. He came out with bruises, broken ribs, and a concussion. That made the late news.

Center was a neutron short of critical, and hanging there, teetering, waiting for some genius or fool to tilt things. News anchors talked about the chances of a veterans' mutiny. Center isn't the only installation with a lot of unhappy old soldiers. High General Staff officers issued soothing reports. Their faces were twisted, like they couldn't figure out why this was happening to them. Bigots ranted. Spokesmen for veterans' organizations claimed neutrality, but with an obvious lean towards the General. Scared politicians yelled for blood. There are a lot of veterans, and veterans tend to vote.

General Billy dropped his rabble-rousing. He talked about staying calm and investigating. Here at Center he kept the lid on. He sent his own men out with the MP patrols till somebody topside had smarts enough to make the MPs less visible.

Tuesday, 28 April

"We're talking Sepoy Mutiny," Mickey said. "We're talking *Aurora*, Battleship *Potemkin*, like that. It doesn't have to do with being treated right. It's class struggle." He was going good. And he had an audience. "Those MPs aren't going to shoot us to shut us up. Ain't nothing we could tell anyway. They'll do it to show us who's boss." I don't know about the accuracy of his historical parallels. I do know you can't always trust them. Sometimes he makes them up.

Fiction or not, his theme attracted interest. He was telling us that no hierarchy tolerates rebellion by its working class. The more rigid and militaristic the hierarchy, the more likely it is to respond by choosing a hard option. He was saying that generals capable of the Dorphat betrayal might be blind and arrogant enough to go the hardest way of all with Center.

Mickey is a little cowardly and a lot imaginative. I can't see it going that far. They could play their games on Dorphat because nobody was watching. They don't have that luxury here. This is getting to be a media happening.

General Billy probably holds the key. If he can keep it cool here, if he doesn't let his own prejudices run away with him, we could come out of this better off than we went in… I hope Harry hasn't talked me into being a complete head in the clouds fool.

Wednesday, 29 April

We've got trouble. Shots were fired this morning. The General couldn't contain it. His own fault, really. He's been whipping the men up for so long. Some of his vigilantes splintered off and started them a guerrilla campaign.

The MPs showed more restraint than I expected. There were only a couple of firefights when those clowns took over the city. They grabbed the port, communications, the arsenal, and the power station. They made some pretty silly broadcasts.

The rest of us are sitting around wondering what to do. We're specials, and it's always been Specials against everybody else, right or wrong.

Harry says our getting out is dead now. Practically a case of suicide. I could cry about it.

"Look at it this way," somebody said a while ago, "our problems are over. No more worries. No more mystery about tomorrow."

No mysteries…

I hope it isn't that bad. I hope it isn't moving so fast cool heads can't tame it.

Thursday, 30 April

Maybe there is hope. The Major talked to the Chancery this morning. He says the Old Earth government will try to stop High Command

Enemy Territory

from making a show of force. They're also demanding an investigation from outside the Service. High Command claims we're all in on this, and deserve a good slapping around. Old Earth says we should be given amnesty. We were provoked.

Tempers are pretty hot. Nobody really cares about the facts.

The Major says the Old Earth people must want our help real bad. That's scary. If they're so desperate to beef up their cops, their law enforcement situation has to be worse than anybody guessed. Gives me the feeling I'm going to be gun-fodder in a desperate delaying-action against the forces of chaos.

The news is all guesswork about using force to straighten Center out. All the pros and cons, with generals and politicos getting red in the face arguing their sides. I saw one series of interviews with enlisted men who might be sent here. They said they wouldn't fire on us, orders or not. They aren't stupid. They understand precedent and getting your turn in the barrel.

The politicians smell blood. For the first time in their generation they have the upper hand on the Service. They want "the Butchers of Dorphat" strung up. They don't much care about justice for veterans. They see a chance to grab back some power lost during the war. They're taking it.

All the howling may turn out to be sound and fury signifying nothing. The public don't give a damn. The war is over. They're safe. They don't want to remember what they owe us, and they don't care who holds the hammer in government. Government is one of the trials of life. It has to be endured, and, as much as possible, ignored.

The Major came in. "They arrested the guy who sent in the MPs," he said. "Charged him with abuse of power."

Mickey grumbled, "Abuse of power? Conspiracy to commit murder would be more like it."

"They did it mostly to put the General on the bad side. He foxed them. Did a song and dance for the news people. Told them he'd take full responsibility for the mutiny if there was amnesty for the rest of us. He really hammed it up. They won't be able to turn him down."

"Good old Billy," I sneered. "Didn't know he had a Jesus complex. Going to die for our sins, eh?"

"That's the general idea."

Mickey made a rude noise reinforced by an obscene gesture. "He's just showing off. He'd love to go out a martyr. Despite all his pissing and moaning about justice, he never attacks the real question."

"What would that be?" the Major asked. There was sarcasm in his voice. He can't take Mickey serious.

"What does society do with its veterans? It takes years from their lives, their sanity sometimes, and maybe wrecks their future by taking away their chance to keep up with guys who didn't have to go. Society owes for that. The question is, how much? How much return can a veteran expect for having met *his* obligation?"

"I suppose you're going to tell us," the Major said.

"No. I can't. It's an ancient question. Nobody has ever answered it. Since societies stopped sending everybody to war, most of them have done what ours has. Tried to forget the whole thing as soon as the blood stopped running."

Silly little Mickey. Always so serious. "You're forgetting this war had a new wrinkle," I said. "The laboratory soldier. The soldier who never was a part of society. Who was made, same as tanks and rifles. What about us?"

Mickey, of course, had thoughts on the matter, but I didn't hang around to hear them. I have the same trouble as the public: Too much thinking gets painful.

Friday, 1 May

May Day. Famous in the history of insurrections. Looks like ours is over. General Billy hasn't said, but the nets claim he made a deal with High Command. He'll take the rap for the mutiny. They'll ignore the rest of us and throw the book at the Dorphat clique. Those people deserve whatever they get. The latest leaks say they weren't just trying to kill us off, they were trying to rack up enough casualties so public reaction would

Enemy Territory

wreck the armistice. They wanted the war to go on. They wanted a more decisive victory.

No wonder the politicians are mad. Somebody was tromping on their power preserve.

Saturday, 2 May

Happy faces everywhere I look today. Harry was fizzing when I saw him. The storm has broken. It's over. Senate voted to take the whole thing away from the Service. An investigative team is on its way. And old Earth Chancery says they'll start placement testing Monday. The Major is out rustling up volunteers from the other commandos.

This mutiny thing woke a lot of guys up. They got slammed in the chops with how fragile our situation is. We don't need the General or High Command's reactionaries to get wiped. Politicians could scuttle us quicker than they saved us, for a handful of votes. We're vulnerable as long as we let ourselves be kept here.

Monday, 4 May

The crowds at the Chancery were impossible. They couldn't handle everybody. Hard to believe how excited everybody is. After two years of doing nothing, any growth of purpose has to run wild.

It's caught on all through Center. A lot of other outfits say they're taking their Harry's along too. A lot, like 454 Codo, are closed bands, almost families.

Mickey is a genius in disguise. This thing could solve most of our problems.

Chancery says they'll move the first shipload the end of this week. They want people so bad they're taking almost anybody who wants to go.

Thursday, 7 May

The first ship is off. 1200 apemen and elephant men. 454 Codo is scheduled out Sunday. We've made it! We're going to slide out the side door before this mutiny business is really settled. The Senate investigators won't get here till next week.

I can't believe how happy everybody is. After two years of dying inside there's suddenly a future.

Friday, 8 May

There's something funny going on. Port traffic is stacked. Chancery is chartering everything. Hauling out all the bruisers they can, like they're racing a deadline.

Saturday, 9 May

I was right. Two heavy attack transports just made orbit. With a division of Force Marines. Somebody told some big lies. And we get the dirty end again. Late news tells it all. All those encouraging news releases were smokescreen. Only maverick Old Earth really stood with us. Senate's true attitude is that treating us right will cost too much. So the Marines are here to put us in our place. And then what?

Guess I could get me an organ grinder and a tin cup.

The part that rankles is that so many of the real rebels have gotten out, leaving us to face the music. 454 Codo went right on just like every other day, and stayed out of it completely, but will that make a difference? Not bloody likely.

All that's left is a big moral decision. Join the guys who want to shoot it out as a sort of final protest? Or sit tight, try to ride it out, and pray for that ever receding brighter day?

Enemy Territory

Sunday, 10 May

There's firing in the northern part of Center. Building Two is burning. Too many men with too little hope, who decided they might as well go out fighting.

Lunatics. I don't care what they do anymore.

The band are sitting round the card tables, eyes vacant, nobody talking. Waiting. Just waiting. Only Mickey fidgets. he wants to fight. The Major made him sit.

Somebody pounds on the door. Nobody moves. More pounding. After a while, the Major sighs and goes over.

It's Harry and a brain-damaged ape man buddy of his named Kenny. Kenny is carrying Harry cuddled in his arms like a newborn. Kenny squats down on the floor. He doesn't say anything. I've never heard him say anything. His eyes are kind of misty.

The Major finally reacts. "What the hell are you doing here, Sergeant?"

"I'm still part of the band, Major." Harry's eyes are wet too. And for the first time since I've known him they hold no humor or hope.

I want to cry.

The Waiting Sea

1943

The sea was an obsidian plain, hard and glossy, flecked with flashes of silver. The moon was a god's thumbnail clipping riding low in the west, a thin crescent about to hit the water. The air was cool and still. Not a ghost of a cloud marred the nighttime sky. The stars blazed down in their billions, indifferent to one insignificant man standing on the starboard bridge wing of a scab of rusty iron doggedly churning across a mote of cold black water.

The sea whispered along the vessel's side, rolling up faces of pale fire as disturbed plankton luminesced. Below, the boilers groaned and the engines grumbled in their soft deep voices. The ship pushed ahead an unchanging eight knots. The sounds were more felt through the metal than heard on the wing. The deck gently pushed against his feet as the ship turned to a new tack.

Zigging and zagging, he thought. Turtle trying to run like a rabbit, or a halfback in the open field.

Now he could see the ship ahead in column, a fat tanker looming a deeper black in the darkness. A hint of stack smoke touched his nostrils, then a whiff of tobacco. Somebody inside the bridge had lighted a smoke. He ached for a drag of calming nicotine.

He raised the glasses to his eyes and slowly swept the sea. How many times had he done so? Put a buck in the bank for every one and he could live on the interest. Nothing out there. A whole lot of nothing.

The sea whispered along the vessel's side, a steady, barely audible susurrus. It could put you to sleep. Or it started talking to you. You started straining to hear the voices, and forgot to watch…

He whipped the glasses to his eyes, searched the night. More nothing.

Those were the real sirens of the deep down there, murmuring and playing in the froth along the hull. Poison, they were. Murderous. Hear them. "Shawn. Shawn. We're coming for you, Shawn. Sleep, Shawn."

Cold sweat stood out on his forehead. He snapped the glasses into position, scanned. Nothing but the wolf-shape of a destroyer across the silvery trace shed by the moon.

He had to get out of this. Those voices again. They were getting to him. This would be his last crossing. It got scary when you started hearing voices.

He stared down at the water rolling from beneath the ship's bows, watched the pale light vanish into the polished stone of the surrounding plain. It was all an illusion. The ship wasn't going anywhere. She was frozen here, like that ship that tried to go to the north pole and got caught in the ice. There was no end to the sea. The sea was eternal and infinite. Tonight's calm was a soft mockery, a taunt thrown at the little mortals who dared challenge it.

He cursed softly. What fool notion had gotten him into this? He hated the ocean. It was a great hungry monster with an appetite that couldn't be appeased. It was sleeping now, or pretending, but soon it would waken or lose patience. The water would turn angry grey and hurl giant's fists against the hull, pounding with an endless, senseless, lunatic rage, till even the Old Man looked grim and green.

He slammed a palm against the rail. Pain obliterated the crazy thoughts. He raised the glasses and looked for the enemy.

The Waiting Sea

A sneer stretched his lips. The enemy. He didn't need binoculars to see the enemy. The enemy was all around him, waiting with the patience of a spider. The ship was caught in its glassy web.

"Shawn. Shawn. Come to us, Shawn." There they were, their faces foaming in and out of focus along the ship's side. They watched with black, bottomless eyes, called with toothless mouths stretched in hungry grins. "Come to us, Shawn."

Their voices were plain now. He didn't misunderstand a word. Before, he hadn't understood. But the voices got plainer and louder every crossing. Angrily, he spat into their restless, formless faces. "Not me," he murmured. "You're not getting me."

"Come to us, Shawn. Shawn. Shawn."

He glanced at his watch, to see how much longer the watch would run. It seemed he had been on the wing for an eternity. But hardly an hour had passed. Still an hour before he could slip inside for a smoke and coffee while Tony gave him a break. Lord God, why did you make the hours of the night so long?

The moonlight was almost extinct. A few minutes and its danger would no longer exist.

The ship's body continued to relay a soporific rhythm of sound and roll. "Shawn, Shawn," the sea whispered. "Come to us, Shawn." His eyelids slid together. He caught himself, shook his head violently. For an instant he thought he saw mocking grins in the foam. He raised the glasses. His eyelids drooped. He should step to the bridge hatch and ask for coffee. Something off the bottom of the pot, the thick black stuff so terrible the aftertaste stayed with you a week. But he didn't. He wasn't going to be beaten by the sea.

The moon was gone. The stars seemed even more cold and remote, turning their backs one by one. His eyelids drooped again.

A deep, rending boom tore the guts from the night. The sea spawned a terrible flower of orange and yellow light. He stared at the tanker, unable to comprehend.

Again that great deep boom as an explosion ripped the tanker's iron hide. Out across the water, a klaxon shrieked as a destroyer protested this maltreatment of her flock. The horn made a mournful cry of, "Too late. Too late."

"Shawn."

He whirled and stared at the sea. His mouth worked. Nothing came out. The luminescent streak arrowed closer and closer, as if in extremely slow motion. Finally, he croaked, "Torpedo!"

None heard him but the sea. His puny cry vanished in the explosion's roar.

Gentle hands tugged him down, urging him deeper. Champagne bubbles boiled around him, whispering, "Come with us, Shawn."

No! Damn it, no! He fought upward, against the undertow of the sinking ship, toward the orange boundary of his own world.

Metal shrieked beneath the sea. The ship was breaking up. Dull screech and thunder as watertight doors yielded to ever-increasing pressure… Was he imagining the screams of the men trapped in the flooding compartments?

He should have seen the torpedo earlier. His woolgathering had killed…how many?

"Come with us, Shawn." The caress of the sea was gentle and intimate and seductive. Watery fingers tugged him down.

No! The orange was right above him now. He broke the surface, gasped violently…and screamed amidst the burning oil from the tanker. The whole sea was aflame. He went under again, all rationality and hope gone, knowing nothing but the pain and the whisper of the sea.

He came to once, clinging to something in an aisle between lakes of flame. The stern of the tanker remained afloat, metal glowing cherry red in spots. Amazingly, men danced and screamed amongst the flames. Somewhere beyond the tanker, an ammunition ship was tearing its own guts out, shooting off all the fireworks of the Fourth. Out in the darkness there was a whoop of horns and rumble of depth charges as the tin can wolves snarled and snapped at the enemy.

The Waiting Sea

Blackness returned.

Awareness again. A bluishness in the east. The tanker was gone. Only small pools of burning oil remained. The flicker of huge fires defined the horizon. The convoy was miles and miles away, maybe scattering. The sea had him now.

A *chwung-chwung-chwung* came from behind him, growing rapidly louder. Diesels. Feebly, he turned till he saw the lean iron shark shape come out of the dark. He saw the silhouettes of the men on the tower. He tried to raise a hand, tried to shout, did not have the strength. The sub swam on, following the spoor of its prey. Its wake rocked him to sleep.

Fingers plucked at him. Hands dragged him out of the cool, dark sea. He screamed. The pain! He had one glimpse of friendly sailors, of a motor whaleboat, of a grey destroyer bobbing in the background. He sobbed. He was one of the lucky ones.

1955

They finally talked him into going to the seashore. "About time you faced up to it," Gladys told him when the kids were out of hearing. "You can't let it rule you. You're not the only man who had a ship knocked out from under him."

All the old arguments. All irrefutable. He did have to face it, to conquer it.

There was a breeze off the ocean, salt and cool. It brought back that wartime sea. He found himself listening... He started shaking. Gladys put both hands on his arm and pushed him forward. The boys put the umbrella up and charged the water, their shouts drifting back like old battlecries fading into the mists of time. "C'mon, Dad. C'mon."

He looked at the plain of blue and the far horizon and froze. He began shaking his head.

"It's all right," Gladys said. "Just sit under the umbrella. I'll ride herd on the monsters."

Umbrella and blanket were too close to the water.

After one gut-wrenching minute of trying to watch his brood, he turned his back, stretched out on his stomach, and tried to escape into sleep.

The surf rolled in behind him, a gentle whoosh, roar, sweep of sand back into the deep. A whisper in the waves, "Shawn, Shawn. Come to us, Shawn."

Shaking, he begged sleep to come.

He wakened to the cold grasp of watery claws on his calves, trying to drag him down the beach. Eager, bubbling whispers. He clamped his eyes shut and clung to the umbrella pole.

Another wave swept in. And another. Oh God. They had him. This time, they had him. They were going to pull him in.

"Shawn-Shawn-Shawn," came in an eager, tumbling babble.

"Shawn! Snap out of it!" A palm hit the side of his face. "I'm sorry, Honey. The boys wanted to go get hot dogs."

1968

A different coast and a different wife, Madelaine. Lean and cool, ten years younger than Gladys. Hip. Almost able to bridge the gap to the boys. The sullen, unpatriotic little bastards. Long hair and pimply faces behind ragged beards, desecrating the flag of the country for which he'd almost died… They didn't even try to understand. Called him a fascist. Him! *They* didn't know what fascism was. *They* hadn't seen the wolf packs maul a convoy and kill a thousand men…

"Here they are," she said. "Try not to mention the war. Either war. Give them a chance. They'll give you one." Amateur psychiatrist. She was good with words. Gladys hadn't been. The boys liked her well enough. They could talk to her.

But why did she have to try killing two birds? This Marineland outing… He exchanged unenthusiastic greetings with his sons. The tension… He could think of only one thing to compare. Salt water in burn wounds.

The Waiting Sea

Madelaine chattered brightly in her false, amateur diplomat way. The boys didn't mind, or didn't detect the phoniness. Or maybe they just accepted it as natural. This was the west coast. And, much as they finger-pointed his generation, the foundation of theirs was sand cemented by willful blindness and wishful thinking.

"Stop dragging your feet, Dear," Madelaine whispered. "Do you want these hippie freaks to think you're scared?"

That was a shot. Just because of what he'd called the oldest because he didn't want to go to Viet Nam... She was right. He couldn't call the boy yellow for not wanting to face enemy fire if *he* couldn't face a little water.

He stared down at the sea and glass-bottom boat. His stomach knotted, but it wasn't as bad as he had anticipated. He seemed to step outside and watch his legs carry him along the pier. Madelaine chattered at him and the boys. They all answered her, but he could not recall what anybody said.

Half an hour out. "Seasick?" his younger boy asked. "I thought you were a sailor, Dad."

He nodded. His stomach was grinding and churning. This was different, somehow. Maybe because the boat was so small. He tried to ignore it, to get into Madelaine's game, to share his knowledge of the deep.

He had to give it up. He closed his eyes and leaned on the gunwale, concentrated on retaining his breakfast. The water whispered past, occasionally licking his fingers.

He was half asleep, one arm extended. A wavetop caught his hand, nearly wrenched his arm away. "Shawn! Shawn! Come to us, Shawn!"

The voices! Still there! Out here. They had him.

He jumped up, yelling, and staggered as the boat climbed a wave. Arms flailing, he went over the side.

He was under for just a few seconds, looking upward, clawing his way toward the sun, a scream locked in his throat by the pressure of the sea. The fire up there... The burning tanker... Better to stay down here with them... His floatation jacket drove him to the surface.

"Shawn. Stay, Shawn." Their fingers tugged at his clothing.

He was back aboard the boat in seconds, sobbing. Far, far away, Madelaine was telling the boys what had happened in '43. He wanted to yell at her to shut up. But she couldn't tell it all. She didn't know it all. Did she?

"It wasn't your fault, Shawn. Don't you understand that? It wasn't your fault. There was no way your ship could have escaped."

He wished he could believe it. Whining, he surged up, pushed her away, threw himself over the side again.

Eager murmurs. Grasping hands. "Shawn. You've come. At last, Shawn. At last."

Yelling and panic above. Salt water in his mouth. The people in the boat were quicker, stronger, and trickier than the sea. They pulled him out again. For a moment he thought he was tumbling into that ill-remembered motor whaleboat.

"Come back, Shawn. Shawn?"

1980

No wife now. Madelaine had died in an encounter with a drunk driver. She would have left by now anyway, he figured.

The younger boy was gone, too. Killed by a mortar bomb outside Khe Sahn. The older boy was in retail sales. Appliances. A college education down the tubes. There were grandchildren. He didn't see them often. There was too much bitterness still.

"Come on down to Florida," the guys said.

"We're taking the company plane. We'll go after the big ones off the outer keys. Remember that marlin Wally hooked last year? That baby has cousins just waiting to jump in the boat."

He had nothing else to do over Christmas, and, somehow, the sea didn't seem scary anymore. He agreed to go.

So there he was, somewhere over the Gulf Coast, staring down at the sharp shadings of color in the shallows, marvelling at the clarity of the

The Waiting Sea

water. Search as he might, he could find no fear in himself, though there was something there that might have been resignation.

The sea rose to greet them. The plane shivered as its landing gear locked down. "Going to refuel," Wally called back. "Won't take long."

The runway ran straight toward the Gulf. He watched the concrete come up, wondering if the plane would overshoot. But the tires touched and squealed almost before his imagination could slip into gear.

The others wanted to eat while they were down. He wasn't hungry. He walked to the edge of the beach and watched the combers roll in from Mexico. He stood there, the breeze teasing the remnants of his hair, listening.

He couldn't hear the voices. Not a hint, not a whisper. Just the sound of warm tropic waters lazily washing the sand.

It was over. Somehow, he had whipped it. He poked around inside, just to make sure, going deep, prodding the old sore spots. There was no pain, no guilt. While he wasn't watching, he had done what Gladys and Madelaine had demanded a thousand times. He had grown up. Somehow, he had accepted the truth. There was nothing he could have done that night. The ship's number had been up, and that was that.

That was that. One boat had sunk three ships with its first spread. None had had a chance.

He shivered again. So long ago. Two thirds of a lifetime, in a different world. A forgotten age. Most of the people now alive hadn't been born.

"Shawn. Hey, Shawn."

He jumped, then lifted a hand to let the guys know he had heard. He looked out onto the Gulf, a grin stretching his wrinkled face. "I don't know if you're real or not, but, damnit, I know I've beaten you." As he walked toward the plane, he wondered how much he had put together retroactively. A man dying of burns and exposure couldn't help going a little goofy. He really shouldn't have survived.

"Holy shit!" Wally yelled in his ear. "Jesus! You guys, get up here! Shawn's got one. Look at the size of this bastard."

The marlin came up and stood on its tail, dancing on the wavetops. It fell back with a slap audible aboard the boat. "He's going down. He's sounding," one of the guys said. "Watch your line, Shawn. Give him some slack."

"He's not," Wally insisted. "He's going to run in on us. Reel it in, Shawn. Reel it in. Keep the tension on it. Make him work."

He'd never done this before. He didn't know what he was doing. He hadn't had a line in the water since the war, when they had fished for sharks off the fantail. He offered the rod to someone more experienced.

"This is your baby, Shawn," Wally said. "We're not going to take it from you."

He began to taste the excitement that drove the others, that sense of a test of endurance and will against something strong and wild… One instant of flashback, flame gouting against the night when the first torpedo hit the tanker. Man. There was an opponent to test your limits. The boats tried to catch the fat-bellied freighters and tankers. The destroyers tried to catch the boats. Losers slept forever in the deep.

"Shawn don't daydream, man! Give me that rod if you're going to…"

He told Wally he had it under control. Now he wanted to do it himself. His victory would be complete when he brought that big bastard alongside. He would have beaten the sea once and for all.

"What's that?" one of the guys asked.

"Looks like a shark."

"That's all we need. Somebody get the rifle."

He heard the bolt slam a cartridge home. Sweat rolled into his eyes. He asked somebody to do something. He couldn't take his hands off the rod. Wally mopped his face with a handkerchief. "Hang in there, Shawn. He's weakening."

"There it is."

More sweat rolled into his eyes.

Bam!

"Missed him."

The Waiting Sea

"Shit, too. Right through his fin."

"Master gunfighter. Like hell. That slug hit fifty feet the other side of him. Give me that thing." The bolt worked again.

"What's the matter, Shawn?"

He shook his head. He couldn't tell Wally he had seen the shark's fin from the corner of a watery eye and imagined it to be a hand with webbing between its fingers beckoning.

No time to get silly. He had to remember he had it whipped.

"Somebody better help him," one of the guys said. "He don't look so good."

He gritted his teeth and refused to let loose of the rod. This one was his, all his. It wasn't much, but, by damn, this was going to be the victory of his life.

Something clicked. He seemed to have been doing this forever. He played the monster perfectly, with total concentration. The voice of the rifle was barely audible as the others took turns sniping at the shark. Their excitement came from another galaxy. "Go, Shawn." "You got him, fellow." "Hang in there, Shawn. It won't be long now. He's ready to give up."

Tension on his line. Keep that tension on his line. The marlin was barely fighting now. Coming in. Closer and closer.

"Hey, Wally. Shawn really don't look good."

"Leave him alone, will you? There you go, Shawn. He's done now. He'll do whatever you want. Bring him on in. Somebody get the gaff."

Right up next to the hull now. He laughed and told somebody to take the rod. He pried his stiff body out of the chair and staggered to the rail, looked down. Obsidian water, rolling along the side. Black, bottomless eyes staring out of the luminescence. "Shawn. Come to us, Shawn."

He laughed.

"Give him the gaff."

He took the gaff and leaned over the side...

The laughter left him. The creature looked back with hollow eyes, and it was no marlin. It had webbed hands. "No! Damnit, no!" He raised the gaff like a throwing spear.

"Shawn? What the hell is the matter?"

Something slammed against his chest. No. It was inside. There had been smaller blows while he was fighting the fish—or whatever it was. This one hurt. Oh, it hurt.

Shouts. Hands grabbing as he dropped the gaff. He staggered. Somehow, despite them, he slipped forward and tipped right over the rail. The thing on his hook grinned.

The yelling faded away, away, far away, even before he hit and the happy laughter surrounded him.

Brine filled his mouth. The bright surface dwindled. Champagne-bubbly chuckling filled his ears. He struggled, but the agony in his chest left him without strength to fight. The gentle hands drew him down, down.

"Shawn. Shawn. You've come. We've been waiting so long." Their caresses and kisses roamed over him. The wrinkly light of the surface receded ever farther away. "We waited so long, Shawn."

But not long in the life of the eternally waiting sea.

The darkness came and took him, and even the happy laughter faded.

Winter's Dreams

1

The light of three racing moons drenched the smoky city. Silver shadows schooled lazily amongst crowded spires and steeples and minarets, making the gargoyles appear to stir and stretch. Mist crept through the narrow, torturous alleys and streets, heavy with odors foul and sweet. The air scarcely stirred. Tall black prayer banners rose toward the weary stars, swaying like kelp beneath a gentle sea.

A broad-winged shadow wheeled like a hunting moth, began a circumspect descent that seemed to ignore but never moved out of sight of a certain open window high in the city's tallest tower. The separation dwindled. Then ceased to exist.

An indeterminate form perched on the windowsill, wrapped in its own darkness. The city was silent but a deeper stillness gathered 'till it seemed a clash of cymbals would not dare speak louder than a whisper.

The darkness stole inside. A faint, cracking acetylene light tickled the necks of the grey towers facing the window. The gargoyles stirred uneasily.

2

The room was cramped with gaunt, pallid, hand-wringing men in black, few of whom had any business being there. Functionaries and menials, there was not a fat cell among them. Senior Magician Ymarjon Shredlu thought they resembled nothing so much as a brood of devoutly terrified mantids.

"What's wrong with her?" a reedy voice demanded.

Shredlu glanced at the only fat man present. "I've only just arrived, my lord. But as a preliminary I suggest she be allowed more air."

Lord Everay Sloot shooed retainers. They continued to hold their long, bony hands before them as they retreated, robes flapping like raven's wings. Agitated whispers stirred like the soft rustle of trampled leaves. They sensed trouble.

Lord Everay continued to bluster and throw his weight around. Though not half so imposing a figure himself Shredlu ignored the man. He concentrated on Sloot's daughter.

Everay Ake Winter was a golden child-goddess, a throwback to the Star Walkers, perfectly proportioned, at fifteen summers swiftly approaching the peak of her beauty. The Everays bred stronger by the generation. Already Winter outshone her mother's best.

Master Shredlu hardened the shell round the spark he was amazed to discover still dwelt within him. There was a fierce and alien taint to the air; a smell of something from the Old Times. It troubled him deeply, as though he recognized it down on some near-instinctive level like an almost-forgotten fear-fragrance from early childhood. He rested the tips of the central pair of fingers on his right hand upon Winter's forehead, each an inch above the eye. He shut his own eyes to the gothic splendor surrounding him.

An electric tingle climbed his arm. "Uhm! Tackoo?"

"What?" Everay demanded. "What is it? Is she in danger?" Winter was his beloved and overly indulged daughter. In keeping with tradition, she carried his successor already, conceived within the fortnight, with

Winter's Dreams

the Senior and Master Magicians chaperoning the rut to guarantee the quickening of a son. Though he saw it every generation, Shredlu did not enjoy witnessing those couplings. But it was essential to the stability of the domain.

Shredlu paid Lord Everay no mind The man was fatter, but weak. Shredlu turned Winter's head slightly. In profile she resembled her mother more strongly. He beckoned his apprentice. "Shubam. Razor and soap. Quickly."

"Instantly, master."

"What is it?" Everay demanded. He indulged Shredlu's moods. Shredlu had been around a long time.

"A moment more, my lord." Shredlu stepped to the window. The alien scent was stronger. He stared out at the grey towers while brushing the sill with the spatulate fingertips of his left hand. The sensitive cells there picked up more of the musk and a strong, ugly taste.

Perhaps the auguries were overly optimistic. Of the thousand futures foreseen for Winter only a scatter in the far estuaries of probability shone brightly.

Apprentice Shubam announced proudly, "Razor, hot water, towels, and shaving lather, master." Shivering, Shredlu turned. His face betrayed nothing. He considered Shubam. The boy was enthusiastic but sloppy—despite knowing what had befallen his predecessor. He had cut no corners with so weighty a witness present, though. The razor was sharp, the towels and water hot, and the lather were of a precisely calculated temperature and consistency. Shubam did well when he concentrated.

Shredlu turned Winter's head farther. "Hold her there, Shubam. Gently!" He daubed lather. Lord Everay continued to fuss but stayed out of the way. Shredlu did not listen. He was old enough to entertain doubts that weight and condition of birth bestowed divinity.

It took just two small strokes of the straight razor to confirm his fears. "Clean her," he told Shubam, dropping the razor into the water. "My lord, she hasn't fallen into a coma at all. A tackoo came in the night."

"Spare me any witchmaster's obfuscations, Shredlu. Speak only with precision and concision. What might a tackoo be?"

Shredlu maintained his bland exterior. Even an apprentice as raw as Shubam—who had gasped—knew, though no tackoo assault had been reported for generations. Magician's generations.

But the dark reaches of the world still harbored many nightmares from the Old Times. Shredlu summoned one or another himself occasionally.

"Tackoo. One of the Artifact Folk. A vampire of dreams. See the mark on her temple." That was a rusty hourglass an inch tall formerly concealed by Winter's hair. "It took her dreams. Now she is trapped in a sleep where no dreams occur. If she does not dream, she cannot awaken as Everay Ake Winter." Shredlu straightened a strand of golden hair, then thumbed open an eyelid, exposing an empty blue iris. It was not necessary for Sloot to know she could be wakened as something else. "My lord. It's going to be a long siege amongst the books."

Lazy Shubam made a whimpering sound.

3

In private, Lord Everay Sloot seldom betrayed the impatience and petulance so often demonstrated before an audience. Shredlu suspected the public Sloot of being a pose. Indeed, he suspected Lord Everay wore several personas, onionlike; the real man might never be found by peeling. Shredlu did not let Sloot concern him overly much. One day he would be replaced by the yet unborn Vonce. Sloot waited quietly while Shredlu consulted his library. Shredlu instructed Shubam who directed a covey of raven men who made haste to comply, lashed on by Lord Everay's unforgiving gaze.

Shredlu sketched a gesture with his right little finger. The light went out of the book before him. It closed itself.

"Magician?"

"This is a matter best not discussed in every pantry and alleyway, my lord."

"As ever, your advice is without flaw, Shredlu. All of you, leave us."

Winter's Dreams

Shredlu nodded at Shubam, who seemed uncertain if the directive extended to himself. Alone with Sloot, Shredlu announced, "My memory betrayed me only in the details, my lord. Tackoo do, indeed, dote on a relish of stolen dreams. They are among the oldest of the Artifact Folk. Literally. They do not die. Neither do they breed. There cannot be more than three left alive in this late age. Our night-visitor will have been the tackoo Syathbir Tolis."

"You put a name to the demon so swiftly?"

"Of the three tackoo known, at most recent report, to survive, only Syathbir Tolis has the capacity for flight. Tackoo are undoubtedly hardy, but I hesitate to credit that even the most resolute non-flyer could clamber past the wards and gargoyles to reach Winter's window."

"Why would even a flyer visit the child? Can her dreams be so much tastier than easier prey found far nearer the lurking places preferred by Old Time things?"

"A flyer would if it were conjured and constrained and placed under obligation."

"A Magician is responsible?"

"Such a conclusion is inevasible, my lord. Your reasoning is apt, no Old Time demon would descend upon us while easier prey is available closer to home. Someone selected Syathbir Tolis from the literature, then found it and bound it to his will. Tackoo appear to be dull of wit and, once located, easily manipulated."

"Who?" Sloot wondered aloud. "Why? I have no enemies."

"We all have enemies, my lord. Occasionally, our enemies do not declare themselves publicly. Often we find the source of their rancor inaccessible or obscure. I suggest we concentrate instead upon freeing Winter, knowing that quest will certainly expose your enemies."

"There is hope?" Sloot brightened. He did love his daughter in more than a carnal manner, as a vessel for the Everay seed, far more than he ever loved their mother.

"The tackoo is a vampire of dreams but seldom a destroyer or vandal. They cherish and keep them. They can be reclaimed. They can be restored. Unless your enemy is so virulent he has compelled

Syathbir Tolis to repudiate his very nature. I choose not to believe this is possible."

"What is accomplished by this blow? Vonce resides in her womb already. The progression cannot be interrupted… She will not perish of this, will she?"

"She will go on as one in a coma. For however long her allotted span. The cruel truth, though, is that Vonce will enter the world with no dreams, either. The Everay progression can be maintained but you will be the last to think and rule."

Shredlu saw the suspicion poison Everay's thoughts. Sloot's eyes narrowed. They became evasive as he examined the possibility that his enemy was his own Senior Magician, bent on rule through a progression of empty-minded puppets.

"Not I, my lord," Shredlu said. Not this time.

"What will you do next?"

"Locate Syathbir Tolls. The tackoo is the key."

"Find him. Be not retiring in assessing his chastisement."

"Fear not, my lord. Rue and woe. Rue and woe betide."

Shredlu watched as Lord Everay waddled out of the library. Sloot was lost in thought, perhaps reflecting on the strange circumstances that had made him master of Everay a generation before his time.

He was not deep and persistent. Thought would abandon him once he reached the pleasures of the bath and seraglio.

4

Not all Artifacts and Old Timers were confined to the shadowed reaches of the world. Only those whose aspect offended or whose talents terrified and who were not otherwise useful on a regular basis. And those considered too dangerous to Real People. Shredlu saw several of them as he passed through the domestics' corridors. They did not see him. Not even the guards. He wore an illusion supplementing their natural disinclination to see the thing that did not belong. They felt him. They moved out

Winter's Dreams

of his path, puzzledly, though even under torture they would recall with certainty nothing concrete.

Shredlu returned to the principal hallways for the final approach to his destination. Manners forbid making his entrance like a servant. He scratched at the appropriate door, waited patiently. She would come when it became clear he would not go away. Someone might pass and remark upon his presence.

Lady Everay Non Ethan appeared beautifully serene when she opened the door herself, more swiftly than Shredlu anticipated. She had prepared herself to receive company. Elegantly gowned and coifed and bejewelled, she appeared a regal vision of Winter, tall, lithe, blonde, her forty-six summers unbetrayed by cunningly engineered lighting. "Shredlu. Will you stand there gawking 'till some roving band of functionaries tramples you?"

The Magician stepped forward. "You surprised me, Ethan. You were waiting."

"Am I so isolated and deaf that alarums and tumults fail to reach me entirely? I hear Winter's name whispered when they think I cannot hear. What disaster has befallen the child so soon after her cheerless nuptials? Has she been laid low by melancholy, like her mother before her?"

Ethan confused melancholy with bitterness, Shredlu feared. Her bottomless well of bitterness was the principal reason he came visiting so seldom anymore. "She is laid low but wicked magic was the agent. Someone sent a tackoo to steal her dreams." His gaze swept the decadence around him. Ethan certainly made Everay pay for her participation in its progression.

"How could that be? Tackoo and dorado and the gell people… They're nightfears you Magicians made up so you can extort a livelihood from the rest of us."

She did not believe that. It was a play-argument from a time when there had been less cool between them.

"This is no game, Ethan. A determined and abiding malice has turned its countenance upon Everay. The weight of its animosity is being born by Winter but it is not she who won the motivating hatred. She's never been out of the tower."

"Perhaps she has an enemy inside. Tuft Yarramal springs to mind. Yarramal hates everyone."

Shredlu examined the proposition from obscure and descant angles. Tuft Yarramal did indeed hate everyone but only as a mannered attitude. Nor did Yarramal hate herself enough to devise her own destruction. "It is a thought, Ethan. I shall consult Yarramal."

"Will you go without so much as touching me?"

"My time is no longer my own. I came as a courtesy, to inform you, to caution you."

"Caution me?"

"Catastrophe has struck once. Forewarned, we need not let it slide into our midst again." Shredlu surveyed his surroundings once more. He turned to the door.

"Don't go."

He steeled himself against her loneliness. "I must. I must reclaim Winter's dreams."

He was gone before she whispered, "And what of Ethan's dreams?"

5

In addition to Senior Magician Ymarjon Shredlu and his varying apprentices, Everay employed Master Magicians Rolo Kintrude and Aleas Dubbing, their several apprentices and Journeyman Magician Tuft Yarramal. Yarramal was the sole female in the magical establishment. She subscribed to none of the purported feminine weaknesses, she considered all soft emotions vices. Shredlu suspected she would become a Master at an early age and a threat to his position, if not his person, soon afterward.

The Magicians and their followings assembled in Shredlu's laboratory in response to his summons. He observed a shadow as they awaited his pleasure, unaware of his presence. Kintrude and Dubbing remained near the entrance, in an area plainly devoid of pitfalls, managing their impatience and that of their companions. They did nothing to temper the curiosities of Tuft Yarramal, however. Yarramal prowled the aisles

Winter's Dreams

between Shredlu's worktables and curio cabinets, here picking up an alembic full of gangrenous ichor, there a moldy book with an angel's feather as a bookmark. Never a word of caution crossed the lips of the Masters. Perhaps they hoped Yarramal stumbled into something. They had no love for her.

Shredlu noted carefully which particulars attracted Yarramal most strongly. He had shut down most of his little protections, partly as courtesy, partly to allow Yarramal's overconfidence to build to the point where she would take the one step too many if the impulse seized her.

Shubam made his entrance on cue, fawning obsequious to the Masters and haughty toward their companions. The lad looked like he was gaining weight on a diet little better than bark tea and gravel. He might find that proclivity a greater source of embarrassment than his inclination toward sloppiness.

Yarramal poked a finger into a case displaying several ancient tintinabula, one of which was said to have come from beyond the stars on one of the ships that brought the First Fold before the beginning of the Old Times. Yarramal did not subscribe to the theory that Real People were not native to this world. She believed all evidence supporting extraterrestrial origins to have been manufactured…

A distinct *clack* reverberated throughout the laboratory. Yarramal yipped in surprise. She tried to withdraw her hand from the display. The case ignored her desire. Shredlu noted that she neither panicked nor yielded to an impulse to implore aid of Kintrude and Dubbing. With her free hand, she rolled up her sleeves and began to experiment.

Yarramal remained unaware of Shredlu's presence 'till he reached past and probed the case with the elongated digit of his right hand. The catch devil recognized him and accepted his admonition against further restraining nosy journeymen. Shredlu said nothing, words had little impact upon Tuft Yarramal. He joined the Masters. Yarramal followed.

Shredlu spoke straightforwardly. "Winter's state is the result of a predatory visitation by the tackoo Syathbir Tolis. There can be no doubt on this point. The tackoo's present whereabouts must be determined.

An expedition must be mounted to collect the miscreant so that we may inquire into the causes of its remarkable behavior. To this end, we will now pool our knowledge and resources, reserving nothing, for we have already staked our reputations upon the welfare of the Everay domain."

Kintrude nodded. Dubbing employed all six fingers of his right hand in a gesture indicating absolute agreement. Only Tuft Yarramal disdained demonstration.

Shredlu issued his instructions, Rolo Kintrude to hunt the craggy wastelands to the west; Aleas Dubbing in all his skill to search the haunted forests to the north. The Senior would employ his own powers seeking Syathbir Tolis in the ugly fens and marshes and swamps to the east, known to be a favorite retreat of the more dark and insane Artifact Folk. Tuft Yarramal would examine the registers of Magicians and associated castes in an effort to determine the most probable villains in the case. She could not handle the south; nothing lay in that quarter but a cold, grey heaving ocean.

"We shall gather here again in four hours," Shredlu announced. "I shall provide a banquet. We will plan our expedition."

6

Nervously, Shubam took down the panels concealing the adonnai orden, each a five foot by seven painting in the neoClassical representationalist mode pioneered by Wensby Strait. Each cast a mythological creature against some well-known attractions outside the city. But for one latecomer by Everay Non Ethan, the paintings reminded himself not to be rigidly intolerant of others' infatuations. Time tended to suppress the inessential and pretentious.

The features of six olive drab faces filled the spaces once covered by the panels, each taller between lip and eye than was Shredlu between head and toe. The adonnai slept, kerchiefs and mist wisps of ectoplasmic matter darting and larking in their breaths, into their nostrils and

Winter's Dreams

out again, to buzz out across the world like worker bees, harvesting the pollen of secrets. Shredlu considered them for several minutes. There were no immediately apparent differences between the six. All would be equally testy if awakened. All harbored an unreasonable resentment over being bound to his service. He had provided the ingrates a warm and secure place to sleep.

"Shubam, have you carried out my instructions?"

"Yes, master." Shubam was a lad of few words, unlike the run of apprentices, who seemed to have automated the hinges of their jaws.

"Then take the table to the very end." He would begin with Xyzzys, the least tractable of the adonnai. If by clever badinage and cunning evasion he compelled Shredlu to waken a second adonnai, more animosity would be directed Xyyzyx's way than Shredlu's. The adonnai resented one another more than any other entity. Shubam positioned the wheeled table. Shredlu stepped up. His apprentice had failed to overlook any items and had positioned all with absolute precision. Shubam had heard rumors about the fate of his disorderly predecessor. Adonnai featured largely in every version. Adonnai did not restrain their irrational rancor when tempted by lax preliminary work.

"Excellent, Shubam. Would you care to cast the invoking incantations?" They were simple enough.

"Master, I would prefer not to enjoy my first exercise with Xyyzyx."

"Very well, I will not insist." Time was passing. Scarcely two hours before the Everay Magicians assembled. As he commenced the awakening, Shredlu asked, "Has anyone approached you about our work here? Particularly about our current course of experiments?"

"No, master." Shubam stirred nervously, warily keeping Shredlu between himself and Xyyzyx.

"Has no one shown any curiosity at all? Tuft Yarramal, perhaps?"

"I have never, to my recollection, spoken directly to the Journeyman."

"Excellent. I urge you to persist in your neglect."

"Thou pestilent Ymarjon," Xyyzyx boomed. "I will not ask thee why thou disturbest mine slumbers. I have anticipated thine importunities. Thou art, in point of fact, tardy in launching them."

The huge olive face opened its eyes. They proved to be the most human of the an's features, being vastly enlarged orbs identical to those of a brown-eyed man—'till ghosts began to wisp in and out of their pupils.

"You understand what moves me to trouble you?"

"Thou wishest to unravel the mysteries surrounding a theft of dreams."

"You know about that?" Shredlu was troubled. The adonnai were seldom so direct. Xyyzyx in particular preferred evasion and misdirection.

"Much escapes me. I spend my life in sleepy reverie."

Shredlu supposed it was too much to expect the adonnai to volunteer anything though it was obvious the Artifact was deeply concerned and quite possibly frightened—if such a creature could make the acquaintance of fear.

"Thou needs must ask the right questions, Ymarjon Shredlu."

It could not shake its nature completely. Shredlu asked questions. Scores upon scores of questions. He studied the huge olive face with every one, taking clue from its swift play of expression whether he pursued the correct will-o'-the wisp. Xyyzyx was doing his best to communicate. This fact continued to impress Shredlu.

In response to a particular inquiry, Xyyzyx replied, "Thou art more intuitive than most would suspect, Ymarjon Shredlu. The call for the tackoo did indeed originate within the Everay domain. Sadly no adonnai can identify the source with precision." Shredlu noted five more pairs of adonnai eyes open and turned his way, though he had done nothing to conjure them forth from their sleep. "The thing was done clumsily, though. As thou hast noted secretly. A lack of skill was revealed both in the summoning itself, and in the concealment of the source and nature of the summons."

The attack originated within the Everay domain and was directed against the Everay domain. If Winter failed to dream, it would be but a few generations till the Everay progression concluded.

"You have placed me deeply into your debt," Shredlu confessed.

"Swift recompense of obligations is urged by all great thinkers. Strike while the mood of generosity is yet upon thee. Let down these prisoning walls."

Winter's Dreams

Shredlu chuckled. "Where is the tackoo Syathbir Tolis? One suspects your reveries might have touched upon this matter."

"Indeed. It was an intriguing task. The tackoo's slow wits reached the inevitable conclusion only after it was too late to desist or recant."

"I presume the tackoo eventually converted to the doctrine that his only hope of salvation lay in hiding. That being what he is, he has long had several refuges prepared."

"Thou art intelligent. For a mere man." The adonnai Xyzzyx's grin exposed hideously deformed teeth. Ghosts fluttered in and out of its sparkling eyes. It was prepared to bargain hard.

7

Master Magician Aleas Dubbing declared, "The tackoo Syathbir Tolls failed to make himself evident in my quarter of the compass. Sources available, however, suggested he might be located by an investigator who turned his eye upon the Dustrake Reach of the Lesser Miasmatic Swamps."

"A suggestion in substantial agreement with my own conclusions," Shredlu said. "Kintrude?"

"I found considerable consternation on all levels Outside. Syathbir Tolis is nowhere amongst the Wastes. Outsider rumor reliably places him within the Lesser Miasmatics."

The tackoo appeared to have confused no one. "Yarramal? Have you contradictory evidence?"

"None such was to be found within the registers, even of a caste so remote and narrow as the Necromancers."

A caste of one, which consisted of Shredlu's cousin the freelance charlatan Ousted Delf. Shredlu was confident Yarramal had made her own locational inquiries. "Did you find a name that can be attached to this dream-theft villainy?"

"None whatsoever, Senior." She frowned thoughtfully, as though taking a last look at a decision already made. "Perhaps it is irrational or unreliable intuition, Senior, but I have arrived at a conviction this crime germinated inside the Everay domain, probably within this very tower, possibly close to the child."

"Substantially my own assessment. Shubam. I see you have returned. Have you extended the invitations?"

"Yes, master."

"And the airmen?"

"They have been alerted; His Lordship expects to launch a spontaneous picnic foray."

"Excellent. You outdo yourself in these times of crisis, Shubam. We shall have to reward you by adding to your duties."

"My gratitude knows no bounds, master."

Shredlu could only suspect that Shubam was being less than honest. "Come, then. Let us be off… Shubam. You did send to the kitchen for appropriate provisions?"

"I did, master."

Yarramal asked, "We are going out to the Miasmatics?"

"It will make a wonderful afternoon excursion."

"It occurs to me that your plan puts all the domain's Magicians in the same place at the same time."

"It does indeed. And one of us may be the villain of the piece. The blackguard may be hoping for this eventuality. A grave risk. Which of us should remain behind?" Shredlu chuckled. There was a dirth of volunteers, it being evident that suspicion would surround whoever held back.

It would be an interesting journey as each prepared for the worst while pretending to share a social jaunt. "I think we need not take our apprentices. Come. Time flees." He strode forth, snatching his cloak and staff from Shubam as he passed. He offered the apprentice a sharp look. Winter would be his responsibility in his master's absence. Winter would be a test.

8

The airmen had brought the sky yacht *Vangier*, there would be no sneaking into the Dustrake Reach. In any event, it would have to do. There was

Winter's Dreams

no time to cover its gaudy paintwork. Lesser craft could not transport the entire party. Nor could he keep an eye on everyone if they scattered amongst several smaller vessels. And it was a picnic, after all.

The picnickers assembled upon the airmen's promenade, eighty levels up Everay Prime. Rolo Kintrude and Aleas Dubbing stood together, conversing in low tones. Tuft Yarramal stood apart, introspective, as was her wont. Lord Everay Sloot stood between his mother, Everay Non Ethan, and grandmother, Everay Tak Arone. In the cruel light of afternoon it was difficult to distinguish which woman was the younger. They did not chat. The Everays had little to say to one another, ever.

The airmen cursed one another as they wrestled *Vangier* into position for boarding. A breeze made the ship difficult to manage. Nevertheless, they performed their task and the picnickers boarded without a festive face among them. Senior Airman Mug Rusale barely waited 'till the boarding steps cleared. *Vangier* sprang upward; grey towers began to slide away underneath. Mists and smoke concealed the streets way down below.

It was an hour's flight to the Lesser Miasmatics. The picnickers remained disposed as before, a group of three, a pair, two alone. Only Kintrude and Dubbing had a word to share and that quite seldom. No one attempted to probe Shredlu's intentions. Questions might bestir presumptions of guilt.

Xyzzyx and his family had been of incomplete assistance in determining the identity of the person responsible for the attack on Winter. Reason and information gathered argued that the villain had to be aboard the sky yacht. Shredlu was inclined to suspect Tuft Yarramal but could not fathom a motive.

As the yacht approached the Miasmatics, the sky outside filled with bizarre creatures more colorful than the airboat itself. The largest of these was an orange-bellied, blue-backed pseudopteronodon with a wicked and intelligent eye. "Hemmaus?" Yarramal asked from behind Shredlu. "It fits the deamon's description."

"Hemmaus," Shredlu agreed. "We have done business before. A dangerous entity, Hemmaus. Intelligent, unpredictable and occasionally treacherous. In no sense should you ever show him your back. But he is a powerful ally when it suits his humor."

A score of Hemmaus' lesser cousins larked around like flickering confetti.

The sky yacht descended. Mug Rusale regaled himself with imprecations, critiquing his own performance. The swamp began to impinge upon more than the eye; its odor, then sound, penetrated the cabin of the airship. The odor alone sufficed to convince even the slowest wit that the wetlands were appropriately named.

Shredlu directed Mug Rusale to a particular stretch of Dustrake Reach. Several thousand acres of vegetation were of a uniform green so dark it verged upon the black. That sprawl consisted of a single million-trunked nedereyya tree harboring an ecology all its own.

Rusale excoriated the yacht for its sudden inclination to proceeded in a nose-down attitude.

Dubbing and Kintrude had come forward. Dubbing asked, "The tackoo is hiding in the canopy there?"

"So my sources indicate. What of yours?"

Both Master Magicians nodded. Shredlu examined them closely. Neither seemed distressed by the swiftness with which the hunt was closing in on Winter's tormentor, not that either would have given himself away easily. Each *was* a master.

Mug Rusale found a bit of solid ground convenient to the vast tree, brought *Vangier* to earth.

Shredlu attended to his host's duties immediately. With the aid of Mug Resale he set up tables and chairs, put out insect repellers on poles at a distance of fifteen feet. There were no protests and no urgings to get on with it. Great stakes were on the board; caution was indicated. Yarramal and Rusale brought out the picnic baskets. Shredlu served a rare wine from his own stock. Lord Everay commented favorably, the first he had spoken since boarding *Vangier*.

Shredlu cast the occasional glance toward the nedereyya, at Hemmaus wheeling high above. Unless he had been anticipated, something would happen soon.

Winter's Dreams

Shadows were long and purple when the swamp suddenly grew raucous with the approach of Hemmaus' smallest cousins. Their reptilian barks and hisses and squalls swept back and forth behind concealing foliage. Shredlu was pleased. Lord Everay's patience had grown lean. Much longer and he would have demanded an end to the outing.

A black butterfly silhouette sprang up against the rosy lilac sky, fluttering in panic. Hemmaus' cousins darted around it. It shifted directions with greater facility than its tormentors, but they had numbers. Where one was outmaneuvered, another flashed in.

With a line of sight established, Shredlu could now bend his own will upon the tackoo. He drew it in, struggling like a fish reluctant to leap into the pan. Shredlu brought it to a perch upon one of the picnic tables. It quivered in terror, surrounded by Real Men. Above Hemmaus' cousins hastened toward their aeries. Night was falling. Darkness would summon forth creatures less condign than they.

Hemmaus himself called down an admonition for Shredlu to mind his debts faithfully.

Shredlu responded in the tongue favored by the flying Artifacts. He always discharged his obligations. Were that not true, Xyzzyx would not have arranged events so that Syathbir Tolis joined the Everay picnickers.

Rolo Kintrude said, "Senior, we should, perhaps, consider going home. Already the night grows aware of our presence."

Shredlu felt it himself. "Rusale, load the sky yacht. Yarramal, lend a hand." The Senior Magician remained close to Syathbir Tolls. He would not allow it out of his sight. He would remain artfully alert on levels natural and magical till he could isolate the creature within his laboratory. Never had the tackoo had another so concerned for his well-being.

Under other circumstances, an attack would not have been a disappointment. It would have exposed Winter's enemy and, perhaps, have defined what motivated such an evil assault. Under other circumstances, however, Shredlu would have had a better notion whence trouble might come. At the moment, he trusted only Mug Rusale and, to a lesser extent, Lord Everay. His imagination was fertile: he could conceive of circumstances whereby Winter's bereavement would profit each of the others.

The entire party was so paranoid that not a sigh expired but every eye registered that fact and every brain sorted implications. Tension mounted as *Vangier* approached Everay Tower. Shredlu began to doubt his reasoning. Everyone seemed to be waiting for someone else to crack.

In the end it proved that he had been anticipated. Winter's enemy had no need to indulge in self-betrayal aboard the sky yacht. An ambush was in place at the dock. Its fellowship, however, were understandably apprehensive about the risks inherent in an attack upon the combined Magical masters of Everay. Nerves caused a premature tripping of the trap.

Events thenceforth were foreordained: the air howled with vortices of color, screams of despair were heard, prisoners were taken. Shredlu paused a moment to help Mug Rusale extinguish a scamp cantrip gnawing at a landing claw on the sky yacht.

Aleas Dubbing and Rolo Kintrude appeared a bit tattered. Tuft Yarramal smoldered at left hip and right elbow. Shredlu himself had taken no part once he determined that the others were adequate to squelch the tumult. He merely observed, hoping the behaviors of others would prove instructive.

Tuft Yarramal did not become involved till the ambushers, in despair, hurled their final efforts her way.

9

"I suspected Yarramal from the beginning," Shredlu announced in his laboratory. "Simply because she was most likely, in character. Shubam was a surprise, though. And the motives of all involved remain elusive." He considered his sullen apprentice, in restraints beside Yarramal. Shubam's motives became transparent instantly. Slothful ambition coupled with passion. And Yarramal's self-destructive behavior became less opaque when her glance fell, as it did often, upon Everay Non Ethan.

Rolo Kintrude and Aleas Dubbing were proficient readers of pregnant glances themselves. Not only did they discern the source of Everay dismay, they also read Shredlu's cautioning frown. Lord Everay would

Winter's Dreams

not hear a word of accusation against the woman who was both mother and sister, however much he detested her personally.

Particularly unfathomable were Ethan's motives for putting together the broad but inept conspiracy in the first place. What hatred could she possibly bear her own daughter? Successful, the plot would have meant the end of the Everay progression.

Senior Magician Ymarjon Shredlu oversaw the bringing together of mothlike Syathbir Tolis and Everay Ake Winter, resulting in the restoration of Winter's dreams. Then, with Winter her sparkling, cheerful self once more, none the worse for her misadventure and full of helpful suggestions and even lending a playful hand, he oversaw the punishment of the guilty. He thought a great deal about Ethan while he worked. He cherished what had been and now could never be again. He thought about the Everay progression. He worried about where he might find a teachable, tractable apprentice.

He was using them up at an alarming rate.